Reality Chec.

Reality Check

VICKI NOTARO

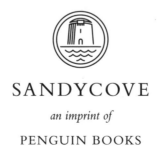

SANDYCOVE

an imprint of

PENGUIN BOOKS

SANDYCOVE

UK | USA | Canada | Ireland | Australia
India | New Zealand | South Africa

Sandycove is part of the Penguin Random House group of companies
whose addresses can be found at global.penguinrandomhouse.com.

Penguin
Random House
UK

First published 2024

001

Copyright © Vicki Notaro, 2024

The moral right of the author has been asserted

Set in 13.2/16pt Garamond MT Std
Typeset by Jouve (UK), Milton Keynes
Printed and bound in Great Britain by Clays Ltd, Elcograf S.p.A.

The authorized representative in the EEA is Penguin Random House Ireland,
Morrison Chambers, 32 Nassau Street, Dublin D02 YH68

A CIP catalogue record for this book is available from the British Library

ISBN: 978–1–844–88657–9

www.greenpenguin.co.uk

To Joe,
for everything

'If you cannot get rid of the family skeleton,
you may as well make it dance.'

– George Bernard Shaw

I

I never thought that the beginning of my life imploding would happen at a gender reveal party, but I've heard since that people have died at those things. I guess they're pretty dangerous.

It was an unseasonably warm spring day in Co. Limerick; I'd gone to the ladies ostensibly to 'freshen up', but really to escape from the chaos that is an Irish party for five minutes. The pub near Croom was a huge, multilevel place resplendent in mahogany, and when I finally found my way to the bathroom and locked the cubicle door, I exhaled deeply. I'd feel better after a little scroll on my phone; I didn't want to be hanging off Jason like a limpet all day, not when he was back home with his family and friends, but I felt decidedly out of place. I was minding my own business looking at Twitter in the cubicle when some giggly women came into the ladies to preen.

'She's kind of stuck up, isn't she? Not what I imagined, her sister seems so down to earth online . . .' said one, followed by a hiccup.

'I think she's just very American? Cool, maybe?' I recognized that voice. Sandra Dempsey, the godmother-to-be. 'She can't have had a normal life, with a family like hers . . .'

They were clearly talking about me, as I was the only American in a ten-mile radius, so I appreciated Sandra's attempt at diplomacy. She was the only one of the WAGs I knew in any real way, as she was married to Jason's older brother, Mick. The rest of The Gang, as my boyfriend called them, I'd only met earlier that day.

'She's a BABE,' another woman slurred. I guessed this was Sinéad, who had secured a babysitter for the day and who I had seen taking shots as soon as she arrived. 'Gorgeous, like a perfect, rich princess. Jason landed on his feet! I mean, I know he's always been the big ride of the group, but he did well for himself!'

'Well, I think she thinks she's better than us,' the first voice sneered. She clearly wasn't a fan of mine.

'She *is* better than us, Niamh. Better than you, anyway.' This, deadpan from Sandra, made me smile. Sandra is one of those women that has a nice, understated way of putting you in your place.

'Well, I'd say she's hating being around all us plebs, especially at a party like this. We're beneath her, and sure doesn't she hate kids, Sandra?'

Wow, Niamh really had it in for me.

'She doesn't hate children; she just doesn't want any. There's a difference.'

'Yeah, but she's the reason Jason hasn't had any yet, that's what Mick told Brian, anyway. He says she doesn't have time for a family, too into her career.'

'I'd have babies with her. I'd leave my babies for her, and Patrick too. He's a useless shite!'

Niamh sounded exasperated. 'Sinéad, would you ever shut up mooning over Portia feckin' Daniels and move? My eyelash is hanging off, I need the good light.'

I sat there waiting for them to leave. I figured I'd spare them the embarrassment of being caught talking shit about me. Then I heard something that stopped me in my tracks.

'Well anyway, Jason told me that they've changed their mind,' said Sandra. 'He says babies are in their future, that they realized during the pandemic that life has no meaning without a family.'

'Oh, *good*,' squeaked Sinéad. 'They'll have gorgeous kids; it would have been an awful shame if they didn't . . .'

They finished up and tottered out, the sound of their heels echoing as I sat in the cubicle, paralysed. Babies were in my future? That was news to me.

I was leaning against the wall smoking a cigarette when Jason appeared at the front door of the pub. He'd always found it amusing that I was an Angeleno with such a filthy habit, and Lord knows I'd tried to quit over the years. But I always gave in to the lure of delicious, disgusting nicotine when I'd had a cocktail.

My sister, Vinnie, smoked too, but didn't all models? Her followers would have been distraught if they knew that their beloved goddess sobbed, scratched and fought when she realized she couldn't smoke while pregnant, that it wasn't just a guideline – 'Not even Lights?' she'd bawled. 'Menthols?!'

Then again, they'd be distraught if they knew a lot of things about Lavinia Rizzi-Schwartz.

I'd sent Jason a text to meet me outside a good fifteen minutes ago, but I suspected he was too caught up in the corn-hole tournament taking place in the beer garden – I don't personally understand the appeal, but men seem to love tossing sandbags into a small wooden box. I was irritated that he wasn't being more attentive; he was aware that I felt a little out of place among a gang I didn't really know. I keep my own circles tight, so meeting a lot of new people was daunting.

I knew that people went all out for these gender reveal parties in the States, and I wasn't surprised they'd infiltrated Irish culture – everyone knows Irish people love any excuse for a celebration – or a 'do', as my mother would call it.

The party was for Jason's younger brother, Tiernan, and his Australian girlfriend, Liza, to celebrate their impending firstborn. The entire Dempsey clan had travelled from across the globe to reunite for the first time post-pandemic, and my boyfriend was on a real high back in the bosom of his family.

There was the obligatory confetti cannon that would reveal whether the baby was a boy or a girl, blue and pink balloons and cupcakes, and disgusting games galore. I'd politely declined eating a melted chocolate bar from a diaper and got away with it because they all presumed people from Los Angeles don't eat.

I'll say one thing for an Irish gender reveal though – they have far more booze than their American counterparts, which are much more sedate affairs. In Ireland, who cares if the hostess can't drink? Everyone else gets lit.

'What's up, babe?' Jason's eyes looked more glazed than they had when I left for the bathroom. 'Sorry, the corn-hole forfeit was a round of Jägerbombs, and then another . . . I didn't see your message until now.'

All the fight left me at the sight of him. After more than 6 1/2 years he still had the ability to melt me with one look – even though his pupils were huge, his smile wonky. Being near Jason always calmed me a little, so it was hard to stay mad.

And those women had probably been full of it, anyway. I know our relationship and child-free status is interesting to people, especially Jason's home friends, who have always wanted him to 'settle down'. But there's no way Jason would have said something so cavalier about our life to his sister-in-law. A man doesn't just change his entire way of thinking about something as massive as having babies without mentioning it to his partner.

If he had said something to make it seem like kids were in our future, he was probably just trying to make me seem a bit less of a baby-loathing demon to these women.

And a baby-loathing demon I was not, but I could see how a roomful of mothers might not warm to the thirty-eight-year-old Yank who not only had the gall to win the heart of the town's prodigal son but was also audacious enough to refuse to procreate with him.

I pasted on a smile. 'Sorry, I was just having a bit of a turn, I got all hot and dizzy. Hopefully a hot flush. Maybe menopause is finally on the way!' I grinned, but he didn't return my smile like he usually would. In fact, he frowned a little.

'Why do you say things like that, Portia?'

'Like what?'

'Wishing for menopause and stuff like that, it's weird.'

Then it was my turn to frown. 'Jason, you suffer with periods for more than a quarter-century and then you get to tell me that wishing for menopause is weird. And anyway, my uterus is basically a vestigial organ.'

He shrugged and then sighed, the fresh air clearly making the liquor hit him a little harder. I decided to keep the peace and not to bring up what I'd heard in the ladies. I linked his arm. 'Come on, godfather-to-be,' I said in my most convincing Marlon Brando voice. 'This is the day of your nephew or niece's gender reveal. In Sicilian culture, that means you can't refuse me anything, and I fancy a quickie in the toilets.'

'I don't think that's quite right.' He grinned, swinging an arm around me and planting a kiss on my lips. 'But I'd never say no to a ride in the loo. Only, you might have to hold me up.'

I woke up the next morning a little worse for wear. I could hold my tequila, but when these Irish events got going . . . well, my mother always says there'll be enough booze consumed to fell an ox. My mother, like Jason, is Irish by birth, but that's where the similarities between them end.

If anyone behaved like Jason's family and friends at a party back in the States, there'd be interventions all round in the morning. I've always thought that drinking is the one thing Irish Catholics don't feel shame or guilt about.

I guzzled the bottle of water next to my bed – thank heavens for turndown service – and turned to spoon Jason, but his side of the bed was empty. Then I remembered I'd left him at a lock-in in the pub around the 3 a.m. mark and got a cab back to the hotel in Adare. I'd had more than enough by that point, and it was getting to the maudlin sing-song stage of the night. But it wasn't like him not to come to bed at all.

I picked up my phone – 10.01. At this rate he'd miss breakfast, and Jason never, ever missed a hotel breakfast. Especially in Ireland – he was forever wistful about the country's superior sausages.

Then I saw the note on his nightstand, scrawled on the fancy hotel stationery.

Gone for a run with T, back soon xo

I sank back against the pillows, feeling a little put out. It made sense that Jason might want to squeeze as much time in as possible with Tiernan before we all went our separate ways again. But to leave me behind, when I'd come all this way to visit his family over the Easter vacation? I tapped out a text to that effect and a reply buzzed back straight away.

Jason: Sorry babe, you looked like a peaceful angel, and I didn't think this would be your scene! Order room service, be back soon and starving ♥

Jason: PS get extra sausages!!!

Not my scene? True, I was more of a Reformer gal than a runner, but it stung to be excluded, especially as he hadn't even come home with me the night before.

6

As I called the extension for room service I was certain that staying at the Manor had been a mistake. Of course, I didn't want to impose on his family, the house was full to bursting with Tiernan and Liza staying, but I also now felt totally out of the loop. Hangxiety, I told myself. Just breathe.

I turned to my favourite comfort activity – doomscrolling through all my apps to assure myself the world hadn't ended as I slept. My routine was news headlines first, then Twitter, then Instagram. Then, if I had time, a quick glance at the *Mail Online*'s Sidebar of Shame, a flick through my fyp on TikTok and another scroll through Twitter.

It was on this last scroll that a link caught my eye. It was a blind item, another addiction of mine: nameless and often defamatory gossip that inspired flurries of guesses as to who any titbit was about – which producer was sleeping with his leading man? what DJ was headed to rehab? I consumed it all voraciously, even though you were never sure what was bullshit and what was true.

> This A-list model-turned-lifestyle-guru might be the picture-perfect mommy and wife, but sources on the ground say that she consistently turns a blind eye to her OH's philandering. This time though, it's gonna go public – he's sick of being an Instagram husband and has been doing more than managing his new protégée.

I frowned. I was well aware that half of these things were completely made up, but this one sounded a little too familiar, and too close to home.

The door swung open and I nearly jumped out of my skin. 'Jason, you scared me!'

He looked like I felt, rumpled and rough around the edges, but also flushed and damp from his run. Jason and Tiernan are action men; they'd never let a silly thing like a hangover stop them from doing a casual 10k first thing. He proffered a cup of coffee, which I gladly accepted.

'I hope you ordered me a cure; I'm bolloxed!' He pecked me on the forehead as he flopped on to the bed and dropped the papers. 'Those were outside the door.'

I ruffled his damp hair. 'Weird of you not to wake me before you went?'

He made a face. 'I wanted to talk to Tiernan.'

I shuffled the *Sunday Independent* to get to the magazines. I wasn't expecting to see my mother's face staring back at me on the cover of *Life*, but I wasn't surprised either. I held it up to show Jason, who fanned himself dramatically. DESSIE DANIELS screamed the headline. IRELAND'S MOST GLAMOROUS EXPORT?

'Everything all right with Tiernan?' I replied, flicking through my mother's shoot. As usual, she was dolled up to the nines and looking fabulous.

'Yeah, he's . . . perfect. Great. In fact, he's the best I've ever seen him, and Liza is amazing.' His eyes took on a misty quality. 'I can't believe I'm going to have another baby nephew. It's kind of the first time it's hitting me, probably because it's Tiernan having a kid and not crusty old Mick.'

'Wow, how hungover are you?' I laughed, sipping my coffee. 'Going all dopey-eyed over your brother? You must be at death's door.' I swatted him with the magazine.

'No, I'm not dying, Portia, literally or figuratively. But I do want to talk to you about something. Something serious.'

He took my hands, and even though I still wasn't sure if he was joking or not I felt an anxious fizz in my chest at the look in his eyes.

'You see, I've realized something over the past year or so, after the pandemic and being back home in Ireland this week

8

after so long. I've been doing a lot of thinking and I never know how to broach it with you, but to be honest, I just can't keep it in any more.' He put down his cup and gulped nervously.

'God, Jason, spit it out. You're scaring me.'

'Well, the thing is, P, I've realized that there's something important to me now that wasn't before, and I need you to be on board with it because I love you and it's about our future. But . . .' He paused. 'I don't know how to tell you. It's just seeing Tiernan so happy, and with my dad gone now . . .'

I raised my eyebrows. 'Please don't tell me you want to move to Australia, babe. I am so not a ginormous spider person. I know you miss Tiernan, but what would I do down there? I don't fancy the idea of writing for *Home and Away*.'

His eyes softened. 'No, no. God, not Australia. Sure, I'm always telling Tiernan that everything down there is designed to kill you!'

'Thank heavens for that!' I laughed and downed the dregs of my cappuccino. Skinny milk, one sweetener, with both chocolate and cinnamon on top, just as I liked it – Jason always got everything just right.

'No, P. What it is, well, it's that I've changed my mind. I've decided I want to be a father. I want us to have kids together, and I want to start as soon as possible.'

I spat my coffee across the beautiful white sheets.

Dessie Daniels: Ireland's Most Glamorous Export?

17 April 2022

Barney Edmonds sits down with the mogul, momager and reality star to discuss big-boob business, being the mother of famous daughters, and still feeling sexy at 62.

When you look at Dessie Daniels in our stunning cover shoot, it's easy to be bewitched by the glamour she exudes in spades. But don't be fooled by her beauty and sex appeal – still apparent in her seventh decade on earth. She is as shrewd a businesswoman as they come, a mastermind of branding and never afraid of hard work. She's also warm, witty and, thanks to her mischievous expressions, the queen of GIFs online.

Her story, of emigration, celebrity, near-destitution and now huge success is both inspiring and fascinating. 'Looking back on it all now, I never could have predicted how my life would have turned out,' she admits, perched on a leopard-print chaise longue in her Bel Air home office. 'I didn't realize that little old Desdemona from Killarney with her big dreams could even begin to achieve them when I followed my sister Celia to the Bronx in 1979. But it hasn't all been easy, mind you.'

I've travelled from Ireland to interview Daniels about her vast business empire. She has been named the richest Irishwoman in entertainment by Forbes, knocking Enya from the top spot she's occupied for decades. This is all thanks to savvy investment, entertainment riches and her eponymous brand empire. And of course, Dessie is still utterly Irish despite more than four decades Stateside – she's never lost her accent, for one thing.

'I am as Irish as a Claddagh ring, as a pint of Guinness. And I think that's what has set me apart as a personality and as a businesswoman. The United States is a nation of immigrants, which is something it likes to forget these days, but I think I was the first true reality-TV star here from the Emerald Isle, and of course that's part of the charm. But I have lived the American dream several times over – and I'm not done yet!'

Dessie started her career in entertainment as a model in New York City after being spotted by a scout for Ford Models when she was working in an Irish pub in Hell's Kitchen. She experienced the last days of Studio 54 and, in her own infamous words, existed on clove cigarettes and the attention of men. One such man, filmmaker Roberto Rizzi, would change the course of her life.

She met the renowned writer/director at the premiere of his 1981 gangster mega hit, *Siciliana*, and swears it was love at first sight. 'He always said he saw my legs first, then my boobs, then my face, and that each was better than the last.' She laughs, throatily. 'He was so tall, so handsome, with that gorgeous Italian accent. And of course, he was already so famous as a director. I was totally starstruck. We were married three months later and spent years living the high life – yachts, film festivals, parties at Barbra Streisand's house. I didn't work, I was a lady of leisure. But I always knew I wanted a family, so when Portia was born in 1983, I was ecstatic.'

Dessie's eldest daughter is the least famous member of her brood, but happily so. She works as a screenwriter based in New York, content in the background – so much so, she's never used her father's surname and goes by Portia Daniels. 'She never wanted to capitalize on Roberto's name, or be accused of nepotism,' says the proud mother.

Second daughter, Lavinia Rizzi-Schwartz, clearly didn't mind using her famous surname and needs no introduction. The former supermodel's online fame almost eclipses that of her mother, as the most followed lifestyle and parenting influencer in the world under the moniker @LifeWithLRS. Married to super-agent Billy Schwartz, they have two sons and until recently lived in a sprawling mansion situated five (gargantuan) doors up from Dessie, her ex-husband Manuel Alvarez, a music industry executive, and their 14-year-old daughter, TikTok sensation Ariel. The Schwartzes have recently relocated to Hidden Hills, where they live in a modern glass enclave already familiar to Lavinia's rapt following.

I ask how it works for Dessie, living with her ex-husband. 'It's an unusual set-up between Manny and I, I get that, but it works for us. He's my right-hand man, and he's a very hands-on father. It may be unorthodox to live with your ex-husband, but love, when have I ever been traditional?' She laughs huskily.

Dessie is known for managing her family's careers as well as starring in *Ladies of Los Angeles* since its inception. But it is in business she has thrived. Rizzi's sudden death in 2000 shocked the world, and his nefarious financial affairs were exposed to all and sundry. The fallout left Dessie almost destitute; she had no choice but to work and support her girls, so that's what she did.

'I would have bagged groceries, done anything, to survive. But this is Hollywood, baby! And one thing Roberto left me with was connections. People felt sorry for me, but they also admired me. I was too old even then to be a proper model, so I started doing commercials and info-mercials, which are big business over here. Then I was approached by a casting director about doing a short arc on *Baywatch* as the mother of one of the lifeguards. I guess the audience liked what they saw, because I worked consistently as an actress after that.'

Dessie was a huge hit on television. The brunette's ample assets, enigmatic green eyes and 'exotic' Kerry lilt set her apart in a sea of blondes. She dabbled in different shows over the years but found herself growing bored with learning scripts. 'I was getting on; I wanted an easier life. By then I'd met Manuel and we wanted to have a child together desperately.'

The couple decided to proceed with what was perhaps the first well-known celebrity baby born by gestational carrier in 2007, and just as the paperwork was signed, Dessie was approached by the V Network to star in a show about wealthy women living and working in the entertainment industry.

'I remember a working title was *Hostesses of Hollywood*, but they changed it when I signed up. They said I brought class to the proceedings, and darling, I still do! I thought it would be great for both my growing lingerie business, and also promoting motherhood later in life.'

The rest is history. The show revolutionized television, coming as it did alongside *Keeping Up with the Kardashians* and *The Hills*. There was a new format in town – scripted reality about beautiful, wealthy people who had problems, just like the rest of us.

Dessie and her family saw their status skyrocket. 'I never wanted the girls or my husband to be on the show, but the network insisted I show my real life. And then I realized it could be good for them, particularly Lavinia, who was going through a tricky period of restlessness. She found her way into high fashion off the back of being somewhat notorious on television. It's been a stepping stone for all of us – you can't buy the publicity the show has given my business.'

Dessie now does it all. Her first foray into becoming a brand name was DD+, her collection of stunning lingerie for the fuller-breasted woman. It grew with the show, and its success enabled her to broaden her empire, which now includes Freckle cosmetics, her own brand of bronzing products ('Irish women need all the help we can get in the tanning department,' she winks), Dazzle, a range of hair extensions and volumizing potions to help keep locks lustrous, an interiors line called The DD Touch with Pottery Barn, and even a spin-off home-makeover show on HGTV, *Dessie Decorates*.

She's started investing in the influencer market also, having seen first hand the success earned by her middle daughter, and is a major shareholder in Lavinia's LRS Inc. 'The secret to staying young is staying relevant – and having an excellent surgeon on speed dial,' she deadpans. 'You need to keep your finger on the pulse. I could just spend my days pottering around my homes, playing with my grandchildren. But I feel like as soon as I stop moving forward, I'm dead.'

Ominous words, perhaps, but there is just no stopping Dessie. Her latest DD+ collaboration with the buxom and beautiful actress Sofia Vergara has just launched, she's being pursued by Spotify to develop a podcast distilling her unique wisdom, and she's still managing Lavinia's and Ariel's social media careers. There's plenty of life in this diva yet, so watch this space.

2

I met Jason Dempsey when I was thirty-two years old. I was just out of yet another long-term relationship, having dumped an insipid pathological liar named Dustin. We'd been living in LA together almost three years when I'd discovered Dustin had been a member of the online cheating site Ashley Madison. I'd looked for his name mostly as a joke when the database of members was hacked and released, but there it was in black and white. Maybe I already knew.

That was the end of that, but I was not even remotely ready to face the dating scene; after a lifetime of accidental serial monogamy with a succession of losers I wanted to focus on myself for once.

You see, I have a history of fondness for absolute dorks. Men that seem nice when you meet them, that always want me to be their girlfriend and don't act out with ghosting or breadcrumbing or any of those shitty things modern daters have to put up with. But in the end, they're always without fail a shower of soul-sapping saps who can't so much as brush their own teeth without guidance – that description comes straight from Dessie, and it's painfully accurate.

My mother says it's a reaction to my father being a charming but often absent figure in my life. My sister says I have the worst taste ever, that I treat men like rescue dogs looking to be rehomed. My retort is that they both have a recessive gene that makes them go for the most clichéd of men – the seemingly reformed bad boy.

But when Jason first shook my hand one fall morning,

it was like being struck by lightning. He was much better-looking than my usual type, which in the past had been strictly lanky and average. Here was a man with sandy hair, a good head taller than me and solid with it, and with the bluest eyes I'd ever seen. I was a goner there and then. I'd heard about the thunderbolt, but I'd never experienced it until that moment.

And I wasn't exactly looking my best that day. I'd been staying at my mother's place in Bel Air since the break-up and debating whether to stick it out with sitcom pitches in Hollywood or head back to the relative safety of my old writers' room in New York. Writing for the screen is far less glamorous than it looks from the outside, and I was getting tired of giving my all to an idea, getting to the stage of shooting a pilot, and the show not getting picked up by a network.

After a couple of years of living in La-La Land, I was desperate to get back into some sort of routine, and that was a more likely prospect in New York, where I'd be welcome on staff with an old collaborator. Still, it was coming in to winter on the East Coast, so I was biding my time in the balmy Bel Air climate.

The morning I met Jason I'd crawled out of bed after a very late night out. I'd been woken by my seven-year-old sister, Ariel, scooting down the corridor and shrieking about wanting another puppy. Coffee, I needed coffee.

I had heard my mom mention she'd be filming that day, but with Dessie, that could mean anything – a YouTube video, an infomercial for one of her brands, or for her show. When I rubbed my bleary eyes and copped that there was an entire crew in the kitchen, I realized it was the latter.

My mother was in full glam, lit to perfection and positioned in front of a camera. In the business, this is known as a 'confessional', where a reality star narrates and analyses the action viewers see unfolding after the fact. It's Dessie's favourite part, because she gets to use her killer one-liners to eviscerate the other women.

My mother is one of the stars of *Ladies of Los Angeles*, or *LOLA*, as it's known on the internet. It's a reality show that follows the lives of affluent, beautiful women in a particular locale. I was interning in New York after grad school at NYU when it all started, so was never really involved – not the way Vinnie was, anyway. But several seasons in, the show had become notorious on cable TV and had legions of devout fans – gay guys and women, mostly. My mother has been well known for as long as I can remember, but by this point she had become something of a zeitgeist favourite. I could barely go online without seeing a meme of her face.

'Oh god, so sorry, Mom!' I called sheepishly. 'I'm just going to get a coffee and then I'll disappear!'

'Nonsense, pet, come over here and meet some of the new guys.'

I've always been taught to be polite to a fault, so I did as instructed even though my hair was a like a bird's nest and I was wearing sweatpants with ice-cream stains on them. I pasted on a smile, prepared to shake hands and make nice.

'This is Sam, the new social media guy, and this is Jason, who is my new story producer, and I simply adore them both! Guys, this is my beautiful daughter Portia.'

I smiled at the first man, who hardly looked up from his phone, and then BAM! I was shaking hands with a stubbled Adonis and feeling a physical shock at his touch.

'That's a beautiful name,' he grinned at me, still holding my hand.

'I got off lightly,' I whispered.

'Sometimes I call her Titty!' trilled my mother. 'She was going to be Titania, but I decided that was too dramatic, even for me. But I couldn't exactly give her a normal name, could

I? I'm Desdemona, her father is Roberto bloody Rizzi, she could hardly be little Mary or Karen!'

Jason was still smiling at me and I felt myself blossoming under his gaze. 'My middle name is Flavia. She really likes vowels,' I smirked. 'I hope she's treating you well?'

'Dessie is an absolute pleasure.' He beamed at my mother and I noticed an Irish accent. No wonder she loved this guy. 'She tells me you work in the business too?'

'Oh, I'm just a boring writer, it's all behind the scenes – the exact opposite of all this glamour.'

'She is talking absolute shite, Jason, darling. Portia has been beavering away on an utterly divine romcom for ever, she's like my little Nora Ephron, but fresh and modern. She's fabulous. She's got a great eye too. I have her sitting in on all my design meetings for DD+ this year.'

I had not agreed to that yet, of course. But that was my mother all over.

He gestured to the backdrop behind him, a sort of brightly lit and perfected version of the room's usual set-up, only with more fresh flowers and a Versace vase I'd never seen before. 'Well, if you've got the eye, how did we do?'

I narrowed my eyes. 'Hmm . . . for Dessie, you could use a little more leopard print. Maybe some added topless men lounging about the place? A bit more leather? She's big with the gay community, you know.'

'Darling, they're coming at noon.' My mother winked a perfectly made-up eye at me. She and Vinnie have the most feline green eyes, and it's always made my brown ones feel completely nondescript. 'Now, hurry along and let me get this finished. I've asked Jason to stay for dinner, because I want to reminisce about the old country with him.' She winked at me again behind his back. 'Join us! Six p.m. sharp. Chef is making bacon and cabbage.'

And that's how I fell in love, over boiled pig and smelly green vegetables.

I developed the most disgusting crush on Jason Dempsey, the kind that consumes your every waking moment and some while you're asleep too. He was working with Dessie most days, so Jason was around the house a lot. I was hyper-aware of him physically, as if I was being drawn towards him like a magnet. But while there was lots of flirting and friendly banter, he wasn't making any moves.

I was mooning about, texting my best friend Suz about him non-stop. Suz is a proper grown-up with two kids and a high-flying TV job as a late-night host on CBS, so she wasn't exactly available to parse every glance and syllable Jason and I exchanged. My other best friend David, on the other hand, is a fiend for gossip and was there to dissect every milli-second of contact with my latest infatuation. He's also my mother's chief hairstylist, so could observe my interactions with Jason up close.

After a week of torture, I was struggling to keep my shit together; my crush had become crushing. Every day I noticed something new and desirable about Jason. He wasn't a fixer-upper; he was a fully-fledged man. He was decisive at work, knew exactly what he wanted. The crew seemed to respect and admire him, and he was funny and smart. Plus, he had amazing arms and shoulders, the kind that could either crush you or hold you tight, and the most perfect little ears. You know you've got it bad for a guy when you're obsessing over their ears.

Dessie was totally on to me. 'I see you watching Jason like a hawk, you know. I don't blame you, either.'

She was lying on the floor of her walk-in wardrobe stretch-ing her back on the sumptuous cream carpet. The closet resembled a small boutique rather than a place to keep your clothes. Shelves artfully displayed dozens of pairs of heels, and the rails were full of bright colours and prints. There was jewellery in glass-topped units, but that was only the costume stuff – anything of value was in the hidden safe.

I was blow-drying my hair at the light-up vanity. I'd started taking more care with my appearance over the previous days – my glossy chocolate bob was styled every morning, my skin holding its summer tan thanks to my Sicilian genes, and raiding Dessie's impressive skin-care collection. I'd also traded in my sweats for cute leggings that showed off my butt, and sun dresses that were cute but sexy.

'Yes, Mother, I have zero chill and I'm well aware of it. But he's not asking me out,' I sighed. 'Maybe he's not into me?'

'Darling, that's impossible. You're a beauty inside and out. You're my brown-eyed girl! But I didn't raise you to sit around waiting for a man to make the first move . . .'

'I'm trying to be a tiny bit cool, Mom.'

'And failing,' she grinned. She swung herself off the floor on to the pink velvet sofa and fixed me with her killer emerald gaze, described as 'devastating' in *Stellar* magazine, 2017. 'Portia Daniels, you might be trying, but you are fooling nobody. Sure, you might as well be dribbling on him!'

I covered my face with my hands.

'I know, love, you're scarlet. But you'll be even more scarlet if you let him get away. Ask him for a drink, for feck's sake. What's the worst that can happen?'

It was easy to be as confident as my mother when you are Dessie Daniels, a glamour puss who leaves men drooling in your wake even in late middle age. She has dark hair like me, but hers is skilfully streaked with copper balayage by David, and her cat-like eyes steal the show even in an otherwise beautiful face. She's got a tiny little nose and a perfect chin, and the kind of appearance where you know she's had some work done but you don't know what exactly because it's very, very good.

But being little old me, it was slightly more frightening. I'm relatively self-assured, in the way that I know who I am and what I bring to the table. But it felt like there was a lot riding on how I felt about Jason Dempsey.

In the end, it all happened by accident. I was out in West Hollywood at a sexy new bar called Laurel Hardware the night after Dessie's pep talk, accompanying David on a quest to find a guy he'd been stalking on Grindr.

'I don't understand why you have to go looking for him, Dave – isn't the entire point of Grindr location-based hook-ups?'

'Well, that's how I know where he is right now, yes. But I don't want this to be another Grindr hook-up. This man is going to be the love of my life!' I rolled my eyes; I'd heard that one before.

He dragged me through a thronging crowd at the bar. It was the latest hotspot in a strip of hotspots, a place where everyone was gorgeous, of indiscriminate sexual orientation, and pheromones were heavy in the air. West Hollywood is the epicentre of LA nightlife, a former hotbed of anarchy and rock and roll in the 1970s and now a gay-focused paradise of late bars and buzzy restaurants.

'How do you know this guy, anyway?' I enquired while David's eyes raked the room.

'I did his hair for a shoot last week, then I followed him on Instagram, but I was convinced he was too hot for me. Then I saw a photo of him with his ex and realized he likes pale and interesting.'

David is certainly that. I've known him since I was six years old; we met when both our families holidayed in Ballybunion,

Co. Kerry. A Kerry boy himself but from the village of Barraduff, he always thought Vinnie and I were the absolute height of glamour with our LA drawls and natural tans.

In contrast, he is white as a sheet and has bright red hair. We fell in platonic love the summer we turned nine, when we raided Dessie's suitcase together and he gave me a makeover. Despite thousands of miles apart over the years, and him working as a session stylist in Dublin, London and then Milan while I was at NYU, we remained as close as can be.

I honed my writing skills with long letters sent across the Atlantic in the pre-internet era, and when dial-up internet reached Co. Kerry, we spent hours on MSN Messenger. When Dessie hit the big time, it was David she hired to head up her glam squad; by then he'd made a name for himself working backstage at various fashion weeks around Europe, but he'd recently lost his own mom. He moved Stateside in 2007 at the age of twenty-four, sponsored by Dessie. My mother is incredibly loyal, to her credit, and their business relationship has evolved to include salons in New York, Palm Springs and WeHo.

David was still talking. '. . . then I saw him on Grindr earlier, and I knew he was, if not single, then at least ready to mingle . . . Look, there he is!'

Before I could say anything, David was off, chasing a beautiful Brazilian guy with several earrings across the room. If I was an accidental serial monogamist, David was a purposefully polyamorous prowler.

I plonked myself down at the bar. I'd give him fifteen minutes to shoot his shot and have a strong Martini while I was waiting. I went to order and came face to face with none other than Jason Dempsey.

'Hey, it's Titty!' He grinned. 'Your mother is some character.'

'Well, let's be glad that didn't stick, because I didn't exactly inherit her greatest assets.' I smiled back. 'What are you doing behind the bar? Moonlighting for tips?'

'Ha, I wish. I pull a decent pint, but there's no call for them here – everyone drinks skinny Margaritas. No, I'm doing a recce for a new show about the sex lives of ridiculously good-looking bar staff in West Hollywood.'

'Sounds . . . great?' I offered, grimacing.

'It's shocking.' He laughed, leaning over the bar. 'They are all terrible, terrible people. I'd much rather get to know you better, now I'm off the clock at your mother's house. Mind if I join you for a drink?'

I glanced over at David, who was coquettishly stroking his conquest's shorn hair – likely offering him a freebie. 'I'd like that very much.'

From there, it was a whirlwind. We'd go for strolls on the beach in Santa Monica, spend hours in dive bars shooting pool, stay up all night talking. He wrote me notes on actual paper when he had to leave early in the morning, preferring love letters written in pen. My heart would almost burst in the mornings when I woke up to a piece of folded printer paper on his empty pillow, proof I hadn't just dreamt him.

From these long conversations in the wee hours, I learned that he'd come to California after a bad break-up in London and that he hadn't lived in his native Limerick since he left for college in Dublin.

'I sort of fell into television,' he told me at 2 a.m., a few weeks after that first handshake zipped straight from my fingers to my crotch. We were in Dessie's guest room, naked in a tangle of sheets, as we had been most nights since we met that evening at the bar. For once I was thankful that I was between projects and had nowhere to be and nothing to do except gaze into this beautiful man's eyes and jump his bones whenever I got the chance.

'I was doing freelance bits in London in the media, and ended up as an assistant producer on a morning talk show, which is where I met the ex. When that relationship ended, I obviously wanted to leave the show – she was the head make-up artist, she'd been there first and I had itchy feet anyway. I got an opportunity to work on a dating series set in Portugal, so off I went. Then when they were making the US version, I got the call, and I've been here ever since. Two years on *Lust in the Sun US*, and now I've crossed over to *LOLA*.'

I was less interested in his professional resumé than his romantic one. 'Why did that relationship end?' I murmured, lying on his chest and stroking the wiry fair hairs.

'Ah, it was a long time coming. We wanted different things.'

'A familiar story,' I grinned. 'Same with me and mine. Mostly, though, I wanted him not to be a lazy, lying layabout who signed up to an extramarital affair website even before we were married.'

'Oh, it wasn't like that with Molly. She was great.' I stored the name away for some light social media stalking later. 'She just wanted to move home to Ireland, have babies and get married, and that just wasn't for me. I don't think it ever will be. She said I was a commitment-phobe, I said she didn't understand me, and that was that. She's already married to someone else, and good luck to her.'

I realized I was holding my breath and tried to act cool. 'So, uh, babies aren't for you, then?' I trilled.

'Shite, have I scared you off?' He rolled on to one arm and looked down at me, concerned. I'm not being cheesy when I say he took my breath away. 'No, I can't have scared the sexiest, funniest girl I've ever met! I'm not some horrible guy that wants to lead women on, I'm just not the most traditional, I guess. My work has always been really important, and I didn't want to just go home and get a mortgage and then . . .'

'Sssshh.' I put my finger on his lips. 'I was only asking because, well, it's awkward to bring this sort of thing up, but I guess it's important to get it out there when you're in your thirties . . .'

He looked worried.

'It's nothing bad! I just don't want any children. Ever,' I managed. 'It's something I've always known, but I realize it's not exactly the norm so I find it's better to say it early. That way we both know where we stand.'

I looked at him as he digested my outburst and was pleased that he didn't seem to be horrified. I hadn't meant to blurt it out like that, but if he was looking for a gal who wanted to be barefoot and pregnant he was barking up the wrong tree, and he might as well know that sooner rather than later.

'I'm not just saying that to appear like that Cool Girl stereotype, the one that's totally unbothered until she has you hooked. I mean it. Ask anyone in my family, I've never seen myself being a mother, never felt maternal. It's just . . . not in me. And I used to think I'd have to compromise myself to be in a relationship. Maybe that's why I spent the last fifteen years dating unreliable, emotionally unavailable assholes.' I paused for breath, realizing I was babbling when I clocked his grin.

'I know this is brand new, and I know it's a lot to take in, but what I'm saying is – I'm not going to ask you to knock me up, or for a ring, even. Not now, not ever. I just want to be with somebody that I respect, and that gives me dizzying but-terflies, and . . .' I lifted the sheet. 'Has a completely perfect dick.'

His eyes went dark, the way I'd noticed they did when he was horny.

'Say no more,' he whispered. 'And put my perfect dick in that perfect mouth.'

And for six and a half years, we'd had what I had thought was the perfect relationship. Of course, we'd discussed our future over that time, and we were on the same page – we wanted a life of freedom and adventure together, a relationship where we came first for one another.

When Jason transitioned from *LOLA* to its New York franchise, *LONY*, we'd bought a place together, admittedly with more than a little help from my mom – a beautiful second-floor walk-up in Greenwich Village that was almost a New York City real estate urban legend. The unicorn property spanned an entire storey of an old brownstone, meaning that it was still compact but it had two roomy bedrooms, an open-plan kitchen and living room and lots of natural light.

My life had been nomadic until that point; I spent my childhood travelling anywhere my parents had to be but was always based in LA until I left for college at NYU. I was happy to be back in my spiritual home with a staff job on a long-running series.

For the first time in my adult life, things felt steady and serene. And no matter what, Jason and I were each other's constant. We supported one another through everything – missing our families, stressful work days (months, years), exciting opportunities, painful disappointments. Despite getting older and witnessing the couples in our circle doing the usual things couples do, our situation remained happily the same. We attended weddings, bar mitzvahs, funerals, naming ceremonies, and never wavered in our opinion – that we were strong as a twosome, that neither of us wanted anything more and that we were as deeply committed as a couple could be.

We swatted away all the 'you're next!' comments, rolled

our eyes when people commented on my bare ring finger. I wasn't just pretending to be fine with our status; I was truly content. We had each other, and that was enough.

And even though we were seen as childless, unmarried heathens by many, we had an inkling that we were also the couple everyone secretly envied – we had money, sure, but more than that, we had so much fun together. We travelled whenever we could, went out to dinner most nights and really talked to one another. We soaked up the culture of the city we loved and we enjoyed our downtime together, the peace that comes with a happy relationship of equals. Ours was a work hard, play hard arrangement and it suited us. Until this.

Jason knew I was in shock after his revelation – being soaked in coffee spit will hammer that home – and he also knew me well enough to know that I would need time to digest what he'd told me.

I've always known that I don't want to be a mother, the same way you know that the sky is blue and that gravity is what keeps your feet on the ground. As long as I've been conscious, it's been clear to me that I never wanted to have kids, from when I was a little girl ignoring baby dolls to an adolescent realizing for the first time that how I felt was unusual.

When I was a teenager my friends and I were all preoccupied with avoiding pregnancy at all costs. But at some point I came to understand that for all of my girlfriends this was but a temporary measure. Eventually, they all wanted to add 'Mommy' to their resumés, when I knew that I categorically did not and would remain fearful of a missed period for the remainder of my fertile years.

And me being me, someone who availed themself of therapy as soon as I got to NYU, I wanted to talk about it and normalize how I felt. But that just resulted in an avalanche of questions from all and sundry. Why did I not want children? Was there some trauma in my past? Was I frightened of pregnancy? Would eschewing motherhood mean a life without meaning, and lonely twilight years?

My answers rarely varied – a) I just don't, b) as much trauma as any child raised in Los Angeles, c) well, it sounds absolutely barbaric, but that's not why, and to d), I'd normally just glare. I realized that talking about not wanting kids only engendered discussion, and my life choices were up for debate. I was the outlier, and I just had to accept that.

Discovering early on that Jason didn't want to have kids either seemed to confirm that he was the perfect fit for me. I just couldn't believe he had now changed his mind. I'd worried that it was always a vague possibility in a sort of abstract way, and other people often told us that we'd get sick of our wandering ways and city life. But I had zero desire to trade in my passport for a pram in my late thirties and was certain I never would. It wasn't about our lifestyle or our careers, or anything except the fact that we didn't want to be parents. Raising a child was not something we felt compelled to do, ever.

Well, that's how I felt. And I had thought Jason felt the same way. Even through the haze of shock, I knew that something had shifted. This wasn't a discussion, a place for compromise or working things out.

If Jason truly wanted to be a father, that wasn't something I could ask him to give up. The simple fact was, if he meant what he was saying, we were no longer on the same page. At that moment in a five-star hotel in Limerick, I had been issued an ultimatum.

3

It's one thing having a well-known mother, but quite another having an uber-famous sister. My mom occupies a niche area of celebrity culture – diehard reality fans screech and cry when they meet her and people my age who loved her on *Baywatch* always want to yap her ear off. Irish people are proud of her doing so well in the US. But with Vinnie, or LRS, as she's known to her legions of fans, it's a different level of notoriety.

In her heyday, Vinnie was the model of the moment. Along with Agyness Deyn and Arizona Muse, her look came to epitomize the noughties – androgynous, lithe, striking. She's softened now, her hair long, golden-blonde and sleek, her style more coastal mommy casual chic. But with this new iteration of Vinnie has come a new kind of fame, and her followers are so devout they're practically feral.

That's why I found myself running into my building a fortnight after my return from Ireland, shielding Vinnie from a pack of yummy mummies with strollers that had clocked her on the corner and were literally chasing her down the block. 'Oh my god, Lavinia, your nipple pads changed my life!' screamed one, rolling her poor baby at my sister with brute force.

I only exhaled once we were in the relative safety of the hallway. 'Jesus Christ, Vin. I have no idea how you put up with that madness.'

She shrugged, looking genuinely unruffled. 'I would've stopped for a selfie, you know. You didn't have to manhandle me into the foyer.'

'I was protecting you! One of those mothers had a mean glint in her eye.'

Vinnie laughed. 'Portia, these women are my bread and butter. Without them following me, liking my stuff, buying my nipple pads and signing up to my mindfulness webinars, I am just another washed-up former model. I'll have to post something now about my schedule being crazy, or they'll all be in the comments calling me a rude bitch.'

Not for the first time I marvelled at her wherewithal. To me, she is my younger sister Vinnie. But to her fans she is a goddess, the ethereal vision Lavinia who blends business savvy and supermom powers. They don't know that it's actually our mom's business savvy, and Vinnie is happy to keep them in the dark.

She is of course also physically impressive; she's six feet tall, and while she has Mom's green eyes every other bit of her comes from our father. A strong Roman nose, an athletic figure and naturally perfect teeth make her beautiful, but more in an interesting rather than just a pretty way. She's been bleaching her hair since she was a teenager, but with dark roots now blended with such flawless balayage by David, it looks as if she naturally has two-tone hair. Vinnie is no sex kitten like Dessie but all jumbled up together; her attributes are literally stunning. The camera loves her, but it makes me freeze like a deer in the headlights.

I could be painfully jealous of my sister because I'm five feet seven and have a softer jawline and less mysterious eyes. But I learned growing up that with great height and striking beauty comes great responsibility – sometimes it's easier to be the cute, normal-looking sister.

Vinnie and I are not just chalk and cheese when it comes to our appearance but in our wildly different lifestyles. Yet our differences have never stopped us being extremely close.

There's a little over a year between us in age. Much to Dessie's disappointment, we're not quite Irish twins – even with her formidable focus she didn't manage to get pregnant in time to produce baby number two within a year. We might as well be twins though, as we are two sides of the same coin. We both love to have fun, we're both creative, both fiercely protective of our family. If Vinnie is the light and bright, albeit with an edge, I am her dark and mysterious counterpart who likes to keep my business to myself.

Knowing the real Vinnie as I do, I don't envy her in the slightest. Her career as a lifestyle influencer is my idea of a living hell. But it works for her – she gets to be a mother, which is all she's ever really wanted, and make a living from just . . . living.

'Okay, that's today's work done,' she declared, posting the photo I'd taken of her at this morning's wellness event downtown with a flourish. She'd been paid a fortune to travel to New York and speak to a crowd of adoring followers, all the while promoting her new line of pre-natal vitamins. 'You make a good photographer, sis.'

'Maybe I inherited some of Dad's "visionary talent"?' I said. Vinnie looked up. She knew that tone.

'It sure as hell beats ending up with his gambling addiction,' I added, elbowing her in the ribs.

She swatted me away; she doesn't like it when I speak ill of our father. 'I'm kidding, Vin. You're an easy subject to make look good.'

We walked into my open-plan apartment and were greeted by absolute chaos. I expected a bit of mess, as Jason and I were hosting Vinnie, her kids and their nanny, Marjorie, for the weekend, but this was . . . a lot. My sister doesn't like hotels; she thinks they're impersonal and worries about the staff going through her stuff. Ever since she watched *Maid in*

Manhattan on a plane a few years back, she's been paranoid. Vinnie has her quirks, and she'd rather stay with us in our relatively small apartment than somewhere more comfortable. Luckily, Jason understands her idiosyncrasies and Marjorie doesn't mind the couch.

I noticed a makeshift teepee in the living room, some sort of foodstuff smeared on my beloved white oak desk, and toys strewn across my teal sofa and beloved Persian rug. 'Jason?' I screeched.

At that moment, two curly-haired creatures emerged from the tent and barrelled at us, chorusing, 'MOMMY-YYYYYYY! AUNTIE P!!!!!' I caught the smaller one before I was headbutted in the crotch, while Vinnie artfully grabbed the other and spun him around. My nephews Sebastian and Silas take after their mother when it comes to grabbing attention.

Jason appeared from the bedroom, looking sheepish. I knew then that he'd broken Vinnie's cardinal rule and given the boys sugar; Sebastian was practically foaming at the mouth.

'Babe, where's the nanny?' I enquired, trying to remove Silas's teeth from my ear. He had sharp incisors, for a five-year-old.

'I gave her the afternoon off.'

Vinnie rounded on him. 'You did what?!'

'Yeah, I thought she deserved it! Marjorie has never been to New York before, I told her to go and see the sights and I could mind these little munchkins. I feel bad she's sleeping on our couch, the poor thing.'

Vinnie was visibly on edge. 'That's not the way we work, Jason. The boys have a super-strict schedule with home-schooling when we travel, Marjorie knows that. I can't believe she'd just up and leave without calling, and she had such excellent references from Victoria and David . . .'

'Relax, Vinnie.' He gave her his megawatt grin, the one that reduces all opponents to a pile of mush. 'I'm family! I love the boys; I've got it covered. We've been having a laugh. She'll be back at dinnertime, and she left me tons of instructions.'

Vinnie and I looked at the boys, who did seem to have all limbs intact, and big toothy grins on their faces. Seb, seven and a half, was positively gleeful. I saw my sister exhale. 'Okay. Thanks, Jason. That was really good of you. God knows their father is often too busy to just hang out with them, so this is . . . nice.'

'No problemo. We've been having *man time*!' At these words, the boys started screeching and giggling, jumping on him as he pretended to drag his knuckles on the floor like an orangutan. My heart lurched at the sight of my partner, so happy playing with my nephews. I felt the weight of everything unspoken between us bearing down on me.

Vinnie took one look at me and made a decision. 'Right, if you've got everything so beautifully handled here, I'm taking my sister for a boozy lunch. You're right, Jason. When in New York, one must do New York-y things.'

'Go, have fun, girls,' he called from underneath two writhing children as we made a break for the front door. 'We'll practise our ABCs. I could use a refresher!'

A half-hour later Vinnie and I were in a booth at the Standard Grill clinking icy glasses of Aperol Spritz. Well, Vinnie's was a mocktail, but you'd never guess. Booze had never been her crutch in her wild years, more uppers and downers, but alcohol was off limits for a recovering addict.

Vinnie was sober more than eight years, since the age of twenty-nine. A year later, she was swept off her feet by Billy Schwartz, a Hollywood agent who married and knocked her up in quick succession. The boys are his clones, compact little dudes of five and seven with dark, curly hair and cheeky grins. It remains to be seen whether they'll inherit their mother's height or their father's lack thereof.

'God, it's so nice to get this time to myself,' she said, beaming. 'I'd better take a picture. My followers love knowing that I'm not chained to the boys 24/7. Moms need a break too!'

'Cheers.' I grimaced. I was still shaken by the memory of Jason looking utterly elated with a feral child hanging off each limb. He has a tendency towards immaturity at times, but he'd been so natural with them.

Vinnie knew all about his bombshell in Ireland, of course. I'd FaceTimed her bawling before we'd even landed back in New York.

'So, it's been a couple of weeks,' she said, finished with her snapping. 'Have you guys talked about the baby thing yet?' She took a sip of her drink.

'No, and I've sort of been hoping we wouldn't have to. That it was a momentary blip brought on by nostalgia and proximity to family, never to be discussed again.'

'Portia, be serious.' I sensed I was about to get a lecture; she was gearing up to use the same ever-so-slightly holier than thou tone bestowed upon her followers when she talked about the importance of breastfeeding and teaching your kids how to use the potty with positive reinforcement.

Vinnie was probably the least empathetic of those closest to me when it came to my stance on kids. But I never held it against her – she's one of those mothers who thinks a woman's life isn't fulfilled without children. She grew up besotted with babies, begging Dessie to have another one every chance she got. I was quite happy just the two of us, and at age seven I told my mother that another baby would 'disrupt the family dynamic'. (What can I say, I've always been precocious.)

34

Vinnie always felt that she was put on earth to be the greatest mother of all time. She believed that even when her track record with men was frightful. She had many a fraught, high-profile break-up: the Oscar-nominated actor who cheated on her incessantly, the rock star with a fondness for groupies and heroin, the clean-cut boy-band star who was bisexual and into polyamory . . . I could go on. But even when she was busy being the *enfant terrible* of fashion, haunting clubs and making headlines, she was always certain that having multiple children was in her future. She was just waiting for the right opportunity.

Since the boys were born, Vinnie has made being a mother her *raison d'être*. In fact, we were all surprised she hadn't had a third yet, but I wasn't rude enough to ask her why. I don't believe in questioning women about procreating, unlike some.

And Vinnie is a fantastic mother. Kind, nurturing, responsible (believe me, I'm more shocked than most about that one), open-minded. I know Seb and Si will grow up feeling valued, like they can be their true selves, whoever that may be. And despite being so privileged, those boys are neither spoilt nor bratty. They're high energy and a lot of work, but they are sweet and loving, and I adore being their auntie more than I can say. I also love handing them back.

Knowing how deeply Vinnie loved being a mother – not only loved it but had a bone-deep sense that it is a woman's destiny – I knew she'd try to talk me around. She took a deep breath, and she was off. 'The man is perfectly within his rights to want a child. It's the most normal, natural thing in the world.' She held up a hand when I began to protest. 'I know he said he didn't want to be a father when you met, but P, things change. Everything has changed in the world since You Know What, and I know where he's coming from.

When I was running around the city taking ket and blowing bartenders, I never imagined I'd be where I am now. Being a parent is the most fulfilling, important . . .'

I cut her off. 'Please, spare me the sermon about motherhood, Lavinia.' I only ever use her full name when I'm pissed off. 'I don't need to hear it, I know how the vast majority of people feel about the wonder of having children. And I know we need to talk, but clearly, neither of us is keen on the idea of discussing how our relationship can possibly be saved if he's serious. And please,' I begged, 'don't blame the pandemic on Jason suddenly wanting to sire an heir.'

Vinnie acquiesced. She's so used to giving unsolicited advice, sometimes she forgets with me.

'It's all I've been thinking about since he told me,' I admitted. 'And you're absolutely right, people change. But I haven't, and I just didn't think my person would either. I thought we were the same.' I hung my head. 'I thought I was enough.'

'You are enough, as a life partner. But this is different, it's elemental, inherent. Man has sex with wife, man make family.'

'Well, I'm not his wife, am I?' I snorted.

'Do you want to be?'

I sighed. 'It's never mattered! None of that was ever important to me because I just knew I had him, he was mine and I was his. This has been a complete bolt from the blue. It's making me rethink everything I've ever known about him, about us.'

Vinnie looked at me sympathetically as she twirled her straw. 'I know I'm not an expert on relationships. Christ, Billy and I are like ships in the night most of the time. But if I can give you some advice, as an old married lady with children . . .'

I nodded, grudgingly. She was going to, whether I wanted her to or not.

'I think you should do the done thing. It's the done thing

for a reason! Give him what he wants and you'll both be happy, in the end,' she stated. 'You'll come around to motherhood, just don't overthink it. You could even surprise yourself and love it!'

I could have been upset with Vinnie. I could have over-analysed the fact that she seemingly knew nothing about me if she thought I could just flick a switch and want to have kids after thirty-eight years of knowing in my gut that I didn't. But I also knew that she's just a glass-half-full kind of person, someone who's been through a lot and genuinely believes that you can manifest anything you want for yourself. It's hard to blame her for it, with the extraordinary existence she's experienced, so I'd learned not to take her advice too seriously. Still, I was rattled into silence. She took that to mean I was heeding her and kept talking.

'. . . humans have kids for a reason, you know? It's not just about propagating the species; they give you purpose and something to think about besides yourself . . .'

Our meals arrived mid-monologue and Vinnie dived on her fries, even though her followers are advised that a low-glycaemic-index-based organic diet is best. 'I know you've never seen yourself as a mommy, but trust me, the reality is different,' she said with a mouthful of potato. 'And if I were you, I would do anything to keep hold of a man like Jason.'

'What do you mean, keep hold of him?'

We were interrupted by a fawning woman doing a little dance beside the table. 'Ohmigod, Lavinia, it is you! I am so sorry to interrupt, but I just want to thank you for always being an ally for working mothers, iloveyousomuuuuch . . .'

Vinnie flashed the megawatt smile she's known for the world over. 'Come, sit down next to me, you lovely, sweet momma you!' She proceeded to allow the woman to cuddle and compliment her for the next five minutes, made a big show of following her back on Instagram, and enlisted me to take a (very nice, actually) photo of the two of them. The woman floated away, thrilled with herself. That was the Lavinia effect.

She turned back to me, and suddenly she was my sister again. She continued talking as if the interruption had never happened. 'Well, sis, you can't expect him to deny a biological desire, can you? If it's not with you, well . . . it's going to be with somebody else.'

I downed the rest of my cocktail.

Four hours later we found ourselves twenty storeys above the High Line, propping up the bar at Le Bain and The Rooftop, looking out over stunning views of Ellis Island and the Hudson. Lunch had turned into drinks, which had turned into calling David, who had been working in Salon O'Shea Soho all day, to meet us and continue the fun.

Marjorie the nanny-slash-schoolteacher was back with the kids. She's Venezuelan and a petite, cheerful presence. After a FaceTime with her and the boys Vinnie was convinced that all was well. Jason was shooting *LONY* at a black-tie gala and my head was so scrambled I could do with the fuzzy reprieve of a drunken evening out.

Vinnie was sober but high as a kite from freedom and the placebo effect of virgin G&Ts. I was forever afraid the old Vinnie would make an unfortunate reappearance and be filmed for social media. Her followers don't mind her letting her hair down, she was a reformed party girl, after all. But any indication of inappropriate behaviour and she'd be cancelled – and that's without them having any inkling that she was actually in recovery.

Perception is everything in Vinnie's industry, and perfection is non-negotiable. That's why her devout followers can never know that she's been in rehab for both substance abuse and food issues. Our Aunt Giulia is also the family publicist and has always managed to keep the more salacious elements of Vinnie's past under wraps. I wouldn't cross Giulia; I'm lucky that being a blood relative means our Sicilian auntie would pretty much die for me.

That night, though, Vinnie was just loving life. Nobody in the exclusive bar was batting an eyelid at her presence so she was letting loose, regaling David and me with stories of her craziest DMs while he and I sipped thirty-dollar espresso Martinis.

'. . . then this woman says, "Your children are sooo ugly," and I will admit, it hurt for, like, a nanosecond until I looked at her profile and saw her own offspring. I'm not one to mock children, but my *god*, like this lady did not have a leg to stand on dissing my beautiful boys! As I always say, hurt people hurt people,' she intoned.

'I'm going for a cig,' I whispered to David, easing myself off the high stool and heading for the terrace. I was lost in a reverie and a cloud of nicotine when David sidled up beside me and poked me in the ribs.

'Do *not* leave me with her when she's on one of her beautiful boys rants, you bitch,' he intoned. 'She's met a fan in there.' He jerked his head towards the bar. 'Some Upper East Side old bag that adores Dessie and just *loves* Vinnie's highlights. Does she get them done at Fekkai, she asked.' David snorted. 'I was about to tell her they're a Salon O'Shea special but thought the better of it.'

He reached for my cigarette and took a lusty drag. 'Right, shall we discuss my sex life when we get back, or are we going to talk about the elephant in the room?'

'Don't talk that way about Vinnie!' I giggled, but he only raised his eyebrows. I wasn't getting away with avoiding Jason talk. David was my boyfriend's biggest fan, and equally horri-fied by the recent turn of events. He thought we were special, a rare couple in a world of 'normies', as he put it.

'Honestly, Dave, I don't have room in my head for all the thoughts flying around. I've had Vinnie's take on my life today, and believe me, that's enough.'

'Let me guess, she thinks you should get knocked up, like, yesterday?' He harrumphed at my nod. 'Portia, I have known you almost your entire life. You are a woman who knows her own mind. Yes, Jason Dempsey is an absolute ride and you two are annoyingly fabulous together. But the woman I know would never, ever, do something she didn't want to do. Espe-cially something as momentous as birthing new life. And I'm not just saying this because I've been depending on you two being my fabulous, fellow child-free-by-choice friends when we're sixty.'

A tear unexpectedly slid down my face, which alarmed him because I am not normally a crier. Vinnie weeps at the drop of a hat, often on Instagram Live (which is apparently 'relatable' and 'vulnerable'), but I'm considered the family ice queen when it comes to showing emotions. At that moment, though, I felt so sad. More than that, I also felt angry.

'I'm sorry, but nobody understands just how shocking this has all been, David. I truly thought he would never hurt me like this. And I am hurt. I'm hurt!' I screeched across the skyline.

David rubbed my back. 'Let it out, girl. Scream it!'

'*I'm hurt!* I feel like he lied! And nobody fucking cares, because they're all too busy feeling sorry for poor Jason and his biological clock!' I was on a furious roll, the rage and fear I'd been keeping tamped down since Jason's revelation spew-ing out into the night sky.

'Nobody cares about the fright I've got, how our whole

relationship has been turned upside down. They just tell me to have a baby, to keep the good man. It's the normal thing to do. But I don't want a baby, David. I've never wanted one, I still don't want one. Why is that not okay? *I really don't want one.*' The trickle of frustrated tears became racking, heaving sobs. David made comforting noises and let me bawl. It felt better to just let it all out, finally.

'Okay, okay, that's enough,' he cooed. 'Your face will never recover if you keep this up. You're not a very pretty crier, Portia.'

That made me laugh, and my sobs slowed to a sniffly trickle. 'Let me look at you,' he said, taking my face in his hands. 'Okay, a little swollen, a lot snotty and gross, but you'll do. You're lucky you've that good, tanned skin, I'd look like a boiled ham if I cried like that.' He wiped under my eyes gently and fluffed out my choppy bob. 'Still, let's be glad it's dark in there.'

David took me by the upper arms and looked in my eyes. 'Look, you don't need an answer right this second. But whatever happens, Portia, you'll be fine. You always have me, okay?'

I nodded. 'I needed that cry.'

'Okay, I'm glad you got all of that out, but it's windy up this high. And I'm sure that Upper East Side queen has a cute homo sidekick, so let's go.'

I threw my arm around his shoulder and we walked back inside together, just in time to see Vinnie dancing with the aforementioned sidekick.

It was going to be one of those nights.

4

I woke up feeling like death. And it wasn't just the hangover, although that was off the charts. My brain was also in meltdown due to Vinnie's prediction that Jason would find a new woman to bring forth his children, as if he was a character in a dystopian novel, driven to propagate his genes by forces beyond his control.

The bout of ugly crying with David had helped a bit in the moment; it had allowed me a brief reprieve from wondering if I was in the wrong, a slight decompression. But still I couldn't shake a feeling of sheer terror – as if I was at the top of a roller coaster about to plummet to my doom.

By lunchtime I had dragged myself into the kitchen for a coffee when I saw a message from Suz demanding I Face-Time her as soon as I felt human. Normally the thought of speaking to anyone when hungover would bring on a bad bout of The Fear, but Suz understood me like nobody else.

Though she had two longed-for daughters and was a wonderful mother, she had always accepted that motherhood was not for me. Not only that, Suz wasn't just one of my closest friends but also my former stepsister – her dad, Kyle Peterson, being Dessie's rebound husband after my father died – so she knew Vinnie and me intimately. She would help me figure this out.

'Well, you look like shit!' was her opening gambit.

'I feel like shit.' I shrugged. 'So that tracks.'

'Oh, honey. I'm sorry. I've only got a minute to chat, I have a production meeting. But I was talking to my other former stepsister this morning and she freaked me out a little. Did she really tell you to just suck it up and get pregnant?'

'She sure did,' I grimaced. Looking at myself in the bottom corner of the screen, I realized Suz was right – I looked exhausted, pale and wan.

'You know that's terrible advice, right? That she's looking at everything through her own lens?'

I nodded. 'I do know that, but thanks for saying it. Sometimes I feel like I'm just being stubborn, so it helps to get a reality check.'

'Honey, I am no expert, but I do know one thing – a single woman in possession of a good fortune needs nothing except herself. I'm paraphrasing Queen Jane Austen, but the message is there – never do anything you don't want to do to keep a man. Even one as fine as Jason.'

I laughed. 'You know I always appreciate a good literary reference.'

'I gotta go, sweetie. Come home soon? You're looking pasty, and I need to squeeze you in real life. Kisses!' She was gone.

It was short and sweet but enough to put me back on an even keel. Suz often jokes that she's like my emotional support dog, that she can tell when I'm about to have a meltdown and is able to nip it in the bud. In my family I was generally the steady, sensible one, but the odd time I wobbled Suz was always able to help me find my equilibrium. Which was funny considering that when our parents first met, there was no love lost between us. We were in the same year in the same Beverly Hills high school and generally steered clear of each other. But getting pushed together, grudgingly, via our parents, we soon realized our personalities were so complementary we'd make the best of friends. I'm an ambivert, someone who likes socializing and being around people, but I also have an insular

43

side where I need time alone to recharge my batteries. She's an extrovert with introvert tendencies, so we tend to balance one another out. As teens, we loved going to parties in the Hills, but we also loved spending the next day relaxing by the pool or watching movies in the cinema room. We both have an off switch, something Vinnie lacks. In the days when Vin was getting high in a Volkswagen van with her stoner friends, Suz became an anchor for me.

By the time we had bonded, the cracks were showing in our parents' ill-advised union, and then we were no longer step-sisters. We joke that I got to keep her in the divorce, and she's still very much part of our family. She and Vinnie became close when my sister got clean, and they lean on each other when it comes to mom stuff.

When Dessie and Kyle got together he was a fledgling anchorman for CNN, having been promoted from the Louisiana outpost a few years previously. Suz went on to follow in her father's footsteps as an entertainment reporter on TV news, and then overtake him. She's the first black woman to host a late-night talk show in the US; *Late Night Chat* has been on air for almost a decade and counting. She was savvy enough to blend social media and YouTube early on, and young enough at thirty to not look silly doing so.

Suz is also utterly gorgeous, which undeniably helped build her fan base – she inherited Kyle's height and gravitas and her Czech model mother's cheekbones, and pictures of what she's wearing are common fodder for the tabloids. She often jokes that she also inherited her father's big ass, and that's why she never made it as a model when Vinnie did. I think it's because she was already well on her way to becoming a broadcast superstar; pouting for the camera full time would never have satisfied Suz.

While Suz and I don't see each other as much as I'd like,

between work, kids and the fact that she's based full time on the West Coast, she's a pillar in my life. We'd been emailing a lot since Jason's declaration and I knew Suz had been worried about me. But at that moment I felt like she had my back. That was assurance enough to know that I wasn't really going crazy.

After Vinnie headed back to LA with Marjorie and the boys, and peace and order had been restored to the apartment, Jason and I continued ignoring our problems and throwing ourselves into work. I knew he didn't want to pressure me but could also sense that his patience with my lack of communication was wearing thin. I am a talker, so my reticence was unusual. But it must have been obvious from my silence that I wasn't capitulating, so we were in some sort of unspoken deadlock.

For the first time in my life I just didn't know what to say. Everywhere I went, I was surrounded by children, even at home. Our irritating downstairs neighbour Frida was a single mother by choice to twins, a boy and a girl she had with donor sperm, and spent what felt like her entire life sitting on the stoop simultaneously breastfeeding them even though they were starting pre-school.

Frida is the type who never, ever wears a bra, she barely wears shoes and thinks fermenting your vegetables on the windowsill is the best thing since sliced bread – only she'd never eat sliced bread. Full of chemicals, she says. She is my worst nightmare – a loud and proud vegan who, not content with eschewing animal products herself, also blogs about orphaned calves, meat being murder, and getting all the protein you require from seitan and tempeh. I read her blog out of morbid curiosity, and as a result I know more about her vagina than I do my own, and how she impregnated herself with a turkey baster.

She's also a hideous flirt and loves trapping Jason in the laundry room for deep and meaningful chats about renouncing meat. He says he gets a kick out of her, but I think he just enjoys the attention. He's also desperate to know more about her life – how she affords her place, what she does for work (if anything) and if, as he suspects, she has an OnlyFans for those attracted to crusty earth-mother types or lactation fetishists. He says it's the producer in him. I'm not really the jealous type, but Frida rubs me the wrong way.

One morning in late May, I heard Frida's loud guffaw as I descended the stairs on the way to work. She must have some poor sap trapped on the stoop, I thought, and was surprised to see that the poor sap in question was in fact Jason, sweaty from his morning run.

'Baby!' he cried. 'Are you leaving already? I brought you an iced coffee.' He held up a cupful of half-melted ice. How long had he been dawdling with Frida?

She beamed at me. 'I love the bag, Portia. Stella McCartney? Vegan leather for the win!'

'Ah, yes,' I managed. 'I bought it because it was cute, not vegan. But good to know.'

'Every little helps,' she trilled. She got to her feet, her breasts threatening to spill out of her vest. 'Gotta go feed my babies. So great chatting with you, Jason, as always!'

She was practically purring as she loped back inside, barefoot as usual. Jason laughed when he saw my raised eyebrow. 'She's a gas ticket, that one. Off to work so early?'

'Yep, duty calls.' I stood on tiptoe and kissed his sweaty cheek. 'Thanks for the coffee. I'm not sure what time I'll be back.'

'Okay. Try not to be too late. I miss you. Have a great day.'

I was perhaps purposely spending long hours in the writers' room for a tween comedy in development for Netflix.

Being a writer for TV means your projects vary wildly – you could be working on a weekly live sketch show, a scripted reality programme or, if you were lucky, a drama spanning dozens of episodes. This show was a luxury, with a big budget, a relaxed schedule and old friends on the team.

The best of those was my former college roommate Amy. She's my age, New York to the bone (born and raised in Chinatown to first-generation immigrants), and an incredible show runner. She likes to call herself the Asian Shonda Rhimes, and while she's not yet quite as prolific, she's on her way.

I took the subway uptown to the rented office space near St Patrick's Cathedral. We'd been working together in person again for a few months after being limited to Zoom throughout the pandemic, so it was nice to have somewhere to go and a routine. Every writers' room is different, but Amy's team is a little brain trust of creatives who spitball ideas and arcs for the characters before the nitty-gritty of the writing begins. It becomes pretty clear when someone has a strong feeling about a particular episode, and they then take the lead on with input from everyone else. I like to do that part of the process alone, and Amy's flexible way of working suits me.

That Tuesday, we broke for lunch a little early. We'd been teasing out a scene between our main character and her BFF; thankfully the series was set around the turn of the millennium, so all the references were things I'd lived through. As the elders, Amy and I were enjoying educating the graduates and twenty-somethings about the Spice Girls, butterfly hair clips and MTV's *Total Request Live*.

I'd noticed Amy was quiet, and as we strolled to Chipotle on Park, I saw she was a little green around the gills.

'Amy Wu, are you suffering from a hangover at work?'

'Ha! I wish!' She laughed. 'It's a little early, but what the hell. You're one of my oldest friends and I know you can keep a secret.'

I must have looked perplexed because she laughed. 'Anyone else would have guessed a month ago when I started excusing myself to vomit every thirty minutes. Portia, I'm pregnant!'

I was stunned. It had never occurred to me that Amy would have a kid; she'd been happily married to our college friend Peter since we were twenty-five, but she'd never mentioned wanting to be a mom, and her baby has always been her high-flying career.

'Oh my god, Amy!' I recovered quickly. 'That's amazing!' I hugged her tight.

'Careful, any squeezing and I'll puke up my decaf. Ugh, I have been so ill. I can't believe you haven't noticed!'

'Either I'm not attuned to these things, or I am the least observant writer on planet earth. Is Peter thrilled?'

'"Thrilled" is not the word. I've been keeping my husband away from everyone because he cries every time he looks at me. It's been a long road to get here, but I'm just over fifteen weeks. We're waiting until we have the scan at twenty to officially tell everyone.'

'What do you mean, a long road?'

'Three failed cycles of IVF, every invasive test known to man . . . and then just when we decided to give up, this little miracle came to be.'

My eyes misted over. How could I work so closely with Amy and have no idea she'd been through all of that?

'Hey,' she said, noticing my shock. 'Don't feel bad. I purposely didn't tell anyone because I didn't want to get my hopes up. Once it didn't happen naturally when we started trying, I was super freaked out. But whatever eggs I have left have finally come through. I think everyone presumed I was some baby-hating oddball!' Amy laughed, and then realized what she'd said.

'Oh, Portia. I obviously don't think that about you!' She was mortified.

I attempted to laugh it off. 'Oh my gosh, don't be so silly! I only mildly dislike babies, and I'll probably tolerate yours,' I joked, and she gave me a weak smile.

'Well, never say never!' Amy twinkled, so obviously delighted. 'I'm glad that's off my chest, now you won't judge me when I order a bag of tortilla chips and extra queso.'

'As if I ever would!' I laughed, hoping I was doing a decent job of looking less shocked than I felt. 'I'll even join you. Eating my feelings sounds good this week.'

When I got home that evening, I didn't tell Jason Amy's news. It felt too weird, not just because our impasse was baby related, but also because I'd always considered Amy and I to be so similar. Now she was going down a path that I never wanted to tread, one that Jason was eager to follow, and it was making me feel decidedly strange.

In the days that followed I saw families with children everywhere I looked. Heavily pregnant women on the subway cradling their bumps, sticky toddlers waving at me in the bagel shop, sweet little newborns strapped to proud dads' chests. Everything was babies, everywhere I looked. And all I felt was abject terror.

24 May 2022

HomelessANDToothless84: Ms Perfect Life is in for a fall . . . I have it on VERY good authority from a friend of mine that her hubby has been caught with his pants down yet again, and this one isn't going away quietly.

JJ767beans: Billy Schwartz is a predator, I hope he gets his comeuppance!

ShowbizGal_RS123: I once saw a little black book from a very disreputable hostelry with his name all over it!

MariaMaria19_92: I worked at his agency right out of college, and he is famous for feeling up the interns. My girlfriend totally hooked up with him in a hotel one night, said he's into strangling.

SxcSugarBby: I knew Lavinia was a faker! Wants us all to think she's so flawless! HA!

DessieIsAPimp: those poor children. But they never had a chance, with a family like that

LoveLavFan1998: You're all horrible! Poor Lavinia, she's a person just like you.

ShowbizGal_RS123: She married a bastard . . . that's what happens! Watch this space . . .

5

I wasn't alone in my workaholism; Jason was spending long hours on *Ladies of New York*, trailing Manhattan socialites from one function to the next and waiting for them to scratch one another's eyes out. As story producer his chief role was Shit-stirrer – he'd tell one of the women what another said about her, and then sit back and let the magic happen.

I was always surprised that Jason enjoyed work that was so shady. As a born people-pleaser, I couldn't cope with the confrontation, the necessary manipulation of the cast. But he said the ladies reminded him of his own family and that he found their shrieking cathartic.

On the rare occasions we were both home we'd eat together, lounge together, sleep together as normal. We were bingeing *Succession* (a show that would make you think twice about having kids) and having more sex than usual; I don't know whether he was trying to slip one past the goalie, to put it bluntly, or if he was just less stressed since he'd made his confession. I was receptive because feeling close to him was all I wanted.

But when I was alone, I couldn't focus on anything. I didn't want to see anyone, didn't even want to talk to Vinnie or my mom because I knew that they were Team Portia-Just-Get-Pregnant. I was having vivid dreams where I had a huge bump but nobody else could see it, or others where I was in some sort of trouble but my hands just couldn't dial Jason's number to come and rescue me. As a result, I was sleeping poorly and I'm somebody that needs my rest. Amy and I were lucky the writing was almost done for the show – she was permanently nauseous, and I was dead-eyed and sleep-deprived.

David staged something of an intervention after he clocked my grey hairs sparkling on my Instagram story and dragged me to his salon for a day of pampering. I agreed on condition that he would not mention the war.

A gorgeous stylist darkened my roots in the fabulous Soho outpost of Salon O'Shea because David was looking after a Broadway diva who'd landed in without an appointment. It wasn't until I was ready to be rinsed that he appeared at my shoulder. It took him approximately seven minutes to mention the war; he waited until I was prone at the basins with shampoo in my hair and couldn't do a runner.

'Well? Have you talked to Jason about your empty womb yet?'

I promptly burst into full-blown sobs, frightening both of us. I was grateful that I seemed to be saving my sobbing bouts for David; he was not thrilled.

Thankfully, we were in the private suite upstairs at SOS and I didn't have his clientele gawking at me. David has done well for himself, taking the opportunities that glamming Dessie presented him with and running with them. He considers himself a New Yorker, but he's been living his best bicoastal fabulous life for years, leaving broken-hearted young men in his wake.

David is family. He comes to Thanksgiving wherever we celebrate, he wears matching pyjamas on Christmas Day in the Daniels household. His mom, who was a friend of Dessie's, died of breast cancer when he was twenty-three, so he's Dessie's honorary son and she loves him like she does her girls. Because she was close to his mom in Ireland, it gives Dessie comfort to support David through life. I know she always secretly wanted a gay son, although she says that's reductive.

He let me cry as he rinsed and didn't even skip a step to expedite the process. When I was all wrapped up in a soft white towel he returned my chair to a sitting position, hunkered down in front of me and took my hands. 'Portia, you and Jason not talking to one another can't continue.'

'I know.' I blew my nose loudly. God, even the tissues in this place were fabulous. 'I just don't know what to say yet, and I'm waiting for a moment to present itself. And Jason's as bad! Drops a bomb and then never mentions it again.'

'But you do know that it is a decision, yes?' His eyes were kind, but his tone serious. 'That Jason doesn't automatically get to upend your life because he's changed his mind?'

My heart leapt into my throat. 'It's not a choice I can make, though, is it? Give up the man I love more than anything in the world, or give up everything I've ever known about myself? How am I meant to do either?'

David got to his feet and pulled me to mine. We are the exact same height, something that bothers him greatly. 'In all honesty, who knows, my love? I don't envy you one bit, and this is why I'm extremely glad that I don't have a womb. But the only advice I can ever give anyone is to go with your gut feeling.'

I snorted, easing into a quilted chair opposite a glowing vanity. Christ, I looked a state.

'Okay.' David was suddenly all business. 'We're not going to make any life-altering decisions today, beyond a straight blowout or a boho one – and one glass of champagne or two?'

'Make my hair as big as humanly possible, let's split a bottle, and please, distract me with your tales of young virile men with thighs like tree trunks, please.'

Walking home afterwards, mildly buzzed and with fabulous

hair, I realized that, in truth, I did have a gut feeling and it was one of pure and utter desperation. I was desperate for Jason. To reconnect with him, to know what he was thinking, to feel close once again.

The worst part of all of this was that I hadn't suspected a thing. I hadn't known that for several months Jason had been trying to tell me something momentous and hoping that I would receive his declaration happily.

While I'd thought we were as great as could be, Jason had known he had a bombshell to drop, one that would alter both of our lives one way or another. One that I probably wouldn't happily receive. And while his timing hadn't been great, it seemed being in the bosom of his family had meant he could no longer contain himself.

The result of it all was that I was so, so frightened. Jason was my rock, my North Star. Things being off kilter with him tinged everything. The world felt tilted, like everything was tinted with a horrible filter.

It's not like we never had arguments or he never pissed me off. Jason could be a bit of a lad, a tiny bit immature and prone to suiting himself. Blowout fights in the past had been about him being too wrapped up in his own head sometimes and not considering my feelings. It always surprised him that I felt he should check in with me before hitting the club with the guys after filming, that I felt it was basic manners in a relationship to let me know what he was up to.

He found my smoking irritating, and my ability to mess up a room in mere seconds – sometimes he'd scold me like I was a child, and it boiled my blood, but those were all little things, silly things. In six and a half years, our lives had never diverged like this.

That May, days were too bright and felt endless. I'd always liked summer, being a California girl, but the warmth and heat felt oppressive and I'd developed allergies out of nowhere. Only at night, when I was in bed with Jason and he was wrapped around me and the air con was on high, could I feel safe for a little while. I didn't sleep much; I just lay there watching him snore, imagining altering my very being to keep him. What if I was wrong about not wanting children? What if I were lacking in some fundamental kick up the ass to do what everyone else was doing? Was it worth trying to find out?

I decided to approach considering motherhood like I would any new project. I would do lots of research, ask lots of questions, arm myself with the facts and try to create a world that was so true to life I could imagine myself living in it.

I may be headstrong by nature, but I wasn't too stubborn to take a long, hard look at myself. I knew I owed it to both of us to give parenthood some serious thought, given the circumstances. I couldn't give up easily; Jason was my life, after all. If romance novels and chick flicks were to be believed, the thunderbolt only strikes once.

I arrived home to an empty apartment. In a fit of gusto and slight tipsiness, I decided to write a note for Jason saying everything that I wanted to say out loud but couldn't, for fear of getting it wrong. Writing letters had always been a thing for us. I was amazed I hadn't thought of it earlier. It was so much easier for me to put my feelings on paper than to utter them. So that's what I did on my special fancy notepaper, emblazoned with my full monogram, PRD – a gift from my mother, of course.

In my letter, I asked him for time and for empathy. In my loopy script, I told him I would seriously consider what he had asked and beseeched him not to pressure me. I wrote until my hand was sore, until I'd filled three pages, front and back. Then I fell asleep on the sofa, my efforts on the table next to me.

When I stirred, it was 2 a.m. and I was in Jason's arms. He was carrying me to bed, laying me gently on my pillow. He kissed me on the forehead and, through blurry eyes, I saw the sheaf of paper in his hand. 'I love you,' he said. 'Go back to sleep.'

6

It's always a whirlwind when my mother comes to town. Her *LOLA* bestie, Graham (who is a woman, despite the name), generally lends her the private jet; Dessie could afford to buy her own, but owning a plane is something she can't quite bring herself to do: 'I'm Irish, darling, it's too vulgar.' I know she doesn't want to get in trouble on Twitter for unnecessary carbon emissions, either.

The city was unusually sweltering for Memorial Day weekend. I was feeling a little claustrophobic in New York for perhaps the first time ever. The writers' room was over, so it was my time to get to work, but I couldn't concentrate. Normally I'd head for the beach in Rockaway or even out to Montauk when it got hot, but something in me wanted to be at home, safe in my usual space. But the tall buildings felt oppressive and the apartment pokey and stifling. I didn't need a psychoanalyst to tell me that the situation with Jason was colouring every aspect of my life.

Despite being Irish by birth, Desdemona Daniels had been an LA creature for most of her life, so New York in the summer doesn't bother her at all. While everyone else is wearing shorts and vests, Dessie descends upon the city in a haze of faux fur and Black Opium by YSL. She has her own fragrance, but she doesn't actually wear it.

'It's almost ninety degrees out, Mother,' I grinned, accepting kisses on both cheeks. 'I'm getting hot just looking at you!' A little head popped out of her gilet and licked my chin. 'And hello to you too, Bubbles.' I scratched the little Morkie (a Maltese and Yorkie cross) under its chin. Mom has six dogs, but Bubbles is her fur baby. Where she goes, he goes.

I was meeting my mother in her Elizabeth Street apartment to accompany her to something she claimed to be dreading – a convention called V-Palooza, where she'd be face to face with the rabid super-fans of her show and all the other franchises on the V Network. Ariel was flying in with Manny later in the day, but for now it was just my mom and me, and her entourage.

V-Palooza is an opportunity to promote *LOLA* and its ilk, to stir the pot with on-stage panels and reveal gossip that will drum up drama for the forthcoming season. Fans pay up to $3,000 for the full VIP shtick including meet-n-greets and photo ops, and while Dessie protests that it's overwhelming and even a little frightening, she forgets all of that once she's in her audience's loving embrace.

My mother is the rare v-lebrity that's pretty much universally adored. She has her moments that are dissected on the blogs and Twitter isn't always kind. But she's never had the fans baying for her blood or trying to get her fired. Graham, on the other hand, is a couple of bad episodes away from the axe.

'How was your flight, Mom?'

'Oh, Graham is insufferable at the moment, love. She banned Fernanda from the jet, so Isabel wouldn't come in solidarity. This weekend is going to be torture, buffering that pack of wagons!'

Her assistant, Natasha, appeared, dragging a massive suitcase and four garment bags. I rushed to help her. 'Isn't this a bit excessive?' I huffed as I lifted the case. 'You're only here for the weekend!'

'A weekend of paps and events and interviews, Portia! I have to be prepared.' She rolled her eyes dramatically at me.

What Dessie doesn't understand is that even in her travelling clothes and minimal make-up, she's utterly divine.

Natasha had no sooner set the bags on the sofa when Dessie descended upon them like a vulture on its prey. Of course, all the outfits were pre-selected and styled for her in LA, right down to the underwear, jewellery and accompanying glam, so I didn't know why she was fussing. But I was glad that my mother was busy and blustering, because it meant no third degree. She was obviously nervous about the day ahead.

Jason was also due to appear at the convention the next day, on a producer's panel. That meant Dessie would be seeing us together for the first time since the news of his paternal desire broke. I was pretending to care about the shoes and dresses she was holding up when I heard the rapid click-clack of heels in the hallway that meant only one thing. Giulia.

The door flew open and in walked my aunt, yapping as always on her phone and gesticulating wildly. You could say that Giulia Rizzi is authentically Sicilian, or that she plays up to the stereotype. I think both are true.

'Ariel, *bella*, I am sorry you have to fly commercial. Your papa does too, okay?! Gray-ham cannot fit your mamma's entire entourage on that little plane! This family, it likes to travel like a shoal of fishes!'

I grinned at Natasha over Mom's head. I'd say the poor assistant was thrilled to have a day away from the whims of my almost-fifteen-year-old sister. Ariel is popular on TikTok, a bit player on *LOLA* and an absolute nightmare at the best of times. I love the kid, but she's like walking contraception.

As always, Giulia was decked out head to toe in Dolce & Gabbana, caring not a jot for the fact that they've kind of been cancelled. She has jet-black hair cropped tight, wears no make-up except for a swipe of MAC Lady Danger lipstick and is frighteningly beautiful – she has a double layer of black eyelashes, just like Elizabeth Taylor. She is my father's younger sister, my mother's publicist and closest confidante, and everyone is terrified of her except me. I'm her favourite, what can I say?

She hung up and tossed her phone dramatically on the couch, flopping down next to me. 'That girl, I swear!' She muttered something in Italian under her breath before opening her arms to me. '*Bella* Portia, you are so beautiful, look at that face! I have missed you, *carina*!' Nobody gives hugs like Giulia.

'Now, Desdemona,' she said, all business again. 'The car will be here in five minutes and Dah-veed-ay is meeting us there. You do your own face, yes? No? Perhaps no. You need more help today. I will summon Axel the make-up wizard; he stands by.'

I love my mom and Giulia's relationship. They're both the kind of women with a do no harm, take no shit attitude, and I'm lucky to have been raised by them. Even before Dad died, Giulia was a constant in our lives. She's never been married, never even lived with a man. She would be my child-free icon if she wasn't so anti-romance and relationships – Giulia is the type who people wouldn't even imagine as a mom, but she's always been like another parent to Vinnie and me.

I figured that Ariel could do with as many parental figures as she can get, so it was a good job Giulia was part of her life despite not being related by blood. Along with Dessie, she tries to manage Ariel's burgeoning social media stardom, but so far, my little sister is proving unmanageable. She goes live on Instagram when Dessie is getting dressed in the background, posts suggestive pictures of herself constantly and even once screenshot Vinnie's teenage diary and shared it on her story. Thankfully it wasn't anything too juicy, but the kid is a wild card.

If Dessie is a master in self-promotion, it's Giulia who makes sure things stay on track. She oversees all the PR for DD+ and my mother's other endeavours, and rules Dessie's schedule with an iron fist. Some may call her a dragon lady (and believe me, they definitely do), but she gets shit done. Together, they're a dream team, but that doesn't mean they don't fight like cat and, er, cat.

For example, Dessie dithering over outfits that have already been styled was sure to set Giulia off. 'Desdemona! If you don't get dressed in thirty seconds, I will sell those photos of you right after your buccal fat removal!'

She never uses Mom's nickname ('it's stupido!') and David has been Dah-veed-ay since he was a child, despite protestations. Over the years though, she has picked up some of Dessie's Irish-isms, which is a delightful affectation. Things are often 'grand', and she 'does be' on the phone to *Entertainment Weekly*.

Her threats worked. My mother stopped flapping and selected a garment bag. Within minutes the four of us were in the limo speeding uptown to the Javits Center, where the glam squad was ready to rock.

I don't know if I've ever been a big enough fan of anything to go to a convention, but V-Palooza is a fascinating experience. Think ComicCon, but without the A-list celebrities and superhero movie announcements. This is reality stars walking among the crowds and making their day with a mere smile and wave. Picture panels of women arguing, hot young singletons flirting in front of an audience, drag queens giving makeovers, and thousands of people queueing for three hours to get a photo with their favourite v-lebrity.

I figured out that the safest place to hang out were the special experience lounges. The green room was full of egos and tension, the press rooms of fakery, but these lounges had alcohol and fans both wealthy and genuine enough to purchase an hour of mingling with their faves. That made for a chill vibe, which was what I needed after the morning I'd had.

Mom had convinced me to get a full face done in case I ended up on the show (cameras were of course capturing content at the event), and like David, waited until I was stuck in a chair to pounce about the Baby Question. In a neat illustration of the nature versus nurture debate, I felt very differently to my mother and sister. Dessie shared Vinnie's feelings about procreation; maybe she planted those ideas because, unlike normal mothers who live in terror of teenage pregnancy, she talked about us having babies as if she couldn't wait. She was so excited to be a grandmother that it felt like she had been practically bugging us to have kids from when we began menstruating. So I knew it was only a matter of time before I got a lecture. If it was going to happen, I decided to let it – a monologue from Dessie was like a force of nature, something to endure and survive.

And it didn't matter to her that Giulia, Natasha, David and her make-up artist, Axel, were all present and thus privy to my business – one, they're part of the gang and already knew everything that was going on, and two, they've all signed iron-clad NDAs.

'Now, pet. I have some things I want to say to you,' she began. She was done up to the nines by this point – in a vintage black Givenchy dress with sheer sleeves, rippling brunette curls and wispy lashes from her Freckle range. She looked ageless. She could genuinely be forty or seventy, you would never know. She draped herself across the sofa, Bubbles nuzzled into her breast, ready to deliver her speech.

'Ever since the sex party in Ireland—'

Axel's head swivelled like the kid's in *The Exorcist*.

'Mom, it was a gender reveal,' I wheezed. 'Not a sex party!'

'Sorry, sorry, you know what I mean. Ever since the gender reveal and what Jason told you, I've been wanting to chat, but I waited until I saw you in person. Darling, I know you've always followed the beat of your own drum, and I admire you for it. With your lineage, you were never going to be ordinary. Kerry Irish and Sicilian blood? A fiery combination!' She loves to talk about our lineage. What she always fails to note here is that I have always been a Goodie Two Shoes; Vinnie was the wild one. I let her drone on, tuning back in when I heard the magic word.

'. . . but this whole never having children thing, I admit that I've never fully understood it. I thought, is it something I've done? Did my own late-in-life mothering frighten you? Because everyone loves children, don't they? Deep inside, you love your own. With Giulia, it's different' – a loud snort came from my aunt's direction – 'but you, sweetheart, you've got a lot of love to give. You're a romantic! You're madly in love! You're maternal with the puppies! Isn't it only natural to want to make a family with your mate? It's evolution!'

'More like natural selection,' David giggled, and I thumped him.

Dessie was still going. 'I mean, for a woman of a certain age, who has a wonderful man in her life that wants to give her babies, why wouldn't you want that? Is it the biological clock, Portia? Has it not gone off yet? Because it will, I'm telling you, and it will be too late! You turn thirty-nine in mere days!'

She didn't need to remind me; my impending birthday was at the forefront of my mind. My mother has always loved that she had me on 1 June, Marilyn Monroe's birthday. Giulia has insinuated that Dessie imbibed castor oil the day before to make sure, but Mom disputes this.

This particular birthday filled me with existential dread in a way no other one ever had. I'd never worried about getting older, because I felt like issues concerned with having babies didn't apply to me. I wasn't worried about my eggs dying off, or my chances of conception lowering with every passing month. But in the wake of Jason's announcement, edging closer to forty made me feel like edging towards a precipice, to a dangerous place where my body might make the decision for me.

'What is this talk always of clocks?' Giulia appeared over my shoulder in the mirror and winked at me. 'I have enough clocks, I don't need another one.'

'Well, love, yours is definitely gone rusty,' Dessie chortled, dodging a swat. 'But Portia's is still in fine working condition, I'm sure! Darling.' She hunkered down in front of me, imploring me with those cat eyes, Morkie struggling to breathe in her heaving bosom. 'I just don't want you to have regrets. That's all. Motherhood is fabulous, especially when you've got the money and the support to do it right. Jason is a wonderful man, love.'

My mother's earnestness meant tears were threatening to ruin the gel liner Axel had just painstakingly applied. I knew logically that Dessie was only concerned about me. That it wasn't about appeasing Jason, or society. It wasn't even about giving her grandchildren, because she already had those. It was that she quite simply couldn't understand not wanting kids, and she didn't want me to have the world's worst FOMO.

'Mom, I mean this with all the love in the world, but please, stop,' I pleaded in a desperate whisper. 'Everything you're saying is all that's been rattling around my brain for weeks on end. Why I'm different, why I don't want what is apparently natural for everyone else. Why I'd risk things with the best man I've ever known. I'm working through it, okay?'

She nodded, happy to have said her piece. 'I just worry, darling,' she said, tears springing into her own eyes.

'If you ask me, you're better off by yourself,' said Giulia, leaning across me to reapply her signature lip in the mirror. 'Men are trouble, and *bambini*? Ten times more. You are a woman of the world, Portia Rizzi-Daniels. Now, I have to visit de jacks before your panel, Desdemona.'

I was relieved when Dessie and her entourage swept out to start a day of glad-handing, posing and petty on-stage arguments, but they left me feeling utterly defeated. I felt a hand on my shoulder and looked up to see Axel's kind eyes. 'For what it's worth, I'd love a baby,' he cooed. 'If you ever want to donate those primo eggs . . .'

That's when I bolted and found the Rosé Room, serving Graham's pink tequila and Fernanda's pastel gin (their competing alcohol lines being one of the causes of their current beef) and settled in to people-watch with a can of Sybil Simpson's Skinny Seltzer in hand. Sybil is one of the *LONY* stars that Jason works with, and I love her. Old-school New York, she's a blousy, sexy divorcée that's seen and done it all and has more than a touch of an alcohol problem.

But as my recent luck would have it, I wasn't the only hanger-on who had found the best seat in the house. I groaned internally as I saw the gossip blogger Simon Katzenberg making a beeline for me. 'I didn't know they allowed bottom-feeders in here,' I said drily as he invaded my personal couch space. Simon wasn't the worst of the media leeches, but he wasn't to be trusted, either.

'Ha! Press pass, baby. Gets me in anywhere.'

'And keeps you well oiled, I see.' I gestured to the array of cocktails he was placing in front of us.

'Research!' he exclaimed. 'The readers of *Simon Says* simply need to know which v-lebrity's cocktail is the best. And um' – he looked a bit shifty – 'you might need a drink after what I have to tell you.'

Simon was always feeding the family titbits in return for an exclusive take, so this wasn't unusual – I was the least likely to play ball, however. 'What is it now? Is Ariel joining a cult? Has Dessie been exposed as a tax dodger? Let me guess – Lavinia is really a man!'

I was laughing until I saw his expression. 'No, it's kind of . . . serious. You can't have avoided the gossip about Billy Schwartz?'

'Unlike you, Simon, I know that most of what I read online is bullshit.'

'Not this time, Portia.' He put down his pink tequila and took my hand. 'You know that Billy isn't as perfect as Lavinia makes out, we all do. But he seems to have gone too far this time. Everyone thinks he's been having an affair with JenKat, his new signing, which is bad enough. But it's worse than that. It's her little sister, Trysta.'

My blood turned to ice. 'Little? But JenKat is like . . . twenty-one? Twenty-two?'

Simon nodded. 'Twenty-one. The sister turned eighteen a few months ago, Portia. She's just graduated high school. And the gossip means other young ladies are telling their stories too. It seems like Billy has come on to every barely legal woman in town.'

When Vinnie married Billy and became a wife, I hoped she was finally in a relationship with proper communication, honesty and respect. I had never thought Billy was a choirboy, or that he was this stupid. He is a classic example of somebody with Short Man Syndrome – small in stature but with an ego the size of Long Island. That makes him good at his job.

He always says marrying my sister is the smartest thing he ever did. Billy is proud of Vinnie, and loves showing her off.

They show up for one another publicly when it matters, on a red carpet or for a photoshoot, and they understand one another's businesses. Their brand is extremely important to her, to both of them. So why on earth would he risk it all, the empire that they've built together, to sleep with teenagers?

'Does Lavinia know?' I whispered.

'The message boards have been lit for weeks. It's only a matter of time before the tabloids get their claws out. The only reason it hasn't happened yet is because everyone loves your sister,' Simon lamented, doing a good impression of somebody who genuinely cared. 'The editors want solid proof, someone respectable to go on the record. And if my sources are correct, that's going to happen soon, because JenKat is livid.'

TikTok teen steals the limelight at V-Palooza

27 May 2022

SimonSays was all up in V-Palooza today, and with record attendance and lots of spicy shenanigans from the v-lebrities, it was certainly the place to be.

The Ladies of Las Vegas pulled no punches, literally, as their cast panel descended into violence and mayhem, while the gang from Camp Mates revealed that the bunks were definitely rocking this season – but you'll have to tune in to find out who gets it on with whom.

But while Dessie Daniels was the undisputed star in terms of v-lebs (much to Fernanda da Silva's disgust) it was her teenage daughter Ariel Alvarez who grabbed the most surprising amount of attention.

Already well known from appearing on the show since infancy, Ariel has a Gen Z fan base all her own thanks to TikTok. And while her DD+ mogul mommy spent hours longer than scheduled taking selfies with fans and got the most rapturous applause from the fans, Ariel was making behind the scenes content devoured not only by young users of the app. It went viral across social media.

In one video, she mugs at the camera while Dessie gives an interview in the background. In between her yawns and eye-rolls, captions proclaim 'When your mom thinks she's Kim Kardashian' and 'Being a Nepo Baby is now officially over'.

It appears no matter how gorgeous and beloved your mother is, she's still incredibly uncool when you're turning fifteen and being dragged around her workplace.

Ariel is reportedly in New York for talks about a Super Bowl commercial with a huge drinks brand. Dessie handles her daughter's career, but both she and publicist Giulia Rizzi were tight-lipped when questioned about Ariel's potential deal.

Dessie's other famous offspring, *LOLA* regular, supermodel and influencer extraordinaire Lavinia Rizzi-Schwartz was absent, not making the trip to NYC with her gorgeous family.

The new season of *Ladies of Los Angeles* premieres on V Network, Sunday at 9 p.m. EST.

7

Back at the apartment later that afternoon, I was stuck between pacing the floor and chain-smoking out on the fire escape. I couldn't worry Vinnie until I'd done some research of my own on what Simon had said. I'd stuck it out for a couple more hours at the convention, posing with the more devout fans who had a clue who I was, before claiming a headache and racing home. It was only once I got there I realized I'd left my laptop in Dessie's dressing room.

My head was whirling, and my phone a constant barrage of concerned notifications from Dessie and the entourage that were interrupting my googling. I put it down, stubbed out my third cigarette and logged into Jason's intimidating iMac. I don't usually touch it for fear of deleting an entire episode of the show, or accidentally tweeting something from his account. But I needed to focus, and the phone wasn't cutting it.

At that moment I didn't even know for sure what I was looking for, but I had to find something to help Vinnie. I wasn't mentioning anything about this to her until I was fully informed.

Jason's email was open, and before I could open a new tab something caught my eye. A new email from . . . Sandra? His sister-in-law, Sandra! In a thread of . . . what? Two hundred and sixty-eight mails? I clicked on it without even thinking. And in that instant, everything changed again.

I'd never understood what people meant by having an out-of-body experience until that moment, but that's what I'd call it. It was like I was floating above my own body, hunched at Jason's computer with a slack jaw and a gaping mouth.

What had I just stumbled across? Without even pausing to consider if I should look any further – looking back, it was an invasion of privacy – I was reading every word of correspondence between my partner of over six years and his sister-in-law at a rate of knots.

Numb and intent on scrolling, it dawned on me in that instant that I didn't know everything about Jason's interior life. That he had secrets, he had desires, and he would rather share them with his brother's wife than with me. All I could think was: *Jason isn't even an email person. He prefers to use a pen.*

That thread of hundreds of emails was only the most recent one. There were more, lots more, ranging from a casual ten-thread chat in the vein of 'saw this and thought of you' to more long conversations spanning nearly three years, and literally thousands of messages.

One particular note was like a stab to the gut. It was from Jason to Sandra, sent on a Tuesday at 3 a.m.

Sandy,

Can't sleep. Feeling really homesick today. Send me one of your lovely, long emails that makes me feel like I'm right there with you all. God, I can't wait until I can fly back! NY is feeling strange right now, both isolated and claustrophobic. It's making me question things.

Hopefully see you very soon.
Love, J x

Sandy? I didn't know what to think. It seemed like an innocent enough message, but the tenderness, the intimacy conveyed in those couple of sentences was alarming. Why on earth would he be emailing his sister-in-law in the middle of the night, looking for comfort? And what did he mean, questioning everything?

I checked the date; it was during the early days of the pandemic, when things in New York were opening and then closing again due to surges in the virus. I totally got feeling homesick – I've never felt at home anywhere except New York, but I'd missed my family desperately when we weren't allowed to get on a plane. But why would Jason turn to his sister-in-law to feel better, when I was in bed in the next room?

I opened the most recent thread again and clicked print. As the pages and pages of emails slid out of the printer, I went to the bathroom and threw up Sybil Simpson's seltzer.

Later that evening, the reams of contraband emails stashed away in my drawer, I tried to make sense of the man who had written them and the man I thought I knew. Scenes from our lives together played on a loop in my brain. Right back to the start. I got to thinking about our first proper date. Since that initial drink in the WeHo bar, Jason and I had texted every day and hung out at my mom's house, but it was our first evening out alone together. He'd asked me two days previously, and I'd spent the subsequent forty-eight hours in a state of high anticipation.

Still, I didn't want to put too much pressure on it. I'd told him I wasn't expecting to be wined and dined, that foamy cuisine and stuffy atmospheres weren't for me. Imagine my relief when the Uber pulled up at a dive in Santa Monica I knew and loved. It served the best New Orleans-style Po'boy sandwiches, had arcade games, a ping-pong table and a classic jukebox. Ideal.

We whiled the evening away drinking cocktails with umbrella embellishments (every one he ordered was girlier than mine), playing automated beer pong and talking a mile a minute. I was dying for him to know me, and to learn everything I could about him.

Time flew, as it does when you're having the best night of your life, and all of a sudden we were draining our drinks (Pisco Sour for me, Singapore Sling with a pink stirrer for him) and grabbing our jackets.

'I'd better get us a ride,' he said, looking at his phone. Then he looked straight at me. 'One stop or two?'

'One,' I whispered, feeling dizzy.

I spent the entire cab ride fizzing at the prospect of being completely alone with him. I was nervous. I was no virgin but being around Jason made me feel like one. Everything about him felt different to any man I'd ever known; not only did I fancy the hole off him (a Dessie-ism made famous in season two of *LOLA*), we had a physical connection that felt electric, and also an intellectual vibe I'd never experienced before. Was this what people meant when they talked about chemistry? Because it if it was, it was brand new to me.

I suspected Jason was feeling a bit timid by the time we got to his apartment. He struggled to get the door open – 'Feckin' lady-drinks,' he laughed – then led me into a swish open-plan living and kitchen area divided by a black island with shiny white countertops.

'Jason, this is niiiice,' I said appreciatively. 'Not exactly your average bachelor pad.'

'Well, I'm not your average bachelor.' He winked, cheesily-on-purpose. 'It's a rental. The network found it when I came out here first, and I decided to keep it on after their lease ended. I'm rarely here, but I like my creature comforts.'

We were consciously avoiding touching one another, knowing that as soon as we made physical contact all bets were off. I was terrified to make a move and he must have been too, because he was dithering around with a corkscrew. Screw this, I thought. In for a penny, and all that.

Remembering one of my favourite movie sex scenes in *Sleeping with the Enemy*, I jumped up on the kitchen island and perched on the edge. 'Jason,' I said softly. Whatever was in my voice, he turned to look at me and almost visibly gulped. Then walked over, wine bottle in hand, and set it and the corkscrew down either side of me.

We were face to face for a moment, him standing in between my open knees. Those seconds just looking at his face, his lips, his eyes . . . well, I've never been more turned on in my life. He leaned in to kiss me, and I'm not joking when I say it felt like fireworks going off inside me. Once his tongue met mine, we were devouring one another, hungry and frantic. My hands were in his hair, pulling his T-shirt over his head.

Then he stopped and pulled away, holding my wrists. Immediately, I thought I must have done something wrong. Did my breath stink? Did I taste of bad booze, or garlic? Was I a shit kisser?! But he just smirked and said, 'Slowly.' Then he started undoing the front of my dress and all I could do was watch.

God, I was glad I was wearing it the second he touched the first clasp. It was just a tea dress, short with capped sleeves and little buttons all the way down the front. I thought it said, 'I'm cute and hot but not trying too hard.' In that moment, though, it felt like the sexiest garment I'd ever worn.

I was frozen as he opened each fastener agonizingly slowly, revealing my skin inch by inch. He sucked in his breath when he saw I wasn't wearing a bra, and my nipples were rock hard without him even touching them. But he kept going down the line, until I was sitting on the cold marble countertop with my dress thrown fully open.

Keeping eye contact, he raised my knees one at a time and took off my ankle boots. Then he reached for the waistband of my lace thong, and my hips rose to meet him. He slid it down my legs and took it off, placing it on the counter beside the wine. Then he confidently slid two fingers inside me and I gasped.

It was all utterly erotic; by this point, I was literally trembling with desire, which was something I thought was made up in Danielle Steel novels. He leaned in and kissed me deeply, before ducking his head and putting his mouth beside his fingers, where I was burning for him. His tongue found my clitoris, and I nearly screamed.

I lay back on the cool island and just gave in to the sensation. I was so focused on how he was making me feel I didn't feel at all self-conscious. I was only aware of the waves building underneath his tongue, the intense pleasure that was about to burst from the centre of me.

My moans were building to fever pitch, and right when I thought I was about to explode, he stood up straight and grinned down at me. In one swift movement, he was undoing his jeans with one hand and grabbing me by the neck with the other. I was so wet, so ready for him, that I would have begged if he hadn't put his erection where his tongue had been. He teased my clitoris with the tip of him, and I lost the ability to speak.

As he drove into me, I automatically wrapped my legs around him. He lifted me up and carried me to his room like that, fused together at the mouth and hips, and I was coming by the time we tumbled on to the bed.

I don't remember much after that, just waves of pleasure, moaning, stroking, moving. But I do remember thinking to myself that I was ruined for ever for other men.

8

Vinnie's prospective marital woes all but forgotten, I was consumed with Jason's correspondence with Sandra. So consumed, in fact, that I texted him inventing an evening drinks meeting, grabbed the sheaf of papers and headed for Mom's loft. I didn't want to see him until I had some sort of grip on what was going on, and I knew Dessie would be out schmoozing and being schmoozed for a while longer.

I didn't even feel the twentyish-block walk to Elizabeth Street. It was a beautiful summer evening, temperate and bright, but I was too busy fuming about Sandra Dempsey to appreciate it.

I didn't know her well; I hadn't thought Jason did either, to be honest. Sure, I knew he and Sandra had grown up together, but she'd never stuck out as a special part of his life.

I'd met her a few times at family gatherings in Ireland, we'd had dinner with them once when they visited New York. Them being Sandra and her husband. She'd been married to Jason's brother Michael, also known as Mick, for eons.

Amazingly, Sandra was also distantly related to David on his mother's side, third cousins once removed or something. They'd met at a funeral not long after Jason and I got serious, and David was thrilled by the connection. 'It's so Irish, and it means Jason and I are basically brothers!' he'd trilled, delighted at the association with my new man.

Sandra and Mick have been together since the dawn of time, and by that I mean since Mick's debs. The Irish version of senior prom is as much a rite of passage as in the States and as Mick was the local heart-throb and GAA star, he had his pick of dates.

Jason, a year younger, had told me everyone was surprised when Mick had asked Sandra O'Malley, who was in Jason's class. She was blonde (a prerequisite for Mick, apparently), but she wasn't flashy or a good-time girl. She was 'sound' and normal, no obvious psycho tendencies. Mick's ex, Annie, was your typical glamour model wannabe, with eyebrows thin as paper and a too-small Wonderbra. But Mick wouldn't have to worry about Sandra making a show of him.

Jason had told me this because the following year, when it was his turn, he took Annie 'for a laugh' and regretted it immediately. She got pissed on red Aftershock, vomited cinnamon-scented bile all over his rented tux and flashed the bus driver on the way home. Any thrill of bringing an older woman as his date wore off quickly. Still, he said it was worth it to piss off his big brother. The two were competitive, as brothers close in age often are. Was this why Jason had chosen Sandra as his pen pal, to get back at his brother? My brain was frantically looking for clues.

Anyway, Sandra and Mick hit it off and became an item. There was never any drama. She cheered him on at the weekends when he played hurling and football and didn't seem to mind his local idol status. They stayed together throughout college, both attending the University of Limerick, and got engaged when Sandra had a pregnancy scare at twenty-three. Three years later they welcomed their first kid, Michael Junior, or MJ. The wedding followed, at which Jason was best man and number-one target for every horny woman in the town. A little girl called Jennifer came three years after that.

Mick was now forty-two, a sales manager for a pharmaceutical company with thinning hair, a pot belly and a teenager and a tween in the house. Jason has never been close to Mick the way he is to Tiernan, who shares his wanderlust and free spirit. In fact, Mick has been held up as something of a cautionary tale; the brother who never left his hometown, married his teenage sweetheart and is old before his time.

Sandra has held up better; she has a job in HR, so a bit of independence. She's grown into her ears (they were apparently quite prominent when she was a child) and has nice highlights. She looks after herself, balances her work with her home life and loves a cheeky G&T with the girls from time to time. I only know this because of her occasional Facebook update – the woman doesn't even have Instagram. She seems like a nice, normal person.

But competition? It just never would have occurred to me. Sandra was . . . well, just living in a parallel universe to Jason – I couldn't see what they had in common. And she was his brother's *wife*. Yes, she and Jason had a shared history, and they're family by marriage. But what would make her a confidante, a secret friend? Was a woman like Sandra what Jason was secretly looking for? I had to find out.

Two hours later, I was wishing I had never sat down at his computer. My mom came home and found me on the floor of her living room (hardwood, herringbone pattern, très chic), with sheets of A4 paper spread out around me.

'Darling, what's going on? Are you . . . are you crying, Portia?'

I must have looked a sight, because she plonked down on the floor next to me, Givenchy dress be damned. I don't think I'd cried in front of Dessie since my father died, so she was genuinely perplexed. She picked up a random page, and I watched her expression go from confusion to curiosity, then to shock. 'Oh, Portia. Sweetheart . . . what have you found?'

I dissolved in her arms, bawling. I've never been the biggest hugger, but in that moment I clung to my mother and shook with sobs. Taken aback, she let me cry and cooed softly in my ear. Eventually, she led me to the couch and covered me in a soft blanket.

I must have cried myself to sleep, because when I woke up god knows how long later she was on the phone, stage-whispering in the kitchen.

'I don't know what to do, Vin. You know what she's like, she's normally so together. I've never seen her like this . . . no, no, you stay where you are! Ariel and Manny are staying at the Plaza on Gatorade's dime. Yeah, she wanted to live her *Home Alone* fantasy, so I let her. I left Giulia chatting up a young lad at the convention. I doubt she'll be back . . . Yes, yes, I'll mind Portia. No, I'm too tired to go out. I'll call you later, pet. Bye, byebyeyeyeyeye.'

She crept over towards me, and I pretended I was just stirring. She handed me a cup.

'Barry's, sweetheart. A good cuppa tae is a cure for what ails you.' Dessie is fanatical about the tea of the motherland. She travels with it at all times and always makes sure her homes are stocked with fresh Irish milk and butter. 'None of that almond shite. Sure, how can you milk an almond?' she cries. You can take a woman out of Kerry, but you cannot part her from her dairy.

She was stroking my head like I was a child, and I was letting her. I noticed that the papers on the floor had been tidied, and Dessie was changed into super-soft cashmere joggers. 'How long was I asleep?' I asked.

'An hour or so. You tired yourself out, so I thought I'd leave you.' Her green eyes crinkled in concern; well, as much as her dermatologist would allow them to. 'Do you want to talk about it?'

I sat up, sighing. 'How much did you read?'

She had the good grace to look embarrassed. 'A decent

79

bit. Enough to get the gist of it all. Did you know Jason was so close to Sandra?'

I shook my head. 'Well, no wonder you've had such a shock, then. Combined with all the baby stuff as well. But love, it's mostly harmless?'

And it was true, it was mostly harmless in that there were no declarations of love, references to transatlantic hook-ups or even evidence of more than mild flirtation.

But it was worse than all of that because it was deeper. It was vulnerable; long, ruminating conversations about the meaning of life and happiness. Conversations about career worries, fears and dreams. It was the kind of intimate stuff that you only share with someone you're incredibly close with, and as far as I was aware, Jason and Sandra weren't that tight. What else was I going to learn about the man I was meant to already know inside out?

'There's an undercurrent, Mom. She clearly has feelings for him. You don't spend your time emailing a man like this unless you're into him, especially when you're married! All of the reminiscing, the remember-whens . . . I'd bet money that she has always fancied Jason, and that poor Mick was her consolation prize.'

'Well, Jason is a big ride!' Dessie exclaimed. 'Don't look at me like that. He *is*. Of course the entire town fancied him, the whole bloody county probably! And if poor bland Sandra – can we call her Blandra, to be bitches? – if she couldn't get the one with his eye on faraway shores and glamour, wasn't Mick the next best thing? Well, he was until he started losing his hair, God bless him.'

I reached for the papers. 'This is only the tip of the iceberg, by the way.' I gestured. 'There are hundreds more. From what I could see, it seems like they started chatting regularly when everything locked down and we were all going crazy in close quarters, and then they never stopped. There was I, thinking he must be working so hard at his computer, making plans for when life went back to normal, but no! He was pouring his heart out to another woman, three thousand miles away. And do you know the worst part?'

Dessie shook her head.

I flung the pages on the table, spilling my tea. 'He told her about the kid thing *last year*. He told her before he told me that he wanted to be a father, and she went on and on about how being a parent is the best thing that's ever happened to her, blah, blah. She was encouraging him!'

I was shouting. 'It's all her fault! Promoting parenthood like it's the next big thing, influencing him! Who does she think she is, fucking Vinnie?'

Dessie, who had remained silent as I roared, spoke quietly. 'Darling, I'm going to say this, and you're not going to like it. Being a father isn't something someone can encourage you towards. You either want to, or you don't. Jason was hardly likely to confide in you about changing his mind until he was sure, was he? You should be glad he had someone else to talk to about it all.'

'*Glad?*' I screeched. 'Glad that my partner, the person who knows me inside out and upside down, confided something so serious about our relationship to his interfering sister-in-law? That this woman knows more about *my life* and *my uterus* than I do?'

Pacing, I was on a roll. 'I don't know him at all, if this is what he wants, Mom. Everything is a lie! He wants someone who will pander to him, who will give everything up so he can propagate his bloodline.'

'It's not *Game of Thrones*, Portia,' Dessie said drily. 'The man wants children. It's taken him longer than most to realize this, but he has and now there's no going back.' She took my hands. 'The cat is out of the bag, sweetheart. You can't force it back in. The question is, what are you going to do about it?'

I deflated like a balloon. 'I want a time machine, Mom. I want things to go back to the way they were.'

'Well, darling. That's not going to happen. They've invented a machine that can freeze the fat arse off you on your lunch break, but not the time machine just yet.'

She got up, fluffing cushions and wiping the spilled tea with her sleeve. You know you're wealthy when you use cashmere as a cloth. 'Now, you're staying here tonight. I've told Jason that I kidnapped you for wine and girl time, and we'll see him tomorrow at the convention. I need my beauty sleep, so I'll say goodnight.'

She kissed my head and gave me a squeeze. 'Don't stay up too late.'

But I already knew I'd spend the entire night dissecting every word on those pages.

reddit.com/VPaloozaGossip

27 May 2022

superstoner_90210: OMG I got a photo with Dessie and she is SO BEAUTIFUL up close!

PablosGirliexx: she's tiny, like a little doll! I saw her daughters too, the one that's not famous is so cute

leonoramcg_22: do you guys know she's with a V Network producer? And he's so fine

superstoner_90210: no!! I wonder did Dessie orchestrate that for ratings

leonoramcg_22: I don't think so, they're 2gthr a long time

leonoramcg_22: I saw Graham's face lift stitches in real life today. She's such a lyin bitch

PablosGirliexx: I did too! She shoulda used Dessie's surgeon

helloVNetties: petition to get Graham fired like yesterday, the old hag. She's only still around cos Dessie wants her there

PablosGirliexx: Team Graham! *LOLA* would be so boring with her . . .

9

I must have fallen asleep at some point because I woke up with light streaming into the loft. Dessie's New York pied-à-terre is quite something. She got it for a relative bargain in the early noughties when she had a bit of *Baywatch* cash. It was a prime piece of real estate that needed updating, but she didn't have the money at the time to do it properly.

She finally got around to renovating a few years ago, her first TV special for HGTV, *Dessie Decorates*, and the genesis of her interiors collection at Pottery Barn. 'Everyone should have access to fabulous things, darling,' was the response when asked why she didn't hold out for a deal with West Elm or William Sonoma. What she didn't tell them was that the deal had originally been with Target.

Most people might expect Dessie's homes to reflect her personal fashion sense, all glitz and glamour and animal print. But while the Bel Air place is Dessie to a T, her interior sensibilities tend to reflect their location as well as her own taste. This apartment is much more me than it is Dessie – exposed brick, soft neutrals with moments of eclectic chic and gauzy curtains juxtaposed with heavy ebony furniture. The only nod to Dessie's signature style are zebra-print cushions and bath towels. It's a super-comfortable place if you're not a spiller, but sadly, I am. I only ever eat there over the Belfast sink.

I had a banging headache and felt nauseous, like a hangover without the fun beforehand. I could hear Mom bustling around in her room, and she was either talking to herself or

David had arrived to do her hair. I poured a coffee and went to investigate.

The latter was true, and they were sitting with their backs to me in front of the mirror, heads together like a couple of cronies. 'Now, see what I mean?' Dessie was saying. 'I can't have Fernanda looking more dramatic than me today. I'm wearing the purple Gucci, so let's do a big bushy ponytail so I look taller?'

David was nodding in agreement when he clocked me in the reflection. I knew straight away by the look on his face that Dessie had filled him on last night's drama. I held up my hand. 'I know, I look like the Crypt Keeper, and no, I don't want to talk about it.'

'I was going to say you looked like one of the zombies from *28 Days Later*, but whatever you say!' He winked at me in the mirror. 'I'll sort you out once I've made your mother look devastatingly formidable. Wash your big greasy mop in the meantime.'

I did what I was told.

To use a Dessie-ism, my head was up my arse for the entire morning. I was going over everything I'd read the night before on a loop in my head, when something clicked.

'Every man in my life is involved with Sandra Dempsey! Of course!'

David stopped packing his kit and looked confused. Mom was thankfully getting dressed and out of the room. 'You mean me?'

'Yes, I mean you! Aren't you distantly related to Sandra?'

'According to my dad, I am. I met her at the funeral in Kerry a few years back, remember? She was nice, although I didn't rate Mick one bit. Not a whiff of Jason's commanding charm off him, or his looks . . .'

He was getting distracted, so I snapped my fingers. 'What

did you make of her? Was she the kind of woman you'd want to be friends with? Did she seem fun, warm? I've only ever thought of her as Mick's wife, not as a woman in her own right. Is that weird?'

'Not really, that's the context you know her in. She was . . . grand! Pretty, nice hair. She was sort of running the afters of the funeral, it was her granny that died. She said my dad told her I worked on *LOLA*, that she knew the producer, and that turned out to be Jason.'

'I bet she had her eye on him even then. She was probably pumping you for information. Did she mention me at all?' I was getting worked up.

'Calm down, Portia,' he hissed. 'She's like, my third cousin once removed. I'm not the one that's been in a two-year-plus email relationship with her. But you know what it's like when you lose a parent, she was probably just looking for comfort.'

I froze. 'What?'

'Her dad? He died, during Covid. From Covid, actually – Dad told me on Zoom in the early days of it all. It was one of those horrible funerals where nobody could go, and people paid their respects in the front garden as the hearse drove by.' I looked at him blankly. 'Your mam said it all started during lockdown?' David looked exasperated. 'Well, maybe he was sending her condolences, to begin with.'

I sat down, taking it all in. It would be just like Jason to do that, of course. His own father died not long after we met, and he's never forgiven himself for not being home in Ireland when his dad passed. Someone losing a parent in those circumstances, at such a frightening and isolated time, would pull at his heartstrings. It was something that had brought us closer when we met; my own experience of my dad's sudden death bonding us.

'Oh.' I exhaled, perhaps properly for the first time since

I'd found the emails. I felt like an idiot. 'That probably explains why it got deep when it did. I only printed out some chats, I haven't properly read them all – it would take days.' I gnawed on my lip. 'But David, why all the secrecy? Why be intimate pen pals with somebody for years without telling me?'

'I can't speak for monogamists, but we all have our secrets. I don't know why you straights insist on knowing every single thing about one another and you're mortally offended when you don't. Life is messy, different people bring out different things in each of us. He has nothing to lose chatting to Sandra.' He was brushing one of Dessie's hairpieces violently, like it had personally offended him, and seemed mad.

'And what, he has something to lose talking to me?'

David sighed, clearly frustrated. 'Jason is a man, Portia. A big alpha male of a man. He doesn't want you to think he's weak or frightened, that he was scared shitless during the pandemic and bored out of his tree. If emailing Sandra is the worst thing that man has ever done to you, you are blessed. Trust me.'

I swallowed. That sort of made sense. In the cold light of day, I was feeling more than a bit silly. Had I totally overreacted? Or was David just unaware of what it meant to be in a monogamous relationship?

David was still going. 'Look, better a few emo emails than ringing sex hotlines, right? Or riding girls he met on Tinder, or Ashley Madison, like Dustin? You'd be surprised at the things I hear in work; women open up about all sorts when they're in the chair. Would you prefer him to start shagging your mother?! That happened to poor Anna Abruzzio . . .'

'Well, none of that would be ideal, David,' I said drily.

He stopped brushing and looked at me. He had tears in his eyes, and I realized then that David was upset about all of this too. Jason and I not being on good terms was hurting him, because we were his family. And he hadn't offered his opinion until now for fear of upsetting me further.

'Look, Portia, I can't speak for hetero men in general, but I don't think Jason was trying to be sneaky or shady – he adores you. But surely a man needs an outlet for his emotions that doesn't involve his partner? He wasn't going to call his straight American mates for a deep and meaningful, he couldn't go for a beer with his brother and get out his frustrations. He probably didn't talk to me about it because he knows that I'm more yours than I am his. If you ask me, you should be grateful.'

That irked me. He was the second person close to me that had implied I should be pleased about the illicit pen-palling. 'Grateful he discussed us having children or not with his sister-in-law?' I asked, my tone ice-cold.

David held up his hands. 'I never said it wasn't a bit shit, Portia. It is totally shit, and I'm annoyed with him too, about the whole thing. I said it wasn't the end of the world. And at least he was talking to someone. Yes, it perhaps should have been a trained professional and not fecking Sandra, but Irish people are suspicious of shrinks. It's not in our nature to pay someone to have a moan when you can do that for free.'

Ugh, he had a point.

'I'm lucky that nobody ever asks me if I want kids or not,' he continued. 'They probably presume I don't, which is fine, but it's not outside the realm of possibility if I meet my very own Ricky Martin someday. I'm sorry that your choices are up for discussion like that. But it is a choice, Portia.'

I slumped down on the overstuffed couch in a huff. My emotions were all over the place, but I was feeling a bit gaslit by my best friend. Who was David to tell me that it could be worse, when my partner of six and a half years was already having a strangely emotional e-affair?

David noticed I was quiet and joined me on the couch. 'I'm sorry, P. I just wanted to offer my perspective. I've never expected much from men, so it's hard to work out what's actually terrible behaviour and what's normal. I'm not sure, but I think Jason's lies in a grey area?'

'And that's the problem,' I sighed. 'Everything is murky, nothing is clear. I just know that it's all making me feel terrible.'

'I know what'll cheer you up. I'll show you my list of men I'd try monogamy with!'

'You have an actual list?'

'I do, and I have it to hand.' He whipped out the Notes app on his phone. 'Okay, let's see. We have Matt Bomer – living Ken doll. Jonathan Groff is my fairytale king. Ncuti 'Cutie' Gatwa, I'd do murder for him. Leonardo DiCaprio because true love never dies, even though I'm too old and too male for him. Antoni off *Queer Eye*, my *god . . .*'

He was on a roll but, luckily, Dessie chose that moment to reappear. She was decked out in a voluminous violet blouse, tailored wide-legged trousers and platform heels. Dripping in diamonds, she was half a foot taller thanks to David's handiwork and looked exactly the part of a reality-TV superstar.

She did a twirl. 'Day two, my pretties. Are we ready?'

10

It's amazing watching my mother at work. She's a truly genuine person, but when the spotlight is on her it's like she blooms. Vinnie is the same, but I practically shrivel up when faced with speaking to an audience. I guess I'm like my dad in that way; he never asked for the notoriety that accompanied his talent, though he got swept up in it.

My dad, Roberto, was Sicilian by birth, something he liked to lord over his fellow movie brats Scorsese and Coppola because they were second generation. His breakout hit, *Siciliana*, came out in 1981, between the first two *Godfather* movies and *Goodfellas*. It was a mafia in America story but told from the perspective of the women in the family.

It made sense; he was raised by a strong mother, was incredibly close to Giulia and was surrounded by powerful women in the village where he grew up. The men got things done with guns and money, but the ladies were the real bosses at home.

He met my mother at the film's New York premiere. Dessie had been modelling for a couple of years at that point and was getting tired of it. She hated the cold winters on the East Coast and wanted to move to LA and pursue a career as an actress. Meeting my dad was the answer to her prayers. She ditched her date that night, some millionaire businessman douchebag, and went home with Roberto.

Their relationship was a whirlwind. She was by his side when he won the Oscar, looking so radiant that people started to write about her more and more. They married in

Las Vegas, lived the high life for a while, and then settled in Los Angeles, in the Hills near Studio City when I was born. But things were already rocky between my parents by the time Vinnie came along in late '84.

Dad doted on us, but he was a workaholic who was rarely home, and he was temperamental and traditional. He wanted my mother to stay at home and be a housewife, but she wanted a career and hated saying no to the jobs she was offered after every appearance on his arm.

He was also involved with some shady characters, the very ones he based his scripts on, and was known for staying up nights at a time in high-stakes poker games. I don't know if Dessie turned a blind eye or didn't have the confidence then to stand up to Roberto, but I know she was always worried something bad would happen to him.

Dad spent the rest of his career trying to recapture the magic of the debut that won him his award and acclaim, but the press became more focused on his personal life than his work. He was a romantic, but he was also a ladies' man, which was a crappy combination.

There were scandals. I remember women calling the house looking for him, and one nasty fight with Mom when *The New York Times* ran a story about him owing millions to the Mob and the IRS. He swore it wasn't true and threatened to sue the paper. A lawsuit never materialized.

As an adult, I'd realized that our dad was forever chasing money like a man with a gun to his head. He never again quite reached the peak of his early career, which devastated him. It's perhaps no wonder that he dropped dead of a heart attack in 2000, before he turned fifty. My mom was a widow at forty with two grieving teenage daughters and no money, a broken, terrified woman in the wake of his death.

I remember spending a lot of time then feeling frightened,

even after my mother rallied. When the full extent of his gambling and dodgy dealings was revealed, it became clear that Dessie would now have to work for us to survive, a challenge she rose to with great gusto.

It took a long time for me to feel secure after that, having learned more about my dad than any seventeen-year-old should by reading his obituaries. But Dessie made sure I wanted for nothing. Sometimes I wondered if she married Kyle when I was a senior and Vinnie a sophomore, so we'd have some sort of stability. They met at a high-school function and tied the knot within a month. He had connections in television, and by the time I was headed for NYU on a scholarship to the Tisch School of the Arts to study film she had money in the bank again from catalogue modelling and infomercials. But for a long time after my father's death, she seemed in many ways fragile.

In contrast, watching Dessie on stage at V-Palooza was like watching a master at work, the audience in the palm of her hand and her natural charm and warmth radiating out to the back rows. The fragility was gone, and it was hard to imagine this woman as the desperate woman she had been, losing not only her beloved husband but her home, her lifestyle and all the glamour of his association.

She enjoyed acting, but it was with *LOLA* that Dessie flourished. Soaps, commercials and celebrity competition shows were fun for her, but nothing compared to anchoring *Ladies of Los Angeles*. She was the only founding cast member with any profile of her own; the others' sole draw was being glamorous and wealthy.

Dessie is the queen of the show, the OG that's survived all the other stars that have fallen by the wayside over fourteen seasons. The V-Palooza crowd loved her just as much as they did when she burst on to their screens. I remember having my doubts about it all at the time, but looking at her now in her element, I just felt proud.

'I have a question for Dessie,' a small voice in the crowd said. It was the audience participation segment of the panel, and the other *LOLA* ladies were fuming that so many fans wanted to speak to my mom.

This woman was barely five feet tall, had a round, innocent face and was wearing a T-shirt with Dessie's face on it. 'Um, I love you, Dessie!' Cheers rang out. 'My question is, do you think you'll ever get married again?' The audience hooted and hollered.

Nobody else would have noticed, but standing beside the monitor at the side of the stage I could see the shadow that quickly passed over her face. 'Oh, never say never, my darling!' she beamed. 'I just have to find a man that's able for me.' The crowd yelled their approval. 'I've been lucky in my life. Two out of three marriages have been very good ones, and the middle one, well, it was blessedly short. Sure, isn't Manny over there still my BFF? Stand up, Manny Alvarez, my darling! Wave!'

Poor Manuel was standing beside me in the wings and awkwardly waved out at the crowd, mortified at the attention.

'To answer your question, I feel like I've enough experience with marriage and love to last me a lifetime. Romance, on the other hand? Well, there's life in this old girl yet.' She winked, lasciviously. Manny snorted and shook his head.

'She can say that again,' he whispered.

Much later that evening we all gathered in the green room. Most of the bigger players were done with V-Palooza, with the Sunday focusing on the network's niche shows about cooking, fashion and real estate. All the *LOLA* ladies had convened for an impromptu party, and the drinks were flowing.

Jason's panel had gone down well; he didn't mind doing this sort of thing but didn't exactly relish it either. His producer's instinct was lit up at the event, though – you couldn't buy this kind of market research, and he made sure his teams were ready to capture any backstage shenanigans. They'd recently started breaking the fourth wall on the programme, acknowledging that their Ladies were now stars. But they still wanted to retain some narrative mystery, so cameras were down for the drinks party and everybody was letting loose.

David's words had calmed me down that morning, and while I hadn't forgotten about Jason's secret pen pal and was still quietly fuming, I decided not to bring it up. Jason looked gorgeous in a black shirt and a teal suit, more like a star than a producer, and I felt that familiar rush of love and disbelief that he was mine when he shone the light of his attention on me.

'Baby!' he'd called when he saw me across the convention. 'I missed you last night.' He'd picked me up and spun me around, before planting a kiss on my lips. 'Don't let your mother kidnap you like that again; I was lonely all by myself.'

Lonely enough to send Sandra an email? I wondered. Stop it, I scolded myself. Not now.

By the time of the afterparty, I was comfortably cocooned in his shoulder nook. He and Manny were arguing about Ariel's burgeoning career, while my mother was holding court with the Ladies of other cities. She looked tired, but happy among her peers. Despite their differences, these women all have a connection, and an implicit understanding of how wild their job truly is.

'Manny, I'm just saying that maybe it's all happening a little fast,' Jason was saying. 'I know Ariel is precocious, Jesus, she's been that way since the womb. But this commercial, it's mainstream. Will she be ready for it at fifteen?'

My stepfather sighed and looked defeated. I still call him

94

that, although he and Dessie divorced ten years ago. He's been around for a long time and has been perhaps the steadiest male influence in my life. I quite simply adore him.

'Look, Jason, you are preaching to the choir, my man,' he said in his Miami drawl. 'I think she's too young and it's too much. But nobody listens to me.' He shook his fist in my mother's direction. 'These women, they'll kill me.'

I scanned the room looking for Ariel, spotting her lurking at the bar. Excusing myself, I collared her. 'What do you think you're doing?'

She turned and fixed me with a gaze so cool, so adult, that I shuddered a bit. Ariel is the spitting image of Manuel, all glossy, straight dark hair, olive skin and serious expression. We have the same colouring, but that's where any similarities end.

'I'm bored out of my mind and looking for something interesting,' she replied. 'Not finding anything here, unforch.'

'Well, you won't find it near the booze,' I said, directing her away from temptation. 'Your dad and Jason are over there arguing about your career.' I grinned. 'If you want to offer any insight?'

'Oh, let the men think they have a say!' Now, she sounded like Dessie. 'Mom thinks it's a great opportunity for me.'

'It's a big deal, though. And very public, especially for a fourteen-year-old. You're my little sister, I want to be sure you can handle it all.'

Another glare. 'Fifteen? Well, in a few weeks.' I remembered RSVPing to her quinceañera then, a spectacular event in the Beverly Hills Hotel later in the summer. Ugh.

'Anyway, they were right to come to Mom. Daddy would have said no, and this is my career we're talking about. I'll be the one dancing in the commercial, I should have a say in my own future.'

'Do you even drink Gatorade?'

'Ew, no. But they don't need to know that. I'll suffer for 500k. And then I'm going to take that money and build my own content studio. I'm going to get my own series on You-Tube, a podcast, maybe a line of jewellery . . .'

She might be incredibly advanced, but the child was showing her years – as if Dessie would even let her see that cheque before she was eighteen. I allowed Ariel to jabber on, showing me pictures of her 'fits' for the next meeting and asking my opinion. 'For an older woman, you're actually quite cool,' she said, guilelessly.

'Why, thank you.' I laughed, swiping around her phone. Most of the outfits looked like bondage-meets-fairy-princess attire, and I was figuring out how to say that appropriately when I noticed Jason was talking to someone. More than talking, actually – as I peered at him over Ariel's shoulder, he had his head thrown back, laughing.

His body was angled towards whoever was so funny, so I strained to see. Then a manicured hand snaked around his waist and planted itself in the middle of his back. It all looked very cosy from my vantage point.

Ariel forgotten, I stared. And that's when I clocked it was Sybil Simpson, she of the alcoholic seltzer, with her claws literally digging into my man. What was worse, he looked happy about it.

She leaned up to whisper in his ear and gave him a squeeze. I saw her put something in his back pocket before flouncing away, boobs and bum jiggling. He looked after her, before shaking his head and sitting back down beside Manny.

What was it? Short of demanding he empty his pockets, I couldn't know. It had looked like a card of some sort – a room key? A love note?

I was livid once again. How could I trust this man?

I couldn't! Not only was he pouring out his deepest, darkest emotions over email, he was probably shagging his leading Lady of New York. All of the bad, dark feelings I'd quashed came rushing back. Jason felt like a stranger to me once again, and I was suddenly very frightened.

'Hello, back to reality?' A finger snap from Ariel brought me back. 'Wow, are you getting dementia already, Portia? I thought you had a few years left before you started spacing out in public.'

I steered her back in the direction of the family and walked out into the warm evening by myself.

Obituary: Roberto Rizzi,
filmmaker, dies in Los Angeles

31 July 2000

The director Roberto Rizzi has died at the age of 49, it has been confirmed. The Academy Award winning filmmaker is survived by his wife, 40-year-old Desdemona Daniels-Rizzi, their daughters Portia (17) and 15-year-old Lavinia, and his sister and manager, Giulia Rizzi, 37.

A formidable figure in Hollywood, Rizzi was at once introspective and magnetic. A physically dominant man standing at six and a half feet, he was known for an innate understanding of the female mind and for writing women's stories. This set him apart from his contemporaries early on.

Rizzi was raised in Palermo, Sicily. His father, Gianfranco, died in 1964, leaving behind his widow and two children. Urged by his mother, Roberto moved to the United States in 1969, where he attended New York University. Rizzi juggled three jobs as he wrote his now infamous debut, snatching hours here and there to work on his screenplay. He spoke at length about how his script was not only influenced by his friends and relatives from the old country, but made possible thanks to their support.

Rizzi was a huge fan of the American gangster film as well as the Italian new wave. His own style was influenced by this, focusing on location shooting, non-professional actors delivering heartfelt dialogue and flashy, violent set pieces.

Rizzi's big break came when Paramount tapped him to make *Siciliana*, an English-language adaptation of a play he wrote in his mother tongue as a teen.

He famously based the characters on the women he observed in his hometown, including his own family, but moved the action of the film from Sicily to New Jersey and set it in the present day. It was a monstrous hit, cementing his reputation as a writer/director who spoke to both men and women, and had mixed brutality and crime with tenderness and even romance in a way not seen previously. His sister, Giulia, came to America when the film was a hit, acting as a bilingual spokesperson and publicist for her older brother.

After winning his Oscar in 1982, Rizzi married model Desdemona Daniels and they settled in a home in Los Angeles. His next films did moderately well, but never quite replicated the critical acclaim and commercial success of his debut feature, and he subsequently found a comfortable spot making independent films.

He was rarely out of the tabloids, however; he and Daniels-Rizzi were known as one of the most glamorous couples of Hollywood in the eighties, and were friends with everyone from Jack Nicholson and Cher to Michael Jackson and Madonna. The couple were dogged by rumours of Rizzi's numerous alleged infidelities (most notably with actress Lana D'Amico, a regular collaborator who won an Oscar for her eponymous role in his 1990 feature *Donatella*). Rizzi himself was never nominated for another Academy Award, despite the performers in his films earning rave reviews and plaudits.

There were also whispers of ties to organized crime. 'These men do what they must for their families,' he once told this newspaper about the underworld bosses his films often depict. 'The ones they're born into, and the ones they create. They must provide, and for some, breaking the rules is the only way they can do that.'

A rule-breaker himself, Rizzi was a keen gambler, visiting Las Vegas so regularly that a suite at the Sands remained open for him at all times until it shuttered in 1996. But the real rules he broke were that of his art – focusing on the inner workings of the female mind in a man's world, and the allure of danger.

Rizzi often talked of feeling divided between the place of his birth and the place of his work. As per his wishes, he will be cremated and his remains will be divided between a niche in the Hollywood Forever Cemetery, and his mother's grave in Palermo.

11

I heard the heavy tread on the stairs, but I was ready for him. It had taken Jason long enough to realize I had left the party; by now it was close to midnight and I was two glasses of Montepulciano deep, livid and spoiling for a fight. I'd switched my phone to silent as I walked out of the convention centre, and made a beeline for his computer when I got in. If I was going to confront Jason, I needed information and I needed ammo.

I learned quickly that other than his email affair (yes, that's what I was now calling it) with Sandra, Jason ran a tight ship. He's an inbox-zero kind of guy, and I couldn't find any receipts for OnlyFans, any randoms lurking in his sent items or essentially anything incriminating. But if you were a cheater, and a smart one at that, wouldn't you be good at hiding the evidence? Jason was a smooth operator in life, and I suspected he'd be one in deceit also.

All these thoughts were solid proof that any trust I had in him had taken a nosedive off a cliff. All it took was one raunchy older woman pawing him and I was lit up like a Christmas tree.

Since his baby bombshell and then my discovery of his correspondence, I had been vacillating wildly between feeling like I'd never really known him and like I was totally overreacting. Reading back further on his emails to Sandra, I realized how much he hadn't been telling me – the extent of his homesickness for Ireland, and how much he loved harking back to his youth when he was the biggest fish in the local pond, and how claustrophobic he often felt in New York.

Reading those letters was like reading someone else's words. It was as if Jason inhabited two different worlds – the one he lived in with me, full of world travel, glamorous (if demanding) work and an exciting lifestyle, and the one in which he was still living at home, happy in the bosom of his family and spending his weekends with the friends he grew up with.

I'd had no idea that this other world existed for him. As far as I was concerned, our life together was his only reality.

The door slammed. 'Portia? Are you here?' He walked into the living area, where I was sitting in stony silence. 'What the hell, P? Why did you just leave me there? I got stuck talking to every Tom, Dick and Harry, and then I noticed you were just . . . gone!'

'Don't you mean every Harriet?' I snarled. This wasn't like me, but I was seething.

'Who the hell is Harriet?'

I set down my wine. 'I know about Sandra,' I said icily. He still looked perplexed, and he didn't even flinch. 'And I saw Sybil all over you like a rash in the corner. What did she slip into your back pocket? Planning a hotel room dalliance, were you? What else have you been hiding from me?'

His frown deepened, and he pulled a Polaroid out of his suit and tossed it on the table. It was a picture of him and Sybil from their panel that afternoon. 'I don't know what the heck you're on about, Portia, but you're starting to piss me off.'

'Starting!' I barked. 'I've been pissed off for *weeks*! And just when I'm thinking of altering my future for you, of going against every natural inclination I have and going along with this baby thing, just to *please you*, I find out that not only do you have a secret little pen pal, but that you've been discussing my empty, inhospitable uterus with her.' I was furious. It's rare that I blow up, but when I do, it's frightening.

Jason also looked angry. 'You've been going through my emails?'

'That's all you're concerned about? That I discovered your emotional affair?'

'Ah god, Portia, you're something else.' He laughed cruelly. He flopped on to the couch and kicked off his Chelsea boots (Isabel Marant, bought by me). 'I didn't think you were the snooping type.'

'Well, I didn't think you were the parenting type, but things change, don't they?'

He was trying to act casual and dismissive, but the air was thick with tension. All the unspoken words of the past few weeks, all of the secrets kept from one another were charging the atmosphere to the point where I almost expected a roll of thunder. I could see my phone flashing. Vinnie was calling, but I ignored it.

Jason sat up, leaned forward and looked me dead in the eye. 'You're clearly very upset, Portia. We've been avoiding speaking to one another in any real way, and that's obviously not working. So, let's get it all out. Talk to me.' The man literally rolled up his sleeves, ready to go.

But I was too wound up to be calm and rational. 'What's going on with Sandra?' I beseeched him. 'Why are you spending all your time writing to her, instead of talking to me? Are you in love with her?'

'There is nothing going on with Sandra. Jesus, Portia. Don't make it sound so sordid. She's my sister-in-law. We've been friends since we were children.'

'You've never told me you were so close. Why would you keep that from me?'

He scratched his jaw. 'I guess we haven't always been, these things ebb and flow. But during Covid when everything was so crazy and her dad died I reached out and we just started talking. Since when is there anything wrong with talking to a family member?'

I was starting to lose my edge a bit; the mention of her dad took the wind out of my sails.

'There is nothing wrong with talking, but there is something wrong with not telling me about it. Does Mick know how close you two are? And even if you're not in love with her, she clearly is with you. She fancies you!'

'Portia!' he exploded. 'You are being ridiculous. My sister-in-law, my brother's wife, does not "fancy" me!' His voice had taken on a nasty edge. 'You're being juvenile. Do you tell me about everyone you email? It's innocent, it's family! She's a good listener, she makes me feel better about . . . things.'

'There, you've said it. She makes you feel better than I do!'

'No, she doesn't, but she's . . . It's different. She listens to me! She has time for me, cares about what I want.'

'Oh, and I don't? Shocker, a mother-of-two cares about your new-found desires for baby-making, especially because it doesn't affect her! You certainly know your audience!'

I noticed Vinnie was calling me again, but at the same time I suddenly remembered what Sandra had said to her friends at the gender reveal. 'Oh my god, she was telling the truth!' I yelped. 'I heard Sandra telling the other WAGs that we were going to have children after all. I thought she'd gotten her facts mixed up, but nope! My partner has been telling her his innermost desires, his deepest secrets! And I first hear about them when she mentions it in the ladies' room!'

Jason was looking at me open-mouthed. He hadn't a clue what I was talking about, because I'd never told him.

'Oh yes, Sandra thinks I should just acquiesce and upend my entire life overnight because you've changed your mind. I should deliver your progeny, give you offspring and then maybe you'll be happy enough with me to not have to email other women for attention.'

He was getting properly riled up now. 'Do you think I want you to "acquiesce"? Do you honestly think I want the mother of my children to have them just to make me happy?'

'Oh, it's *children* now! Multiple! Sure, why don't we go the whole hog and I'll be an octomom!'

I knew I sounded irrational, even a little crazy, but I didn't care. All my pent-up feelings were exploding out: my anger at him for disrupting our gorgeous life, my fear of losing what we had, my worry that I was truly a weirdo for not wanting what everyone else thought I should.

'And besides Sandra, what was with you looking extremely cosy with Sybil tonight? Here I am thinking she's brilliant, a legend, and all the while she's literally sinking her claws into my boyfriend.'

'Yeah, that's it, Portia,' he sneered. 'I'm fucking Sybil Simpson on the side, just to get back at you for avoiding me. Actually, I'm fucking all the cast members. I'm not fussy!'

'You're probably fucking Frida downstairs too. She has loads of kids already – what's one more!'

I knew I'd crossed a line, and he was properly furious now. But I couldn't back down.

Jason's demeanour changed. All of a sudden, he became quiet and cold. 'You clearly think so little of me, to believe these things,' he spat. 'I spent over a year trying to work out how to tell you that I wanted to be a dad.'

'Oh yes, I remember you telling me that *you* had decided you wanted to be a father. That you had made a decision without even talking to me!'

'I was trying to work out how to tell you I wanted a baby with *you*. I knew it was a long shot, I tried to fight my feelings and just let things be, but in the end, I just couldn't. You can't make me feel bad for wanting kids, Portia, it's not right!'

'But it's okay for everyone to want me to go against my own feelings, my own desires? I'm the baddie for not wanting a baby, not wanting to give up my body and my life?'

'Oh my god, you're being so dramatic. Your body for a while, yes. Your work perhaps would take a back seat for a time. But your life? Portia, what else is there in life besides family?'

I felt like I'd been physically winded. All the air went out of me, and I sat down heavily on the ottoman. He just didn't get it. To me, we were a family, just the two of us. To him, that would never be enough. I realized right then and there that everything I thought about who we were had changed, and the gap between us felt like a chasm.

He wanted children, I didn't. The whys and why nots didn't matter; only the facts did. He must have had the same realization at the same time because we both sat in stunned silence.

At that moment, my phone started flashing yet again. I answered it for something to do, anything to break the horrible nothingness. 'Oh my god, Vinnie, what is it?'

My sister was sobbing. 'Portia, it's Billy. He's gone. He's just left me here with the kids, and I don't . . . I can't get Mom, Portia, what do I do?' She was hyperventilating, becoming hysterical. I could hear the boys crying in the background.

'What do you mean, he's left?'

She was struggling to breathe on the other end of the phone. 'His stuff is gone. I came home from a shoot and there was a letter on the bed. Portia, if what it says is true, he's finished! I'm finished! My life is over!'

'Vin, I'm on my way,' I announced, surprising myself. 'I'll come back with Mom to LA. I'll be there in the morning, okay? Take the boys and go to her place, it's more secure. We'll be there as soon as we can.'

She was panting, but I heard a vague 'okay'. Vinnie had suffered from terrible anxiety as a teenager, so I knew she could help herself with a little guidance. 'I'm calling Suz to come and stay with you, okay? Vinnie, I love you. We'll get through this.'

I hung up to find Jason staring at me agog. 'You're leaving?' He was incredulous.

'It's Billy, he's left Vinnie. I kind of knew it was coming, I . . . I've just been so wrapped up in myself the last few days that I didn't . . . ugh, I should have prepared her for this. I have to go to her.' I was pacing back and forth.

'So that's it, you're just going to go to a different time zone for an indeterminate time without resolving this? What about work?'

'I can write anywhere, you know that.'

'Okay then, what about me?'

I hung my head. 'Jason, I don't see a resolution here. I don't know what to do, do you?'

His shoulders drooped. 'No,' he sighed. 'I don't.'

'I have to go and be with my sister. It's important.'

'Fine, whatever. Maybe a bit of space will do us some good.'

A chill went down my spine.

'Space? Like a break? You want to break up?'

'I . . . I don't know.' He put his head in his hands. 'Portia, my head is wrecked. I don't have a clue what to say to you to make you less angry.' He looked up. 'Right now, I don't know the right thing to do. Call it whatever you want, a break or a break-up. If you're going to go, just go.'

Jason strode towards the spare bedroom and slammed the door behind him. I wanted to go after him, but I was so angry. How dare he make such declarations? I was the one who was supposed to be mad, not him. Was he threatening me? Did he want me to go after him?

But at that moment, even in my blind rage, I was more worried about Vinnie than I was about myself. There'd been a desperation in her voice I hadn't heard since she'd got clean.

I looked at my watch before I called Suz. She had just come off air; the show isn't actually live but shot a couple hours before transmission to allow for some quick edits and a more lively, awake audience.

'Hey, baby girl, you got me at a good time! I'm taking off my lashes,' she drawled. Suz grew up in New Orleans before moving to LA as a pre-teen when her dad got transferred. She's modified her accent for broadcasting to a sort of neutral American, but when she's off duty, so is her professional voice. I could picture her sitting at the light-up mirror in her dressing room, pulling off her eyelash strips and rubbing cold cream on her face.

'Suz, it's Vinnie. Billy's left her, I'm not sure of the details, but I was tipped off that he's involved in some sex scandal that may or may not be illegal. Either way, he's upped sticks and ran off. She's hysterical.'

'Oh no, I had a feeling something was going on,' Suz groaned. 'I'd heard rumblings, but I hoped it might just be nasty gossip.'

'I did too,' I admitted. 'But I've been so preoccupied I didn't get around to investigating more. Look, I'm going to come west with Dessie first thing. Can you get over to Mom's tonight? I've told Vinnie to go there, it's a little less exposed than her place if the paparazzi start swarming. You know how fast gossip travels in those parts, and I think it's best she's not in her own house with everything there reminding her of Billy.'

'Know it? Child, I'm too familiar with it. Fret not, the girls are away at cheer camp all week. I'll go and scoop Vinnie up and bring her to Bel Air.'

'Thank you.'

'Portia, are you okay? You sound awful.'

'I'm uh, just worried. Call me when you have eyes on Vinnie.'

I knew Suz would be as good as her word, so I relaxed ever so slightly. My phone lit up again – my mother. Sighing, I pulled my Louis Vuitton luggage out from under the bed as I answered.

An hour later, it was all arranged. Dessie had sprung into action in true momager fashion. Graham's plane was taking off at 7 a.m. New York time, meaning we'd be in LA for breakfast. I didn't know how long I'd be gone for – I didn't know anything at that moment and was throwing items haphazardly into my case.

Laptop, Kindle, skin care, my Pill. I looked at the packet wryly and flung it in anyway. I found myself grabbing random sentimental stuff – the bear Jason won for me at Coney Island, my dad's work notebook, a family photo album from 2007.

I surprised myself by sleeping for a couple of hours. I woke up confused, the bed empty beside me. And then I remembered that Jason was next door, and that our relationship was in tatters. I thought I could actually feel my heart break.

But I didn't have time to sit there and give in to the pain. I dressed quickly and comfortably for the journey – Graham's plane is fabulous, all cream leather and brass fixtures, and people don't exactly slob out on it. I threw on my favourite DD+ cotton maxi slip dress, a pair of Chucks and my denim jacket. The beauty of having the smallest boobs in the family is that I never have to wear a bra.

I was about to walk out without saying goodbye but relented at the door. I peeked into the spare room; Jason was snoring softly on his back. I crept in and snuggled into him, the little spoon. He responded sleepily, pressing his front to my back and throwing his arm around me.

I could have stayed there for ever. I can't describe the strength it took to get up and leave, not knowing what was going to happen with us. Last night, something had shifted and, for the first time since I met him, I didn't know where Jason and I stood.

But my sister needed me. Maybe the three thousand miles between us would give us some space to figure things out.

I slipped out from under his arm and kissed him softly on the cheek. 'I love you, Jason,' I whispered. Because I really did. And then I was gone.

TMZ.com

Schwartz's sex shocker! Supermodel wife is nowhere to be found

30 May 2022

Hollywood super-agent Billy Schwartz has gone on the lam after three women all still in their teens have claimed to have slept with the married father-of-two.

We're told 19-year-old TopTier intern Sally Morgan, actress Penelope Frank (18) and Trysta Priest, also 18, are only the tip of the iceberg, and there are many more young ladies that have carnal knowledge of the 41-year-old showbiz Svengali . . .

All three women have now made statements about mixing business with pleasure when it came to Billy. Trysta, a high-school SENIOR, is the younger sister of pop sensation JenKat, who also happened to be Billy's client . . . but no more, as Schwartz has been officially fired from TopTier Representation, the agency he co-founded with his pals James Wilson and Lamar Phelps.

Trysta and JenKat are said to be going on the record with a huge (and reportedly damning) TV interview with a major network very soon . . .

No doubt everyone is thinking of Billy's wife, the supermodel turned lifestyle guru Lavinia Rizzi-Schwartz – she's the daughter of reality star and mogul Dessie Daniels, and the momager is doing a good job of keeping Lavinia and her kids away from our cameras. She hasn't been spotted since the rumours swirling were confirmed by the young ladies in question. Her social media has gone dark.

It's quite a turn-up for the books, considering how happy the Schwartz family have always appeared. Nobody was shocked when they fell in love, the powerful, self-made agent and the fashion darling seemed like a match made in heaven – or at least, in Hollywood.

We'll keep you all posted on any updates in what's sure to be a shocking developing story . . .

I woke up on a fluffy pink cloud in a room filled with sunlight. Ah, heaven, I thought woozily. Wait, no. In heaven surely there wouldn't be a cacophony of loud K-pop music. And I wouldn't have a weird taste in my mouth. And wait, where was Jason?

Sitting up abruptly, it took me a second to realize where I was. The fluffy pink cloud was the beautiful salmon velvet sectional sofa in Dessie's family room, the feeling of fuzzy well-being due to the edibles visible on the table beside me, and the music coming from Ariel's room down the hall. The sun, which now felt oppressive, was that Los Angeles speciality. Oh, and it was my thirty-ninth birthday. Reality bit, and ouch. It hurt.

It appears I wasn't the only one disturbed by teen spirit; Vinnie appeared at the door, hovering like a ghost. She looked awful, drawn and gaunt in a way I hadn't seen since her party days. 'Happy birthday, sis,' she whispered, eyeing the jar of edibles. 'Too bad I'm an addict and can't partake,' she smirked wryly. 'I get sober and California legalizes pot, go figure.'

'I'm surprised you're not selling them anyway, to be honest. Your followers don't know you're addicted to mood-altering substances – flog away!' I had hoped to make her smile as my gentle mocking usually does, but she didn't even grimace. I wasn't surprised. I'd been lucky to get two sentences out of her since I'd arrived a couple of days prior.

If I was in a bad way, Vinnie was worse. Yes, I had left my boyfriend of nearly seven years. I was three thousand miles away, and I couldn't even sleep in a bed without him, so had taken to the couch. And it was my birthday. That was bad. But Vinnie's husband of eight years had been outed as a sex pest chasing every barely legal starlet in Los Angeles, and he'd been damn successful at it as well.

The news was everywhere. Not just on the message boards and Twitter, but on TMZ and Page Six, and quickly working its way towards prime-time chat shows and the evening news. The night before, Billy had officially been fired in absentia from TopTier, the agency he co-founded, for gross misconduct. No criminal charges had been filed by the LAPD, but all it was going to take was one young woman under eighteen in California or seventeen in New York to come forward, and he could be arrested.

Regardless of the legalities, Billy was done, cancelled, deemed gross and skeevy, and there was just no coming back from that in the entertainment industry any more. Even before the #MeToo era, agents were meant to be respectable, above reproach, a reflection of their clients' good images. Any bad behaviour on an agent's part could potentially harm their roster of actors, singers, influencers – not just the hassle of having to click with a new representative in the event of a scandal but the jeopardy of deals in progress.

And that was just his professional life. If his clients were tainted by his dodgy sexual activity, his wife was even more so. The brand that Vinnie had so carefully built was all about their family: a loving husband and wife living their best life together with their gorgeous kids. Aspirational, photogenic, #powercouple.

Vinnie curled up in a ball on the other end of the gigantic pink sofa and closed her eyes. I knew she wasn't sleeping or eating, and I worried non-stop she was going to slip back into her old ways of self-medicating and starving herself.

At that moment, I didn't know what was making Vinnie feel worse. Was it her husband's betrayal? Because she had married such a creep and had children with him? Her life being so nastily turned on its head, or the fact that her brand was going to suffer as a result? The whole shit show was packing such a punch and affecting my sister so deeply I believe I would have killed Billy Schwartz with my bare hands if he dared to show his face.

But no such luck. He had fled in broad daylight, leaving only that note for Vinnie, which she'd been clutching so tightly for the past couple of days I was surprised it hadn't totally disintegrated. She hadn't let any of us read what it said.

Everyone was fussing over us both, but I was redirecting most of the attention towards Vinnie. By everyone, I mean the family – Dessie, Manny, Giulia, Suz and David. Ariel knew what was going on and was interested in a ghoulish way because it turned out she was friendly with one of Billy's alleged conquests. Once Mom heard that, Ariel was declared out of any family meetings.

We were all acting totally normal in front of the boys, which was a colossal effort. As far as Si and Seb were concerned, Billy was on one of his frequent business trips, and staying at Glammy's was a fun adventure they didn't dare contest. Yes, my mother makes the boys call her Glammy because Granny or even Nanna are too ageing for her to contemplate.

As for me, Vinnie's more high-profile and distressing drama meant I could focus entirely on that and not on my own shattered heart. If I even thought about Jason or our future, I went practically catatonic with panic.

In a rare moment of lucidity, the night before at 3 a.m. Vinnie had taught me some breathing exercises when I was the one freaking out. She said that they would take me out of my brain when the feeling hit. I let her think they worked and took an edible instead. Seriously, you can get those for anything these days. My preference was gold shimmering gummies that tasted like vanilla ice cream and promised a euphoric high.

I wasn't experiencing euphoria, but they were definitely taking the edge off. And it was so handy being able to buy weed in a glamorous Beverly Hills store these days, instead of from one of Billy's agency suppliers. People are often surprised that such a thing exists, but there's a whole industry that discreetly provides the rich and famous with whatever they want or need, whether they're just passing through town or in need of regular supplies.

What was surprising was that Mom wasn't taking any of this well, which was totally unlike her. Dessie is a physically powerful woman, always in motion, always a consummate professional. She always knows what to do, regardless of how it affects any of us personally. I'd heard her crying the day before when she said she was taking a nap, and felt afraid.

Once Vinnie settled into the couch and her breathing became regular, I went in search of my mother. I found her in her bed, wearing a leopard-print silk eye mask and lying like a corpse with her hands crossed over her chest. 'Mom?' I whispered.

She lifted the mask. 'Portia, pet. Happy birthday. Come in, I was trying to fool my body into sleeping.' She lifted the duvet, which was a comforting childhood memory. I clambered in, allowing myself to forget I was a thirty-eight – no wait, thirty-nine-year-old adult with myriad problems.

Dessie's room is pure luxury, of course. The best-quality Egyptian cotton sheets, silk pillowcases and the softest goose down known to man, all atop a mattress fit for a queen (and custom-made in Encino). Mom would rather have the air conditioning on full blast and sleep under a heavy quilt than actually experience the California climate, but I had to admit it was really comfy.

'So, you're not sleeping either?' I said.

'Lord, no. I'm stressed to bits, love.' She sighed. 'I don't want to depend on tablets, you know? After your sister's rehab trips and seeing poor Graham geeked out of her mind on the yokes, I avoid them like the plague. Manny left me some Xanax last night, but they're not for me.'

'You should try the edibles, Mom. They're not really addictive.'

'No, spliffs have always turned my stomach, pet. I'd be afraid. Anyway, I need to remain sharp. I have to work out how to spin all of this, but I'm drawing a blank.' She lay back down and sighed again. For the first time in my entire life, I thought she looked her age.

'Giulia said it's best to say nothing and lie low for the moment, right?' I said. 'I think the right moment to say or do something will present itself. And Vinnie is safe here, at least.'

'I know, I know. I'm just so worried about her. And I'm so angry at that bastard. I mean, Billy has always been a charming character, and slick with it. But I never thought he had this in him.'

'That makes two of us,' said Vinnie from the doorway. Dessie and I shot up. 'You're like two little meerkats,' she grinned. 'That's the first time I've smiled in days,' she said as she joined us under the duvet.

'Oh, Vinnie, darling. I'm so sorry I couldn't protect you from all of this.' Dessie looked truly wounded.

'Mom, my marriage is literally none of your business. Remember, you wanted me to marry that nice rich tech guy from Colorado who would have looked after me for life, and I said no, I want to marry for love?' She snorted. 'I should

117

have listened to you and just settled for someone who worshipped me.'

'Jesus, Lavinia, don't make it sound so sordid. I was trying to matchmake, not sell you to the highest bidder!' My mother was horrified at the insinuation. 'He was a nice man.'

'Yeah, and it helped that he was richer than God.' I laughed, remembering the poor eejit Dessie had dragged to dinner when Vinnie was officially a year clean and therefore on the market. She would have eaten him alive. Weeks later, Vinnie had been introduced to Billy at a party, and the rest was history.

My mother huffed. 'Yes, well, at least he wasn't a sexual predator.' She saw Vinnie's face turn ashen. 'Oh, I'm sorry, love.'

'No, no, you're correct,' Vinnie sighed bitterly. 'I'm going to have to get used to it, aren't I? I married a sleazebag who gets his kicks fucking girls barely out of high school!' She was building steam. 'I mean, I knew he liked them young, his taste in porn told me that. But why couldn't he just have an affair with one of my friends like a normal Hollywood husband? Why couldn't he limit himself to hookers, or have a secret account on Tinder? I mean, at least they vet people's ages.'

It's always amazed me how cynical the women in my family are about relationships in the entertainment industry. As a true believer in love, I can't imagine being okay with any philandering or deception, but Vinnie and Dessie are different. Their rule is, if you're going to screw around, be smart about it. I know they've both built up thick skins, but surely it would hurt regardless?

Vinnie noticed my appalled face. 'Sorry, little Miss Romantic, I don't want to burst your bubble, but faithful partners aren't all that common around these parts.' She sounded bitter, but that was understandable. I knew she was putting on a brave face, and that she was smarting and mortified.

'You think every husband in LA cheats, is that what you're saying?' I said.

'The vast, vast majority, pet,' chimed my mother. 'I was hopeful like you too, once. But it's just too easy for them in Hollywood. Sex can be like a commodity, a transaction, and there's temptation everywhere. You'd want to be a blessed saint to not dabble occasionally. But I didn't think Billy was this much of a fecking eejit.'

She stretched and went to get up. 'I think of it like I think of my dogs,' she said, pulling on a raw silk kimono from DD+. 'I love and adore them, but do I want to pet and kiss more dogs? Of course I do!'

That was what finally broke the black pall that settled over the house. Vinnie and I burst into convulsions at our mother's analogy, so much so that Vinnie fell off the bed. Dessie was perplexed, then annoyed. '*What* are ye laughing at?' she demanded. 'I'm serious! *It's a good way to look at it!*'

As I struggled to breathe, all I could think was one thing – thank the gods for Dessie. Even in the worst situation she always managed to make things better, even when she wasn't trying to.

Manny appeared at the doorway. 'I heard a pack of laughing hyenas. Is it humour or hysteria?'

'A bit of both,' I managed.

'Happy birthday, honey.' He blew me a kiss. 'It's good to have you here for it.' He ambled off, likely in search of coffee. The man drinks multiple cups of espresso a day, from a machine too sophisticated for the rest of us to figure out.

I drifted outside to the patio off the main suite and looked out over the beautiful, hilly expanse. Being back in LA and back in my mom's house for my birthday felt strange, not that my birthday would be a big deal, considering what was going on with Vinnie. *Maybe this is where you're meant to be right now*, I thought to myself.

A low-key birthday this year wouldn't be much different from previous years. I always liked my birthdays — it marked the beginning of summer to me, and Dessie always made a fuss. But Jason and I didn't usually do much in New York. He just wasn't the sort to make a big deal out of stuff like that. He didn't like it for himself and couldn't see why other people needed it either. When I turned thirty-eight, he'd been so busy filming under pandemic precautions that he'd obviously totally forgotten until he checked Instagram at lunchtime and saw our friends' posts. A rushed picture of us followed, with a birthday crown GIF on my head. I ended up going for a drink with Amy that night while Jason worked late.

I looked at my phone then — New York was three hours ahead, and there was no word from Jason yet. He hadn't contacted me at all since I left, and I was too mad to get in touch with him. I sighed and went in search of Manuel and his complicated coffee machine.

The Los Angeles Times

Who Is Billy Schwartz?
Inside Hollywood's latest sex scandal

2 June 2022

Unless you live in Los Angeles and work in the entertainment industry, the name Billy Schwartz might not be familiar to you. While he has been a power player in the industry for almost two decades, the agent and founding partner of TopTier Representation is someone that people outside of showbiz normally wouldn't recognize. However, his marriage to Lavinia Rizzi-Daniels in 2015 changed all of that.

Now Schwartz is known not only for his work in Hollywood but for his association with one of its best-known families. Lavinia is the daughter of the late director Roberto Rizzi and reality star, former actress and entrepreneur Desdemona Daniels. Herself a huge fashion star in the 00s, Lavinia is famous for documenting her life not only on her mother's reality show, *Ladies of Los Angeles*, but on her own social media. All this has meant that Billy Schwartz is, if not a household name, more well known than your average industry executive.

Born and raised in Brooklyn, New York, Schwartz moved to Los Angeles at twenty, having dropped out of pre-law in Colombia University. In his wife's 2019 autobiography, *Life and Love with Lavinia*, she claims that he didn't want to 'waste time in college, preferring to learn on the job and willing to do just about anything to make it in the movie industry'. Scrappy and likeable, Schwartz did as many have done before him and started working in the mail room of an illustrious PR firm. Deciding that he'd rather be an agent than a publicist, he charmed his way into an entry-level agent position at United Artists at the age of twenty-two. Five years later he started his own firm with his former college roommate Lamar Phelps and UA colleague James Wilson. The trio, backed by Phelps' tech millionaire father, went on to become one of the most successful agenting teams in the business, representing stars of stage, screen and airwaves on both coasts.

But now, revelations about Schwartz's pursuit of barely legal women have thrown his career into ruin. Although technically legal, these sexual relationships with much younger women are diametrically opposed to his image as a loving and committed father and husband. And as one of the women, Trysta Priest, is the younger sister of Billy's biggest client, pop superstar JenKat, things are even more complicated. JenKat threatened to leave the agency, but the partners acted quickly in distancing themselves from Schwartz and ousting him from the company.

'Billy is a bit of a charming rogue,' an anonymous source close to him told our reporters. 'He likes the ladies, always has. But everyone thought he and Lavinia were this golden couple, so we were all really surprised. I've never known him to be dishonest. In fact, he prides himself on being a man of honour. Either he's been misrepresenting himself, or he's recently gone rogue.'

Lavinia has also gone to ground and hasn't been spotted since the news broke last Sunday. Her followers, initially sympathetic, are growing restless with her silence, and many are becoming convinced that she has been complicit in her husband's pursuit of young, vulnerable women. Others are sure she had no idea and has been blindsided by her husband's actions. 'How would this benefit Lavinia in any way?' one tweeted. 'She has nothing to gain and everything to lose.'

'Some men are just never happy,' another source familiar with the couple told us. 'Billy had it all with Lavinia, but there's something in him that means he's always striving for the next big thing. He couldn't just be content with a beautiful wife and children, a gorgeous life. He wanted younger, sexier, more exciting. I don't think he'll bounce back from this one with his cheeky wit. He's gone too far.'

13

My mother had turned the dining area into something of a war room. The heavy drapes were closed to prying eyes, in case a neighbour found themself seduced by a cash offer from a salacious tabloid. The long marble-topped table was covered in iPads, laptops, chargers and phones, and she'd even erected a whiteboard at the top of the room. This was Operation Protect Lavinia & Sons, and Dessie was approaching it in military fashion.

Thankfully, the boys still hadn't cottoned on to anything unusual. The adults were doing their best to act normal around Si and Seb, giving out lots of cuddles and spending hours on the floor with them and their toys. My heart ached every time I saw my nephews, thinking about how all of this would affect them in the long run. Silas is a sensitive little boy and can be clingy. Seb is a bit more rough and tumble, but growing up with a sex pest for a dad? Their lives would never be the same.

Vinnie and I were huddled together on one side of the table. Mom had forced us to clean ourselves up, so we were reluctantly freshly bathed and swaddled in her softest DD+ loungewear. With her hair swept back and her skin gleaming, Vinnie looked a little better, but the same couldn't be said for me. It was like a light had gone out inside of me, my already fine hair was like mousy straw and my lips were all cracked and sore. I was having a physical reaction to being separated from Jason.

Dessie had put on her favourite power suit, living up to

her motto, 'How you do anything is how you do everything', and she looked more like herself. Manny was preoccupied with his phone, David looked like a bold child at the back of the classroom and Suz, who had just swung by to check on us, had been dragged in as the voice of the press. Giulia was on the phone outside, as usual. You can say one thing for our extended family – we're good in a crisis.

Suz was looking radiant. She has the kind of skin most women would commit murder for and striking cheekbones she inherited from her mother, practically the only thing that connected them. Her mother fled back to Europe after her divorce and Suz doesn't have any contact with her. So she's another one of Dessie's honorary children – and at least had been her stepchild, while David can only wish.

Giulia swept in. 'Okay, *ragazzi*, here's what is going on.' She paused for dramatic emphasis. 'My source says Billy is in Mexico, which is just unoriginal, if you ask me.' She shrugged. Vinnie sucked in a breath. 'If he has run away, we will not be able to rely on him making a statement, which means we are on our own with this. *Stronzo!*'

Vinnie put her head in her hands and started doing her breathing exercises.

'We are not on our own, we have each other,' soothed Dessie, albeit unconvincingly. 'Now, let's make a plan. If that fucker won't admit to his wrongdoings and issue a mea culpa, he's leaving our Lavinia to fend for herself with the press. Beyond cruel. But we have some of the brightest minds in the biz here so let's get to work. Suzanna, any suggestions?'

Suz stretched out like a cat then leaned in like she meant business. 'Okay, we all know how this story goes. Everyone is horrified and feels sorry for the wife and children in the beginning. But if the man doesn't show culpability and/or his wife doesn't outright condemn him, the tables can turn on her quickly, because everybody *loves* to blame women for the actions of men – especially when she's as famous and fabulous as our Vinnie.'

I grabbed Vinnie's hand and squeezed.

'Now because of the children and because we're not sure what is even going on here, I'd be reluctant to condemn Billy publicly just yet. But we have to prepare ourselves for people both blaming Vinnie and also being gleeful about her perfect life falling apart . . . we know that the public live for a fall from grace, and an influencer being humiliated is titillating. But in this case, her fans may also feel like Vinnie has been in on it and they've been sold a lie.'

'Maybe they have,' Vinnie croaked. 'I knew he wasn't perfect. I knew our marriage wasn't as shiny and saccharine as we made out, but whose is? I just never thought . . .' She trailed off, but we got it. Nobody had ever thought it would come to this.

Giulia was frank. '*Carina*, when you sell your life, sometimes it bites you on the behind. You are lucky in that you do not *need* Billy, you are a self-made woman and you have financial stability and the loving support of your family. It will be rough for a while with the fans, but you are strong enough to withstand that, no?'

Manny cleared his throat. He is a man of few words, but when he talks, people listen. 'I've been reading everything I can, and I'm afraid the tables are already starting to turn on Lavinia on the message boards. We need to do something before this anti-Lavinia rhetoric trickles down to the media at large.'

Dessie sat down, holding her forehead. 'Are you okay, Mom?' I asked.

'Fine, sweetheart. Just a bit dizzy. David, love, do you have anything to add?'

126

David looked uncomfortable. 'Are we sure we can't just throw Billy to the wolves? Literally all of this is his fault. He's the bad guy here. And I'm just not surprised – he's always had overgrown frat-boy energy.'

Giulia shook her head, earrings jangling. 'It would not be wise. Lavinia needs to figure out how she feels about things. And the second we say anything, it gives people the licence to comment and cause even more of a sensation. And think of the *bambini* . . .'

'I'm just saying, in this day and age, when there's a sex scandal, the woman scorned is often selling merchandise about men being dicks and rising from the ashes stronger within a week.' He shrugged. David had a point, but Vinnie went green at the mere thought of that.

'I'm not strong enough,' she muttered, so quietly that only I could hear.

I spoke up. 'We're not going to say anything at all about him. This is about my sister and her children and how they recover best from having their lives fall apart in public.'

Everyone went quiet.

'Vinnie is not only devastated, she's frightened that this will be the end of her brand, the end of her career, because it's all so tightly wound up in her family life. We have to focus on salvaging her reputation, first and foremost.'

Giulia nodded. 'I agree. Let's make a strategy. Vinnie's social has been dark for a couple of days, yes? Let's leave it that way for now. The press and public can only parse what they can see, so the less we say and do, the less there is to analyse.' She turned to Vinnie. 'I'm sorry, *bella*, that means not leaving the house for a few more days. The boys are grounded too.'

'I have a few friendly paps on the books,' Dessie said. 'I'll mull over who might be the kindest one, and Giulia, we can set up some sort of deal for the first pictures of Vinnie when she's had to time to prepare a little. There won't be any of the boys, understood?'

Giulia nodded curtly, tapping on her iPad.

'David, do you have any clients in this week that can help us?'

He nodded. 'I can certainly do some whispering, yep. What's the official unofficial line?'

'That Vinnie is totally blindsided and heartbroken.' Dessie looked at her for confirmation and got a nod. 'At least it's the truth. But you don't know any more than that and you haven't seen her, don't know where she is.'

'It's no harm to ad lib a bit about how Billy seemed totally devoted,' said Giulia. 'We did not know he was acting like a maggot.'

'It's acting *the* maggot, pet.' Dessie patted her hand. 'It's true. We thought he was a fantastic husband and father and had no idea he was a perv, in so many words. Agreed?'

'Isn't that the truth?' I managed.

'Well, yes, honey. But anybody that's met the man knows he's a slick operator. We can't pretend we thought he was an angel. Is that clear?'

Everyone murmured their assent.

'Um, what do I do?' Vinnie croaked in a tiny voice.

'You do nothing, sweetheart,' said Mom. 'You give us your phone and devices so you're not the slightest bit tempted to do anything until the time is right.'

Giulia agreed. 'If he calls, I will tell you. You let us do our jobs, and when it's time, we'll craft the perfect statement for you to put out. We'll get a friendly snapper to "leak" pics of you.' She mimed air quotes.

'Until then, let me mind you and the boys?' Dessie said.

Vinnie nodded and looked sadder than I'd ever seen her. I squeezed her hand again.

'You better take my phone too,' I said. 'Because I am sorely tempted to blast that fucker from here to Uranus.'

Giulia snatched my phone from my hand. 'Is good you don't hear from the Irish boy either. You two can be in this together.'

Everyone swept from the room, off about their business. Vinnie and I, under house arrest, looked at one another. 'Want to play Scrabble?' I offered. She burst into tears.

I was getting accustomed to taking naps, but never in a bed. I woke from a snooze on Manny's leather recliner that evening to the sound of raised voices in the kitchen. Sparrow the Spaniel and Halle the Lurcher were at my feet and looked perplexed at the racket.

'It's not *fair*!' Ariel was screaming. 'I don't want to be on your stupid show any more!'

My mother was sitting at the island with Bubbles on her lap, looking utterly drained. It always puzzled me why Dessie had wanted another baby in her forties, when Vinnie and I were finally out from under her feet and she was coming in to her own in midlife. Of course, everyone adored Ariel when she was born, and I realized when I saw them together with their baby that it was a must for my mom and Manny. But I don't think she really thought about having a teenager in her sixties at the time, or else she'd forgotten what it's like to have an adolescent in the house. It was draining enough watching my little sister on social media; I couldn't imagine what it would be like to parent an almost-fifteen-year-old at sixty-two.

'Ariel, lower your voice,' Manuel said darkly, and she quickly shut up. He's the only person she's truly respectful of.

'*Bambina*, just listen to us for a minute,' said Giulia. 'We are just asking you to consider letting production film behind the scenes of your Gatorade commercial. The people, they want to see you do well! And they might not even use it; it's just to have in the bin.'

'It's in the *can*!' Ariel screeched.

'Shh, love,' soothed my mother. 'Look, the audience has watched you grow up from a little baby. They'll be so thrilled to see you succeed, don't you understand? We weren't even sure about you doing this gig, pet, but this is a way that ties it back to the family . . .'

Ariel can be quite frightening when she's angry. Her eyes were black and her mouth was set in a firm line. 'I never gave permission to be raised on camera, Mother,' she said. 'I watched an old movie last week, *The Truman Show*? And OHMIGOD, was that not my life? I don't want these old weirdos watching me. I want to do my own thing. I have my own fans.'

'You only have fans because of the show, duh,' I offered as I went to the fridge for a drink. Mom's fridge is a thing of great beauty. It's baby pink with glass doors, and she has every flavour of San Pellegrino lined up perfectly as if in a shop.

'*Mom*, she is not allowed to be insulting!' Ariel shrieked, and I stuck my tongue out at her and winked.

'Darling, your older sisters are going through some problems right now . . .'

'Oh, you don't have to tell me,' Ariel crowed. 'I know that neither of them can keep a man.' She grinned triumphantly in my direction. 'Women my age' – a communal snort went up at this – 'know that relationships are for idiots. Self-sufficiency is everything.'

Ariel was worrying for many reasons, not least the fact that she consumed vast amounts of vapid psychobabble on the internet. Dessie and Manuel tried to limit her screen time, but it was like trying to control a tornado. She'd scream

130

censorship and control, slag them off on her friends' TikToks and generally make life more difficult until they gave in.

And while we were glad she wasn't boy (or girl, who knew?) crazy just yet, she was displaying signs of being difficult in every other department. She was desperate for independence, incredibly ambitious, almost to Lady Macbeth levels (at least, I hoped only almost), and clawing to establish her own identity away from the family. Poor Manny was getting greyer by the day from worrying about her.

Neither Vinnie nor I had been this much of a handful at her age. We were quite innocent until we were legal adults, something I credit to summers spent in Kerry instead of running wild around West Hollywood. I never had a wild streak and Vinnie was a late bloomer. She dabbled in all sorts once she was of age and was already twenty-three when the show catapulted her from – let's be honest – a bit of a stoner lay-about who dabbled in art modelling, to a superstar.

Vinnie had been chronically lazy in her youth. She lasted only a semester in a local college, preferring to see the world courtesy of rich boyfriends with yachts and going on tour with her grungy friends (who all had trust funds). She hadn't a clue what to do with herself, and her beauty hadn't quite crystallized until she was that little bit older. Suddenly her look became hot, and *LOLA* was her launchpad to big things.

Her fame soon eclipsed the show, but Vinnie's problems only worsened under the glare of the spotlight. Her anxiety was assuaged by pills and sex, and her body image issues took a turn from being problematic to very dark.

The final straw came when she disappeared for two weeks, and when she turned up she was frighteningly thin and looked totally strung out. She admitted to smoking heroin, eating literally nothing and falling in with some dodgy characters she met in a bar. We were so glad when she asked for help and seemed to mean it, because other attempts at getting her to rehab hadn't worked. But the heroin experience had truly rattled her. Everyone was beyond thrilled when she cleaned up her act. Then she had married Billy and had the boys, and things were great . . . until they weren't.

I felt bad, because my mom had experienced just a few years of not having to worry about any of us, but it seemed like that was well and truly over. Ariel had turned from a precocious but sweet little girl into this whirlwind of constrained energy and frustration, and it was difficult to watch. But I could also see her point. I wouldn't want to be on the show either if I were her, and it was true she'd never had a choice in her fame – she'd grown up on camera, watched by millions. I went to defend her, but Manny spoke first.

'Ariel, I have no problem cancelling the whole Gatorade deal if you don't listen to your mother and your aunt. They have your best interests at heart.'

'She' – Ariel glared at Giulia – 'is not my aunt. She is my mother's dead husband's sister, and somebody that just wants to make money off me.'

'*Ariel!*' Dessie shouted, and everyone jumped. 'I will. Not. Tolerate. Disrespect.' She seethed. My mom rarely blew her top, so this was highly unusual. 'You are grounded. Get out of my sight.'

'Are you stupid? It's the last week of school! I have activities, parties . . .'

'You have nothing!' Dessie roared. 'Go to your room!'

Ariel burst into dramatic tears and stormed out of the kitchen. Dessie looked shaken.

'Mom, are you all right?' I asked, putting my arm around her shoulders. She felt smaller, bonier somehow, and I was concerned that all the stress of worrying about the three of us was taking its toll.

132

'I'm just exhausted, sweetheart. And I have no idea what to do with that girl . . .' She trailed off. 'I'm going to try and get some sleep.'

As Dessie stalked out of the room with Bubbles at her heels, Giulia put her hand on my arm gently. '*Carina*, there's something I think you should see.' She passed me her phone, which was playing an Instagram story. The video was in a dark bar, and a man appeared on screen, a tall, gorgeous one. Then the person taking the video slithered into his side before turning the camera on the pair of them and planting a kiss on his neck.

My stomach dropped. It was Sybil Simpson, and the man she had wrapped herself around was Jason. I watched in disgust as they canoodled on camera, Jason laughing with this other woman who wasn't me.

Jason looked the exact opposite of heartbroken. Here I was, mooning around my mother's mansion three thousand miles away, while he was out on the town with the cougar I suspected him of shagging.

'I knew it,' I whispered. 'That fucking liar!'

Giulia shrugged. 'I do not trust the men in general, but it's not that damning, *bella*. They could just be friends. Sybil is always playing the fool like this.'

'No, Giulia. He's always been a flirt, but he wouldn't be this . . . obvious if he thought we were still together. I wasn't a hundred per cent sure, but here's the evidence. Six and a half years, gone just like that. I hope she gives him an STI!'

I was right back to livid. Maddened. Incensed. Which was something of a relief, considering how numb and empty I'd been feeling. A scant couple of days after I'd left town, and the man was out carousing with his colleagues in sexy bars. Even if he did consider us to be over, the disrespect was galling.

Through my rage, I felt a glimmer of vindication. I'd been right not to trust him. And even if he wasn't sleeping with Sybil, or anyone else for that matter, he was out enjoying himself, probably scouting for someone to knock up.

'Has he even called?' I asked my aunt. She shook her head.

'Then it's really over,' I said.

Giulia held up a bottle of gin. 'Want one of my special Negronis?'

'What makes it special?'

'Twice the amount of alcohol.'

'Perfect.'

14

Early the following week I was already suffering from cabin fever. I'd finished my episode for Amy's show ahead of deadline, but I had a feeling it wasn't my best work and there'd be revisions required. Normally an utter perfectionist, I surprised myself at how little I cared. How was I supposed to make-believe when my real life was like a soap opera?

I was just working for something to do. Dessie's home may be a modern farmhouse-style mansion with eight bedrooms, ten bathrooms, a tennis court, swimming pool, movie theatre and pool house, but anywhere can feel stifling when you're not able to leave. It has a distinctly Spanish flavour typical of Southern California and undoubtedly influenced by Manuel. They'd bought this place when they married, so while it was never exactly my home, it had been Dessie's for a long time.

Technically, I was permitted to be out in the great wide yonder; paps and reporters don't know me, I could disguise myself easily with a hat over my long bob and a big pair of sunglasses. But Dessie didn't want anyone leaving the gated community unless necessary; she herself was fleeing under cover of darkness in her jeep with tinted windows and heading straight for the DD+ offices off Rodeo, which had ample security.

Luckily, filming for *LOLA* was on hiatus during the summer as the show aired, but the weekly episodes only added to the buzz around the family. The neighbours in the exclusive development were not pleased with the commotion at the entrance every time they tried to leave but were LA enough to understand that when the paparazzi smell blood, there's no calling them off.

In an attempt at solidarity with my sister, I was on a self-imposed house arrest. It suited my mood because all I wanted to do was fume about Jason. I found willing ears in both Giulia and Manuel, the former helping me bitch about feckless men, the latter just listening and making soothing noises. Both helped, but my heart felt shattered.

'Do you think it's actually over?' I beseeched Manny late one night. 'Do you think he's really that selfish and immature?'

He shrugged in that louche way of his. 'I don't want to speculate,' my stepdad intoned. 'But I think Jason would be here fighting for you if he wanted to.'

I nodded, unable to speak. He was right.

I didn't want to offload on to Vinnie because she had enough to deal with. I was helping her with Si and Seb, keeping an eye on her behaviour and diet, and just being there for my sister in case something else happened. I've never felt like it's my place to police Vinnie, but she's worked so hard at her recovery it didn't hurt to be more watchful. But her only vice seemed to be smoking like a chimney, which was expected.

For the first time, I was glad that the boys were being home-schooled for elementary. I had been against it when Vinnie first told me of their plans, suggesting they needed to socialize and be exposed to different cultures, religions, languages and backgrounds. But as I watched them doing their lessons with their beloved Marjorie, I realized that being the kids of the rich and famous in this day and age was utterly terrifying and quite exposing. And Marjorie has a Ph.D. in early childhood education, so she's no slouch in the teaching department. It was quite therapeutic helping them finger-paint (Silas) and learn spellings (Sebastian). I opted out of the language classes, though. Mandarin is not my strong suit.

Regardless, I was relieved when I woke up one morning on my bedroom floor to a note under the door from Dessie calling a family meeting, because that meant something was finally happening. I realized I was already late and scooted down to the dining room in my pyjamas.

Vinnie was nowhere to be seen, but Dessie and Giulia were sitting at the table with a man I didn't recognize.

'Portia, love, meet Noah Frost.'

I held out my hand, and the guy shook it firmly. He was about my age, maybe a little younger, and cute in a sleepy-eyed, messy-haired way.

'Nice to meet you,' he said. 'Nice bed head.'

I put my hand self-consciously to my scalp, and at the same time realized my white vest was see-through. 'Thanks, you too,' I managed, sitting down and crossing my arms.

'Noah is a freelance photographer,' explained Giulia. 'He's here to help us.'

'Oh, you're the pap that's going to play for our team, huh?' I smirked. 'Nice work if you can get it!'

'As it happens, I'm a wildlife photographer who fell on tough times during the pandemic,' he grinned back. 'And it turns out shooting the wildlife in Los Angeles is more lucrative, so I've stuck with it.'

His delivery was just sweet enough that he got away with a bit of cheek. And while I was all for a gentle ribbing, I was glad we had friendly professionals on our side. It wasn't like my mother was above calling the paps when it suited her. And this one seemed normal, unlike some of the menacing men with video cameras and a dirty mouth, the ones that wanted to provoke you so they could get the best shot.

'Noah is a pro, darling,' Dessie said, giving me the eye.

137

'Of course. So, what's the plan of action?'

Giulia went to answer, but Noah beat her to it. 'My plan is to hang out here for a bit, chat to your sister and all of you. I want to get a feel for what's natural for her, for the family. I'll find out where she usually goes, what she gets up to, and that way any pictures I take of her won't seem set up or rehearsed.'

'Great, but what about the paps stationed outside the gates?' I asked. 'They're not going to let Vinnie swan out to Erewhon for a seventeen-dollar smoothie without snapping, are they?'

'That's where you come in, *bella*!' exclaimed Giulia, beaming. Suddenly I knew why Vinnie wasn't at this meeting. 'We want you to be her decoy. Lead the paparazzi astray!'

Normally I was dead against this kind of thing. Let my family play all the games they wanted with the press, but leave me out of it. Anyway, I didn't even look like Vinnie, a fact I stated.

'If you're in your sister's car, wearing a blonde wig with a bit of my Freckle fake tan so you have a California complexion, they'll believe it's her. Especially if I tip them off beforehand,' said Dessie.

The three of them looked at me expectantly. I knew they had me; I would never turn down an opportunity to help my sister in her hour of need. There was no point fighting it.

'Where am I going to get a blonde wig?' I asked.

'Oh, sweetheart,' my mother scoffed. 'Leave the glamour to me.'

And that's how I found myself sitting in Vinnie's Tesla Model X two hours later, covered in sticky instant tan and wearing a honey-blonde hairpiece, LRS baseball cap and dark Celine sunglasses, ready to face the throng of snappers at the gate. They were feral, whipped up into an expectant frenzy after days of waiting, as Dessie had promised they would be.

The plan was that the paps would chase me, leaving the coast clear for Noah and Vinnie to sneak out in Giulia's car a few minutes later. Then my sister would just casually appear on Melrose, and Noah would surreptitiously snap her grabbing a coffee, talking on the phone and acting like a woman in control of her life rather than a cuckolded wife in a swarm of shouting paparazzi.

These would be the photos Noah would sell to the press, turning a nice profit at the same time as protecting Vinnie. It paid to be in cahoots with the who's who of Hollywood.

Giulia plonked into the passenger seat. 'Okay, your mamma has the children and Lavinia is ready to go,' she announced.

'How does she look?' I asked. Vinnie had given herself a facial and a manicure but, up close, she was still dead behind the eyes.

'From a distance, *perfecto*. A little thin, perhaps, but that's to be expected. What's most important is that she's ready to put on a show.'

I nodded. 'Okay.' I switched on the engine. 'Let's get this over with.'

Even before we pulled up to the electronic gates, the yelling started.

'Lavinia, have you heard from your husband?'

'Did you know he likes teenagers?'

'Is your marriage over?'

None of the questions were even aimed at me, but I felt sick to my stomach. The security guard let us through, and I kept my head down in the driver's seat. It didn't matter if their pictures revealed that I wasn't my sister – I could never fake her distinctive nose – because by then, Vinnie and Noah would be out.

Giulia was muttering in Italian under her breath, and my

novice ear picked up a few swear words. 'Giulia, there are too many of them. How do I get through?'

'Just drive, slowly and carefully. The second you're sure you're not going to crush one of them, speed off.'

That's just what I did. Three cars followed in hot pursuit, which was deeply unnerving, as they swerved all over the roads to keep up with us. It took all my concentration to keep driving and not have a full-blown panic attack.

Giulia had devised a route, so I was following Google Maps as if on autopilot. It was meandering and twisty, around the Hills and down into the Valley. By the time we reached Studio City and the V Network offices, there was only one pap who'd kept up. We drove into the parking lot, past the security barriers, and I shut off the engine.

'That was marvellous, *bella*,' my aunt whooped. 'Well done! They totally bought it, yes?'

'I don't see why they would've followed us if they didn't,' I panted. 'Great idea on your part.'

We both sat in the car catching our breath.

'You know, it's so good to have you here, Portia,' Giulia said. 'I don't know what your family would do without you right now. Your papa would be proud.'

Both of our eyes filled with tears at the mention of my dad. It struck me that Giulia losing Roberto would be like me losing Vinnie – unthinkable. I squeezed her hand. 'Sometimes I wonder what he'd make of all this,' I said. 'This strange life we live. Our choices in men.' I giggled, the adrenaline making me feel slightly hysterical. 'I always thought he'd have loved Jason, but now, I'm not so sure.'

'Portia, your father did not know his arse from his elbow when it came to the emotions of the fairer sex. He was good at charming women, but not wise about love. But I know he was always so proud of his girls, and that would never have changed. My brother would have trusted you to make whatever choices you had to make, and always encouraged you to follow your heart.'

'I love you, Giulia.'

'And I you, *carina*. Now, let's take the private exit out the back and go back to your mamma's. The wild chicken chase is over.'

'Goose,' I said. 'Goose chase.'

'These birds, they are all the same to me.'

15

There were no paps at the gate when we reached Dessie's community, which was a good sign that our plan had worked. But we all waited nervously for Vinnie's return.

When she got back an hour after we did, she looked exhausted, but Noah was triumphant. The two of them and Giulia retreated to the dining room to review the shots, while my mom and I sat quietly. I was still coming down from the whole experience.

'I don't know how you do it,' I said, breaking the silence. 'That was terrifying.'

'It's rarely like that, darling,' Dessie explained. 'This is a crisis, higher stakes and all that. You did great.'

'Let's hope it worked.'

Vinnie eventually came into the kitchen. 'Well, we got some decent ones anyway,' she said. 'And I'm starving for the first time in days.'

At the mere suggestion of Vinnie wanting to eat, Dessie leapt into action. She's a wonderful cook when she has time. Having sent the chef home for the evening, she was pulling ingredients out of the giant fridge, and I recognized the elements of her specialty, veggie lasagne.

'How was it? Did anyone recognize you?' I asked my sister.

'I saw one woman taking photos.' Vinnie sighed. 'But she didn't say anything, so it was fine. She'll just have a closer version of what Noah has.'

'Where did you guys go?'

'Erewhon in Beverly Hills, as you suggested. Nothing says

I'm fine, really like spending twenty-seven dollars on a take-out macrobiotic vegan salad.' For the first time since I'd been in LA, there was a mischievous glint in Vinnie's eye.

By the time the oven pinged to signal Dessie's lasagne was ready, the five of us were refreshing every news site around the world to see if the pics had landed. They were already on *Radar Online* and TMZ. 'Lavinia breaks cover!' screamed the latter. The *Mail Online* declared an exclusive (as they'd been the only ones to buy shots without Vinnie wearing sunglasses), stating, 'A supermodel scorned! Beautiful wife of sexual predator Billy Schwartz is seen in Los Angeles for the first time since scandal.'

The result was exactly what my mother and aunt had hoped for. Getting the first photos over and done with under our control was pivotal in framing the narrative. Vinnie, who looked fresh-faced and striking in the pics, no longer had to fear a flood of snappers trying to get those initial photos. Once she'd been seen, a huge part of the value of shooting her was gone for the paps.

Plus, she looked sufficiently strong and capable, not a withered mess. The message was that Lavinia Rizzi-Schwartz had nothing to hide, she was a victim of her husband's cheating but not complicit in his lies. Her head was held high, her shoulders back. And it helped that she was wearing her own merch, which would no doubt sell out overnight.

I was slightly worried, though. She almost looked too good, like she hadn't a care in the world. My suggestions that she looked a little ragged had been dismissed, and I hoped her naturally photogenic face wouldn't make Vinnie less sympathetic.

When Vinnie went to bed with the boys for an early night, Mom and Giulia cracked open a bottle of Bollinger. It had been a difficult day, and I was proud of my sister. Noah had stuck around, delighted with his success. He clearly got a kick out of my mom.

As I clinked glasses with them, I realized that the day had been a nice distraction from my own problems. Giulia had returned our phones to us at dinner, and the plan was for Vinnie to release a statement on her Instagram the next morning that was all about her and the boys, with no direct mention of her errant husband. She would acknowledge her absence and her heartbreak and ask for privacy at a difficult time. She and Giulia were still fine-tuning the exact wording.

Yet while my phone was back in my possession, I hadn't much desire to look at it. I felt so removed from it now, and what it possibly contained, that I was a bit scared. Noah saw me fingering it gingerly. 'It's not going to bite, you know,' he grinned, when we were briefly left alone.

'Oh, I know. I've just sort of got used to being without it,' I said. 'Broken the back of the addiction, you know?'

'Not really, I'm glued to mine. Professional hazard.' He topped up my glass.

'How do you know the gruesome twosome?' I asked, nodding towards Dessie and Giulia in the kitchen.

Noah laughed. 'I do some work for the V Network,' he said. 'You know, snapping shots of the Ladies seemingly unaware, as well as stills at events they're filming at.' He wiggled his eyebrows. 'I met your mom a few months back, and we've been friendly since. She's quite a lady.'

'That she is,' I laughed. Looking at him up close, he was very cute. He had greyish eyes, straight white teeth and full lips. His hair was cropped tight but curling at the ends.

'Are you from this neck of the woods?' I asked. 'You seem a bit too normal.'

'God, no. I'm from Philly.' He stretched to retrieve his glass, his T-shirt sleeves riding up to show a toned bicep with a line-drawing tattoo around it. 'I used to be a news photographer, covering court cases and crime scenes. Then I started getting into birdwatching. Don't laugh!' he said when he saw my face. 'It's calming.' He laughed. 'I decided to do some travelling, got some commissions from *National Geographic* and hoped to make taking pictures of animals my day job. But then that bubble burst when everything closed down in 2020.'

He must have heard his name, because Bubbles barrelled into the room and made a beeline for Noah, landing right on his crotch. Seven pounds of Morkie doesn't sound like much, unless applied directly to the scrotum at speed. Noah roared, and I almost choked laughing.

'I guess Bel Air toy crosses count as animals?' I said between giggles. The poor man was purple, while Bubbles was enthusiastically licking his face.

'When they're this dangerous, they do,' he winced. 'More champagne?'

We whiled away the evening together, the four of us and Bubbles. At some point we switched over to spirits, and everything had become hilarious.

Noah was flirting with me, and I was letting him. It was nice to feel attractive, and I was still so angry with Jason. He'd barely waited for me to leave the city before painting it red with Sybil fucking Simpson. Every time I thought about it, a white-hot rage descended from the top of my head. Dessie said it was good that I was angry, that it was better than being sad. I wasn't sure I agreed.

Noah accompanied me outside for two cigarettes and even joined in, which was oddly nice. Jason always made me feel so guilty about my social smoking habit. Maybe he wasn't so perfect after all, my drunken brain thought. Yeah, looking out for your health and well-being is awful, said another internal voice, and I shivered dramatically.

'Hey, you okay? Are you one of those chicks that gets cold when it's eighty degrees out?'

'I'm not a chick, first of all,' I laughed. 'And no, I'm half Irish! It's just been . . . quite a day.'

'I was impressed with your willingness to cosplay as your sister. And you could handle that Tesla too.'

'I was impressed myself. I'm a New Yorker, I don't drive in the city. But you know, it was fun. And I felt like I was doing something to help my sister for once.'

'You make a cute blonde, you know,' he said, giving me a cheeky grin. 'But an even cuter brunette.'

'Something tells me you're not fussy,' I laughed.

'You'd be surprised,' he said. 'But I know gorgeous when I see it.'

I flushed ruby red, unused to such direct compliments. I was a long time out of the game, but I couldn't deny that I was enjoying every minute.

We went back inside, and I steered the conversation into slightly less sexually charged areas; we talked about show business, the weather, even the birds in the trees. It was all very light, and totally the vibe I needed.

I felt more chilled out that evening than I had in weeks. Part of it was my worry about Vinnie had lifted ever so slightly, another part was the brief reprieve I'd had from house arrest. It had been oddly fun, careening around West Hollywood with my aunt and leading the paps right off the scent. It had stoked something in me, some hankering for adventure.

By 11 p.m., I'd decided that Noah was incredibly hot. He was making me feel something, and I quickly realized what it was – enough. Here was a thirty-something man who just thought I was fun and sexy. He didn't want anything from me, except perhaps my body and a good laugh. He wasn't trying to impregnate me or lie to me. It's amazing how your perspective changes when your heart is broken.

Mom and Giulia eventually peeled off to bed, leaving Noah and me with the dregs of a bottle of tequila.

'I'm drinking too much lately,' I said. 'I ought to go on the dry for a while.'

He laughed as I filled my glass again. 'Drowning your sorrows?'

'Something like that.' I winked, flirtatiously in my own mind, but I probably looked unhinged. 'Man trouble.'

'Ahh, I see. I was going to give you a cheesy line earlier about how a woman like you could possibly be single. I noticed the bare finger.' He indicated my left hand. 'You know you're old when you're checking if girls you're into are married. But of course, it's complicated.'

'Oh, that it is,' I proclaimed, standing up to go to the bathroom to put some space between us. He said he was into me. 'Excuse me.'

As I left the room, my phone pinged. It was a new WhatsApp voice note, and it was from Jason.

I sat on the toilet in the downstairs bathroom and pressed play. I was more than a little buzzed, and my heart lit up when I heard his voice. But then I heard the sombre tone of it, and I remembered.

'Portia, I haven't contacted you because I'm giving you your space. I saw the photos of Vinnie today, I . . . uh, I hope she's doing okay. And you, obviously . . .'

He paused here. 'Look, I'm going to go home for a while. To Limerick. There's some stuff going on and, well, it doesn't feel right being here in New York. I uh . . . I have a break from work for a while. So, yeah. I'll be even further away, but look, that's probably for the best. I never know what to say on these stupid voice notes. Eh . . . Take care.'

147

I sat there, stunned. Take care? After more than six and a half years, he was telling me to *take care*? And he was going back to Ireland. For how long? Why did he sound so . . . shifty? It was one thing me leaving to be with my family in a crisis. But him heading in the opposite direction, over an ocean, to get further away from me?

As I sat there, it could have gone either way. I was drunk enough to either dissolve into tears, or to laugh hysterically. I admitted to myself in that moment that I'd hoped Jason would follow me. Catching a flight to LA was nothing to him, and in my wildest dreams I expected him to turn up at Dessie's and beg me to come back home. He may have let me go, but I dreamt he'd soon learn he couldn't live without me.

But no. The opposite was happening. He was leaving the country, the continent. Crossing the Atlantic, returning to the bosom of his family. And Sandra.

I stood up and looked in the mirror. My hair was messy from the wig, but my skin was gleaming – thanks, Freckle – and I was flushed from the tequila. I looked better than I had in weeks, and something defiant sparked inside me.

I walked out of the bathroom and back into the kitchen. Noah was lifting his glass up to take a sip, but before it reached his lips I took it from him and placed it on the table.

Without a word, I took his hand and led him to the bed I hadn't slept in since I'd got here. I pulled my tank over my head and stepped out of my denim cut-offs. Within seconds, Noah's tongue was in my mouth, his hands roaming all over my body, and I was giving in to the sensation.

@LifeWithLRS

9 June 2022

Sometimes it's best to say nothing when you don't know what to say. But I wanted to let you all know that I am okay, or at least I will be. I am a survivor. Thank you for giving my family privacy at this difficult time. When I can explain more, I will. Love, Lavinia xo

👍 1,239,443 Likes

@glitterbbz_123 omg you want us to know YOU are ok??? What about the girls your disgusting husband preyed upon?

@sandysweetie4eva love you L! Stay strong!

@princessshadyxo @glitterbbz_123 you are so right. There is no way she didn't know what he was up to! Maybe you should have kept a closer eye on your husband and not your business, Lavinia

@valerielewis89 @showpony_247 is it wrong that I'm loving this drama?! She's not coming out of it looking great, she must have known

@noseyparker2023 we don't care about you, we care about the teenagers he GROOMED

@lavinialuvah4eva Leave her alone! She didn't do anything!

@ConservativeMOM911 I feel bad for the children

@DessieFan2015 Lavinia, I have been through something similar. Not everything is always as it seems. Remember being kind, everyone???? I support you!

16

I read Vinnie's post and hundreds of the comments underneath it from the safety of my bathroom floor. I was hiding there, with the shower on full blast, because I'd woken up next to Noah Frost and I didn't know what to do with myself.

I knew I'd have to go back to the bedroom soon, but what I was reading on Vinnie's profile gave me momentary pause. Then, like a bolt from the blue, I had a flashback of my hands snaking down Noah's writhing back and sinking my nails into his ass. Jesus.

In the two hours since Vinnie had posted, the tide had indeed seemed to turn against her. She did as we agreed and kept it succinct and about her and the boys. But these commenters were baying for her blood. It was no use trying to reason with them; they wanted to hold somebody responsible for Billy's behaviour, and he wasn't around to take the fall.

I texted Vinnie.

Where are you?

Vinnie: I'm in Mom's gym. I'm trying not to look at the internet.

Portia: Yeah, don't. Work out hard, get those endorphins. I'm sure Giulia has a plan. Xo

It was time to leave the bathroom, mostly because I was drowning in steam from the spa shower function I didn't know how to turn off. I wrapped my naked body in a fluffy white towel and opened the door cautiously. The first thing I saw was Noah's penis, and I yelped.

'Woah! Jesus, Portia, you frightened the crap out of me!' He was struggling to get into his jeans.

'I'm so sorry, I got a fright!' I was utterly mortified.

'Did you forget I was here or something?'

I felt vaguely insulted. 'Uh . . . no. I don't sleep with random guys often enough to just not remember they're there in the morning.'

He frowned. 'Random? Hey, thanks . . .'

Ugh, I was handling this all wrong. What could I say, it had been a while since I'd seduced somebody under my mother's roof.

'Look, Noah, I'm sorry. Last night was great.' Another shiver up my spine as an erotic moment involving roving fingers replayed in my head. 'Really great. And you're a lovely guy . . .'

'But, it's complicated.' He shrugged on his T-shirt. 'Look, I get it. When you're our age, nothing is ever straightforward, right?'

I nodded, grateful that he understood. 'You're probably better off leaving via the front door. Nobody ever uses it. And thanks for being so cool. Maybe I'll see you around?'

'I'll see you around for sure, Portia. You're quite a . . . chick.' Noah grinned, leaned in and kissed me on the cheek, and then he was gone.

I flopped down on the bed, feeling a million emotions all at once. I'd had the best night's sleep I'd had in a while, in an actual bed, but the effects of alcohol and good sex would do that to a girl. I didn't feel at all hungover – the night's exertions and adrenaline put paid to that. But I did feel guilty, mostly because of how much I'd enjoyed it.

I'm not normally the femme fatale type that commands men to ravage me, but after the couple of months I'd had it had felt good to just be in control. Noah had been more than a match for me, strong and lean, and well endowed. Even better, he knew what to do with it all. I suspected he was a man about town, the kind of guy who snapped starlets and then took them to bed. For my first rodeo in a long time, it had been extremely satisfying.

But what about Jason? Guilt rolled over my shoulders and made me shiver. Had I just betrayed him? No, we had split up. And he was definitely shagging Sybil, wasn't he? The language had been clear; we were estranged. Or were we just taking time apart? Was I as much of a cheating asshole as he appeared to be? I pulled a pillow over my face and let a scream rip. Why was everything so complicated?

There was a knock at the door. '*Bella*, I didn't want to interrupt, but I just saw Signor Frost sneaking out of your bedroom so I thought now might be a good time?' I pulled the pillow off my face and smiled sheepishly at Giulia. 'What is it the kids say these days? Get it, girl?'

I threw the pillow at her retreating back as she click-clacked down the hall. 'Family meeting, ten minutes!'

An hour later, it was clear our plan had flopped hard. As I'd feared, the pictures of Vinnie were being used as proof that she was doing too well, that she should look more shocked and devastated if she had been blindsided, and her brief statement had confirmed that she was only thinking of herself. The more salacious tabloids were running the commentary that her statement was too bland, didn't acknowledge the young women Billy had taken advantage of and that she was selfish and spoilt. Never mind that she had been betrayed; in not condemning her husband's actions, Vinnie was now under fire for them.

She was losing followers at a rate of knots – perhaps small potatoes when your count is in the millions, but if it continued to drop then she would be in trouble with her investors.

Vinnie was a rare influencer in that she had editorial control over a lot of her own stuff. Her Instagram was all her own; only she had the password, and she didn't farm that out to assistants. She even took her own pictures, occasionally roping a trusted friend or family member to snap her outfits.

This was good because it allowed her to connect with her followers in an authentic way. However, it also meant that she had no line of defence between herself and the trolls when the shit hit the fan.

Vinnie was understandably taking it badly. She was shivering and shaking, sitting at the kitchen table googling her name over and over. When I came back from getting dressed, I found her deep in the bowels of Reddit, hungrily consuming every nasty thing her supposedly devoted following was saying about her. The whole situation was awful, but the bile spewed by non-fans getting a sick thrill from her pain was truly vile.

'This is all of my worst fears come true,' she was shrieking. 'Dessie, I cannot let him take everything away from me! It's bad enough he left the boys and me with a fucking note, that he slept with these poor girls and he's a disgusting creep, I can't let him take my livelihood as well!'

Mom was sitting at the island, white as a sheet. She had her hair in a silk turban and was wearing gold under-eye gel masks and a taut expression. I wanted to reassure her that everything would be all right, to see that megawatt grin of hers. But in reality, I didn't know if everything *would* be all right. Instead, I gave her shoulders a squeeze.

Sebastian appeared at the door looking scared. 'Mommy, what's going on?'

Vinnie sprang into action and swooped down on her elder son, enveloping him in a hug. 'Oh, nothing, sweetheart. Just some stuff going on with Mommy's business, okay? Why don't you go and get Ariel to teach you a new dance? Good boy.'

Marjorie appeared and ferried him away, my mom following. Vinnie was lucky her boys were so well behaved. And to her credit, Marjorie had been at Vinnie's side throughout the entire debacle. I hoped she was being paid what she was worth, which was her weight in gold.

'Lavinia, it is time to bring in reinforcements,' Giulia said. 'This is beyond the family's control now.'

'Beyond our control? Are you not a high-powered Hollywood publicist with friends in all the right places? What do I pay you for?' Vinnie screeched.

'Well, you don't pay me at all, actually. Your mamma does.' Giulia was getting mad now. Her plan had failed, and she was taking it personally.

She sat down next to Vinnie and wrenched her away from her laptop. 'Look at me.' Vinnie grudgingly turned to face her. 'I am on your side. I am sorry if you think I steered you wrong, but I was doing what I thought was best. I am a publicist, a good one, but the internet is like the Wild West and getting more lawless by the day, Lavinia. In Desdemona's day, there would be a story in a paper, in a magazine, and we would say our piece. Now? Every man and his dogs can say whatever they want on your own space! It's crazy!'

Vinnie hung her head. 'You don't know what to do, then.'

'I'm not sure, *bella*. Part of me wants to let it blow over, but a bigger part of me thinks there's a crisis manager out there who knows best. I am going to bring in the best people money can buy. I am also hiring an investigator to find that worthless piece of shit you married and drag him back. And I will do everything in my power to make this right. You believe me?'

Vinnie nodded. 'And what do I do, while all this is happening?'

My mother reappeared, hair loose and eye gels gone. I had the feeling she had been waiting in the hall for her cue, so dramatic was her entrance. 'You, my love, are coming away with me.' She pointed at me. 'You too. We are getting away from it all, to the kind of privacy and luxury only absurd wealth allows.'

'Away? What about the boys?' Vinnie gaped.

'We won't uproot them. They'll stay here with Manny, Ariel and Marjorie. They'll have a ball. Giulia needs space to work, you two need a change of scenery, and I'm going to bet we all need a colonic! There's nothing like one when you're feeling bad, trust me.'

I winced. 'Where is this magical place, then? Of obscene comfort and invasive procedures?'

Dessie flung out her arms. 'Why, Palm Springs, of course!'

Within the space of an hour, Dessie had packed matching Louis Vuitton weekend bags for all three of us from her vast closet. She had a whole Desert Chic section, so it wasn't difficult – athleisure wear, flowing kimonos, wedge flip flops and a selection of oversized linen shirts all went in the bags. A few turquoise statement necklaces and mid-heel sandals for dinner, and we were all set. We were off to the sexiest spa in all of California to rest and recuperate, while Giulia set up a brain trust of specialists to figure out Vinnie's next steps.

Ariel was outraged. 'You're all going away together, without me? I'm the *only* daughter not invited?'

'You're still grounded, darling,' Dessie stated matter-of-factly. 'And unfortunately, the resort is adults only. So, yes, you are staying here with everyone else.'

'*Aaarrrghh!*' Ariel's scream was ear-splitting. 'You don't even care about me! You clearly only like your elderly children – I'm an afterthought! I hate this family. Why did you even have me, you old hag?'

Dessie stopped folding, straightened up slowly and turned around. She walked over to Ariel, standing almost nose to nose with her. 'Sometimes, I ask myself that very question,' she said.

Ariel was shell-shocked. Her mouth dropped open and she stood there like a goldfish for a long moment. Then she turned on her heel and ran from the room.

Vinnie and I didn't dare move, shocked at Dessie's words. Granted, I'd have probably strangled Ariel if she was my child, but my mom is normally so calm and composed, even in the face of an adolescent tantrum.

'God, Mom,' Vinnie managed. 'That was harsh.'

Dessie didn't respond. She finished packing her own bag, zipped it up and turned around to us. She had painted on a brand-new expression, one of serenity and warmth. 'Ready?' she said, twirling on her heel and exiting the room. We didn't know what to do but follow her out to the car.

17

The journey was quiet, each of us absorbed in our thoughts. Dessie asked her driver, Ronald, to take the most scenic route, and she spent the ride alternately staring out the window and tapping away on her phone. Business never stops when you're a mogul, and a control freak to boot. Bubbles was in his carrier by her feet, softly snoring.

Vinnie was listening to a meditation podcast, so I put Jessie Ware in my ears and gazed out as the landscape changed from smoggy Los Angeles to sandy desert. It was greener than I remembered; after a wet spring, the succulents were thriving, and the landscape was even prettier than usual.

A notification popped up on my phone, a follow request on Instagram. My social media is locked tight; it doesn't even have my full name. I was surprised and more than a little intrigued to see that it was Noah Frost who had asked to follow me.

I saw he was friends with Dessie, which would explain how he found me. I gave his profile a cursory scroll, but the mere sight of him brought back vivid memories of the night before – my big toe in his mouth? – and my cheeks flamed. Luckily, my family were too caught up in their own stuff to notice. I accepted Noah's request and put my phone away before I did something stupid, like DM him.

Dessie normally stays at the Parker when she's in town; it's a home away from home. Most women in her position own properties in nearby La Quinta or Palm Desert, but Dessie says she can't be arsed maintaining yet another home. She prefers the ease of staying at the quirky sixties time-warp of the upscale resort. This time, though, we were eschewing her beloved Parker in favour of a more zen setting, the uber-fabulous Ritz-Carlton Rancho Mirage.

Dessie being Dessie, she'd reserved the best suite for herself and Bubbles, but she'd booked Vinnie and me adjoining terrace suites with fire pits. We told her to save her cash; we'd share one room. Vinnie and I had become quite co-dependent of late, and neither of us loved sleeping alone.

We spent the afternoon settling in, getting our bearings and checking out the amenities. There's something about the desert that just calms me. Perhaps because Palm Springs is a kind of easy-going place, where the gays dominate and the wealthy let loose, it feels kind of lawless and freewheeling – like West Hollywood on acid.

After checking out our rooms – spectacular, plush and luxurious, though I'd expect no less – the three of us decamped to the spa for the first of what Dessie promised would be many intense pampering treatments. We started relatively slowly, with a Thai deep-tissue massage. While it did involve grown women walking on our naked bodies to release knots that hands can't reach, there was thankfully no penetration just yet. It was quite simply divine.

Mom opted to forgo dinner, which surprised me, but I guessed there was a lot going on. Plus, she's always a bit iffy after a deep-tissue massage. It meant Vinnie and I could order pizza and watch a movie.

Before bed, we were outside sharing a cigarette. It gets chilly in the desert when the sun goes down, even in midsummer, so we were also sharing a fluffy throw and listening to the crickets chirp. There was something about being out in the middle of nowhere, a flat, dusty expanse all around, that was making me contemplative. There were no paparazzi hiding in the cacti, and the night was silent apart from the sound of crickets. The sky was full of stars, and I felt something akin to peace, just for a moment.

But while silence is golden, the quiet soon meant that the thoughts I'd been trying to block out were creeping in.

'How are you feeling, Vin?' I attempted. It felt like as good a time as any to approach a serious conversation, and I was dying to get out of my own head.

Vinnie sighed. 'Honestly?' She looked me in the eye.

'Of course! It's me.'

She took one last drag and stubbed out the butt. 'I feel a million different things. Frightened, hurt, worried, upset. But also . . . sort of relieved.'

That hadn't been on my bingo card. Seeing my curious expression, she sighed again, grabbed a cushion and tucked her legs underneath her body.

'I'm someone that always expects the worst, right? I learned my first stint in rehab that I'm prone to catastrophizing.'

I nodded in agreement. She's always been someone who will envision the worst-case scenario, but your dad dropping dead when you're barely through puberty will do that to a gal.

'They tell me, these shrinks, that I can build new pathways in my brain and become a positive person. I've tried, Portia, and I don't think I can.' She lit another cigarette. 'My entire brand is about this positivity that I don't ever really feel, these affirmations and aspirations. And in the back of my mind, I live with this niggling doubt that it's all complete bullshit. Or that there's something wrong with me because I don't feel positive or upbeat. And that I'm trying to fool myself and, in turn, fooling everyone else. I've been quite good at it up to now. Fake it till you make it, right?'

I remained quiet. When Vinnie was in the mood to talk, it was best to just let her.

'I've been trying these past few years, trying to be a good wife and a good mother and a good businesswoman. But it's never felt entirely genuine. I mean, I love the boys with every fibre of my being, they're probably the only thing I've ever done I feel truly fantastic about. But with Billy, with work, I guess . . . I've always been waiting for the other shoe to drop.'

I digested this. 'You're saying that you're relieved because . . . it's dropped?'

'Not exactly.' She lit up again and took a deep drag. 'I think . . . I think I'm relieved that I don't have to pretend any more.'

I knew to tread carefully. 'Pretend about what?'

'That I'm perfect!' she yelped. 'That Billy is this amazing husband, that my marriage is the ideal. That I know it all, and thus can help other people. Sometimes I feel like I just want to run away, to hand everything except the boys over to somebody else and let them deal with it. To stop sharing so much, to just be myself and take a break from all the bullshit. Unfortunately, the bullshit is my life.'

Vinnie inhaled, the cigarette tip glowing in the dark. 'Like this!' She gestured to the ashtray. 'My followers don't know that I smoke, don't know that I'm an addict. They think I never eat pizza, that I meditate every day and recharge my crystals in the light of the full moon. Did you know that vaginal crystals are the bestselling product on my site?'

I shook my head.

'I think I'm relieved in one way that Billy has shown his true colours, because I've never felt able to show mine. I mean, it's completely terrifying and I'm feeling twenty different things all at once, but he's done it. He's messed up his life by following his . . . proclivities, and his dick. And by extension, he's messed up mine. I feel like I have this opportunity to find out what I do want, like my life has cracked open just enough to let a little light in. The worst happened, so what now? Do you know what I mean?'

'Not really,' I admitted. 'I don't feel relieved at all. I'm furious with Jason for fucking up our life. Everything was ideal, just as it was. Then he launched a grenade right into the core of us. I just want to go back to how things were three months ago.'

'How could things be perfect if he was emailing Sandra behind your back?'

'David says there's nothing wrong with that, that he needed an outlet.'

'David has never really been in a proper relationship.' She had a point.

'Maybe Jason is having a midlife crisis too?'

'Ha!' Vinnie barked. 'Both our guys freak out at the same time, but my husband manipulates teenagers, yours decides he wants kids after an emotional affair with his sister-in-law.'

My stomach turned over.

'But do you know what I think is most telling, P? How we're reacting to what they've done. You want to go back in time, while I'm seeing this as an opportunity to cut and run.' She inhaled deeply on her cigarette.

'What do you mean? Run to where?'

An exhale. 'Well, away from the marriage, anyway. I don't want to be married to a man that thinks it's okay to sleep with teenagers. God, I don't think I could ever let him touch me again. And it's just like him, you know, to be on the edge of the law – he loves a bit of danger. But he's probably been just careful enough that he won't land his ass in prison.'

'Couldn't he just gamble, like Dad?' I attempted a feeble joke.

'Oh, he does that too. Our first year of marriage, he lost two hundred thousand dollars in one night in Vegas.'

I sat fully upright. 'He *what?!*'

She shrugged, seemingly unbothered. 'Yeah, I didn't want to freak you and Mom out so I didn't tell you guys. Giulia and I dealt with it. He went to a few Gamblers Anonymous meetings, promised not to do it any more. As far as I knew, he never lost that big again. Or if he did, he either fixed it somehow or it wasn't significant enough for me to know about.'

This was a lot to take in. My experience of our father's habit had deeply affected me. I had core memories of Dessie being distraught because she couldn't reach him. She knew where he was, or at least where he'd said he was going, but Roberto hung around with such dodgy characters she always feared the worst – a high-stakes game going awry to the point of violence, him totally losing his shirt or overdoing it on the pharmaceuticals he took to stay awake for days on end.

She also knew there were women at these things, sex workers designed to cool tempers, celebrate wins and soften the blow of losses. Showgirls on the Strip, actresses and singers on big weekends at the Sands.

Dad would always come home, eventually, either thrilled with a big win or stonily silent for days, sometimes weeks. I remembered being so relieved he was okay, but furious that he'd made us all worry. I never let him know that, though – I was always extra attentive and loving to our father, hoping that if I was the best daughter I could be, he wouldn't leave us any more. At least that's what my therapist says. Looking back, I don't know how Dessie ever coped with any of it. It was why I liked to be clued in to Jason's whereabouts – he often made me seem needy for wanting to stay in touch, but it was a reassurance that made me feel safe.

'Do you remember that one time, not long before Dad died? When he was gone for, like, five days, and Giulia and Mom thought he'd been murdered?' I asked.

'Not really, no. Everything from that time is fuzzy for me. My therapist says I'm protecting myself by not remembering what happened, or that I was just a self-absorbed kid. Both, probably.'

'I remember it. He came home reeking of booze, pot, god knows what else. He only had one shoe, and he was covered in sand. Eventually Giulia got him to admit that the mobsters had dragged him out to the beach in Malibu as a threat – like, you mess with us and don't pay us what you've lost, you'll sleep with the fishes.'

'Are you sure you didn't imagine that? That sounds like something from *The Sopranos*. I don't know if we have the Mafia in Malibu.'

'The Mob has tentacles everywhere there's money, Vin. And I'm sure. Mom didn't speak to him for, like, a month, and Giulia was pissed too. I remember he grovelled after a while, and they forgave him. But not long afterwards, he was dead.'

'Imagine the stress he was under.' Vinnie shook her head, sadly. 'His poor heart.'

'I know. That's why I can't cope with gambling.'

It's also why I've never been big on Las Vegas, a town my father adored. If I suspected a man got his kicks from taking dangerous financial risks, then he'd never get close to me. In trying to escape the sins of our father, I'd gone for the good guys in life – or so I thought. I avoided anyone flashy or wild and gravitated towards seemingly nurturing men, kind men, safe men. I wanted stability, someone reliable. What you want and what you get, though . . .

I knew Vinnie had a fondness for wildness, but I hadn't thought it extended this far. Not with the man she married, anyway. I expressed this, and she barked a harsh laugh.

'Oh, Portia. Grow up! I married Billy because I loved him. I was infatuated with him in the beginning – he was so confident, even though I was a head taller than him! He's smart, funny, sexy. But I also married him because it was time.'

'Time?'

'Yes, time! I was sick of dating, sick of random hook-ups, sick of all of it. I was clean, starting over. I wanted to settle down, and Billy was the first guy I truly fell for once my light was on.' She saw my face. 'Yes, I am using a *Sex and the City* analogy. I'm a millennial, sue me.'

'Hang on! You agree with Miranda's theory that men are like cabs – that their light goes on when they're available? And you apply it to yourself?'

'Sure! I mean, I'm not totally cynical. I was in love, or else I would've married Mom's billionaire guy. But I was ready to settle down.'

'You would have married anyone you were into at that time?'

'Not anybody, no. But someone I was attracted to, had chemistry with, shared goals with. Someone I thought I could be friends with, have a nice life with and who would be a good father. Despite Billy's flaws, and recent horrifying behaviour, he has been that for nearly eight years. Not a choir boy, don't get me wrong. But a good husband. And we made a promise that whatever happened, we would never lie to one another. Ha!' she barked bitterly.

I was flummoxed. I never thought Billy and Vinnie were the great love story the public imagined, but it all sounded so . . . unromantic.

'I'm sorry, Portia, but life isn't always black and white, you know? People do things for different reasons. I loved him, I was ready to have children, ready to stop thinking about myself all the time. My clock was ticking, and so was Billy's. We had a great marriage for a long time, as far as I knew. But there's something inside of him that makes him act like a selfish prick, his ego probably. Maybe he's cheated before and just hasn't been caught. Only this time, he's done irreparable damage.'

'So, you're done?'

She shrugged. 'Yeah, I think I am. I'm still figuring it all out.'

We sat in companionable silence for a while. What she'd said was a lot to digest.

Then Vinnie spoke. 'Do you think you and Jason will figure things out?'

'I don't see how we can, Vin.' My voice was flat, which was just how I felt. 'We want different things. His biological clock is deafening. I don't appear to have one. For me, it's just always been about love. For him, that's changed.'

'It's still about love. Maybe he just has a broader definition of it now. He wants that love to include children, that's the future he sees.' She moved closer and put an arm around my shoulders.

'Portia, are you a hundred per cent sure you don't want kids? Like, surer than sure?'

'I've never been so sure of anything in my life,' I said. 'And that's what makes this so hard. I thought I could change my mind for Jason if I willed myself hard enough. But now I feel like I don't know him. I've barely heard from him since I left New York. I can't quite believe that we're at this place. I didn't expect us to grow apart so suddenly, or maybe we'd been drifting apart without me really noticing. Maybe that's why he hasn't been communicating with me. I never thought we'd be here.'

She was quiet for a minute. 'I kind of get where he's coming from in a way, because I struggle, you know. To understand the kid thing. You're so amazing with the boys . . .'

'Vinnie, it's not the same. I love my nephews madly, but I don't want any children of my own. I could not be more certain I don't want to be a parent. I know that as surely as I know my own name.'

Vinnie looked sad.

'I don't need other people to get it. I don't even need you to understand or empathize. But Vinnie, I need the people I love to believe me. Just trust me that I know how I feel, because sometimes it seems like I'm going crazy.'

'You're not crazy, you're just weird.' She gave me a sisterly punch in the arm. 'But I can handle weird. Okay, let's get some rest. God only knows what Dessie has planned for us tomorrow.'

Radar Online
Lavinia left distraught!

11 June 2022

After her non-statement and the public backlash, it seems Lavinia Rizzi is on the run as well. Our spies in LA tell us she's left the city for some R&R, distraught at being so misunderstood.

'Lavinia is devastated about her marriage and her husband's betrayal and abandonment. She doesn't know what to say or do publicly but felt she had to say something. Now she knows it wasn't the right thing to say,' a source close to the family tells us.

They say the former supermodel turned super-guru is also really embarrassed and horrified that her husband preyed on young women. 'She really had no idea he was like that. She would never have married him if she did! Lavinia's concern now is for her boys alone. She's trying to block out all the noise from the press, she's not thinking about creating content or promoting her brand. She's just trying to figure things out.'

More as we get it

18

The next day dawned hot and bright, and Dessie had indeed booked us in for colonic irrigation, as promised. My mother is old school; there are other more modern methods of aiding digestion, but she comes from a generation in which flushing out your intestines is a balm for the soul.

Thankfully, after a morning of becoming intimately acquainted with our bodily functions, it was time for a relaxing lunch at the resort's terraced restaurant.

'Those things are far swankier now than they were in the good old days,' Dessie was saying as we got back into our fluffy robes. 'They even have heated seats! I remember when you just lay there and thought of Ireland as they shoved a length of rubber tubing up your –'

'MOM!' Vinnie and I chorused.

'Oh, girls,' she laughed. 'It's only an asshole, darlings. We all have one. Now, shall we lunch?'

This was Dessie to a tee. She looks like the fanciest lady you've ever seen, someone who could take tea with royalty or even Oprah, but she is ferociously frank. This is what the *LOLA* viewers love about her – that, and her filthy laugh.

'You go ahead, guys. I want to send a quick email and then I'm all yours,' I said. This was a white lie; what I wanted to do was take a bikini selfie. Heartbreak had me looking taut, and I was interested to see if Noah Frost would take the bait of a thirst trap. I didn't know why, exactly, other than he piqued my interest. Following me on Instagram seemed to invite a bit of harmless digital flirtation, surely?

I decided a mirror shot was the least obvious, so I tried out a few poses, bending forward to give the illusion of a smidgen more cleavage. My hair was wet, and a lot of skin was on show. It was a pretty hot picture I ended up sharing to my Instagram story, if I did say so myself. I wasn't sure who I'd become, posting sexy shots for attention, but I had decided to go with the flow. And if Jason happened to see it too, well, so be it. He wasn't exactly active on the app, but then, who knew what that man was up to.

By the time I joined my mother and Vinnie on the terrace, we were all ravenous. We ordered a smorgasbord of delicious starters – lobster salad, rice-paper wraps filled with slivers of duck fillet and crunchy vegetables, avocado gazpacho and, of course, Parmesan truffle fries. You can't walk a block in California these days without inhaling the scent of truffle, weed, or both. Dessie added some deep-fried goat's cheese balls to our order, declaring that calories don't count in the desert.

She also took no heed of the no alcohol after a colonic rule and asked for a magnum of their finest rosé. 'I do love Jon Bon Jovi's Hampton Water, if you have that,' she twinkled at the waiter. 'Jon asked me to do a collab with him. I must call him back,' she said to no one in particular, scribbling a note in the hot-pink patent-leather Filofax she carries everywhere.

'Now, girls.' She eyed us both. 'I want you to tell your mother how you're feeling. Think of this as a trust circle, a sisterhood safe space.'

'Where did you learn those terms, Mom?' I smiled.

'Graham, of course! The mad bitch is obsessed with her mantras and the power of femininity, blah, blah.'

The wine arrived, an outrageously ostentatious bottle with a carved glass bottom and glass lid in place of a cork. 'Madame, our concierge thought you might prefer a jeroboam, with our compliments,' said the sommelier, who was struggling under the weight of the gargantuan bottle. This sort of thing was a regular occurrence where Mom was concerned, the irony being that freebies are so often bestowed upon those who can most afford them.

The sommelier poured us all a glass; I hoped Vinnie's would remain untouched. She spoke first. 'I'm thinking of filing for divorce,' my sister announced.

I choked on my wine, surprised not by what she said but by her candour.

Dessie took a long sip. 'Is that because you want to, or because you think it will look good?'

'I don't give a crap what it looks like, Mom. I don't want to be married to a degenerate, or have our sons think that cheating is okay, especially with girls barely out of school.'

'Good, that's what I hoped you'd say.' Another glug of her wine. 'Giulia's team are working their magic; I saw some sympathetic coverage online this morning. But when it comes to marriage and family, I never want you to pander to the public, Lavinia. It gets one nowhere – you must be true only to yourself.'

I snorted, earning me a pointed look from my mother. 'Do you have something to say, Portia?'

'Yes, actually.' Two sips of wine on an empty stomach was making me brave. 'Vinnie gets to be true to herself, while I'm told to shut up and get knocked up to keep a man?'

'She has a point, Mom,' offered my sister.

Dessie was flustered. 'I never said that! Oh, maybe I implied it, and if I did, I'm sorry, darling, but I just wanted to make sure you weren't making a horrible mistake. You and Jason have been so in love, and well, I've had such a wonderful experience of motherhood . . .' She trailed off and reached across the table for my hand.

'Portia, I'm sorry. You should of course be true to yourself.

If you don't want a baby, if you're not a hundred per cent sure, you shouldn't do it. Lord knows, it's not easy, and it doesn't get any easier as they grow up . . .' She trailed off again and took another swig, gazing across the desert vista.

'Are you talking about Ariel?' I asked.

'No . . . yes, well, all of it. I think I let myself and Manny's desire for a child later in life cloud our judgement. I didn't think through what it would be like, being this age and trying to parent a teenager. I didn't know the world would be the way it is now, so divided and instantaneous. And now there's AI to contend with! I don't even know what's real on the internet any more. I didn't know I would be so . . . exhausted all the time.'

'And she's also a pretty special case.' I shrugged. They both looked at me. 'What? She's got a . . . strong personality?' I offered, grinning.

'Ah stop it,' Dessie scolded. 'She's feisty, and vocal. I won't deny that she's tough. But I suspect it's my own fault, putting her on television fresh from the womb, and then being too busy to be a good mother. Thank god for Manuel, or she'd probably be a criminal.'

I made a face at Vinnie. 'Probably' was kind.

'Have you heard from Jason?' Dessie asked, mouth full of rice-paper roll.

'Not since that voice note the other night. He couldn't even ring me, just sent an impersonal soundbite to tell me he wasn't coming to get me. Bastard.'

'Did you want him to come and get you?'

'I didn't want him to go further away.'

More deep sips of rosé for both of us, while Vinnie lit a menthol. They're what she smokes when she's in company. I'd say we looked a right sight, the three of us and a disproportionately gigantic bottle of booze, sunglasses on, hair scraped back, idly munching on ludicrously expensive appetizers. If Palm Springs is where the rich and famous come to decompress, we must have looked like a caricature in that moment.

My mom laughed drily, clearly thinking along the same lines. 'We make quite a trio, don't we?' She nodded at Vinnie. 'You've been made a complete and utter show of by the gross misconduct of the father of your children, and your business is probably going to be fucked because of it.' She pointed at me. 'The man you thought you'd live happily ever after with has turned that on its head and upped sticks back home six thousand miles away. And me? The last long-term relationship I had was with a gay man!' She dissolved into peals of laughter. Vinnie and I looked at each other, and then back at our mother.

'Sorry, what?' I squeaked.

'We're a right pack of sad articles!' Dessie exclaimed, wiping tears of mirth from her eyes.

'No, back up there, Mom,' I said. 'A gay man?'

'Oh, Portia. You're not that innocent, are you?'

I looked at Vinnie, whose face gave nothing away.

'Manuel? He's as gay as Christmas!' She was keening now; it was unclear if she was laughing or crying.

I was stunned silent. I tried to articulate a thought but found I quite simply couldn't. Manny was gay? My mother's ex-husband, Ariel's father? The macho, sexy Latino that oozed charisma? My gaydar had not only never pinged, it hadn't even whispered.

Dessie was coming to the end of her hysterical laughing fit and realized I was completely bewildered. 'Oh my god,' she said. 'You really didn't know. Didn't even suspect?'

I shook my head. Vinnie, on the other hand, shrugged. 'I had my suspicions. Actually, no, I totally knew.' I gaped at her. 'I live nearby!' Vinnie protested. 'I hear him blaring Kylie Minogue.'

'Be serious, Vinnie. Did you know? For how long?'

'I don't think I ever had an "aha moment", to quote Oprah. I've just always thought he and Mom were more besties than lovers is all. I haven't been imagining him sucking . . .'

'Don't!' I yelped.

'I'm so sorry, my loves, it shouldn't have come out like that. I do apologize.' Dessie tried to refill her wine glass but couldn't lift the colossal bottle. A waiter appeared as if from nowhere and obliged. 'I never wanted to make a declaration in the past because I didn't think it mattered that much who we slept with, and it's Manuel's business. We've always loved each other very much.'

I found my voice. 'Mom, did you know? I mean, when did you find out?'

'Oh, I always knew, my love. Manny and I have been friends since the Studio 54 days. He was a stud muffin back then. Swung both ways, but I knew he preferred the company of gentlemen.'

'Why did you get married?' This from Vinnie.

'Because he asked me,' Dessie replied. 'After your father died, the pain was immense. Then I met poor Kyle, and he swept me off my feet. That marriage was doomed from the start because it was all based purely on sex – I'm sorry,' she said, seeing me grimace. 'So, I swore off romantic love altogether after that. I wanted an easy life, darlings. Company, friendship. Manny was a confirmed bachelor, but he desperately wanted a baby. This was before gay men were having children of their own; Elton and David hadn't even had their boys yet. To be gay in Hollywood in the noughties was still tricky, you have to understand. Manny is a confident man, but he's never felt safe enough to be out publicly. He was afraid the rock stars he was paid to look after wouldn't want to work with him, and his bread and butter is entertaining

174

the entertainers. He didn't want the head honchos at his label to find out. It takes a self-assured type to be out and proud, even still. And then he'd managed for so long as he was . . .' She sighed.

'You girls were all grown up, and I was lonely. One night after too much champagne he suggested we should get married and I thought it was a great idea. You know I had my eggs frozen when I was thirty-five? It was all the rage among the Hollywood housewives in the nineties. So, we said, let's do it. And then, in the cold light of day, it still seemed like a good idea.'

'Mom, are you saying you were a beard?' I was incredulous.

'Ugh, Portia, don't make it sound so déclassé. I was having a baby with a man I loved, still love, deeply. He just doesn't fancy me, which has made my life so much less complicated.'

I couldn't believe what she was saying. I've always considered myself to be an astute person, but I was learning that I was lot more easily led than I'd ever believed possible. Imagining my beautiful, ravishing mother in a sexless marriage was blowing my mind. I hadn't been around much over the last decade or so, true. But I couldn't believe she'd never confided in me.

'Why did you divorce him?' Vinnie asked. I got the feeling she had wanted to ask our mother these questions for quite a while.

'Oh, *LOLA* brought so much attention on to us. It was getting more difficult for me to date other men!' Dessie laughed. 'We never knew the show would become what it is; we thought it would be one season, maybe two, and a nice pay cheque. But the longer it went on, the we knew we'd get caught out with our, um, extracurricular activities. We thought it was better to part ways legally so that another cast member couldn't throw suspected infidelities in our faces.'

'Manuel sleeps with men?' I spluttered. 'I can't believe it.'

'Of course, Portia. Do catch up! He does it discreetly. And I have my own dalliances from time to time.'

Vinnie turned to me. 'If she's going to talk about her sex life, can I have a vodka Martini? Just this once?' she pleaded.

'Slippery slope,' I intoned.

'Girls, you're truly being terribly old-fashioned. I hope you're still having sex after menopause. The rumours about becoming a dried-up old crone are greatly exaggerated. Anyway, Manny and I wanted to live together for Ariel's sake, and because we're still the best of friends. People think it's weird, but everything is weird in bloody La La Land. And do you know what, mad stuff goes on at home in Kerry too. The things I hear from my cousin Niamh! It happens everywhere – deceit and intrigue and sex and secrets. It's the way of the world.'

This was all a lot to take in. I had questions – many, many more questions – and they required a bit more privacy. My mother must have read my mind, because she was summoning the waiter to send the rest of the jeroboam, fresh glasses and ice to her suite.

19

By golden hour, Mom and I were quite drunk. They say a problem shared is a problem halved, but what is a scandal multiplied by three?

We retired to Dessie's fabulous suite with a view of the majestic San Jacinto mountains, where Bubbles was thrilled to see us and whirled in circles. We had all plastered on the new sheet-mask range Dessie was testing for Freckle and changed into DD+ comfies. We would order room service – cacio e pepe, chicken Caesars and champagne, it was decided – and talk like we hadn't in ages.

Despite our mother being a warm and present person, it occurred to me that I didn't know her that well as a woman. After our father died, she had had to step into the role of both parents to Vinnie and me, and also took on the worry about how to provide for us when Dad's financial situation came to light. She wanted to keep us in the lifestyle to which we had become accustomed and that meant she was often all business, or too preoccupied to just hang out with us. She never spoiled us; she couldn't afford it. But she was determined that we could continue to live in a nice area, go to good schools and never want for anything.

And I guess it's not exactly normal to discuss your parents' romantic lives. When she first met Kyle, Vinnie and I both thought it was too fast but said nothing. We were teenagers, not yet able to understand the complexities of adult relationships. More than anything, we wanted Dessie to be happy. And we were absent by the time they divorced two years later, both caught up in our own fledging lives and independence.

By the time the wedding to Manuel came around, I was living in New York and Vinnie was flaking around the world with her friends. They tied the knot on the beach in Miami, where Manuel grew up. There was no bachelorette party, and we didn't have girl talk with our mother or ask her about her love life. But now I wanted to know more.

Dessie was reclining with her pooch on the balcony, her brunette hair glistening in the setting sun. She had sunglasses on, and the only reason I knew she was still awake was the iron-clad grip she had on the stem of her rosé glass.

'Mommy?' I surprised myself, calling her that. 'Was our dad the love of your life?'

A funny smile played on her lips. 'You know, Portia, I often told myself that he was. We were together for twenty years, he was certainly a great, great love. A passion, you know? Life with him was a whirlwind; he swept me up in it all. I'd been floundering in New York, homesick for Kerry once your Auntie Rosalind went back and Celia moved to Boston with her husband. I was idly thinking I'd marry a rich man for shits and giggles. But then I met Roberto Rizzi and my life changed for ever. I fell for him and he made me forget my pain.'

'Pain?' asked Vinnie.

'I don't think I've ever told you girls the reason I left Ireland, did I?'

I shrugged. 'Famine? I'm kidding, kidding,' I protested. 'No, I figured you left why everyone left back then. America being the land of opportunity, and all that.'

'Not quite. Rosalind was planning on following Celia over in 1979. Ireland was on a bit of a downswing, politically and economically, and Cece's letters from the Big Apple sounded so glamorous. She was working on a beauty counter, going out to dances, meeting Jewish and Italian and Polish boys, and having the time of her life. But I was quite happy at home. I was young and in love and wanted to stay put. You see, I'd fallen for a sheep farmer.'

I couldn't imagine it. It was hard to picture my mother as a girl at all, never mind one who would choose a small village and a farmer over the glamour of emigrating to New York.

'He was the most beautiful man I'd ever seen,' she sighed. 'Proper Kerry Irish, that Spanish Armada look about him. Black hair and black eyes, and he danced like a dream. I first saw him at a hooley in Killarney, and I was a goner there and then. But everyone was after him, sure he had a big family farm out the way in Barraduff. I didn't think I stood a chance. But then he asked me up for a waltz, and it was like magic, girls.'

Her voice had taken on a dreamy quality. 'We courted for a couple of months, and it was about to get serious. My mammy and daddy wanted him to come over for Sunday dinner and an inspection; they were expecting a proposal. But once he heard that, he clammed up on me. He was older than me by a couple of years but still a young man. He wasn't ready to marry an eighteen-year-old and settle down. So, he broke it off. A few weeks later, I heard he'd taken up with my friend and my heart was broken. When Rosalind asked me to go with her again, I said I would. I wanted to put as many miles between myself and himself as possible.'

'Wow, Mom, that's quite a strong reaction to a break-up,' said Vinnie.

'Oh, I could have moved up to Dublin and got a job, I could have gone to London. But everyone said I was the beauty of the family; I was the one with a spark and a devilment in my eyes. My mother said I could make it in New York, just like the

Frank Sinatra song. She said I could be on billboards in Time Square. I just thought *feck it*, and I went.'

I noticed then that Dessie had started crying. She sat up and wiped her eyes. 'To answer your question Portia, no – I think the love of my life is the man who broke my heart and, in doing so, drove me out of Ireland. At least, he could have been. But that's ancient history, now.'

'What was his name?' I asked.

'Don't be so nosey. I'm not telling you, because you'll only be googling him and looking at his Facebook.'

She wiped her eyes. 'Anyway, that's enough reminiscing. We've enough to focus on in the present, am I right?'

'I thought Jason was the love of my life,' I blurted. 'I genuinely thought we were soulmates, twin flames, all that stuff.'

'And you don't any more?' my mother asked.

'Well, how can I? I doubt my true soulmate would act like this. But I'm terrified that this was my shot at happily ever after and I've blown it.'

'Do you know what, love? Something I've learned is that when someone is obviously good-looking, they often tend to have an easier life than others.'

'Meaning?'

'Meaning that Jason is used to getting what he wants. Which was all well and good when all he wanted was you, but . . .'

'Now he wants more,' my sister finished. 'And he can't take it. I get what Mom is saying – I never had to have much of a personality when I was younger. Nobody cared what I had to say. I was a terrible friend, a lying addict, and people didn't care. They still wanted to be around me.'

'The Sybil thing is crazy, though,' Dessie cried. 'Of all the Ladies to shag, she wouldn't be my choice!'

'Mom! Not helpful!'

'Oh, feck off, Lavinia! I'm hurt by all this too, you know! I'm the reason they met; he was part of my world for a long time as well. And Billy Schwartz is the father of my grandchildren. I never really understood you two together when you could have had anyone – darling, he was also so . . . agent-y and slick. But he seemed to adore you and those boys. Why are we besieged with these men? Are we cursed?'

The three of us all looked at one another. In that moment, it certainly felt like we were. We all burst out laughing.

'The power of three, huh?' Dessie was keening. 'More like the three witches! Double, double, toil and trouble!'

'Fire burn and cauldron bubble,' Vinnie and I joined in.

The phone in the suite started to ring. 'Ah, saved by the bell,' she said as she shuffled across the lush, carpeted floor.

But when she said hello, her face changed. 'Giulia, why are you ringing the room? Oh, I'm sorry, my phone is on si— She's what? How? I'll kill her!'

Dessie hung up and immediately started throwing things into her bag. 'Get packing, girls. Ronald will be here in an hour.'

'What? Why?' I managed.

'I have to get home and throttle your younger sister, that's why.'

'I really am sorry, Mom.'

'Look at the absolute state of you! A black eye!'

'She hit me first!'

'Your father let you out early even though you were meant to be grounded, and this is what you do?'

We were all having brunch on Dessie's terrace. It's my favourite place in the house, especially as a New Yorker with limited outside space of my own. There's a fabulous striped awning in claret and white, and an elevated dining area in front of the pool. Dessie had massive folding doors installed in the house's back rooms, so she could open them all up as she pleased and enjoy that famous Southern California indoor/outdoor living. The property itself overlooks the Los Angeles Basin, and because it's south-facing, it's sunny all day.

Despite Ronald having broken the speed limit to get us back from Palm Springs the previous night, Ariel had been in bed when Dessie came raging into the house, and Manny had put his foot down – there was to be no confrontation until morning.

'She's a child, Desdemona,' he'd soothed. 'And you need to calm down.'

'She's a little rip!'

But my mother had eventually acquiesced, seemingly content to hear the full story from him before taking the night to calm down and confronting Ariel in a more civilized manner in the morning.

Apparently, Ariel had been defending Vinnie's honour. She'd gone to the beach to play volleyball when the day cooled off a bit, and one of the girls on the other team had called Vinnie and Billy some choice words. A scuffle ensued, hands were thrown, and the other girl had a three-inch-deep gash on her right cheek. The parents were threatening to sue for loss of future earnings, as Ariel's opponent was a beauty queen – and a savvy LA family could see a payday from a mile away.

'Did you have to gouge her face?' Dessie was saying to Ariel at brunch, as my sister picked at her yogurt.

'I didn't mean to; I was just wearing those new Freckle press-on nails.'

'Yes, well, every cent I'd have made from them will now be spent on a settlement, so thank you,' Dessie huffed. Ariel started whimpering again.

'I'm not going to stand by and let stupid bitches call Vinnie an enabler, Mom!' she screeched.

I looked at Vinnie, who'd gone pale. 'Who said that, Ariel?'

'Everyone is saying it! Sally Morgan's sister is in my English class, and Penelope Frank is my friend from TikTok! I see her at events. Like, I actually know someone who had sex with your husband! It's so gross!'

Ariel's whimpers turned to full-blown tears. She looked so sad, with her bruised face and broken nails, I wanted to hug her. But when I went to, she shrugged me off and ran to her room.

Vinnie was white as a sheet. 'I didn't think about how this would affect her, or any of you,' she whispered. 'I'm so sorry. This is all my fault. Not long ago, everything was peaceful and quiet.'

'It's not your fault, Vin. And you're not alone, either. And in some small way, I can relate.'

I tried to soothe my sister, but it wasn't lost on me that barely three months ago, I was living my own very different life. Working away, coming home to the man I loved, in ignorant bliss. Now my life was like an episode of *90210*, the nineties version with Shannen Doherty. I sighed deeply. In that moment, I felt desperately homesick. I missed my apartment, I missed New York and I missed Jason. The pain was so visceral, it was like I'd been stabbed.

Giulia strolled into the kitchen in a cloud of Versace Crystal Noir. I knew she'd been on conference calls since 7 a.m., trying to sort out Ariel's mess.

'Well, I have managed to stop the story getting out,' she sighed, kicking off her Jimmy Choos. 'The families have all signed the NDAs.'

'What did it cost me?' Dessie sighed again.

'You do not want to know. I have to say, though . . .' Giulia raised a bushy brow. 'If I wasn't so angry, I would be impressed.'

'Impressed?'

'*Sì, certo*. By all accounts, it sounded like a scrap worthy of a soap opera. Ariel has the kind of energy that works well in this town.' Giulia looked pensive. 'Maybe we should look at getting her an acting coach . . .'

17 June 2022

Which celebrity offspring throws a mean right hook?
Sources say this TikTok teen was involved in a physical
altercation, but her family have used their considerable
influence to make the news go away. We hope her face
heals soon because she has a big job coming up . . .

20

I awoke the next morning in my bedroom at Dessie's. It occurred to me that since my night of passion with Noah Frost the previous week, I had been sleeping better than I had in ages, and on a mattress to boot. The power of a decent orgasm. Then I remembered my thirst trap Instagram story, which had been all but forgotten in the drama. It had long expired but, sure enough, there was a fire emoji reaction from Mr Frost in my DMs. No message, though. My gut reaction was disappointment. Would a few words have killed the man?

There was nothing from Jason, still. I checked his profile, but there were no new posts, stories or tags. It was like he'd disappeared from the face of the earth.

I wandered out of my room in search of coffee and found Suz in the kitchen. I kissed her on the head, not even bothering to ask how she got in – all of Dessie's pseudo children have their own keys and codes and tend to congregate here. Dessie's house is something of a family HQ.

'You're a sight for sore eyes, sis,' I said, and she was. Despite working late nights, wearing inches of TV make-up, and having two teenage girls to care for without a father figure in the picture, her skin glowed, and she looked chic in a simple orange shirt dress and studded Valentino flats.

'Oh, honey, I barely slept after Manny called,' she said. 'Poor Ariel fighting to defend Lavinia's honour! And teen girls leaving marks on one another's bodies? I'm terrified for my babies. All this privilege and exposure just cannot be good for their development.'

I knew she didn't need to worry – Suz's daughters are like the anti-Ariel. Sabrina is seventeen and an honours student and champion cheerleader. Willa is thirteen and following in her big sister's footsteps. They're such great kids, creative and smart.

'Where's Vinnie?' I asked, helping myself to an everything bagel and cream cheese. Suz always brought the good stuff.

'Your sister is out running errands with the kids and Marjorie. She said, and I quote, "I don't give a damn about the paparazzi or this town any more," and flew out the door. The negative comments are ongoing.' Suz sighed. 'Your mom had an appointment and Manny went with her. Ariel is locked in her room.'

I could feel her watching me as I demolished my bagel. 'How are you doing, kid?' she asked.

I laughed at the use of my teen nickname. Suz is nine months older than me, so it's been a running joke.

'I'm up and down,' I admitted. I could always be honest with Suz. 'I was just beginning to enjoy myself in the desert, relaxing for the first time since it all went down in Ireland. And I felt like I was properly bonding with my mom, in a way I hadn't ever before. And then last night everything was turned upside down.' I felt tears rush into my eyes. 'I miss Jason, Suz.'

'Of course you do, baby,' she cooed, reaching for my hand. 'Jason was your whole life. The reason I've never tried too hard to keep a man in my life is because it's too damn scary.'

Suz had been engaged twice, but never made it down the aisle. Both the girls had different fathers; Sabrina's dad was a basketball player who had never been faithful, and Willa's was the man who broke Suz's heart and turned her off love for life. I knew she was rumoured to be having a long-term affair with a well-respected and married morning-show anchor, but I never brought it up. Behind the public persona, Suz is an intensely private person. And really, it was none of my business.

'What about the girls?' I asked. 'Do they ever wish they had a man in the house?'

'Child, no! We love our little ladies' club. They see their dads all the time, they have Manny and David, they have my other friends and my father. And they have me!' She popped a plump strawberry in her mouth. 'To paraphrase the great and powerful Cher, I am essentially a rich man. Those children have never wanted for anything.'

I had to agree with her there.

'And while I know it's none of my beeswax, may I make an observation on your situation?' she asked. I nodded, thinking I might as well get someone else's perspective on my mess.

'I know you'd make the most fantastic mother, sweetheart, but only if you wanted to. You are nurturing and warm and kind and wonderful. But I don't think that any woman has to have a child to complete them, especially to appease somebody else. I am of the opinion that motherhood is not something that should be entered into unless you are one million per cent sure. My god, parenting is hard enough when you want it more than you can say.'

I squeezed her hand. 'Suz, you have no idea how much I needed to hear that today.'

'Any time.' She looked at me slyly. 'I hear you've been getting some, though.'

'No, "getting" is an exaggeration,' I laughed. '*Got*. I got some. Giulia can't keep her trap shut, huh?'

'Giulia, David, your mom. And?'

'And . . .' I stretched out. 'And it was pretty damn good. He was hot, I felt sexy, and it cured my fear of sleeping in a bed without Jason.'

'Yes, girl!' She laughed. 'I know good sex is no fix for a broken heart, but it certainly passes the time. Let's get you some more of it?'

'Oh no! Noah Frost was a happy accident, I think. And I'm not going trawling Beverly Hills for dick either.'

She threw her head back and laughed. 'Portia Daniels, as if you would have to! I have been single in this city on and off for more than twenty years. I have a Rolodex of men that would make your head spin. Tall, short, thin, muscular, straight, bi . . . I could go on.'

I cocked an eyebrow. 'Bi?'

'Pansexual, non-binary, whatever! What I'm saying is, I can hook you up with anyone you want. No strings, just fun. You're out here, you're not working much, what else are you going to do?'

She'd hit a nerve about work. Shockingly, my episode for Netflix had been approved with minimal rewrites, and I wasn't required on set as a freelancer. But with everything going on, I was feeling creatively clogged. I'd been affording myself this downtime to rest and recover, but I knew it was getting past time to get back on the horse. Maybe a little extra-curricular fun, as my mother had put it, would do me some good and get my juices flowing.

'I'm not feeling a set-up,' I said. 'I know you're saying no strings, but Hollywood is like Ireland. Everyone knows every-one, and I'm not ready to enter that domain.'

She shrugged. 'Fair point. You don't want Jason to hear.'

'No, it's not that,' I said. 'For all intents and purposes, I am a single woman. He didn't follow me; he didn't wait for me to come back. There's been no contact other than him telling me he's leaving the country, and I know he hasn't been sit-ting around moping either. I presume Giulia also filled you in about the video with Sybil Simpson?'

'I saw it with my own eyes.' Suz shook her head, disappointed. 'I liked that chick.'

'Yes, well. It's more that I don't want you to, like, recommend me to guys. It just feels . . . wrong, like you're setting them up for a fall with me because I'm a mess.'

'Okaaaaaay,' she drawled. I could tell she didn't get it. 'Well, what about the dating apps?'

I grimaced. 'It's been a long time, and I know they're full of creeps . . .'

Suz squealed. 'I've got just the one for you, baby. Raya!' She took my phone and started downloading an app. 'Here, let it recognize that beautiful face,' she demanded, and I did as I was told.

'Don't you need an in for Raya?' I asked. I'd heard of the exclusive dating app for the world's elite but didn't know much about it.

'I am your in, honey. I know the creator. One text from *moi*, and you'll have the most eligible bachelors in Los Angeles at your fingertips. Don't tell David, though – he's been bugging me to get him on it, but they're maxed out on gay dudes right now. Beautiful, successful women, though? You're like an endangered species, a shoo-in.'

'Are women like me not ten a penny on dating apps?'

'There aren't many women like you, honey.'

By 3 p.m., my profile was ready to go. Suz and I had carefully chosen pictures where I looked both striking and vaguely mysterious and thrown in my thirsty bikini selfie for good measure. She knew all the tricks.

'Nothing overly made up or glamorous; it looks too try-hard. We want teeth, we want shiny eyes. A flash of those abs, since you don't have much up top . . . hey, I'm just being honest! The vaguest outline of an ass, without being too OTT. Okay, perfection!'

She told me the rules. 'No screenshotting. Set your location to Los Angeles only; you don't have time to be waiting for Lewis Hamilton to come home from Grand Prix season, or Andrew Garfield to finish up on Broadway. We are not in this for a pen pal, we are in this for some discreet, high-end entertaining.'

'Geez, Suz. You are making this feel way seedier than it needs to be. And anyway, I'm not ready. This is just a bit of fun.'

Suz relinquished my phone to me. 'Well, when you are ready, it's there. Remember, you only get so many swipes a day, so be discerning and not too rash. Now that I'm done pimping you out, I have to go get Willa from her study group. Keep me posted?'

She picked up her fuchsia Birkin and kissed me on the cheek.

'Remember,' she shouted as she made her way to the door. 'No screenshots!'

And with that, she was gone, leaving me with a phone full of opportunities and a pit in my stomach.

21 June 2022

This month: David O'Shea

Hi, David! We are totally stoked to finally be talking to you. You're a tricky guy to pin down . . .
Oh, my clients keep me busy! If I'm not working on a shoot or on a work trip, I'm in one of my salons making sure things are running as smoothly as possible.

And smooth might as well be your middle name. Your signature style is sleek locks, after all!
Yes, almost everyone except Dessie Daniels goes for the sleek look this year. Dessie likes to have hair even bigger than her personality, and it has been an honour to craft her coiffure for almost fifteen years. I owe her everything.

Is it true that you've known Dessie, the queen of LOLA, since you were a kid in Ireland?
It is. She was a friend of my late mother's. I've always been close to her daughters and, as I got older, I became just as close to her. I mean, come on! She's the greatest. She's been a huge supporter, investor, even a mother figure to me. She's the reason I got a work visa for the US, she financed my first salon.

We've been told by your publicist not to ask about the fabulous LRS, but is she doing okay?

She's as good as can be expected, and being looked after really well by her mom and sister while she figures stuff out. Oops! Maybe I shouldn't have said that . . .

Okay, let's talk hair – do you have a favourite client besides Dessie and Lavinia?
I couldn't possibly play favourites, but I love doing Anne Hathaway. And another Irish superstar, Paul Mescal. He's adventurous with his hair, rare for an Irish guy.

And who is your hair idol?
I have so many – Vidal Sassoon, Jay Sebring, even Chris Appleton – and may I say, what a hottie he is too! Hi, Chris!

Um, he's married now! Would you love to follow in his footsteps and release a hair-care collection?
All I can say is, watch this space! It's a lifelong dream, and something I definitely see myself realizing sooner rather than later.

And how is your own love life? We heard rumours about you and a certain Mr Jonathan Groff . . .
He does have lovely hair, and an Irish complexion, but sadly, I myself started those rumours. Call me, Jonathan!

To join the wait list for appointments in Salon O'Shea at locations nationwide, see salonoshea.com

21

All it took to set me off was one post from Jason. Well, not even from Jason, but from his cousin Sarah. It was a group shot of ten or so of his family members out on the town, not a care in the world. In the picture, which appeared on his Facebook profile, Jason was beaming. It was like a week or so in Ireland had entirely recharged him. He looked young, vibrant and . . . happy. I felt nauseous as soon as I saw it, and that was before I even read the comments.

> Sean Dempsey: @Jason Dempsey the big man is back, slaying the women of Limerick as he always has! They're queueing up!
> Tiernan Dempsey replied: Jayo the Lady Killer! We never stood a chance with him around. I'm glad I'm settled in Oz and not competing . . .
> Jason Dempsey: 😃
> Sarah Dempsey: Just stay away from my friends, okay?! They're all married!

With shaking hands, I deleted the Facebook app from my phone. Shocks like that on social media just couldn't be good for me, and I was sick of mentally keeping tabs on Jason.

In a fit of rage, I opened Raya and started to edit my profile. Just having it on my phone had been giving me itchy feet the past few days, like there was a beacon fanning out from the screen. I felt guilty in possession of a dating app, then curious and then guilty again. But Suz had made me promise not to delete it, seeing as she had called in the favour.

Once Vinnie heard me blaring Taylor Swift's 'All Too Well' (the ten-minute version), she knew there'd been a development. The song had become my call sign for distress, like my own personal Bat-signal. She appeared at my door, and I screamed, 'The bastard!'

'Not in front of the k-i-d-s,' she gestured, and I noticed Silas and Sebastian at her hip.

'I can spell, Mommy,' said Seb. 'And I'm not a kid!'

'Of course you're not, sweetie. You're a fully grown man who should be out earning a living and not freeloading!' She launched herself at him, and they had a tickle fight on the floor, with Si leaping around, shrieking happily. Through my misery, I could acknowledge that the children had a cathartic effect on my sister. But I knew she still wasn't sleeping. When I was lying awake at night, I could hear her roaming the halls.

I filled her in. 'Ew, gross. I'm sorry, P.'

'Yeah, well, two can play at that game.'

'What are you going to do, hook up with Noah again?'

'No, Suz signed me up for that app. You know the one, where you have to be accepted to start swiping? I've just given my profile the Portia Daniels pizzazz.'

'OHMIGOD! Raya! Give me a go!' She had my phone in her hands before I could stop her.

'Vinnie! There are rules, will you stop . . . just . . . stop swiping!' I wrenched it off her to see the damage she'd inflicted.

'I love playing with my single friends' apps. It's so fun when you're married.'

It took her a second to realize what she'd said, and she visibly deflated. It had now been a month since Billy absconded, but it was still hitting Vinnie in waves. I indicated the boys with my eyes, and she nodded. But just like that, the wind was gone from her sails, any shred of positivity extinguished.

Marjorie appeared as if by magic and took the kids out to swim. It was like she was trained to sense bad vibes emanating from my sister, like an angel of mercy and childcare.

David had made a boo-boo a few days previously and confirmed to *Cosmo* that Vinnie was still at our mom's place and inferred that she needed looking after. This single quote gave the news cycle new life and the haters more to hate. David was mortified to be the one responsible for Vinnie's Google Alerts kicking off once again. Giulia had half-heartedly scolded him, but knew he had meant no harm. But Vinnie was irritated by the renewed intrusion and the fact that fans thought she was continuing to play the victim.

I knew @LifeWithLRS was still losing followers. Giulia's crisis convention had been interrupted by Ariel's scrapping antics, but it had tied off the artery – now the great unfollowing was more of a trickle than a haemorrhage.

As Vinnie wasn't posting anything, sales on the site had ground to a near-halt. Influencers must keep up a steady stream of content for the algorithm to remember they exist, and without views, there's no money to be made. They say all publicity is good publicity, but nobody wants to be seen wearing the merch of someone whose husband has been cancelled.

Even vaginal crystals sales had waned – word on the blogs was, if the creator's husband had strayed, they were clearly useless. There hadn't been a single brand enquiry since Vinnie's statement, and it wasn't like she even wanted to be hawking stuff. It was like we were all in limbo – waiting for Billy to break cover, for someone to have a great idea, or for the situation to somehow resolve itself.

To cheer Vinnie up, I opened Raya on my phone. 'Okay, hands off, but let's have a snoop?'

She snuggled in beside me. The beauty of an app like this was its automatic curation. No obvious creeps with crotch shots, no time-wasters and everyone was hot. You paid to be on it, and you had to pass muster with the app's creators. And as promised, it was like a who's who of LA high life – entrepreneurs, singers, reality stars and even a couple of famous actors. I swiped left on every model that materialized because pretty boys have never been my thing.

Vinnie was giving a running commentary. 'Too girly. Too muscular. That one has the eyes of a serial killer. Nope, he gives me the ick. Why is he making that face? Babies in pics are a red flag. Oh yeah, I like his dog! Too old. Too young. Too . . . squirrelly.'

I did as I was told, enjoying this more than I'd thought I would. The next eligible bachelor popped up and I gasped. 'Is this who I think it is?'

Vinnie squealed. 'Arrrrgh, it is!'

It was Brandon Leary, the former boy-bander turned serious musician we had both been obsessed with as teens. I think I felt my first stirring of sexual awakening when his group 4PLAY transitioned from teeny-boppers to balladeers and he shaved his head for the artsy black-and-white music video.

My sister was straight on Google. 'He's forty-six, lives in Malibu. Never married but has had a *lot* of famous girlfriends. Hmm.' She scrolled. 'A lot of models. I wonder how I never encountered him?'

'To be fair, Vin, you might have and you just don't remember. You spent most of the noughties incoherent.'

'True, true.' She continued to scroll. 'He split from Kendra Milan during the pandemic, and it seems like he's been single since. Portia, this is a sign from the universe – you have to swipe right.'

So I did.

Later that afternoon, I forced myself to sit at the laptop. I was never going to get over a dry spell by avoiding work, and in the past I'd always taken solace in writing. I'd emailed my agent, Frank, about some script-polishing work, but so far nothing had come back.

I tried working on my own screenplay, the one I'd been tinkering with for years between jobs. But after two hours of working on one scene and not getting anywhere, I became frustrated. Jason had not only set fire to our relationship, but he appeared to have stolen my creative spark and taken it back to Ireland too.

It was another picture-perfect Los Angeles day, and I was restless. I decided a walk would do me good, maybe even a drive out to the beach. I went in search of my mother to see if she'd come with me.

She wasn't in her suite, or her office. I looked in the kitchen and the living room, but no Dessie. I found Ariel sulking in the cinema room; she was being punished for her fisticuffs because her parents were trying to show her that physical violence was never okay, even in defence of the family. Her devices had been confiscated, and her big blowout birthday party cancelled, which is why she was deigning to watch Netflix in the home theatre instead of in the privacy of her room.

'Have you seen Mom?' I called from the door.

'Try the gym.' She scowled. 'I heard Hector arrive a while ago, to try and train her decrepit ass.'

I sat down on one of the green velvet recliners. 'Ariel, you have to stop being so hard on Dessie. She's just trying to do what's best for you.'

She looked up at me, and for a second I saw a shadow of the sweet ten-year-old girl she used to be, before the hormones corrupted her. She shrugged.

'I don't care that they cancelled my birthday party. Nobody would come now – I'm persona non grata at school. I don't want to go any more. Thank God it's the summer now.'

'You must remember that Mom is out of her comfort zone raising a teenager these days, and God, I don't envy her. It's a whole different ball game.'

'Is that why you don't want kids?' Her question was guileless, and it cut me. I swallowed.

'No, I've just never wanted to be a mom,' I said gently. 'Way before Instagram was invented, I knew I didn't see myself raising children.'

She nodded, sagely.

'And Ariel, I want you to know that that's okay. A lot of people seem to find it difficult to understand that women have different desires beyond what's "normal" or "usual". But you weren't put on this earth solely to procreate, okay? You can do whatever you want to do with your life.'

She laughed. 'Obvi, P! My generation isn't bound by the social constructs of the patriarchy. But I like babies. I'll probably have about ten of them, so they're never by themselves.'

I vowed then to sit Dessie and Manuel down and talk to them about Ariel. In a world so connected, her sense of isolation was palpable. She may be a child of the digital age, but loneliness didn't discriminate.

I kissed her on the head and continued my search for Dessie. Following Ariel's instruction, I headed out to the pool house. Of course, it was more than just a pool house – as well as hosting the various floats and toys pool owners accrue, it also contained a guest suite with a full bath and a wet bar, a home gym and a massage nook. There was also a state-of-the-art outdoor kitchen under a pergola, a fire pit and lots of cosy seating. I realized that I'd made a mistake staying in the main house and should immediately set up camp out here; it was the perfect writer's retreat.

I pushed open the French doors and peered through the gauzy curtains into the workout space. My mom was bending over a bench and her trainer, Hector, was standing behind her. At first, I thought he was helping her do a complicated stretch, until I realized my sixty-two-year-old mother was naked from the waist down. I stood there mute and horrified as it dawned on me that I had walked in on Dessie being taken from behind by her personal trainer.

I turned to run away but got caught in the curtains and landed on the sprung floor with a thud.

'*Jesus!*' Dessie screeched. She wrapped a towel around her waist and ran over to make sure I was okay.

'What the fuck are you doing, Portia? You gave me the fright of my life there!'

'What are *you* doing?' I yelped. 'My eyes, they'll never feel clean again!'

To his credit, Hector did a slick disappearing act, tucking his bits back into his shorts and exiting through the side door stealthily. By the time Dessie helped me to my feet, he was gone.

My mother and I looked at one another and both burst out laughing.

'I'm sorry, darling,' she bleated, as she struggled into her DD+ leggings. 'I usually lock the door, but I got carried away today.'

'Usually? You mean this is a regular occurrence?'

I was dumbfounded. I knew my mother claimed to have lovers, but it didn't occur to me that thirty-five-year-old Hector might fit the bill.

'Let's just say we play as much as we work out.' She winked lasciviously. 'Oh, Portia, don't be such a wet blanket! Am I meant to be able to resist that man?'

She had a point. Hector was almost too good-looking, a personal trainer to athletes and movie stars – he counted The Rock and Sandra Bullock among his clients. And of course he was interested in my mother, still beautiful and seductive as she was. I always struggled to separate Dessie's blatant hotness from the fact that she's my mother.

'It started a few months back, when he bench-pressed me,' she giggled. 'Like, used my body instead of a bar. He put me down after twenty reps, and I jumped right back on top of him.'

'Is it serious?' I asked.

'Serious? God no,' she pealed with laughter. 'Portia, it's just fun. That's what life is all about, having sex with someone doesn't mean anything, especially at my age.'

She strutted back towards the house, still laughing, and shaking out her dark hair as she went. I was left sitting at the fire pit contemplating why I had a more archaic attitude to sex and relationships than my sexagenarian mother when my phone pinged.

I had a new match on Raya. Opening the app, a surge of energy went through me. It was Brandon Leary, and he'd sent me a message!

'Hey Portia, wow, you are beautiful,' it read. 'I've always been a fan of your mom's. I'd love to meet up. Would you like to come visit my studio tonight?'

I dropped the phone like a hot potato. He'd clearly googled me before replying, if he knew about my mother. This was happening very fast. And it was Brandon sex-on-legs Leary! I'd seen him in concert half a dozen times, and I'd had his poster on my wall when he was in 4PLAY and I was too young to know what that meant. Could I possibly?

I needed the moral support of the group chat. I sent a text instructing Vinnie, David and Suz to meet me in a bar in WeHo at 6 p.m. for a summit.

'What position were they in?' David was incredulous as I recounted the afternoon's events. He'd thought Hector played for his team.

'Oh, just casual doggy style while balanced on a gym bench,' I said drily.

'Noooooo,' they all keened in unison.

'I definitely didn't need that detail, Portia!' Vinnie was predictably much cooler about the whole thing than me, but the image of our mother being railed from behind was a step too far.

'And you fell over? I cannot –!' Suz howled. She found the whole thing hilarious.

We were in TomTom, a sexy bar on Santa Monica Boulevard owned by a rival reality-show maven. The crowd was a mix of wannabes, tourists and gay guys, but the setting was undeniably chic and, importantly, devoid of anyone we knew. We had a booth in the back, but Vinnie was having a day where she was defiant about being seen out and about. 'What else can they say about me?' was her reasoning, and I didn't have a good enough response to deter her. I knew her mood changed like the weather, and she'd probably be feeling insular again by the next day.

The real reason for our meeting was to decide whether to take Brandon Leary up on his offer. Thanks to Suz's intel, we'd learned that the studio he spoke of was in fact in his sprawling home. It made sense that he wouldn't want to meet in public, what with his level of fame, but I felt kind of seedy being asked to go straight to his house.

Suz was all for it. 'You said you just want a good time,

Portia. That means no dating, no going out with these men. How can you be offended when a guy is upfront with you?'

David nodded wisely. 'You're lucky he was even this polite. Guys on Grindr just send a dick pic and an address. This is practically romantic, P.'

Vinnie eyed me. 'For someone who claims not to want to go to this guy's place, you're looking pretty hot tonight.'

I was rumbled. I'd made an effort for the first time in ages, styling my sharp bob straight, wearing some eyeliner and lip-gloss, and I had a cute thong on under my signature minidress. 'Okay, I obviously want to go, I admit it. I'm just nervous and need some moral support, you guys. It's been a while since I've had a date with anyone other than Jason, and Brandon Leary isn't just some guy.'

'You need some more Dutch courage,' Vinnie proclaimed, heading to the bar to order another round of chilled tequila shots, and an alcohol-free beer for herself.

'Right, Portia, this is what you do when you get there,' David was saying. I listened, because he was undoubtedly an authority on LA hook-ups. 'Walk in as if you own the place. Shrug off your jacket, let him see those beautiful shoulders! And look him straight in the eye. Accept his offer of a drink, and ask to see the studio, seeing as that's the line he used.'

Suz was nodding. 'Stars love to talk about themselves, it turns them on, so just let him tell you how fabulous he is. I mean, I'd like to know all about his house so please take in all the details. And if you're feeling nervous, let him make the first move.'

'Okay, I'm going to message him back,' I said, and I did just that, fingers trembling. A minute later, a response with the address and a smiley emoji landed.

'Where is Vinnie with that drink?' I shrieked, the nerves hitting hard. I glanced around, and saw my sister at the bar, chatting to a stunning black woman. She was tall, with long, curly hair flowing down her back and abs that were visible from twenty feet away. I vaguely recognized her, but I didn't know from where. I waved at Vinnie, and she excused herself and came back to the table.

'Sorry, I was talking to India! Remember, she used to train me? I haven't seen her in ages.'

That's where I knew her from. She was my sister's personal Pilates instructor, and I knew Vinnie had always been in awe of her. She'd featured heavily on LifeWithLRS for a while; I wondered had there been a falling-out. If there had, I sensed a detente, because Vinnie seemed a bit giddy after their chat.

There wasn't time to ask, though. A shot was placed in my hand, a cheers executed to wish me good luck, and before I knew it I was stepping off the kerb and into an Uber destined for Brandon Leary's house.

22

The house was fabulous, a low-slung, sprawling ranch off Mulholland, with high-spec tech discreetly embedded into the rustic setting. I'd driven past two cameras, at least that I could see.

There was a video doorbell at the entrance, and I stood there awkwardly for a good two minutes after I'd rung it. Then Brandon appeared, shorter than I'd imagined, like basically all celebrities. He was barefoot, in jeans and an artfully dishevelled T-shirt.

'Portia!' He greeted me enthusiastically with a kiss on each cheek and ushered me inside with his hand on the small of my back. If the outside of his home was pastoral, the inside was slick and modern, and the juxtaposition was jarring.

He held me by the upper arms with both hands, and took a long, hard look at me up close. Then without another word, he started off down the hall. I followed him silently, noting the gold and platinum records displayed on the walls, for both his 4PLAY days and his solo stuff.

He must have heard the heels of my boots click on the concrete floors, because he spun around. 'Ooh, no shoes in the house, I'm afraid. Please go back to the door and take them off.'

'You want me to . . . walk back? I can just take them off right here?'

'Oh, no, no. Please take them off at the bench and leave them underneath.'

Vaguely miffed, I did as I was told while he waited for me

in silence. When I returned to his side, he sprang back into action as if nothing had happened. 'I was so pleased to match with you, Portia. You have a rare quality that's often missing on those apps.'

'Dare I ask what that is?' I cocked a brow.

'A certain . . . homeliness, I think. You're not flaunting large breasts or a tight ass or trying to make yourself younger with filler and blonde hair. You're sort of a girl next door, a little plain for LA but quite pretty.'

Was this guy for real? I didn't know what to say, so I followed him into a mammoth kitchen designed in an industrial style. The cabinets were stainless steel and the island was built from what looked like reclaimed brick. Copper pots and pans hung from the ceiling, and I spotted a smart fridge and barista-style coffee machine. It was stunning.

'Can I offer you a drink?' Brandon asked.

'Sure, what have you got?'

'Oh, let's see . . . I have kombucha or . . . water.' He looked at me expectantly, his blue eyes freakishly bright.

'I thought you meant a real drink.' I laughed nervously, but he held my gaze.

'Those are real drinks, Portia. Do you mean alcohol?'

'Uhhh . . .'

He was rooting in the island. 'I keep some red to hand for when my drinker friends come . . . aha!' He uncorked a bottle with ease and noted my expression. 'I personally think alcohol is the devil, Portia. But I understand others partake, so I know my grapes.' He grinned at me as he handed over a measly glass of wine.

I was starting to feel uneasy, perhaps because he kept saying my name like it wasn't an actual word, rolling it around in his mouth.

Brandon sat on the stool next to me. 'Tell me about

yourself.' He smiled, and I thawed ever so slightly. Maybe the dude was as nervous as I was. I couldn't help but notice that up close he had a line of tiny little skin tags under his right eye, and possibly even a twitch. Plus there was a faint musky odour that seemed to be emanating from him. But this was Brandon Leary! I had lusted after this man since before I knew what it was to lust. I needed to just live in the moment, I decided.

'Well, I'm a writer. Mostly for TV, but I've done some script polishing for the movies.' He nodded for me to continue. 'I'm a New Yorker, but uh, some stuff has been going on lately that brought me out here, to my family.'

'I just love your mother, Portia,' he said, leaning in close. 'She is super-sexy for her age and seems so sweet. I'm just addicted to the V Network.'

This was surprising; Brandon Leary was not exactly the target audience. 'Oh, so you googled me and found out Dessie was my mom . . .'

'Oh yes, I don't just invite anyone to my home. I did a full check on you, and I was thrilled to match with Dessie Daniels and Roberto Rizzi's progeny!'

He was gesturing around the room, and that's when I noticed the posters. Massive prints from the theatrical releases of my dad's movies were framed around the room. I gulped.

'Maybe when we fall in love, I can make a cameo on *LOLA*,' he said, completely seriously. Then he sort of barked. 'Ha! Ha!'

I was officially unnerved.

'Come, Portia, let me show you my humble abode.' He took me by the hand, and I noticed his was sort of clammy. He then proceeded to wax lyrical about himself and his career, just as my friends had predicted.

207

When we reached the famous studio I'd ostensibly been invited to see, he had me sit down in front of an impressive, sprawling deck. Then he turned on a light in the other room. 'That's what we call the live room,' he explained. 'It's where the magic happens.'

He left me sitting there and went to the other side of the glass and sat at the piano. He started to play, and I recognized the tune of The Beatles' 'Dear Prudence'.

'Dear Portia,' he crooned, with feeling. I wasn't sure what to make of the look on his face as he sang at me about coming out to play.

I just sat there, smiling stiffly as he played this mini concert. I expected him to stop after a chorus, but he kept going until he'd sung the whole song. Then he beckoned me to come in to him.

I've always had a bit of a thing for pianos. There's a scene in *Pretty Woman* where Richard Gere's character is playing alone in the ballroom of the Beverly Wilshire, and Julia Roberts' Vivian comes to find him. He ends up lifting her on to the piano and going down on her there and then.

I'd always thought it was so horny when I was a kid, surreptitiously watching the movie after Mom went to bed. Right at that moment, though, I was beyond turned off.

Brandon had me sit down beside him on the wide leather stool. He leaned over to whisper in my ear. 'What's your favourite song of mine?' He gave my lobe a light nibble.

'Uhh . . . I guess it's "My Soul"?' I stuttered.

'I can tell you that, nine times out of ten, women I bring in here say that song.' Brandon sounded irritated. 'I'm not going to play that one, because I want you to hear something new.'

He started to play a song I'd never heard before, which was beyond awkward. If I'd been slightly creeped out before, the ick was now enveloping me at a rapid pace. How could I get out of this without making a scene?

He finished singing and took my hand. I hadn't notice him undo his fly, so I was shocked when he placed my palm on a flaccid penis. I shrieked.

'Don't be scared, Portia,' he cooed. 'You just hold him tight, and he's going to get big and strong for you after a couple more songs.'

Horrified, I snatched my hand back and bolted for the door. As I was struggling to get my boots on at the door, a disjointed voice filtered down the hall through an intercom. 'Portia, sorry this didn't work out, but please give your ravishing mother my regards . . . and perhaps my address?'

It was after ten by the time I got back to Beverly Hills. I was furious with Brandon Leary for being such a disappointing creep, and with myself for being such a wannabe star-fucker. And I couldn't even do that right!

It was a balmy night, and the house was quiet. I decided to head out to the pool house to try and write off my rage. I was picking my way across the lawn steps when a shadow of a man appeared as if from nowhere, and I screamed.

'Sorry, I'm sorry, miss!' He stepped into the light. 'I didn't mean to frighten you!'

The man was a giant, over six foot five, and had long hair tied up in a bun. Tattoos covered his arms, and I could see a well-built chest underneath his vest. If I had to be scared half to death in the dark, I guess it was a good thing the guy scaring me looked like Jason Momoa.

'I'm cleaning the pool. Ms Daniels prefers it to be done at night.'

I thought I could discern an Aussie accent. 'Oh, I didn't know. I got a fright,' I managed.

'Are you Ms Daniels' daughter? I'm Andy,' he said, extending a hand. 'I'm not just a pool guy, I do other things for her as well.'

I cocked an eyebrow. What other things? Robotically, I held out my hand and, when he took it, I didn't want to let it go. Maybe it was the let-down with Brandon, maybe my confidence was knocked, maybe I was just into his man bun, but I suddenly had a vivid erotic waking daydream in which I mounted this man mountain astride a pool chair and had my wicked way with him.

In reality, I was still standing there holding this Andy's hand and staring at him, slack-jawed. Extremely awkwardly, he extracted his palm from my now sweaty clutch.

I started to laugh and found I couldn't stop. Andy joined in at first, but tailed off as I got louder and the noise coming from me started to sound more like a roar than a giggle.

'Uh, I better go . . .' I heard him say. 'It was nice to meet you.'

This was it; I was finally losing my mind. I lay down on the couch by the fire pit and focused on regulating my breathing as I wondered how I'd become the kind of woman who can't meet an attractive stranger without imagining fucking their brains out in the great outdoors.

I don't know how long I lay there after I calmed down, but eventually I started to feel chilly and knew I should head to bed. The entire evening had been oddly distressing. Was I losing control of myself?

I'd gone to Brandon Leary's place basically looking for sex, and when I hadn't got it I'd had a kind of sexual catatonic episode. I was starting to worry myself. Once again, I cursed Jason for upending my life and making me the kind of woman that trawls apps looking for men to ease the loneliness and hurt.

As I made my way back towards the house I thought

I heard a shuffle in the foliage, but nothing appeared. I hoped it wasn't a coyote – Dessie lived in fear of one getting its paws on her beloved Bubbles. Then I heard it again, so I went to investigate.

I found Ariel sitting under a massive banana leaf tree, scrolling frantically on her phone. 'What are you doing?' I hissed. 'And where did you get that?'

'Ssssh,' she hissed. 'It's my burner, duh.'

I dragged her up by the arm and tried to snatch the device, but she was too quick for me. I decided I wasn't wrestling my teenage sister; it had been enough of a day.

'Leave me alone, or I'm telling Mom.'

'One big difference between you and me, Ariel, is that I'm a thirty-nine-year-old adult and you can't get me in trouble with our mom. Now, go to bed.'

'How about *you* go to bed, Portia?' she taunted as she followed me down the hall. 'And if you're such an adult, why don't you act like one instead of embarrassing yourself in front of Andy!' She slammed her bedroom door.

I cringed. For all her cheek, Ariel was right. I needed to get my shit together.

RAYA
Chat with Lamar Phelps
1 July 2022

Lamar Phelps: Hi Portia, nice to match with you. What is it you do?

Portia Daniels: Wow, people in LA just really come out with that question. Okay, I'm a writer.

Lamar Phelps: Nice. Would I have read your stuff? You look familiar.

Portia Daniels: It's mostly for TV. I know you're an agent?

Lamar Phelps: And how do you know that? Are you looking for representation on an app?!

Portia Daniels: You used to work with my brother-in-law.

Lamar Phelps: . . .

Portia Daniels: Billy Schwartz?

Lamar Phelps has left the conversation.

Chat with Brandon Leary
2 July 2022

Brandon Leary: Hi Portia, did you manage to give your mom my details yet?

Portia Daniels has left the conversation.

Chat with Brad Pitt
2 July 2022

Portia Daniels: Hi!

Brad Pitt has left the conversation.

Phinneas McLean: Hi, if you wanna fuck I'm at 1075 Palm Lane.
Portia Daniels: Are you normally that straightforward?
Phinneas McLean: Hey, if it ain't broke . . .
Portia Daniels has left the conversation.

23

In the following days I rose early, working out in an attempt to shake off the gnawing anxiety that enveloped me as soon as I woke up. I was spending night after night tossing and turning, having awful dreams about Jason. In one, Sandra was pregnant with his baby. In another, he'd dropped dead just like my dad.

I'd often wake up crying and sweating, and with a pain in my chest. Once I came to, I knew a disgustingly difficult workout was the only thing that could make me feel remotely human.

I'd get up around 6 a.m. so there was no fear of catching my mother in flagrante delicto again; for all her work ethic and girl-boss vibes, Dessie has never been a morning person, so I'd been exercising as the cock crowed.

One morning I was walking into the kitchen afterwards, dripping with sweat, when I nearly collided with Vinnie. She was wearing the same clothes she had been the night before and looked sheepish to have been caught creeping around at this hour.

'Are you just getting home?' I whispered.

'Yes, but it's not what you think!' She looked very happy. Slightly radiant, even? 'I spent the night talking to India – remember, my old trainer? We saw her out in TomTom last week?'

Ahh, yes. The scene before the crime that had been my date with Brandon Leary.

'We swapped numbers again, we've been chatting. She told

me Billy hit on her like a hundred times, P. That's why she stopped coming around.'

'Well, at least she's somewhat age appropriate,' I huffed.

'Yeah, but he was totally barking up the wrong tree. She's gay.'

I wondered why Vinnie looked pleased about this further confirmation of her husband's loose morals. 'And you're happy about this?'

'Of course not, but I'd always thought I'd done something wrong and that's why we stopped working together. Turns out it was just Billy and his wandering dick.'

I winced. If it were me, I didn't know if I could ever come to terms with Jason having had an adventurous penis. She seemed so blasé.

'Vinnie, did you ever cheat on Billy?'

'Me? No! When would I have time to cheat? I have two kids and a business.' She started a fresh pot of coffee. 'Well, I *had* a business.'

'You seem convinced he was up to no good. I thought maybe you were too.'

'Now I know he's been lying to me I don't believe a word that's ever come out of his goddamn mouth. But Portia, I haven't been interested enough in sex to go looking for it. Work and the boys took up all my time. And I'm not like Billy, anyway. Likes and followers are enough validation for me.' She tried to make a silly face but didn't get there because the idea was so preposterous. I felt so bad for my sister.

'Were you two still sleeping together?'

'Occasionally. What's with the inquisition?'

'I'm just trying to understand . . .' I trailed off.

'Our sex life isn't the reason he started sleeping with teenagers.'

'Of course not!' I was mortified. 'I'd never think that.

I guess I'll just never understand people who cheat, and I'm trying to.'

'I'm sick of talking about him right now, it's harshing my vibe,' Vinnie complained, pouring us both mugs of her favourite blend. 'Back to India. She invited me over last night for some dinner and to catch up, and we ended up just talking all night long. She's amazing,' Vinnie swooned. 'Total girl crush.'

I eyed her mooning around the kitchen. 'Uh, that sounds like just a regular crush, Vin,' I said.

She made a face.

'You don't stay up all night talking to a woman you have a vague non-sexual crush on. Especially if she's into women herself.'

'I have kids, Portia. My time to myself is when they're asleep.' Vinnie looked chastened. I hadn't meant to dampen her mood.

'Sorry, sis,' I said. 'I'm not feeling great this morning . . .'

I was interrupted by our mother appearing at the door, hair matted and eyes wild. 'Lavinia, it's happening!'

'What is?'

'JenKat's sister, Trysta. She's done an interview. It's on the *Call Your Mom* podcast, and it's out in less than an hour.'

We hadn't anticipated a podcast. If Trysta had given an interview to Anderson Cooper, or even Drew Barrymore, we would have been given a heads-up and the right to reply. But independent podcasts didn't play by the rules of traditional media. They'd announced the episode's drop at dawn, and it was going live at 8 a.m. Giulia had received the Google Alert when she woke. Now she was walking in the door. She was livid.

'I was *this close* to getting you an interview with Oprah!' Giulia said to Vinnie. 'And I had Kelly Clarkson lined up as a reserve. I wanted you to do an interview with a broad-caster that has gravitas, a bit of celebrity glamour, and now we get scooped by this . . . *podcast!*' She practically spat the last word.

'It's the smart move,' said Vinnie. Her earlier lightness was fully extinguished, and now she was nibbling at her nails. 'It's what a cool kid would do, and Trysta seems to be one cool kid. "Kid" being the operative word.'

'Darling, I don't think you should listen,' Dessie appealed. 'It will do you no good, so let us.'

'No, Mom. I'm sick to death of saying nothing and wait-ing.' Vinnie was defiant. She stood up, her fists clenched. 'This is the fork in the road. I'll listen, and then I'll go on In-stagram Live and speak to my own followers directly. It's what I should've done already, but I was in shock. The time is now!'

I was amazed at my sister's strength. I looked at Giulia. 'That okay with you?'

'*Bella*, all else has failed. I am officially crappy when it comes to Lavinia. So, you do what you think is best, because you know best,' Giulia said, giving Vinnie's shoulder a squeeze. 'I'm going to watch it in the office, alone.' She stalked out.

Vinnie, Dessie and I settled in to stream the podcast on the big screen. *Call Your Mom* was a huge, billion-dollar interview-style podcast hosted by a bubbly brunette named Louisa Lorenzo. Regularly topping the charts on Spotify and iTunes, it wasn't just audio; accompanying footage was the norm nowadays, even more so for a big tell-all.

We all gasped in unison when Trysta came on the screen. She may have been a legal adult, but she was diminutive, fresh-faced and a natural blonde. It was only when she spoke that her husky voice belied her tender years.

'Thank you for having me to tell my story,' she rasped.

'Thank you, Trysta,' said Louisa. 'Your sister, the incredible

JenKat, will be joining us later to share her side of the sordid tale, but let's start at the beginning. How did you meet Billy Schwartz?'

'He was my sister's agent. Billy had been working with Jen for about eighteen months, helping to build her profile and getting her gigs and jobs after Covid. Her record company looks after the music side of things, but Billy was involved in all her promo and brand deals.'

'So, it was his job to act on her behalf, and in her best interests?'

'Yes. Jen trusted Billy, so I did too.'

'Did you know that Schwartz was married?'

'Yes, to Lavinia Rizzi,' Trysta replied. 'But he told me that they had an arrangement.'

We all sucked in a breath.

'Now, though, I think that's bullshit.'

Collective exhale.

'Why do you say that?'

'Because a) he's full of it. And b) my sister told me so,' Trysta replied. 'She says that Billy's colleagues and clients know that Lavinia wouldn't ever be okay with him dating anyone else, especially somebody my age.'

'Remind our listeners, how old are you, Trysta?'

'I'm eighteen. I just graduated from Malibu High.'

Louisa paused for a moment, and let that sink in. 'Tell us how your relationship with Billy developed.'

'A few months ago, I was backstage at *Jimmy Kimmel*. Jen was the musical guest. I'd always thought Billy was cute, and that evening he was wearing a nice suit and seemed busy and important. But that was the first time he paid me any attention. While Jen was on stage, he sat with me and we talked. About regular stuff, mostly. But then he asked me if I'd ever been with an older guy. I said, sure; my sister is a celebrity, so

I've dated some athletes and other singers. But then he said, how about anyone my age? Then he asked me to guess his age, and seemed kinda annoyed when I got it right, but in, like, a flirty way?'

Trysta stopped speaking then, and Louisa gently coaxed her to go on.

'He asked me out to dinner after the show. Jen had to get home; she was on a red-eye to New York the next morning. I didn't tell her who I was meeting, just that I had a date and would uber home later. She told me to be safe, and to call her when I got home. We went for a drink in this dive near the studio, just Billy and me. And after a couple of hours of talking, I knew I really liked him. He was cute, kind and really funny. He made me laugh. He gave me a ride home, and that was it. All very PG 13.'

'Didn't you wonder why a forty-one-year-old man was interested in taking you, who's not even legal, for a drink?'

Trysta narrowed her eyes. 'I'm not naive, Louisa,' she said. 'I might be young, but I grew up in LA. I've been going out for years. And I know what guys like. It's the whole blonde hair, sexy voice thing.'

'Okay, fair. So, what happened next?'

'We followed each other on Instagram, we messaged back and forth for a few weeks. It was just basic flirty stuff – fire emojis and heart eyes sometimes, compliments and shooting the breeze other times. I followed Lavinia, saw her gorgeous pictures of their family, and presumed he just wanted his ego stroked by me. I thought they were happy. Then Billy told me that his wife and sons were going to New York for a long weekend, that he'd have the place to himself. He invited me over.'

'That fucking bastard,' Vinnie whispered. 'That's when I was staying with you,' she said to me, and I nodded.

219

'I went over, and one thing led to another,' Trysta was saying.

'You mean, you had sex?'

'Yes. But not just sex. We had dinner, we watched a movie. I slept over, and he made me breakfast the next morning after we had sex again.'

'Did Billy definitely know that you were eighteen years old? A senior in high school?'

'Yes, we talked about my future and if I might go to college after a year out. I love to act, and he talked about representing me, maybe putting me in JenKat's next video with a romantic lead. Jen hates playing opposite guys, but I love it.'

'Did you feel that, even without the age discrepancy, there was a power imbalance?'

'Not really. I mean, it would have been great to get an agent, but he's not the only one in town. I was conscious that he was married, that things could get messy. And then they did.'

'How did they get messy?'

Trysta's eyes filled with tears. 'A couple of weeks later, I told him I might be pregnant.'

Vinnie let out a scream. My mother put her head in her hands. This was worse, much worse, than we'd imagined. Louisa cut to a commercial break, to maximize the drama. We all held our breath until it was over.

'Are you pregnant, Trysta?'

'No,' she said, and I sagged with relief. 'I never was; it was a false alarm. I was just late, and I panicked and asked him to meet me at the beach. But by the time I took a negative test at the doctor's, the damage was done. By then, he'd left his wife, left LA.'

'Do you think he told his wife that he thought you were pregnant?'

'No, I know that he didn't. Because I threatened to, and

he begged me not to. I never even got to tell him that I was wrong, that I'm not having a baby; he's been off the grid ever since that night.'

'What do you want to say to Lavinia, Trysta?'

'I want to tell her that I'm sorry. I knew he was married, and I didn't care. It was only when I thought I might be having his baby and saw his reaction that I knew how terrible it would be for her. He was like a wild animal, ranting and raving about me ruining his career and his family.'

'Why do you think he took off?'

'Because I know now that all of this is shameful, that he must be deeply ashamed. The other young women that have come forward, we were all under his spell. But it's not okay to be sleeping with teenagers when you're in your forties, even if you're not married with kids. If I had been pregnant, he'd have left me high and dry, and he deceived his wife and everyone else around him. Instead of holding his hands up and being a man, he's just disappeared.'

'That's very mature of you, Trysta.'

'Like I said, I'm from LA. I've had a lot of therapy in my life, and even more lately.'

'That's fair. Okay, we'll be right back after this commercial break with Trysta and her sister, JenKat.'

I looked at Vinnie. She had pink blotches on her cheeks, but her eyes were bright. 'Am I deluded, or did all of that just vindicate me?' she asked.

'I think it went some of the way there, sweetheart,' Dessie answered. 'It's still awful, and we're still tainted by association. But that girl just did us a favour she didn't have to do, no doubt.'

My sister nodded. My mom's assurance unlocked something in her because silent tears started to slide down her face.

The second part of the interview was less explosive.

JenKat told how she found out about Trysta and Billy messaging when she saw a DM from him on her phone and started asking around town about his true character. Quickly, she realized that her beloved agent, Mr Schwartz, wasn't the reputable guy he presented himself as.

'What do you think of LRS in all of this?' asked Louisa.

'I was sad about his wife's public response, because I wanted her to acknowledge the young women who have suffered due to her husband's indiscretions,' she said, in her characteristic drawl. 'I'm twenty-three, and he never tried anything with me. Maybe I'm too old, too weird, for his tastes.' She shrugged. 'But I do not agree with any backlash against Lavinia Rizzi-Schwartz – women should not have to pay for, or even apologize for, the actions of men. We've seen it with Kim and Kanye, with Harvey Weinstein and his wife, Georgina. Predators, liars and inciters of hatred and violence should be held to account, not the wives who have the misfortune to love them.'

Dessie and I clapped. Vinnie was still leaking tears, but she'd developed a resolute expression as JenKat spoke.

The interview wound up with Trysta saying she and Jen had a new, reputable agent, and she was in fact playing the love interest in her sister's new video. 'I guess I should thank Billy for that idea,' she grinned.

Vinnie went to the bathroom to splash cold water on her face. Dessie's phone was already lit up, but we'd agreed to let Vinnie handle it herself, so she was studiously ignoring it and started giving herself a manicure for something to do with her hands.

My sister picked up her phone, got comfy on the couch outside and opened the Instagram app. Mom and I joined the live from the kitchen island so we could hear what she was saying.

'Hello, my friends,' Vinnie started. 'I want to begin by apologizing for my own shortcomings lately. I've shared my life with you all for many years, and you've been loyal and wonderful. I should have made more of an effort to communicate with you all when my life imploded over Memorial Day weekend. But I was in a great deal of shock, and it's difficult to know how to navigate things when you are both numb and in a lot of pain.'

She took a deep, shaky breath. 'I want to thank Trysta and JenKat for their words on this morning's broadcast. I haven't spoken to either of them since news of my husband's disappearance spread, and for that, I am sorry. But I didn't know how they would receive me, or what I would even say.

'Like all of you, I heard their story for the first time this morning. I learned of my husband's affair, which is by all accounts just one of many, from a note he left on our bed on the day he left. He said that he had been cheating with a much younger woman, and that it had blown up in his face. He said he was sorry, and that's the only contact I've had with him since. I went to our closet, and his things were gone.

'Like you, I am shocked and appalled at my husband abusing his position of power and authority to hook up with young women. I am utterly disgusted that this went on under my own roof while I was away with our sons. I am all the things you might expect me to be – hurt, galled, violated, angry, upset and terrified. But I am a strong woman. As Jen said, I won't let the actions of the man I chose to marry reflect on me or define me.

'I was afraid to condemn him in case it affected our children, but now I see that, sadly, our boys will learn what kind of man their father is regardless. Part of me even hoped that Billy would be vindicated, or that he would show up to face the music. But he has been gone now for weeks, without a word to defend himself, to apologize to his family or his partners, or to the young women he deceived.

'Just so I am very clear – I did not know about these young women. I did not encourage or condone him cheating, and we didn't have an open relationship. I certainly had no idea that he was pursuing high-school-aged girls. His actions may technically be legal, but they are immoral. He is also a coward, leaving us all to fend for ourselves in the aftermath of a scandal of his own making.

'Wherever he is, I'm sure he knows that the tabloids and online commenters have been decimating my character because he's not here to take the fall. I'm sure he knows he has inflicted pain and damage on several families. I will be filing for divorce immediately. I will let the courts decide if Billy is a fit enough parent to be around his sons in the future. I am officially finished with him, and I am taking back control of my own life. Thank you for listening.'

Vinnie signed off and came into the kitchen, where Mom and I whooped and hollered and smothered her in kisses. Giulia emerged from the office clapping, with red eyes. She took Vinnie's face in her hands. '*Brava, bella.* That was perfect.'

Vinnie looked depleted, but relieved. Whatever way her speech was perceived, she had spoken her truth, and it had set her free.

'Right,' Dessie said, rubbing her hands. 'I'm calling in the pros. Let's get this divorce on the road. Giulia, can you get me Laura Wasser?'

Vinnie spent the rest of the morning talking to the boys. She wanted to pre-empt what Si and Seb might pick up on out in the world and tell them that their dad's heretofore unexplained absence may go on for a good while longer.

The fact that they took it so well was testament to Vinnie's amazing relationship with her children, and Billy's status as a loving but largely absentee father.

Dessie, Giulia and I were monitoring the news cycle. The story was dominating online media worldwide, with reporters frothing at the mouth not only about Trysta's interview but also Vinnie's immediate response. So far, every major outlet was positive about my sister's diatribe.

'Lavinia handles herself with style and grace,' said *Us Weekly*, while the hashtag #WeLoveLavinia was trending on Twitter.

JenKat had called too, and Mom was in the process of setting up a sit-down for that afternoon with Vinnie and the two sisters. 'And afterwards, we're going out to celebrate,' said Dessie. 'We will sit in the Polo Lounge in full view of everyone in Hollywood, with our heads held high. Let them talk!'

BlindGossip.com

10 July 2022

Which A-list influencer thinks that the coast is clear now she's addressed the elephant in the room? Well, she's mistaken. There's a lot more to come out in the wash about her skeevy husband!

Comments (673):

SxcBB23: Watch out, princess Lavinia!

JenKatStan: Maybe we should just leave her alone now.

LUVLRS: What more can this woman endure??? I'm worried about her!

PrincessH8er: Lavinia can suck it. She's done, over, cancelled by association.

Tanya22379: I hate her stupid face.

GoodTimeGal: I heard that she's started a secret cult. And I kinda want to join tbqh

24

'And he put my hand on what I can only describe as a limp, soft member . . .'

The table erupted as I recounted my non-date with Brandon Leary. It felt like an eon had passed since all of that had happened, but it hadn't even been a fortnight.

Vinnie's chat with JenKat and Trysta that afternoon had gone as well as it could. When they turned up at the house that afternoon, I'd been struck by how young they both were in person, especially Jen, without her trademark raccoon eyeliner. Pop stars that seem larger than life in videos and on the red carpet wearing couture are just people, and often very young ones with a lot of pressure on their shoulders.

There was a lot of crying and hugging between the three of them, as well as the exchanging of numbers and noting of important dates Vinnie would need for her divorce filing. Forget no contest, Vinnie was filing on the basis of adultery. The trio even took a sombre selfie, for posterity, if not to post right away.

Now, the family was settled in a booth in the Polo Lounge. It's my mom's favourite place, at the Beverly Hills Hotel, and it reeks of old-school Hollywood glamour. We had to stop her ordering the ridiculous $2,000 Anniversary McCarthy salad, which comes with twenty-four-carat gold leaf, caviar and lobster, and a souvenir plate. Dessie loves a gimmick.

The whole gang was there, except Ariel, Seb and Si, who were under Marjorie's control for the evening; my mother, Manuel, Vinnie, David, Giulia, Suz and Natasha, who was technically still on the clock and monitoring my mother's calls and emails. I felt safe, cocooned with people I loved.

It was Suz's night off, and she was crying laughing at my Raya experience from hell. 'I'm sorry, Portia. This is all my fault, but it is totally hilarious.' She wiped her eyes.

'Look, it's a story to tell someone else's grandkids,' I quipped. I was enjoying myself: the champagne was flowing, the food was delicious and the atmosphere jovial after Vinnie's vindication.

'Darling, if you don't want him, can I call him?' Dessie asked, and we all erupted again.

As we ordered another bottle of champagne, Vinnie texted me from across the table.

India is coming to meet me for a drink and a debrief.

I raised my eyebrows at her, and she shrugged. It was good she had someone she could trust outside the family.

After a luscious dessert of the lounge's infamous chocolate soufflé, some of the elders peeled off into the night. Dessie, David, Suz, Natasha and I were chatting when we noticed Vinnie returning from the restroom, accompanied by the dazzling India. I don't think I'd ever seen a better-looking woman; India was utterly stunning in a body-skimming black minidress that looked like SKIMS. She was all soft brown skin, long hair and toned, endless legs.

'Are they holding hands?' David wheezed.

'Girls can hold hands, Dave,' I snapped, trying to get a better look myself.

Dessie was snooping on my Raya. 'This is mad – you only get fifteen swipes a day? And they charge you for more?'

'It's a smart business model, I guess,' Natasha said. 'Suz, can you get me on it?'

'I mean this with love, baby, but you're not enough of a somebody.' The younger girl pouted.

'Why aren't you on it?' I asked.

'Because I'm too much of a somebody!' She laughed. 'I was a member in the early days, before the press knew about it. But I got off, because I could foresee the headlines . . . "Late-night host scours app for elite sex!" The network would love that.'

I was half watching Vinnie and India when I noticed an older man in one of the other booths who looked vaguely familiar. He was staring right at me and gave a little wave in our direction.

'I *knew* he was looking at you!' David said. 'Portia, don't you recognize him?'

'Sort of . . . ?'

'That's Chris Adams! You know, the Marvel dude? He's like the eldest of the Hot Superhero Chris gang.'

'Oh shit!' Natasha squealed. 'He plays the sexy dad that's kind of a bad guy! I love him!'

I hadn't recognized Chris Adams with hair; in the Marvel movies, he's bald and built like a brick shithouse, as my mother would say. This guy was average-sized with a full head of salt-and-pepper hair, and some artful stubble.

'OMG, he's coming over!' David whispered. 'Act cool!'

Chris appeared at the table. He was even better-looking up close, with kind, crinkly eyes and a gorgeous smile. 'Suzanna,' he said, in a smooth-as-butter voice. 'It's great to see you.'

Suz slid out of the booth and kissed him on both cheeks. Of course she knew him; Suz has interviewed every major movie star there is, twice over. She introduced us all, leaving me till last.

Chris leaned in and kissed my hand, keeping eye contact. 'Portia, what a beautiful name.'

I tittered awkwardly, momentarily thrown off by the charisma that seemed to be radiating from his pores.

'Would you do me the honour of having a drink with me at the bar?' Chris asked me.

I looked around the table and saw everybody nodding. 'Sure,' I managed. 'Let me just visit the ladies, and I'll meet you there.'

I half ran across the beautiful hotel lobby to the restroom, and when safely locked in a cubicle took out my phone. Google told me that Chris Adams was fifty-eight years old, twice divorced and highly eligible. I'd never had a drink one on one with a man old enough to be my father before, and I was intrigued.

Chris had been something of an action star in the eighties, appearing alongside Tom Cruise and Kurt Russell, and these days he was on the Marvel payroll quite happily, voicing video games and animated spin-offs as well as appearing in the flesh. His last big relationship had been with his second wife, a fellow actress named Kayla Stines. I recognized her from playing the best friend slash sidekick in a variety of romcoms. Chris had three grown-up kids, and no salacious scandals following him around the internet. Okay, I was game.

After reapplying my lipstick and brushing my hair, I strutted back out to the bar, where Chris was waiting. 'Would you join me for a Martini?' he asked smoothly. This guy was suave.

'Sure, extra dirty with three olives,' I told the barman, who disappeared to make the drinks.

'I noticed you from across the room,' Chris said, and I laughed.

'There's a line I haven't heard in a while!'

'I know, it sounds corny, but it's true. And when I saw you were with the effervescent Suzanna, I had to go and introduce myself. It's lovely to meet you, Portia.'

'And you,' I said, clinking glasses with him.

We whiled away an hour, swapping stories. He told me about his work, which he clearly adored, and I told him about mine. 'I'm going through a dry patch at the moment, though.' I shrugged, taking a long sip of my drink.

'And why is that?'

'A long story, involving a broken heart and subsequent lack of inspiration.'

He nodded. 'I've been there. But tell me, what would you do if you knew you wouldn't fail?'

Nobody had ever asked me that before, although I had seen it printed on one of Vinnie's LRS Manifestation Cards, only $39. I was at a loss for words when asked such a deep question directly.

'Forgive me if I'm being presumptuous here, Portia, but from what I can gather, you're quite a lucky and privileged woman, yes? You're not desperate for work, for money, for a roof over your head?'

I nodded. 'Of course, I know I'm not a starving artist, and I'm grateful that I'm able to flee my home and shack up at my mother's palace . . .'

'Right, and you say you're getting itchy feet and feeling uninspired. So, now is the time to ask yourself, what is it you really want to do with the rest of your life? You have time, there's no pressure – what is it that you want to write?'

'A romantic comedy,' I answered right away. 'But a good one. Not something fluffy or silly, or where you can see the ending a mile off. I've always wanted to write a sort of *When Harry Met Sally* for the millennial generation. I've been trying to get back into it lately, but it's proving tricky.'

'Then that is what you'll do.' He smiled. 'Just keep trying until it clicks.'

I liked this guy. In the time I'd been talking to him, I'd felt present and at ease, possibly for the first time since that wretched baby shower in Ireland. I felt a million miles away from it all now.

'Chris, I'm going to go now because, all of a sudden, I've a strong desire to be in front of my laptop,' I said, putting down my glass. 'But thank you so much for the drink and the conversation, and here's my number if you'd ever like to do it again.'

I scribbled my digits on a napkin, shook his hand and strolled into the night. It was all remarkably civilized and what I thought dating as an adult would be like – almost enough to erase the memory of Brandon Leary's flaccid penis in my hand.

The rest of the gang had dispersed so I walked the thirty minutes home, enjoying the balmy midnight air. My mind was abuzz with what Chris Adams had said, and I was itching to sit down and let it all out.

I let myself into Dessie's house and heard voices in the kitchen. It was Vinnie and India, whisking a bowl of something and looking very cosy indeed.

'Hey, P! You remember India?' my sister chirped.

I smiled and shook the trainer's hand, noting how firm her grip was.

'We're making protein pancakes. Would you like one?' India offered.

'Oh, I'm totally stuffed and I've got some work to do, so I'll leave you ladies to it.'

It was good to see Vinnie energized. It had been a huge day for her, emotionally draining no doubt, but India was putting a pep in her step. I was again glad Vinnie had a new friend – and a super-healthy, sober one at that.

I wrote in the pool house until three in the morning. My hands were cramped from my frantic typing, where I filled page after page with ideas, outlines, dialogue and instructions for my romcom. An idea was crystallizing in my mind, one I knew would shake up the plot point I'd been stuck on for years.

When I looked at my phone, there was a message from an unsaved number.

Great to meet you tonight, Portia. I would love to take you for dinner soon – let me know when suits? CA

It was a classic older-guy move to sign off texts with his initials – Manny does the same. But I would have known this was Chris Adams from the gentlemanly vibe regardless. No messing around, making his intentions clear. I felt a buzz of excitement in my chest. I would text back and accept in the morning and make a date.

I'd become fond of my bed in the main house over the last few days, so I yawned, stretched and decided to head back there. I found Vinnie and India watching a movie – or at least India was, as my sister was asleep with her head in her friend's lap. I mimed a goodnight to India, who waved back.

I spreadeagled on the bed, and noted that, for the first time in ages, I was genuinely feeling okay. Motivated, inspired, energized, and if not exactly happy, then at least not depressed. I didn't dare hope that this new project might be the kick I needed to get me out of my funk. I fell asleep feeling hopeful.

25

The hopeful feeling didn't last long. I woke up a few mornings later to find my mother sitting on the end of my bed, looking serious.

'What is it?' I bolted up. 'Is it Ariel again? Is Vinnie okay?'

'Sssh, pet, relax. Everyone is safe.' She handed me a coffee.

'Okay, then why are you watching me sleep, looking like the Grim Reaper?' I asked, exasperated.

'Well, I've had some news from your Auntie Rosalind. She's friends with David's cousin Martha, who's Sandra O'Malley's aunt?'

I nodded, slowly. When an Irish person got going with connections, it could take a while.

Dessie sighed. 'You're not going to like it, Portia. But they're saying Sandra has left her husband and run off with Jason.'

This time, I managed to avoid ruining the sheets, and spit the coffee back into the mug.

'Tell me everything,' I spluttered.

And so she did, recanting her entire conversation with Rosalind. As the eldest sister of the Daniels clan, Rosalind's the head honcho and chief local gossip back home. She works in the local doctor's surgery in Killarney and knows everything about everyone in the entire county of Kerry, and most of Limerick too.

She had heard through the grapevine that Sandra had indeed left her husband, Mick, and taken the kids with her. The rumour mill said it was because she was in love with his

234

younger brother Jason, *my* Jason, and that they were shacked up somewhere remote together.

'I wanted to corroborate this before I came to you, so I got David on the case. He's in Las Vegas this week, but he wants to FaceTime. Is that okay?'

I nodded, mute. I'd had my suspicions about Jason and Sandra – more than just suspicions – but leaving Mick? Shacking up? This was more than I could take.

David's face appeared on Dessie's screen, his head covered in bleach. 'Going blonde, are we?' she asked drily.

'It's the only way to get the hot young guys these days, Des. Believe me, I wish it wasn't the case. It's stinging the shite out of my poor scalp!'

'David, I'm with Portia. Tell her what you told me.'

I struggled to take his grave expression seriously, topped off as it was by a crown of peroxide. But he at least tried to hide the pain in his eyes as his scalp likely blistered away.

'Okay, P. It is not confirmed that Sandra and Jason are in fact together anywhere. She has definitely left Mick and taken the kids, but the rest is just idle gossip because he hasn't been spotted around the town. If he is still in Ireland, hopefully he's just laying low and not actually riding his sister-in-law.'

I flinched. '*Sorry,*' David protested. 'My head is distracting me. Anyway, I have people back home on the case. So, let's not worry too much for now? I have to go rinse; I'll call you later.'

As the screen went black, Dessie turned to me with a smile. 'There! I knew Rosalind was exaggerating. She can be a silly bitch like that.'

'Mom, it's hardly good news? Why else would Sandra have left Mick? Why would Jason be hiding out?' I fell backwards and keened. '*Why is my life like thissssss?* It's not a fucking soap opera! This is meant to be reality.'

Dessie stroked my head. 'Sometimes truth is stranger than fiction, my love. I've learned that the hard way.'

Somehow, I must have fallen back to sleep because, when I woke up a couple of hours later, I was absolutely livid. Just when things were starting to go okay, just when there was light at the end of the tunnel with Vinnie and I was enjoying my work again, everything was going to shit once more. At that moment, I rued the day I ever laid eyes on Jason Dempsey. Then, in my troubled mind, that became my mother's fault.

If she wasn't such an attention seeker, she wouldn't be on a reality show and I wouldn't have fallen head over heels for her sexy Irish producer. Not for the first time, I cursed my parents for having me. Why couldn't I have been born into a nice, normal family? Why wasn't I 'belonging to' Auntie Rosalind, as Dessie would say, the spinster maven of the family? I'd have had a lovely life in her house. Ordinary, content, comfortable.

Instead, my life was the exact opposite. Privileged, undeniably. But with that luxury came a whole heap of its own unique shit. Paparazzi and pop stars, cheating husbands and wayward partners, reality television, tabloids and social media. Gossip was universal, but everything was heightened in Dessie Daniels' orbit, and I was feeling very hard done by.

I was back to thinking about Jason and Sandra together on a loop, only this time it was much worse. This wasn't images of forlorn people sending long, yearning emails flitting across the Atlantic – this was illicit rendezvous and dramatic love-making in vivid Technicolor. I was utterly disgusted by it all and couldn't shake the image of them in a passionate clinch out of my mind's eye.

If he had wanted a woman like Sandra, why had he been

with me for nearly seven years? Why had he ever left Ireland if Sandra was his type? Was I just an exotic stopgap before his real life began, a fun and shiny plaything with a direct line to glitz and glamour, until he got bored and returned home to PTA meetings, coaching football and going to the local on a Friday night? I felt dirty, like I'd been used for a distraction until he grew up.

If was honest with myself, I had been wondering why I hadn't heard from Jason at all since he'd been home. We used to talk all day every day, and it had been radio silence. I'd thought he might be giving me space, respecting my boundaries. Now I knew. This was the crisis he needed to go home and tend to. This was the final nail in the coffin of our relationship.

I had a sudden thought that made my stomach lurch. Was Sandra who Jason truly wanted to have babies with? Would he go so far as knocking up his brother's wife? Have his nieces and nephews be half-siblings to his spawn?

I felt like I was going to be sick. It was all so . . . depraved.

I went in search of Vinnie and found her doing something she hadn't done in a long time – filming a beauty and skin care look for her social media. 'Hey, sis!' she trilled, pausing the recording. I noticed she had all her professional gadgets in situ.

'When did you move all that stuff over here?' I asked.

'India helped me bring it all over from Hidden Hills this morning. I felt like making a video. *Vogue* asked me to do their *Get Ready with Me* series.'

'Why here, though? You have your own new fabulous house, with a studio. And all your stuff is there, all the boys' stuff?'

She paused the recording, turned, and looked at me.

'I will never live in that house again. God knows how many

girls Billy had sex with under that roof! It may have been featured in *Architectural Digest*, but it's sullied for me now.' She turned back. 'Besides, the boys know the community and love it here, and I know Mom loves having us all. At least until I figure things out. Marjorie is going to move into the pool house for a while.'

There went my writing refuge, but I didn't even have the headspace to complain in that moment. If Vinnie, Silas and Sebastian were happy here, well, that's all that mattered.

'Anyway, you're a fine one to talk. Why aren't you hotfooting it back to New York, now Jason isn't there and I'm okay?'

She mustn't have heard the latest, or she wouldn't have mentioned his name. But she did have a point. Why was I hanging out in LA when my real life was supposed to be back on the East Coast? My apartment was sitting empty, my plants would all be dead – it wasn't even like I was friendly enough with Frida to ask her to check on things there, and Amy was too pregnant to bother.

I didn't have an answer. I guess Dessie's house did feel like something of a safe haven. Suz was here, David was spending more and more time here, and it was nice waking up every day and seeing my whole family. Except . . .

'Does Ariel know you have all this stuff here?'

She made a face. 'No, and don't tell her. She'll break in and start messing everything up. I've caught her sneaking around at all hours of the day and night.'

'I have too!' I exclaimed. 'I keep meaning to tell Mom about it, is she here?'

'Nope, she and Manny took Ariel to some therapist in the Valley before school. Ariel was screeching about being dragged to the seventh circle of hell and demanding to be home-schooled through twelfth grade.'

I shuddered.

'I'm going to finish this and then take the boys to the Grove with India, do you want to come?'

'Nah, I'm not in the mood for shopping. You're spending a lot of time with her,' I noted, keeping my tone neutral.

Vinnie smiled. 'She's amazing, P. India is all about energy and looking after yourself from the inside out. I want Silas and Sebastian to just be around her chill vibes and healthy attitude, you know?'

'Sure, and it seems to be doing you some good too.'

'It's just easy. Like I said, she's amazing. I feel like India is who I've been pretending to be for the best part of a decade. And with her, I'm just myself.'

What could I say? The way I felt about straight men at that moment, maybe hanging out solely with women and gay guys was the way to go.

But I had made a date for early that evening with the handsome Chris Adams, and I didn't want to cancel it – it was something to do besides ruminate, and it might get me out of my own head. We were meeting at 6 p.m.; I'd made an early-bird special joke, which didn't exactly land via text. But it was amusing that my older man wanted to eat so early – it was giving pensioner vibes.

I spent the afternoon getting ready, taking my time so I wasn't wondering what position Jason was making love to Sandra in at that very moment, or thinking about how her kids felt about Uncle J. sleeping in their mammy's bed. Every time it crossed my mind, I felt like puking.

I took a long bath, blaring Carly Simon's Greatest Hits. I was going to make myself look good, so maybe I'd feel it. I shaved, buffed, moisturized and exfoliated. I used a lot of Dessie's expensive La Prairie body lotion and did a 111SKIN sheet mask. I plucked, polished and even slathered on the Freckle bronzer I'd worn when impersonating my sister.

239

I straightened my hair, glossy after a treatment, and took extra care with my make-up. For once, my eyeliner behaved and my wings were perfect. By the time I strutted out of Dessie's closet in borrowed shoes and a pilfered dress, I felt a million bucks – on the outside, at least. My silver fox wouldn't know what hit him.

His reaction didn't disappoint. We were meeting at the London hotel for cocktails before heading to Craig's. Chris had told me he was a vegan, and loved the food there – plus, his Marvel trainer approved of the menu.

His eyes roamed over my body; I was wearing one of Dessie's vintage Tom Ford dresses, black and slinky with cut-outs on a tight bodice, and long earrings that drew the eye down. It gave the appearance of cleavage, even on me. Teamed with sky-high Christian Louboutin lace pumps and all my grooming, I had to admit I could understand why heads swivelled when I entered the hotel.

It didn't matter, though. I felt hollow inside, unnatural even. I hadn't given Jason what he'd wanted so desperately. Was there something wrong with me? Was I odd?

No! I had to snap out of that train of thought: it was dangerous.

I pasted on a happy face and beamed at Chris Adams, looking fabulous himself in a dark suit and pale blue shirt. He had a nice, light tan, perfectly manicured fingernails and an easy air about him. I was going to enjoy myself if it was the last thing I did.

'So, how is the writing going?' he asked cheerfully, and I burst into tears. I was mortified, having done more crying in the past few months than in the twenty years previous, but I couldn't stop. Poor Chris looked horrified, guiding me away from prying eyes at the bar and towards a secluded table.

'I'm sorry, I'm so sorry,' I was saying. He pulled a clean

handkerchief from his pocket and handed it to me. I blew my nose loudly.

'You can talk to me, Portia. I know we just met, but you can trust me.'

And I just felt like I could. As an older man, I knew he'd been around the block himself. I found myself telling him everything.

'Wow, that's quite a pickle,' he said when I'd finished, revealing a hint of the native Texas accent disguised by decades in Hollywood. I laughed, despite myself.

'Poor, poor Portia. I'm sorry you've been so badly disappointed. It happens to the best of us.'

'It does?'

'Of course! My first wife ran off with my best friend, who was a stunt man. And my second, well, she was deceitful in a different way. She liked to gamble a little too much.'

I gasped. 'My father was a gambler!'

'I know. Well, I'd read about it around the time I was begging Kayla to go to rehab. She wasn't into high-stakes poker, her downfall was online betting, and also extreme shopping. She could lose or spend a hundred grand overnight, and I had no idea because she had her own accounts from her movie work. It broke my heart when it all came out in the wash.'

I felt a sudden kinship with this man. He was kind, empathetic, and it helped that he was incredibly handsome. I felt safe beside him, like we had a different kind of chemistry than I'd experienced before.

'Why do you like me?' I blurted out, mortified the second the words left my lips.

He laughed. 'Well, initially I liked that you were beautiful and seemed like a lot of fun,' he said, looking into my eyes. 'And now I see we have a lot in common too.'

Chris took my hand. 'Look, I've learned to be upfront

241

about myself and my life. I want to tell you that I'm not looking for a wife, Portia. I've had two of those, and I've had my children. I'm looking for companionship, sex, fun. And I'm looking for a woman that I can talk to. Now, you've been through a lot in the last few months, so I'm not going to pressure you. In fact, I want you to forget about dinner, and go home tonight to rest.'

I protested, but he held his hands up. 'I insist. I want this to maybe go somewhere, and that means being wise enough to let you heal before it becomes a thing. Okay?'

I felt burned. I'd imagined myself having an elegant meal with him, taking my mind off everything thanks to his easy manner and intellectual conversation. And then I'd thought about him taking me home and unzipping my dress, worshipping my body. Okay, I was thirty-nine and not twenty-five, but I was in good shape and I thought a man in his late fifties would appreciate me.

I knew logically that Chris Adams wasn't rejecting me, he was respecting me. But it didn't feel like it in that moment.

26

Too antsy to go home, I told Chris I'd had friends waiting nearby in case things went left. 'Modern dating, you know?' I offered, weakly. He'd kissed me goodbye chastely, on the cheek.

I waited in the booth for fifteen minutes so the valet would bring his car and, once I was sure Chris was gone, I attempted to totter elegantly back to the bar. I so wasn't a high-heels girl. Once there, I ordered another extremely dirty Martini, and then another. I was losing the run of myself, and I just didn't care.

I had to give him credit: Chris Adams had laid his cards on the table. In many ways, we were looking for the exact same thing – love, respect, happiness. But when he said it like he had, it all seemed profoundly unromantic. Like an agreement, an arrangement – the thing Vinnie had been accused of having in her marriage.

Maybe I wanted to be wooed. Maybe I needed to feel like a man wanted to be my everything. When I was younger and I met Jason, I was so wary of men offering me the world and weary when they didn't live up to their promises. In being so upfront with Jason about my lack of expectations, maybe I'd given him the wrong impression and let him off the hook entirely. I'd meant it when I told him I wouldn't be waiting for a ring, or to be his wife. But maybe I'd spoken too soon. Maybe I deserved the whole package regardless.

I didn't need a piece of paper declaring us to be soulmates or even legal partners, but perhaps it was worth having after all. Perhaps the solemnity of marriage would have forced us to address issues as they arose, or to communicate when our paths diverged. As heartbroken as I was now, I wasn't getting a divorce, with the gravitas that brought to the situation. I wasn't even separated. I was a woman pushing forty with yet another ex-boyfriend, and an offer of sex and companionship on the table from a charming older man.

The truth was, I'd just never wanted to be a traditional bride, a traditional person. Maybe because my mom was married three times, and I never wanted children, I just thought the whole white-wedding thing was pointless. But there were other ways to get married without diamonds and bachelorette parties. Why hadn't I just done that? Who was I trying to fool with my 'I'm not like other girls' act?

As I drained my Martini, I felt indescribably sad. I was suddenly worried that I'd messed things up with Jason right from that first night, that this was inevitable and all my fault. Maybe I'd misrepresented myself; in trying to communicate my lack of desire for motherhood, I'd let on that I was too cool to be a wife.

And because Jason and I had never broached marriage, we'd never talked deeply about the things people getting hitched do – *Are you totally sure you never want kids? What would happen if you change your mind? Do we need a pre-nup?*

In the middle of a WeHo hotspot hotel, I buried my head in my arms on the bar. It felt so heavy, so burdened with unwelcome thoughts, that I just couldn't keep it upright. After a minute, I felt a hand on my shoulder. I was certain it was going to be the manager, telling me I was desecrating his glamorous establishment with my emotions. But when I turned around, I was looking into the grey eyes of Noah Frost.

Only I was in no mood for them, or him. I was smarting,

and men, all men, were the enemy – even cute ones that were great in bed and boosted my ego on social media. He looked concerned, which only irked me further.

'Portia, are you okay? Did something happen?'

I laughed cruelly. 'No, nothing at all. I'm just dressed like a high-class hooker and crying in a bar because everything is hunky-dory!' I yelped, my voice rising. Those Martinis were strong.

'Okay, let's get you home,' he said, taking me by the arm and frog-marching me out of the bar. I noticed then that there was a woman shuffling after us, and realized Noah was on a date. She was your typical Hollywood gal – massive boobs, blonde hair, Ozempic-honed body and plumped-up lips. She was probably in her late twenties and gorgeous, but even so, Noah had me by the arm and was asking the door-man to hail me a cab.

I don't know if I've ever felt as awkward in my life as I did when he insisted on getting into the cab with me and dragged his date along too. 'Portia, this is Sara,' he said graciously as we crammed into the back seat together. Through my tears, I managed to shake her hand. It was clammy.

When we got to Dessie's and the guard waved us through the gates, Noah insisted on seeing me in. 'You're not get-ting a repeat performance,' I hissed meanly at him as he helped me out of the car. 'Or a threesome, if that's what you're angling for! I don't care how much you flirt with me via emojis.'

'I'm just making sure you don't break your neck,' he replied curtly, slipping the driver a fifty and asking him to wait. Who even carried cash any more, my drunk brain wondered.

I scrabbled for my keys in my vintage Guy Laroche purse, a flea-market find on a trip to Paris with Jason. Everything reminded me of Jason.

When I found them, Noah took them off me and easily opened the door.

We walked into a scene of domestic bliss – Vinnie and India were surrounded by fresh produce, cooking up a storm, while the boys sat obediently colouring at the island in their pyjamas.

'Oh, give me a *break*!' I barked, before Noah steered me down the hall.

'You remember where my room is, then,' I said. 'Okay, you got me home, Mr Hero Man.' I kicked off the ridiculous shoes and tried to wriggle out of my dress, but I couldn't reach the zip, so I flopped dramatically on to the bed.

'Are you going to be okay?' Noah asked.

'Yeah, yeah. Get back to your date.'

'I mean it, Portia. You were in a bit of a state back there.'

'Well, of course I am! My life is in tatters! I hate everything!'

He didn't reply, but feeling his weight on the bed beside me was somehow calming, and eventually my tears subsided. I looked up at him, not even daring to consider how much snot and mascara was on my face. 'I can't get my dress off,' I sniffled pathetically.

'Allow me,' Noah said.

I struggled up, and as soon as his fingers touched my skin I felt warmth flooding through my body. He was sitting behind me as I held my hair off the nape of my neck, and if he were to kiss me there, I would have let him. I didn't care about the girl waiting in the taxi, or about anything else. But he cleared his throat and stood up.

'Who's that with your sister?' he asked, suddenly all business.

'Why do you care? Are you looking to cross off another line on your Daniels family bingo card?'

He ignored me. 'I saw photos of them come through on

the wire earlier. They were at the Grove with the kids, and they looked . . . well, they looked a lot like they did just now in the kitchen. And . . .'

'And what?'

'Well, it's rare for paps to be at the Grove unless there's an event on, or someone calls them. And we got an anonymous tip that Lavinia had been spending time with someone unexpected. The tipster said they had "intimate photos" but then went quiet when we pressed.'

'Does my mother know about this?'

'I told Giulia,' he said, and shrugged. 'These tips come in all the time. It was only when I saw Lavinia looking so friendly with the same woman from the photos, I remembered.'

'That's her friend India,' I said, rolling my eyes. 'Women can be friends, you know? It's not all about sex and scandal, Noah. Even though that's what pays your bills.'

I knew I was being unkind, but I couldn't help it. I was mad as hell, and he was there. I eyed him suspiciously. 'Why are you nice to me?' I was feeling upfront, just as I had been with Chris. 'Do you like me or something?'

'Um, not right now, to be honest. But when you're not having a meltdown, well, you're great. Normally you give off good vibes. Normally.' I could see him concealing a grin.

'Yeah, well, I'm all out of those right now. Go back to Sara. Thanks for your help.'

He held up his two hands in an act of submission and left me alone. I shimmied out of my dress and crawled into the relative safety of my duvet, where I planned to stay for as long as physically possible.

Over the next few days, Vinnie tried to get me to go out with her and India several times, but I swatted her away. I didn't want to go on a hike, play pickleball, do reformer Pilates.

247

Nor did I want to go skating in Venice, bowling in Pasadena or take the kids to Universal Studios.

Vinnie and India's healthy, positive vibes revolted me, and the idea of attempting to have fun seemed foreign and fake. I was content to be left alone in my misery.

My parents had lifted Ariel's grounding to allow her to film the Super Bowl commercial of her dreams for Gatorade. Thankfully, her battle wounds had healed – that good teenage collagen. She and three other famous TikTok teens would be duking it out in an imaginary obstacle course, powered by the sugary beverage. I knew Ariel would come out on top, even if it wasn't in the script. That's just how she rolled.

Manny had taken Ariel to Chicago for the shoot, her Swarovski-encrusted phone back firmly in her paws and creating all sorts of behind-the-scenes content. My mother was on a 'girls' weekend' in Sonoma with some All Stars from the other Ladies franchises. It was a new thing the network was trying, and of course they chose Dessie to spearhead the trip. 'I couldn't be *arsed* with this *shite*!' I'd heard her exclaim as she packed, but Dessie the pro always perseveres – especially when there's money and an opportunity to be Queen Bee involved.

With David still in Vegas, it meant I was left largely in peace, except for when it came to my sister. Vinnie accepted my refusals brightly, chirping 'Okay!', but never stopped asking me to come out with her.

'Doesn't India have a job to go to?' I spat one morning.

Vinnie didn't take the bait. 'India has her own Pilates studio with a staff of nine, and is currently scouting another location,' she beamed back.

Her glee was offensive. Why couldn't Vinnie and I be miserable together?

I was also ignoring texts from Chris Adams. He'd sent me a couple of messages days apart, just checking in. While I appreciated the thought, it was his rejection that had sent me into this tailspin, so I wasn't engaging.

The only person I spoke to was Suz. She FaceTimed me each night as she was getting ready for the show and didn't care that I looked like hell and sounded worse. She was surprisingly astonished by the whole Chris situation.

'Girl, I know a hundred women that would *love* an offer like that from that man. Hell, they'd settle on being wined and dined and occasionally felt up by him.' She laughed throatily. 'He's gorgeous, straight, successful, and he doesn't want any more kids – what's stopping you?'

'Nothing is stopping me, Suz, it was just all so . . . unromantic. I'm too young to be agreeing to companionship! I want love, I want fireworks and passion and to be cherished. Is there anything wrong with that?'

She raised one beautifully arched eyebrow. 'No, Portia, there is nothing wrong with that. Only you might find yourself waiting until kingdom come.'

When I wasn't sleeping, eating or crying, I was frantically stalking Facebook and Instagram for news of Jason, Sandra and Mick, and finding little. No updates from any of them, or the kids. It occurred to me that they may all have me soft-blocked so I couldn't see what they were doing.

By my fifth day of hibernating, I was smelly and sick of myself.

Dessie had clearly had enough too. She'd come back from wine country complaining about her cast mates and their manufactured drama.

'I don't know how much longer I can take it,' she told me, while forcing me out of bed to change the sheets. My mother has a rule about making your own bed and washing your own underpants, something her own mom taught her, but she was sick of my stagnating. 'I know I say that every time there's trouble, but I'm really getting too old for all the bullshit.'

'It's not like you need the money, Mom.' I was sitting on the floor scrolling while she faffed about with the mattress protector.

'No, but *LOLA* has been a big part of my life for a long time. It afforded me opportunities in business that I wouldn't have had otherwise. And I say this without ego, but I think the show would suffer without me. I mean, it's a strange old world when I'm the normal one of the bunch.'

I nodded in agreement. When Dessie had finished making the bed, complete with seventeen pillows and a velvet throw, she flopped down on it and gestured for me to join her.

'I'm worried about you, Portia.'

'Join the club,' I grunted.

'No, I mean it. For the first time ever, I'm truly worried. You've never given me a moment's concern in life, you were always so sure of yourself. You've always had this innate confidence that was lacking in poor Lavinia. And Ariel, well, she has too much of it.'

I snorted.

'You're my well-balanced child. So, to see you off kilter now is . . . well, it's frightening.'

I felt awful. My mother had enough to worry about without throwing my messed-up life in the mix. I should never have burdened her with my problems. I should have gone back to New York and got on with my life.

When I said as much, she was even more annoyed. 'For God's sake, will you stop with the martyr act. I'm saying that I'm here to help you, here to mind you. I know I haven't been as involved in your life as other mothers might have been, and I often thought that was a good thing, to give you your independence and neither crowd nor bother you. But I don't care what age you are, Portia. If you need me, I'm here.'

I let her spoon me, and for a moment felt content.

'You really do reek, though, darling. When is the last time you washed yourself?'

'Um, it's been a while,' I said sheepishly.

'If there's one thing I won't stand for, it's bad hygiene. I'm drawing you a bath and then we're going to hunker down and gossip about your sister and her new best friend.'

BlindGossip.com

24 July 2022

Which ageing superhero has been spotted out with
a very sexy, much younger woman? Sources in West
Hollywood spied the sexy 'dzaddy' seemingly consoling
a beautiful brunette last weekend. Could this be the
beginning of a beautiful friendship for the star? He hasn't
been lucky in love, so let's hope so . . .

Which former supermodel turned lifestyle guru is seeing
someone new . . . and surprising? It seems after her
bombshell divorce announcement, this B+ list celebrity
offspring has been swimming in the lady pond. Rumour
has it there are pictures confirming a sexy sapphic
coupling is happening.

27

Something clicked on day eight of my moping, and I started writing again. I was pouring my heart out into my script, all my bitterness and sadness and loss of faith. I didn't know if it was any good, but I was relieved to have an outlet for my feelings. And what's a decent romantic comedy without true experience of heartbreak? Maybe women my age would relate to whatever this screenplay would become. Maybe it would even help them, if it ever saw the light of day.

I'd been tinkering around with the fundamentals of the same story for the best part of a decade, but it needed an update every time there was an advance in technology and culture. My heroine was growing older with me as I dragged out the process of writing the damn thing.

In her current iteration, she was a divorced, heartbroken woman pushing forty whose dancer husband had cheated on her with his celebrity partner on a dance competition show, and she was back in her hometown licking her wounds. That's where she rekindled a friendship with her first love, who she had left behind for the bright lights of showbiz. But he was struggling with issues of his own – what exactly these were was the plot point that had thus far eluded me, but I'd finally cracked it.

The setting was partly inspired by Dessie's stint on *Dancing with the Stars*, which came at the same time I first started writing it. I'd been working on a cheesy soap and tinkering with my script to keep myself sane and occupied while coming up with ridiculous dialogue for my actual job.

Dessie's pro partner had been a cute but very young Polish guy. She had recently divorced Manuel and loved that everyone thought she was a cougar sinking her claws into poor Pavlov, when she was in fact having a fling with the older head judge.

I was typing around the clock, forgetting to eat and ignoring my friends. But it felt good to be selfish for a reason, withdrawn for a project. I deleted social media from my phone, played with the boys when I needed a break and worked out in the home gym to clear my head before I started every morning.

Vinnie was supportive, supplying me with green juices and matcha lattes. She'd stopped inviting me to accompany her everywhere she went; I suspected our mother had had a word, or maybe she was just sick of being rejected.

I had sent some pages and an outline to my agent, Frank, who had been delighted to hear from me. He promised to shop the project around to a few producers on his speed dial, but I wasn't holding my breath. Romantic comedies are notoriously difficult to get made, and even more difficult to sell at the box office. But I wasn't even focused on selling the thing; I was happy just to be writing again.

I was also Zooming with Amy, who was being forced to lay low due to suffering from hyperemesis gravidarium. She was going stir crazy cooped up, so was delighted to help me out.

'Portia, I think you've got something great here,' she said one Friday night. 'If you want to wait for me to come back from maternity leave, we could tease it out into a series . . .'

'Amy Wu, I love you,' I beamed. 'But something in my gut is telling me that this is my movie, my big shot. If I'm wrong, well, I'll hold you to that.'

'If I ever birth this baby and get back to work, you're on.'

Dessie was around the house a lot as well, working in her office with the door closed. I knew she was stressed about the *Ladies of Los Angeles* reunion taping, which was coming up in the middle of August. She was contractually obligated to appear and dissect the happenings of the season, and she knew she'd get questions about the whole family. She and Giulia were prepping, and the glam squad was working on Dessie's look – poor Natasha was constantly on the phone to the other Ladies people, trying to find out what they were all wearing so Dessie could outdo them.

I was writing one afternoon a few days later when Manny came into the family room with two pizza boxes. 'Is Lavinia here? These came for her.'

I wrinkled my nose. 'Really? Vinnie doesn't eat that junky pizza, and neither do the boys.'

'Security dropped it off, said it was for her.'

My mother appeared, sniffing the air. 'Do I smell pepperoni?'

Vinnie was summoned, and confused. 'I didn't order that.' She shrugged.

Dessie was instantly on alert. 'Manny, do not open that box. Bring it into the island, and call Andy.'

'Andy?' Vinnie and I chorused.

'You know Andy, my Man Friday. Huge, big Aussie fella that does a bit of bodyguarding, a bit of manly work around the house. Surely you've seen him?'

I remembered and shrank inwards when he stalked into the kitchen. In the bright light of day, Andy the Jason Momoa-alike was even more beautiful than I'd remembered and looked carved out of marble. I saw Vinnie gulp at the sight of him.

Andy eyed the pizza warily, even leaned in and appeared to listen to the boxes intently. Was he . . . oh my god, he was listening for ticking. That's when I realized that my mother suspected something truly dangerous.

After a few shakes of the boxes and taking some pictures, Andy flipped the lid of the top one. There was indeed a pepperoni pizza, but there was also an envelope. Donning a pair of latex gloves, he appeared to have had in his pocket, Andy opened it carefully as we all stood back. Inside, there was a typed note.

I'm watching you, you stupid bitch.
Now I know how easy it is to reach you.
Enjoy the pizza, enough for you and your little angels.
And your new friend too. Xo

Vinnie paled dramatically, while my mother shrieked. Andy scooped up the boxes and immediately made himself scarce. I wondered absent-mindedly if he was going to eat the pizzas, or dust them for prints. Both, probably. He seemed to be a jack of all trades.

Dessie was on to Giulia pronto. 'Fuck this!' she yelled, her olive skin reddening. 'Lavinia, I'm on my way over anyway because there are things we need to discuss. See you in ten.'

I wondered if Giulia was going to tell Vinnie about the photos being shopped around. In truth, I'd half forgotten what Noah told me, drunk and emotional as I was that night a couple of weeks before. Once he said our aunt knew about them, I'd relaxed because she's the professional tasked with keeping distance between our family and the media. Plus, I hadn't wanted to upset my sister, not when she was showing signs of recovering from the shock and trauma of Billy leaving.

Giulia arrived minutes later, clearly having done some speeding. But she was calmer than she had appeared on

FaceTime, and all business. Manny went back to his office, and us four women congregated on the sofas.

'*Allora, ragazze.* Are you all okay? Shaken up?'

My mom looked pale. 'You could say that.'

'I understand, a nasty shock. But really, just a pizza, yes? Anyone can drop stuff here for you guys, and if they seem legitimate, the lads bring up?'

I tried not to smile at the word 'lads' tripping off her tongue.

Vinnie nodded. 'I mean, they know when something seems unusual. Manny says it was just a regular DoorDash driver, nothing out of the ordinary. There was no house number on the box, just my name and the street.'

'*Sì*, I think it is somebody chancing an arm, you know? Trying to scare you. There are bad people out there, Lavinia. But this is something we keep an eye on, yes?'

We all nodded. Vinnie looked a little less ill.

'I want Andy to stick around you a bit more, and to check all of the packages that come to the door,' Dessie stated.

'Where did he come from, by the way?' I asked. 'I saw him a while back cleaning the pool in the dead of night.'

'Graham recommended him, darling. His brother Stan is her bodyguard, they're two divine creatures. Handy and protective, and really lovely guys. They do a bit of body-doubling as well.'

'I did background checks on them, *ovviamente.*' Giulia shrugged. 'Good lads, good references. Lots of training, good with hands.' She mimed what I guessed was meant to be some sort of heavy lifting but just looked obscene.

'There's something else,' said Giulia, and my sister stiffened once again. 'There have been some photos making the rounds of you, and some tips going into the paparazzi agencies.'

'What photos? When?'

'I'd heard that too, Vin,' I offered sheepishly. 'Noah told me, but he said Giulia had it in hand.'

'And I do, but they continue, I'm afraid. Pictures of you and your new friend, what is her name?'

'India,' Mom and I chorused.

'*Sì, bellissima* India. Lots of pictures on different days, different places. Well, now the blind items, they are saying she is your lover.'

'My *what*?' Vinnie screeched.

'Calm down, love,' Dessie soothed. 'Sure, you'd be doing well to pull a cracker like that.'

'Yes, these bloggers, they see you looking happy with anyone, they will say you are having sex. And she is gay, yes?'

'Well, yes,' Vinnie spluttered. 'But how would they even know that?'

'Oh, *bella*, you know they have their ways. This India, she doesn't hide who she is. This is a small town.'

Everyone went quiet, until I asked the question we were all thinking.

'Is there any truth to it, Vin?'

'No! Well . . . no, nothing has happened! She's been an amazing friend, and she's obviously gorgeous and amazing with the kids, but no. We haven't been involved in that way. I'm not into women.'

'What about that time . . .' Dessie started.

'Oh god, everyone has experiences when they're younger. I was a model, for God's sake, and high most of the time!'

'Yes, darling, but you have been down to Lady Town,' our mother offered. 'And there is absolutely nothing wrong with that! I often wish I fancied women; men can be so tiresome.'

'Oh, Lord . . .' Vinnie looked like she was going to faint. 'Poor India . . .'

'It's okay, calm down,' I said, rubbing her back. 'Look, there could be far worse rumours. Don't worry about it.'

'Don't worry? Portia, I'm only just starting to get back on my feet after Billy threw my life under a bus. You know, the one built around me being a perfect mother and squeaky clean? I don't care if they're good or bad rumours, I just can't face any of this right now.'

'Unfortunately, my love, this is the life we chose,' Dessie intoned sagely. 'We don't get to pick and choose.'

And then, because sometimes the universe has a funny way of messing with you and it never rains but it pours, Silas tore into the living room like a bat out of hell. '*MOMMYYYYYY!* Sebastian is on the phone to Daddy! He wants to talk to you!'

From: leothelion2K23@gmail.com
To: editorial@people.com
Subject: LRS and her new friend
Date: 5 August 2022; 11.47am

See attached images of Lavinia Rizzi-Schwartz at home.
Email me if you want the pics in hi res.

28

It was only a matter of time before Billy Schwartz crawled out of whatever hole he was hiding in, but what made him reveal himself said a lot. He was furious about the rumours that his wife was seeing another woman.

'Are you crazy?' Vinnie screeched at him. I could hear him ranting and raving on the other end of the line. 'You pursue *teenagers* and fuck them *in our bed*, and then have the audacity to disappear when you get caught, and *now*, after months of zero contact, you're pissed off because I was spotted having coffee with a friend? You're unbelievable, Billy.'

She put the phone on loudspeaker so I could hear.

'Vinnie, people are saying you're gay. How does that look for me, for our sons?'

'Uh, a whole lot better than you sleeping with women that just got their driving licence, you fucking sicko! Where are you? Where did you disappear to?'

'I'm, uh, south of the border. Staying at a friend's place, keeping a low profile. I thought it would be for the best.'

Giulia made a grab for the phone, but I blocked her and gestured for her to be quiet.

Billy's tone altered; he was clearly changing tack. 'Look, Vinnie, I'm sorry for everything I put you through. I was afraid I was going to be arrested, that Trysta had lied about being eighteen. When she told me she might be pregnant, my life flashed before my eyes. I needed to just get away so you wouldn't have to deal with all of that. I didn't want the boys to see me cuffed!'

Dessie stepped forward as if to give him a piece of her mind, but Vinnie held her hand up.

'Billy, you left me to clean up your mess. I was a prisoner, and so were your sons. But none of this matters any more, because I'm divorcing you, whether you like it or not. What I do now is none of your business.'

'Vinnie, baby,' he pleaded. 'Can't we work it out? I love you. I can be home in just a few hours.'

'No, Billy. I'm done. Truly, honest to God, totally over it. DONE.'

His voice hardened. 'Fine, fuck you. Go make out with some Pilates instructor and generate more headlines to embarrass me and your sons. I loved you when you were nothing, a down-and-out junkie with no prospects. I made you who you are today. Divorce me, but if you think you're keeping my boys from me, you have another think coming.'

The line went dead. Vinnie was shaking like a leaf, but I was so, so proud of her in that moment. She'd stood up for herself. She was so much stronger than she gave herself credit for.

'Mom, he can't take the kids, can he?' Vinnie was white as a sheet.

'Of course not, love. He's just acting out, trying to be Billy Big Bollocks Schwartz. No judge in the country would let him have custody after what he's been up to.'

'You're right, you're right,' Vinnie whispered, almost to herself.

By 6 p.m., there were photos of Vinnie and India looking cosy together all over the internet. Pictures of them walking on Venice Beach at sunset, laughing at the park with the kids, and having coffee, just the two of them. The photos were strictly PG, but the tabloids knew India was gay and were running with the assumptions presented by the obvious chemistry in the pics.

'Where the blind items start, chaos follows,' Dessie muttered as she scrolled through the stories. 'At least you look fabulous, darling!'

'How long have these paps been trailing me?' Vinnie fretted. 'And why? Those images go back weeks. Why have they been sitting on them? Has Billy had someone watching me and reporting back, to make me look bad?'

'Vinnie, you spending time with another adult woman doesn't make you look bad,' I said.

'But this all feels like an attack. Oh my god . . .' Vinnie visibly paled. 'Do you think it's all coming from India? Is she using me for clout?'

'Oh, pet,' my mother cooed. 'I hate thinking the worst of people, but it wouldn't be the first time we've been betrayed. Remember that stylist who was selling the knickers I'd worn? Until we have an idea where these pictures are coming from, we can't trust anybody.'

I had an idea of someone who could help us, and reached for the phone.

An hour later, Noah Frost was pacing the terrace. He was making calls to try and get to the root of the stories and the pictures. As soon as I'd called, he'd leapt into action. I didn't know why he was being quite so helpful, but I was immensely grateful. I'd apologized profusely for being nasty the last time we met. Noah had been gracious, which only served to make me feel worse.

'You're going through some shit, Portia. Nobody's perfect.'

So succinct, so correct – I was learning that that was Noah. 'Honestly,' he said when he saw me squirming with fresh embarrassment. 'We're all good, I swear. You can be an absolute bitch to me three times before I'll officially dislike you, okay?'

'Okay.' I laughed. 'Strike one.'

While Noah wasn't exactly compromising the integrity of his sources, he was doing me a favour by trying to find out more. My soft spot for him was becoming a little softer as I watched him frowning by the pool, iPhone clamped to his ear.

India had been calling and texting, the volume increasing as the other woman realized that her image was splashed all over the world's media. But until we determined that she wasn't the leak, it was best to keep her at arm's length. Vinnie dashed off a quick text saying to hang tight and say nothing, she'd be in touch asap.

Ariel was mooching around trying to earwig because she knew something was up, and Manny, Giulia and Dessie were huddled around their laptops and tablets at the island. The three of them are able to communicate almost telepathically, like a benevolent coven.

Noah came back inside. 'I've a guy calling me back, and then we should know more,' he said. 'For now, we wait.'

My mom sprang into action. 'The best thing for waiting is eating,' she announced. 'Giulia, put your apron on. We are going to make your mamma's famous pasta alla norma.'

Giulia did what she was told, and I decided to help for something to do. Before long, the kitchen was rich with the smell of simmering tomatoes, frying aubergines and fragrant garlic. Dessie dished up lavish portions of rigatoni drenched in the rich vegetable sauce, and Giulia grated fresh pecorino on top before finishing with a sprig of basil. Red wine was poured, and we gathered to eat.

Ariel declined to join us, preferring to dress Bubbles up in a series of ridiculous outfits for her Instagram. She was well and truly back living in her own little digital world.

'Noah, tell us about yourself!' Dessie exclaimed. 'I know

264

you, but I also know so little about you. Have you got a big family? Ever been married?'

I narrowed my eyes at her. 'Mom, leave him alone.'

'It's fine.' He laughed graciously. 'Nobody ever asks me about myself in LA. I have one sister, a twin. She lives back in Philly. I've never been married, but I came close once.'

Seeing our expectant faces, he continued. 'High-school sweetheart, we got engaged after college. But then I guess we grew up and apart. I wanted to be a hotshot *National Geographic* photographer, she went to law school at Penn State. I realized I was a bit of a nomad, whereas she wanted to have it all – a high-flying career, kids, a stay-at-home husband, or at least one who was in the same city as her. So, it ended, but we're still friendly. My mom sees her all the time back home.'

'And there's been nobody special since?'

'Mom!' This was Vinnie.

'I'm only asking. It's human nature to be curious.'

Noah laughed. 'That it is, Dessie. Uh, I mean . . . I guess not. Not really, although I thought there was. The older I get, the more I think I'm better off being a lone wolf.'

'Just like me,' said Giulia. 'No muss, no fuss.' She mimed dusting off her hands.

Just then Noah's phone rang and brought us all back to earth. It was his contact, so he went outside to take the call.

'Why the third degree, Mom?' I asked.

'Honey, he could be the leak. I don't trust anybody, but I get good vibes from him. And in case he is a good guy, I wanted to find out if he had any ex-wives lurking.' She winked lasciviously at me, and I rolled my eyes.

I busied myself clearing plates, while Vinnie chewed her fingers and ignored her flashing phone. Mom poured herself, Manny and Giulia another glass of wine.

When Noah returned minutes later, he looked deadly serious. 'It's not good news,' he said.

'What is it? Who broke their NDA? Who do I have to sue?' Dessie moaned.

'The call is coming from inside the house.'

'Whose house?' she trilled.

'It's a line from a movie . . . never mind. Dessie, this person called the editor of a very well-known publication from a number that's been traced back to this home. They were very obviously disguising their voice and got spooked and hung up when asked for more information. Since then the only communication has been via email.'

'Wait, which phone?' I asked. 'The landline?'

Dessie looked confused. 'Manny? Do we even still have a landline?'

'Sure,' he confirmed. 'It's in my bedroom, in case of emergency.' Manny looked around at our bemused faces. 'What? I'm old school! And it's a cool old rotary, goes with the decor.'

'Okay, well, if my contact is to be believed, then the tipster in possession of photos and video of Vinnie and India is someone close to you, because most of the photos, the ones that haven't been published yet, were taken right here.'

We all gaped at him. 'What?' I said, bewildered. 'In this house?'

He nodded. 'My contact has seen pictures of them in the kitchen, by the pool and in the family room. He recognized the interiors from *LOLA*. It's somebody you know and trust.'

Our family kept our circle small and well protected in terms of who was allowed on the property. But it was impossible to police everyone. There were drivers, personal trainers, a chef, a housekeeper, and that didn't even account for our friends . . . my stomach dropped. Mom ran a tight ship, but it wasn't the White House. Anybody could have snuck pictures, maybe installing hidden cameras or recording devices. This wasn't paranoia, it was the reality of being famous in the twenty-first century.

'It's that Marjorie. I never trusted her!' Giulia screeched. 'She is too sweet to be genuine.'

'It's not Marjorie,' Vinnie seethed. 'I trust her with my life. Do you think I'd let a weirdo look after my children?!'

Dessie was deathly pale, gripping the table.

'What about Andy?' Manny offered. 'He's new, he's been around a lot.'

Giulia shook her head. 'I just don't think so. He's got great references from Graham, and I know the Kardashian girls have used him in the past too.'

'They don't know who's behind it yet. It's someone who goes by the name Leo and only communicates via email,' said Noah. 'They don't even want big money for the photos, just to get them out there. That alone is unusual. I think you're all right to be worried. Someone in your circle is doing this and they're doing this purely out of spite.'

My head was spinning. Who on earth would want to expose Vinnie like this, after all she'd been through? Especially when nothing was even happening with India – at least nothing she wanted to admit.

'Could it be the same person that sent the pizza?' Manny asked.

'It could be.'

'Noah, why hasn't an editor run the shots from inside the house yet?' I asked. 'Surely they're absolute gold?'

'Whoever is behind this clearly doesn't know the right people to get them out there. A reputable editor would never publish pictures from inside Dessie's home, particularly when there's nothing sinister or illegal going on. If this Leo reaches an unscrupulous outlet, though? They'll put them out and deal with the consequences later. Or Leo could get fed up and decide to put them online themselves.'

Vinnie finally answered the phone to India, and curtly asked her to come over. 'I need to look her in the eye and know she hasn't set this up,' she explained as she hung up.

I felt another wave of longing for New York. In my apartment, I didn't have to worry about people spying on me, or who I could trust. How could my family live like this, so publicly? Was the money and adulation truly worth the down sides?

Right then, I guessed they would say no. Vinnie was pacing, waiting for India to drive over from Marina del Rey. Giulia was interrogating Noah about indiscernible spy equipment and how to root it out, and Dessie was in a daze, clutching her glass of red. She looked oddly frail.

'I'm not able for these frights, love,' she said. 'I'm getting too old for all of this.'

'Well, if it's any consolation, I've aged at least ten years in the last few months.' I grinned weakly, trying to make her feel better. 'It'll be okay, Mom. It always is.'

She smiled wanly. 'I bloody hope so.'

When India arrived, Noah left, and we all gave her and Vinnie their privacy. India looked distraught, so unless she was a very good actress, I didn't think she had anything to do with leaking images. Besides, she was a private person. She had her own successful business and didn't need any of this family's drama. If she was willing to get involved with us at all, it was because she genuinely cared for my sister.

They talked for a long while, and then I heard Vinnie walking India out to her car. There were muffled voices, and then the noise of an engine running, and the car driving away.

Vinnie knocked on my door. She looked exhausted, but her eyes were bright.

'It's not her,' she declared, flopping down on the bed.

'I didn't think it was. Do you feel better?'

'I think so, but she thinks her ex is behind the pizza delivery. She told her she had feelings for me, and the ex freaked out. They only broke up a couple of months ago. But now I'm more confused than ever, because her admitting that has changed everything between us. And . . .'

'And what?'

'Portia, I kissed her.'

I sat up. 'Tell me everything.'

Vinnie explained that India had been really spooked, fielding calls all afternoon from concerned friends and family, and dealing with a tirade from her ex. It hadn't even occurred to her that Vinnie might think she had something to do with it all, until her calls to my sister went unanswered.

'She was so upset I took her in my arms for a hug, and it just felt so right,' Vinnie whispered. 'I realized I'd been wanting to hold her for weeks, but I'd been stopping myself. Then it was like my body just took over. When I kissed her, she pulled away at first – but then she kissed me back and . . . Portia, it was like I'd never been kissed before.'

They'd talked then about everything. Vinnie's confusion, India's reluctance to complicate their friendship, the difficult position they now found themselves in, being watched by the world. But they acknowledged that their feelings went deeper than just those between friends.

'How did you leave it?' I asked gently.

'We agreed to cool it, for now,' Vinnie said in a small voice. 'India said we'll find our way back to one another when the time is right, or we won't. She's quite matter-of-fact like that. And I think it's for the best, you know? Instead of jumping into something with both feet, and then figuring it out later? That's what I've always done in the past, and well, it's never exactly worked out for me.'

I patted her on the back. 'Vinnie, that's so mature. I'm proud of you. And count yourself lucky!'

'Why would I do that?'

'Because your conservative followers will all ditch you now before you confirm anything. A mere whiff of homosexuality, and they'll be off. That's millions of bigots fewer to deal with right off the bat.' I saw a way to lighten the situation. 'Now, where did I leave that rainbow flag? And let's figure it out, are you bisexual or is it more of a pansexual thing?'

She pushed me off the bed.

29

For the next few days, everyone laid low. I was writing for ten hours every day, breaking only to eat and pee. At night I was tumbling into long, dreamless sleeps, spent from emptying my brain on to the page. I'd wake up early, work out until I felt like I'd collapse, and then retreat to my room with my laptop and AirPods.

Before the boys went to bed, I'd help Vinnie bathe and feed them and then we'd play for a while. I was getting pretty good at *Minecraft* and was secretly enjoying watching endless episodes of *Bluey* – it was surprisingly well written.

Vinnie's fondness for the outdoors was no more, and she had become a hermit once again. If she did go out, Andy went with her, and she took to wearing a mask. 'Thank the Lord it's LA – everyone is a health nut, so nobody even looks twice at me,' she told me when I asked if it didn't make her stand out. 'Some things we can thank Covid for.'

She was also spending a lot of time writing for her resurrected blog. Social media had long ago taken over from long-form online posts, but she said there was something appealing about going back to basics and writing from the heart. Vinnie's posts weren't that deep, mostly about parenting and things she was into at the moment. I saw it for what it was, a distraction, so I acquiesced when she asked me to take some photos of her in the gym and modelling some stuff she had bought online. It was keeping her going, keeping her sane.

Ariel had been behaving, which was a relief for my mother.

She seemed to have calmed down since she shot her commercial and was dutifully going to school and her extracurricular activities. When she wasn't acting out, it was easy to forget my little sister was even in the house sometimes – until she started blaring Olivia Rodrigo and Kim Petras.

On Friday night, David came over after work and he, Vinnie and I took some wine and charcuterie out by the pool. It had been a hot day and was a balmy evening, the perfect setting for a frosty glass of rosé and cured meats as the sun set.

We lit the fire pit, and things got a little rowdy, as they normally do when David is around. Before too long, we had set up a Prosecco pong station, and were raucously taking it in turns to land as many little plastic balls as we could in flutes of sparkling wine within a minute.

Once we'd exhausted ourselves, we brought blankets to the outdoor sofa and huddled up together under the stars.

'You know, I'm thinking about moving out to LA permanently,' David said after a while.

I sat up. 'What? What about New York? What about it being the centre of the civilized universe?'

He sighed. 'New York has changed, P. Since the pandemic, it's honestly a little bit grim downtown. The vibe is different. Everyone is working from home, and so many of my favourite little bodegas and cafés have shut down. The rent is crazy, and only getting higher. And you're not even there now, either.'

'Well, that's temporary.' I baulked.

'Oh yeah? Well, when are you coming back, then?'

He had me there. As it stood, I had no firm plans to go anywhere, and my apartment was lying empty.

'Yeah,' he snorted. 'I thought as much.'

'I don't know, Dave,' Vinnie mused. 'I just don't see you as an Angeleno full time? You're too pale, to start.'

'I'll be buying shares in SPF, that's for sure. OMG, maybe I should do a diffusion line of Freckle for men! Is your mam awake? I'm a genius!'

'No, Einstein, her light is off,' I said, indicating the darkness behind her French doors. 'She has the *LOLA* reunion first thing. Write it down. It'll keep.'

'Okay. Well, Vinnie. I hear you're a lesbian now?'

I almost fell off the sun lounger at David's delivery, drier than the Sahara. Vinnie was red-faced and huffing, and I dissolved into Prosecco-fuelled giggles.

'Don't worry, I'll walk you through all of it,' David was saying. 'I've already told Dessie, I may not know vaginas, but I do know gays. And to be honest, I think the community will welcome you with open arms. You've always had sort of butch vibes, like, no offence.'

'*David!*' I yelped, howling with laughter. 'What is butch about Vinnie?'

'Well, she's tall and strong-looking. Muscly shoulders, and that nose. Like you're not the girliest girl to have ever girled, Vin. Am I wrong?'

Vinnie was starting to see the funny side. 'Okay, I'm no shrinking violet. And before I had the boys, I was a bit androgynous, played with gender norms. But that doesn't make me a lesbian.'

'Fancying a woman does, though. Or at least bisexual.' David had a point. 'Do you fancy India properly? Or is it more of a crush? Your mother can't hold her piss, I know all about the kiss, and the crazy ex sending threatening pizza. I wish my exes sent free food.'

She groaned. 'I don't know. I mean, I have feelings for her that go beyond friendship, but I don't think I realized that until I was kissing her. And as Mom so kindly pointed out in front of everyone, I have been with girls before. But I was so

273

off my face during that time of my life I didn't think it meant anything.'

'And maybe it didn't, other than you're open to experimenting,' David said. 'But if you were a million per cent straight, drugs wouldn't make you want to eat pussy. I'm just saying!' he protested as we loudly objected to his phrasing.

'I'm not a million per cent straight, no,' Vinnie admitted. 'But is anyone?'

'Uh, I am,' I offered. 'Like, I find girl-on-girl porn hot, but who doesn't? The guys are gross! But beyond thinking women are beautiful, that's about it. I've no desire to go downtown; I don't even want to squeeze a boob.'

Vinnie looked thoughtful. 'Did I ever tell you that Billy and I went to a swingers' party once?'

David and I both sat up, agog. 'You did not!' I screamed.

'We did. I was in disguise, wearing a red wig and a butterfly eye mask. But it was a high-end party; nobody there was in the business of ratting anyone else out. There were politicians, even royalty, at it. It was before Seb was born, and I mostly went out of interest, and to keep Billy happy. He wanted to "spice things up",' she said, rolling her eyes.

'Did you . . . participate?' I asked, disbelieving.

'No, but we did watch. And now that I think about it, it was two women together that got me hot. You'd all know one of them, she's an actress. No names, no!' She swatted us as we begged for intel. 'It was a safe space. But yeah, looking back, I probably would have got in between them if it wasn't for my reputation and fear of going wild again. I definitely wanted to.'

'What do you mean?' David asked.

'Well, everything changed when I met Billy. It was the end of my wild days, the end of the substances and crazy parties. With him, I had to be this show wife, you know? Like go to dinners and functions, take gorgeous pictures, smile and talk to everyone. Sometimes I felt totally out of it, like I was floating and watching myself in these social interactions. It all felt sort of false, but I thought that was just because I wasn't on drugs. I thought that's what being an adult was all about, because I'd never been a lucid one before.'

I'd never thought of it like that, but it made a lot of sense. She kept going.

'The only thing I knew I was good at was being a mom and creating content, so it made sense for that to be my job, to use my privilege to help and advise other people. I thought that's what was right for me. When Billy wanted to get a little crazy, do these wild things, I was intrigued but I found it all too frightening. Like how could I do anything crazy sober? And as a respectable parent? Imagine if the pre-school WhatsApp Moms found out.'

I nodded, and David looked like his mind was blown. 'You mean, you just switched that side of you off?'

'I guess so. I figured I could meditate everything away, my instincts as well as my anxieties, and make a buck doing it. But now I realize I was faking it. Big time!'

She threw her hands up. 'My therapist says I was looking to Billy to save me, and my followers to complete me, that my self-worth was tied up with my perception of what it is to be Mrs Schwartz. She says that now I have to learn to look after myself, to ask myself what Lavinia actually wants to do.'

'And talk about yourself in the third person, it seems.' I grinned.

Another silence followed. I couldn't believe that Vinnie had divided her life into such distinct phases – the loose, free-wheeling chapter, then the complete opposite. I felt sad that she thought she needed to be perfect to stay clean, but it made everything that had happened so much more understandable.

'So, you knew Billy was unfaithful, then?' David asked.

'No, I didn't. But I don't know of many marriages around here that don't inevitably become less traditional over time. We always said we'd never lie to one another, that was our promise. But at that party I was too in my own head to let loose, and it ended up being a bust.'

'You're not the only one surprised by all of this, Portia,' David said. 'As a proud gay man, I see all sorts of things going down. True monogamy is so rarely a thing in my community, especially in LA and New York. But I thought heterosexuals were different. Like, in this day and age, you don't have to get married, so why bother if you're just going to cheat? You'd never get that carry-on in Ireland, let me tell you.'

'I bet you would, because people want to have it all.' Vinnie sighed, sounding jaded. 'It's just more extreme in a place like this. They want the public partner at home, the one they bring to dinner parties and awards ceremonies. And then they want the dirty, exciting little secret they bring to cocktail bars and fancy hotel rooms. Sometimes they even want to pay for it, so it's a business arrangement with no mess. And in Billy's case, that seems not to have been enough for him. He also wanted to skirt the law and screw the youngest legal women he could possibly find just for thrills.'

'He couldn't just take up skydiving?' I said drily.

'What are you going to do about India?' David asked.

'I'm waiting on the universe to give me a sign,' Vinnie said, totally seriously. She saw my cynical face and said, 'Look, I've been hawking this stuff for so long, some of it seeps into your brain. But I do think I need to just wait and see. I don't want to rush into anything too soon, I want to take my time and listen to my gut. And the universe.' She winked.

I smiled at her. 'You know, people always say models are

dumb, and deep as a puddle. But you, Lavinia Rizzi, are at least a little bit deeper than that.'

An hour later, my phone buzzed as David and I were chatting after Vinnie went to bed. I looked at the screen – Noah Frost.

'Noah, it's after midnight. Is this a booty call?'

'Portia, there's been another leak. I asked the agency to keep me posted, and more stuff was sent in by this Leo guy. This time it's you, your sister and your friend drinking by the pool.'

I sucked in my breath.

'And there's more. There's a video, and you're talking about Lavinia's marriage in it.'

David clocked my expression and gestured for me to put the call on speaker. 'Thanks for telling me, Noah. I cannot tell you how much I appreciate it. Are they going to buy the video?'

'No way, man. It's filmed on private property. But if this sort of thing is out there in the industry, people will talk.'

'Thank you,' I whispered, and hung up. 'David, who's here?' I managed.

'I . . . I don't know. It's Marjorie's night off. We said good-bye to her earlier. I haven't seen the Momoa-alike . . .'

'Andy,' I breathed.

'Yeah, that big ride. And the chef left at, like, 7 p.m., right?'

'Right. Can you record film with a long lens? Like is some-one out there hiding?'

'Not with audio, no.'

That just left immediate family. I kept hearing Noah's voice saying that the tip-off call had come from inside the house. Something was niggling away in the back of my brain, but I couldn't quite get a handle on it. It had been a long even-ing, and my mind was fuzzy from the drinks.

Who was this Leo, and what did they have against my family? Who could be leaking pictures and footage from inside Dessie's house and tipping off the paps about Vinnie and India's whereabouts?

Everyone was a suspect, even Noah Frost himself. I didn't think it was beyond a professional pap to play double agent. Hell, there was even a brief moment when I thought it might be Giulia, because a publicist is trained to keep their clients in the headlines. But then I caught myself; my aunt would never do anything to hurt us.

My brain kept whirring, so I picked up a dog-eared copy of *Cosmo* I'd brought outside earlier to distract myself as David went to fetch us something stronger. It was from the beginning of the year, and Vinnie was on the cover looking beautiful in ecru loungewear and an open linen shirt. ' "I'm not perfect," says the perfect mom' screamed the coverline.

I laughed sharply because nobody would be accusing my sister of that now. In just a few months, everything had changed. Her marriage was in tatters, a good chunk of her following had turned on her, and the weirdest thing about it all was that she didn't seem to care.

The magazine had twenty-four pages dedicated to a New Year astrology special, which pricked at something in my mind. Normally I have no interest in star signs; in fact, I think anybody who lives their life based on what some hack writes in a magazine has a screw loose. But something compelled me to read on.

A hideous thought crystallized when I reached the fifth sign of the zodiac. I tried to dismiss it because it was so awful, but I found I couldn't rationalize the thought away – it made a sort of terrible sense. Everything clicked into place, and in that moment, I knew for sure.

I jumped up, frightening David, who was drunkenly pouring

out shots of Casamigos. Stalking down the hall, I burst into my mother's room and woke her, not caring that she was due in studio and on camera in a few short hours.

'Mom, I know who Leo is.'

'Jesus, Portia, what's going on?

'Leo, the leak. Mom, it's Ariel.'

30

Perhaps it's because Ariel grew up on television and surrounded by cameras, but there's something innate in her that
knows to be always 'on' around other people. It's a quality that
neither Vinnie nor I possess; when we're around our family
or in the safety of our own home, we let it all hang out. But
never Ariel. Every moment is a moment to be captured for
social media, documented for posterity.

Maybe it was this compulsion that led to her filming us
unawares, but I had no idea what made our little sister leak
private photos and videos of the family – especially when
she'd been literally fighting to defend us so recently.

When I finally got my mother to understand what I was
saying, she was instantly in denial. But when I told her about
the burner phone I'd nearly confiscated, and the intimacy of
the content being shopped around, I saw realization dawn-
ing in her eyes.

'How can you be sure?' she'd wept.

'I had a feeling she was up to something,' I said. 'I'd noticed
her haunting the house when she was grounded, and I kept
wanting to sit you down and talk about her behaviour. Maybe
if I had, it wouldn't have gone this far.'

'Don't you go blaming yourself,' Dessie scolded. 'But I still
don't know how you put it all together from that.'

'It was the name, Leo,' I said. 'It was knocking around
in my head, but I couldn't quite get there. Then I remembered that Ariel is a Leo and wanted a tattoo of a lion
because . . .'

'Ariel means "the lion of God",' Dessie whispered. 'Oh my god, Portia.'

'I'm sorry, Mom,' I said.

'I am too, pet. This is all my fault.'

In the end, the confrontation wasn't dramatic. When Ariel was woken up and presented with the evidence, she sang like a canary. She handed over both phones and had the good grace to bawl her eyes out.

'I'm so sorry, Mommy,' she wept, looking even younger than her fifteen years. 'It was just a joke; I didn't think anybody would pay attention to me. I was bored, and you were never around. Then I just kind of wanted to see how far it would go.'

As I'd hoped, it had all started innocently enough; Ariel said it was unusual for her to have her sisters in the house constantly, and she was interested in us. We're much older, and something of an unknown quantity to her. Plus, Vinnie is famous, and there was definite hero worship at play on Ariel's part.

But the devices didn't just reveal photos of Vinnie. There were candid shots of my mom with no make-up on, taken in her bedroom. Selfies of Ariel posing with her hair in nineties space buns, pictures of Manuel dozing in the sunshine, countless shots of the dogs and lots of images of Si and Seb. There was even a video of me lying dazed on the sun lounger. It took me a second to even recognize myself, I looked so out of it. The little wench had been papping us all.

Then something had gone sideways with Ariel, and she'd decided to go rogue and cause havoc. Maybe it was the cancellation of her quinceañera, or the fact that myself, Vinnie and the children were dominating our mother's attention. I felt guilty then. We had definitely been ignoring her.

By the time the sun came up, the family was all gathered

on the sofas. David had skedaddled, declaring, 'I had enough teen angst of my own to last me a lifetime. Laters!'

Manny was the most upset. 'Ariel, what possessed you to tip off the paparazzi? How did you even know how to do that?'

'I googled it,' she said, as if it was the most obvious thing in the world. She looked at Vinnie. 'I wasn't trying to hurt you, Vinnie, I swear. It was just that I knew they'd be most interested in you.'

'Why were you fighting with your friends on your sister's behalf if you were doing this behind our backs?' I asked.

'Because they were full of it! I wanted to get the truth out there!'

To her credit, Vinnie was kinder to Ariel than I think I could have been in her shoes. 'I'm just glad you approached an agency with some integrity with the photos you took.'

'Ew, as if I'd go to TMZ. I tried *People* first, but they never got back . . .' She trailed off as she realized she was digging herself a deeper hole. 'Guys, I didn't want to hurt anybody. I just got carried away. I really am sorry.'

'If you're so sorry, why were you still at it only hours ago?' I asked, not wanting to let her off the hook. 'Recording private conversations about your sister's marriage is far worse than hawking photos.'

'Because I want Billy to get in more trouble for what he did! He's so disgusting!'

'But don't you realize, Ariel, in trying to hurt Billy, you're hurting me and the boys?' Vinnie said softly.

Ariel's little face fell. 'I hadn't thought of it like that. I just . . . I loved Billy. He was my brother-in-law, my neighbour, and I thought he was my friend. Sometimes it felt like he was the only one that listened to me, when Mom was so obsessed with you and the kids. I'm totally freaked out by him being such a creep.'

'Ariel, he never . . .' Mom couldn't finish her sentence, but the seriousness of her tone gave us all horrifying pause.

'No, he never touched me,' Ariel spat. 'He was only ever kind to me. But Penelope Frank was my friend, and he slept with her! Do you know how embarrassing that is? And gross? And everyone in school was calling Billy a paedophile because Naomi Morgan said he was one because he hooked up with her big sister.'

She stood up and started pacing. 'I miss him, and I'm angry with him, and I just want him to pay for what he's done.' The tears were flowing freely again. 'Penelope won't speak to me any more, and it's not fair.'

We were all quiet. We'd forgotten what it was like to be a teenager, to do something wildly stupid because you felt slighted or angry or afraid. And we hadn't even considered the effect Billy's actions would have on Ariel.

My mother spoke. 'Ariel, I am sorry that you've felt so neglected lately, and that we haven't taken how you might feel into account with everything that's been happening. It's my job to be a mother to you, to parent you and show you right from wrong, and I'm afraid I haven't done a good job of it. I've been preoccupied for . . . well, for years. And while you will be punished for this despicable betrayal, this goes deeper than that. We have to figure out how it got this far, and how to make things better for all of us. I will talk to your father and with some professionals, and we will work this out. Okay?'

Ariel nodded, sniffling.

'Okay. I have a commitment today that I cannot put off. It's bigger than me, unfortunately, and I'm already holding everything up. So, you go and wash your face, have some breakfast and get ready for dance class, and your father will take you. We'll discuss all this properly when I get home tonight.'

I don't know what I'd been expecting from Dessie, but it

certainly wasn't that. Vinnie and Manny looked surprised too, but we all let it go. My mother always knew best, so if she felt like an anticlimactic talking-to was more effective than a showdown, we trusted her.

'Do you want me to come to the studio with you?' I asked.

'No, love. You stay here and relax. Oh, and make sure you tell Noah that we got to the bottom of all of this, will you? He was so good to us, playing detective on our behalf.'

I nodded, then helped Dessie out to the car with her garment bags. Of all the days to be filming a reunion. Dessie certainly wasn't going to be on her A game after the night she'd had. But my mother was a pro, so I knew she'd rally as best she could. Maybe one of the other Ladies would experience the wrath that Ariel had thus far escaped.

I tapped out a text to Noah.

The mystery of Leo has been solved. I owe you a drink asap to explain everything.

Three dots appeared, and then a thumbs-up emoji. The man couldn't even send a few words back? He mustn't care as much as I'd thought. We were obviously just another famous family to him. Whatever, I thought. I was exhausted, so I headed to bed.

Hours later, I was working when my phone buzzed. It was Frank, which was jarring. Agents rarely call, only if there's very good or very bad news, and it's usually the latter.

'Hello?' I said cagily.

'Portia, honey!' he boomed. Frank looks more like an old-time newspaper editor than an agent; he's as round as he is tall, wears extra-stretchy braces to keep his trousers up and is permanently smoking a cigar. I loved him ardently. He'd

284

known my father and was terribly kind to me when I said I wanted to write, but on my own terms. I never wanted to be known as the second coming of Roberto Rizzi; it was simply too much pressure.

'Apple is crazy about the script, honey.'

'Apple who?' I was confused. 'Gwyneth's daughter?'

Frank barked out a laugh. 'No, dummy. Apple TV? As in the streaming service? As in *Ted Lasso*, *Bad Sisters*, consistently good original content?'

It took me a minute to catch on. 'They like my script?'

'They love it, honey. They've been looking for a project for a hotshot new director, you know, the girl who everyone is calling the next Nancy Meyers? They think this is a perfect fit.'

I nearly dropped the phone. He could only be talking about Katie Carlton, the woman single-handedly attempting to revive the romantic comedy genre. If she wanted to be the next Meyers, and me the next Ephron, well, it was a match made in heaven.

'Frank, you're not kidding me, are you? Because I've had a strange few months, and I'm not able for this kind of joking . . .'

'I'm not playing, hon. They want to meet you tomorrow in Pasadena. Can you make it there for 11 a.m.? I'll text you the address.

'Of course I can,' I spluttered. 'Can I bring Giulia?'

'Bring whoever you want, honey. I'm gonna fly out from New York too. I'll see you there.'

Frank hung up, leaving me dazed. Agents only flew cross-country when there was a very big deal on the table. Frank rarely flew at all because it meant he couldn't smoke for hours on end.

I sat there, trying to take it all in. What was strange was the fact that I was starting to get used to my life being a series of utterly bizarre events. Mere hours previously, I'd been involved in an intervention with my kid sister. Now I had less than twenty-four hours to prep for a meeting that could change my professional life for ever.

I screamed for Vinnie, filled her in, and the two of us spent the next while flitting between our mother's vast closet and Vinnie's. I called Giulia, and she looped in Frank's office to get all the details. Vinnie phoned David, who was backstage with Dessie at the reunion, and he sent his best stylist, Pansy, over to touch up my roots. She even added a few subtle highlights. 'Anti-ageing,' she commented, and I chose not to take that comment personally.

By early evening, I had decided what to wear the next day. A sleek camel-coloured linen blazer with gold buttons, with a black V-neck DD+ body suit and leopard-print cigarette pants from Zara. Céline sandals, chunky gold jewellery and Dessie's weathered, tan Mulberry Alexa completed the look. It said, 'I'm professional, but also sexy and chic.' At least according to Vinnie, anyway.

Vinnie gave me a facial and helped me choose some make-up. 'You want to look polished and defined, but also like you're wearing very little,' she instructed. 'Lit from within, subtle, glossy. *Capisce?*'

I nodded, fizzing with excitement. I didn't know how I was going to sleep that night. This was even bigger than the break I'd always dreamt of.

We'd just finished laying everything out on the bed in my room, right down to my underwear, when the phone rang. David again. 'Probably calling to see if Pansy did a decent job,' I said to Vinnie, rolling my eyes as I answered.

'Portia? You guys need to get to Cedars-Sinai right away. We're headed there right now in an ambulance. Your mother has collapsed on set.'

TMZ.com
Dessie Daniels – DOA?!?

12 August 2022

Word reaches us from the set of the *LOLA* season 15
reunion that OG and star Dessie Daniels has collapsed
during filming, and was unresponsive when taken to
Cedars in LA.

She appeared faint during a row between cast mates
Graham Townsend and Isabel Lopez, and insiders say she
went to go get some air and keeled right over.

'It wasn't just like fainting,' says our mole. 'She was totally
out of it, and when she was lying legs akimbo, you could
see bruises on the skin that had been hidden by her
Carolina Herrera gown. Nothing could revive her.'

More as we get it . . .

31

Vinnie and I sped to the hospital's emergency department on Beverly Boulevard. She was driving like a maniac, cutting people off and flipping beeping drivers the bird.

'I thought Mom was a bit shaky lately,' I whispered as we sat at a set of lights. 'I thought it was just all of our drama.'

Vinnie was chewing her nails. 'She's been under a lot of stress. God, we never should have inflicted any of our problems on her. Dessie is getting older, and she's just been worrying non-stop about us!' She tore off as the lights changed, leaving actual skid marks on the road.

'She'll be fine,' I said, more to myself than to Vinnie. 'She's a tough old bird. She's just been taking too much on.'

David met us outside at the valet – because only hospitals in LA have valet parking. 'I need you guys to be calm, okay? Your mother is fine. She's awake and sitting up and she wants to talk to you both.'

I didn't know what to expect, but he was telling the truth. When we tiptoed up to her room, Dessie was hooked up to a couple of intravenous drips and a heart monitor, but she was awake and alert, and even looked kind of fabulous in her reunion glam and hospital gown.

Manny was there, as was Natasha, who looked much worse than my mother – Dessie's loyal assistant had obviously had a major fright. She excused herself when we arrived, probably going to stress-eat in the cafeteria.

It was only when I gave Dessie a big hug that I realized how frail she felt in my arms, and that she recoiled ever so slightly at the ferocity of my squeeze, as if I was hurting her. It was then I noticed that her arm was covered in angry bruises, all at different stages of healing. She always keeps her arms covered, even when she's swimming and working out – she says it's unseemly for women to inflict their bingo wings on the world.

'Mom?' I whispered, shocked.

'Girls, sit down, sit down. Have a cup of tea.'

David appeared with a box of Barry's, presumably from my mother's stash, and a kettle he'd seemed to procure from the nurse.

Dessie was holding court from her bed like a queen, so we obeyed her. 'Portia, Lavinia, I have something to tell you both, and I just want you to listen to me, okay?'

We nodded.

'About ten months ago, I was diagnosed with a condition called CML. It's a serious and chronic but – and this is important – not exactly life-threatening form of leukaemia.'

I was stunned silent, but Vinnie let out a yelp. Undeterred, Dessie continued.

'I know "leukaemia" is a scary word, but my condition is quite manageable. As I said, it's chronic as opposed to acute and immediate, and it can be held off with medication. We caught it early, and I've been doing great. There's a possibility down the road for a stem-cell transplant, but not yet. My doctors see no reason to worry right now, okay? You got that?'

We nodded in unison again.

'David has known, because it was him that noticed the bruising on my body and told me I should get checked out. Manuel has known because he lives with me and accompanies me to all my appointments. I was going to tell you both in person as soon as possible, and I need you both to understand this part.' Dessie paused for breath.

'I wanted to give you this information privately, but also swear you both to secrecy face to face because I didn't want you to tell your men just yet. I couldn't risk the news getting out and I was afraid that telling Billy or Jason would increase the likelihood of that happening. And then everything happened with the two of them . . .' She trailed off. 'I haven't wanted or needed to worry either of you with my diagnosis thus far because, as I said, it isn't that serious at the moment, and I have access to the best possible healthcare there is.'

I was struck completely dumb. Our mother had kept something so huge from Vinnie and me, something so frightening, because she didn't want to bother us?

'I am one of the lucky ones,' Dessie continued. 'But stress exacerbates everything, and I took a bit of a turn today because I haven't been minding myself. I'm exhausted and dehydrated, so I passed out. And because it happened on bloody set, the news will be everywhere in a matter of moments, if it's not already.'

Vinnie looked as shaken as I felt. 'Mom, you have . . . you have cancer, and you didn't tell us?'

'"Cancer" is such a terrifying word, and yes, while I technically do have cancer, it's not the really scary kind,' Dessie implored. 'No chemo, no losing my hair, no radiation. I don't even need a bone-marrow transplant, not yet anyway. I just take a cocktail of drugs every day, get regular blood tests, and see my doctor once a month. I'm meant to lead a healthy and mindful lifestyle.' She rolled her eyes dramatically. 'I swear, if I was seriously very sick, I would never have kept it from you for a second.'

'But you did!' I shouted. I was so upset, I couldn't help it. 'You let us all go on like we had real problems when you have cancer!'

Manuel moved to stand behind me and put his hands on my shoulders. 'Portia, your mother didn't want the public to

290

know until she came to terms with it. She wanted to tell you both together, but then everything happened so fast . . .'

'And you two!' I screeched at him, and David. 'You knew, and you didn't tell us?'

David looked ashamed. 'She made me promise not to tell a soul, Portia. You know how things get out in this town. It's been so hard not sharing it with you guys, but Dessie swore blind that if it got any worse, or there was any reason to tell anybody else, she would.'

'I don't believe this . . .' I muttered.

In that moment, I felt utterly betrayed, yet again. Yet another secret being kept from me by someone I loved. More lies, more hiding, more sneaking around. I felt like I couldn't trust anyone, even my own mother. Why couldn't anybody just tell me the truth?

Vinnie, on the other hand, just looked worried. 'Can you take my bone marrow?' she asked, matter-of-factly.

'I don't know, darling. You'd have to be tested. But I told you, we're not there yet.'

'Well, if and when we are, I want you to take it,' Vinnie stated. 'I'll give you anything. You fixed me when I was broken, so it's payback time.'

Dessie gave her such a beatific smile, her whole face lit up with warmth. 'You owe me nothing, my pet. But thank you for being so kind.'

'*Kind?*' I was screaming now. 'She's offering you her literal body parts, and you're thanking her for being kind? This family is so messed up! What is wrong with all of you?'

The four of them stared at me, as if I was somehow the one in the wrong.

'This is real life! It's not a TV show! When somebody is sick, they tell their family. When somebody needs something, they ask for it. I feel like I'm in an alternative universe!'

I was furious, practically seeing red, as if a lens was clouding my vision.

Manuel interjected. 'Portia, you can see how your mother wouldn't want this to get out. She's a busy, dynamic woman. She doesn't want to be seen as someone that's sick.'

'Manny, no offence, but I am her daughter. Telling me is not this "getting out". I'm not Ariel, I don't tell the family secrets when I'm upset!' He backed off, holding up his hands. It was perhaps a low blow, but I didn't care. 'And right now, I don't give a flying fuck about her businesses, her reality show or anything except her health and the fact that she's clearly yet another pathological liar.'

Natasha re-entered the room. 'You told me to keep you updated,' she squeaked. 'TMZ broke the collapsing at the reunion story, and Page Six have confirmed it with the network.'

Everyone but me reached for their phones. 'Dessie Daniels reunion collapse!' David read. 'The OG *LOLA* rushed to hospital, status unknown.'

'Sorry, Dessie, but TMZ is questioning if you're alive,' Natasha said.

'*Fuck it!*' my mother shouted. 'I knew my idiot cast mates would run straight to the press. I bet you a hundred dollars Isabel rang TMZ before she even knew I was conscious. Manny,' she barked. 'Call Giulia, get her to release a statement right now. Blame low blood sugar, stress, anything. Tell them I am very much alive and kicking, and not to be pitied!'

I couldn't believe the circus that was unfolding around me. Disgusted, I left the room.

I don't even remember dialling Noah Frost's number, but the next thing I knew, I was climbing into his car on Robertson Boulevard.

Noah didn't say anything. When he pulled into a parking garage, I came out of my trance and looked at him properly for the first time.

His grey eyes were concerned. 'It's okay, we're at my place. I didn't know where to go, so I just came here. Are you okay?'

'I'm really not,' I managed, and then dissolved into his arms, sobbing. He let me cry, and then wordlessly helped me out of the car and into his place.

I was still bawling like a baby when he settled me on the sofa, an Afghan throw around my shoulders. The tears just wouldn't stop – it was as if I'd turned on a tap and every crazy, awful thing that had happened over the last few months was hitting me full force.

I cried for my mother, keeping her poor health from Vinnie and me for fear of worrying us, or of being seen as less than fabulously capable. I was sad and angry that she felt we couldn't or wouldn't keep a secret, that she knew on some intuitive level that our men weren't to be trusted. That her life was like this, a constant worry that someone was going to screw her over. That made me sob harder.

I cried for my old life, happy with Jason in New York City.

I cried for Ariel and her loneliness and terrible behaviour, for Vinnie and her disgusting husband, and for the boys who had to endure the consequences of their parents' choices. Everything just seemed so sad, so desperate, so beyond repair.

Noah poured me a glass of brandy, and one for himself. He sat on the couch, put my legs on his lap and let me weep until I cried myself to sleep.

He shook me awake a while later. 'Portia, wake up. Your sister keeps calling you.'

Before I was even fully alert, I had thrown myself at him. I kissed him desperately, loosening his belt at the same time.

I wanted to feel something, anything, other than scared, betrayed and devastated.

But he wasn't kissing me back. In fact, Noah had pulled away and was holding my wrists. 'Not like this, Portia.'

'Not like what? Are you turning me down?'

'Not when you're this upset, this frantic. I think you're amazing, Portia, but I'm not here to bang your pain away.'

In that moment, I deflated. 'I'm so sorry, Noah,' I groaned, my head in my hands. 'I have never felt more fucked up in my life than I have the past few months. And every time I think I'm getting a handle on it, something else happens.'

'Hey, I've lived in Los Angeles for over a decade. I am well versed in feeling fucked up.' He grinned kindly. 'Portia, I can see that you're having a tough time. I've been there – someday I'll tell you about it. But I want you to know that it's okay not to be okay.'

I nodded, tears threatening again. 'Thank you for being so nice to me.'

'Nice, shmice. Before I had a lot of therapy, I wouldn't have stopped a few minutes ago – yes, even with all the crying. It's actually quite interesting, thinking with my brain and not my dick.'

I laughed, despite myself.

'Call Lavinia,' he said, rubbing my back. 'Then I'll bring you back to the hospital.'

'What about the paparazzi?'

'I *am* the paparazzi.' He grinned. 'I might get fired, but I told them Dessie was taken to White Memorial.'

32

The hospital let Dessie go early the next morning. As predicted, she'd been dehydrated and fatigued, so she was sent home with strict orders for rest and proper nutrition. The press had been informed that she was, in fact, alive, and that her collapse was due to recently diagnosed hypoglycaemia. Apparently, it was more desirable to suffer from low blood sugar and fainting spells than to tell anybody the truth.

The network and three of the other Ladies sent ostentatious flowers, food hampers and cards, and Dessie received them while propped up on half a dozen pillows in her fabulous California king bed.

Vinnie, Ariel and I were all tucked up with her. I'd apologized for my behaviour in the hospital, and Mom had shooed it away. 'Pet, I owe all of you an apology. David tells me I should have trusted you both to be able to handle my news whatever was going on, and I acknowledge I did you a disservice by not telling you. I'm just so used to keeping everything to my goddamn self.'

'What about me?' Ariel whined. 'Didn't I deserve to know the truth? I live here!'

'You can't handle the truth,' Dessie answered. 'Oh my god! I've always wanted to say that line seriously! How fabulous.'

Even on her sickbed, she was making us laugh like only Dessie could. Ariel snuggled in closer to her; she'd had a terrible fright when she saw the headlines online before Manny managed to reach her, and was remorse personified.

295

I was texting Frank, trying to reschedule my meeting, but it wasn't going well. Dessie noticed me frowning at my phone.

'What's wrong, Portia?'

'Nothing. It's nothing,' I said, flapping her concern away.

'It's not nothing,' Vinnie piped up. 'She's trying to cancel a super-important meeting with Apple TV+ this morning so she can stay here and keep an eye on you.'

'Vinnie!' I hissed. This was no time to be bothering our mother with my silly script business.

'Portia Flavia Daniels!' Dessie exclaimed. 'I am not being used as a scapegoat for you not following your dreams. I am absolutely fine; I have round-the-clock care and attention, which you know I simply thrive on. You are going to that meeting. Nobody stands up Apple.'

'It's not just Apple,' Vinnie said wickedly. 'It's a chance to have her movie made by the next Nancy Meyers.'

'Nancy bloody Meyers?' Dessie nearly leapt from the bed. 'I based the kitchen in this house on the one in *It's Complicated*! She's an icon! Are you insane?'

Ariel giggled, until a glare from Dessie silenced her. 'I'm serious, Portia, I won't stand for this.'

'The *next* Nancy Meyers – she's called Katie Carlton. And I'm sure she'll understand that there are much more import-ant things than a development meeting. I'm not in the right state of mind for it right now.'

'Bullshit, you're not. You're going to summon every ounce of energy you have and put on a show. You are going to this meeting, or so help me God, I will drop dead on the spot and it will be all your fault.'

'She's right, Portia,' Vinnie offered. 'Go to Pasadena. We have everything covered here, I swear.'

I looked between them. Even Ariel was nodding at me encouragingly.

'If you leave right now, you'll make it, if the traffic isn't horrendous,' Vinnie said.

I felt a rush of adrenaline. They were right, of course. Dessie was being well cared for and had everyone at her beck and call. The only one I'd be hurting by blowing off this meeting was myself.

Screw my fabulous outfit and flawless glam. Bless my family. I kissed each one of them on the cheek and ran to grab my keys.

Giulia was dealing with the media fallout from Dessie's collapse, so I was on my own in Mom's car with the top down, cruising down the freeway towards beautiful Pasadena, the part of Los Angeles that's so clean, you could eat your dinner off the sidewalk. It's peak Nancy Meyers country, all white picket fences and Spanish-style homes, and I love it there.

I hadn't had time to practise my presentation, I had hair dye stains on my forehead, and I wasn't wearing any makeup. I threw on my signature minidress and boots combo, and it would just have to do. I had wanted to dazzle everyone in the room, but if that wasn't going to happen, I might as well feel the breeze in my hair and focus on being as present and in the moment as I possibly could be.

One positive was that I did know my script back to front. It wasn't a hundred per cent finished, and I didn't even know how much of it Frank had sent over to the team at Apple. I had to trust him, and remember that I was being asked to meet them urgently because they liked my work. I was going to channel Dessie at her ballsiest, and bowl them over with enthusiasm and eagerness to get this project off the ground.

Writers in Hollywood are at the bottom of the totem pole, I knew that. But every good show or film starts with a good story, and a visionary that's able to bring it to life. My father had been a consummate filmmaker, one involved in every aspect of getting a project made. I didn't inherit his producing or directing skills, but I did have a sliver of his charm. I was going to knock Katie's cashmere socks off.

She was everything I hoped she'd be, and more. A former sitcom actress, she'd used that notoriety to get her own directorial debut off the ground, one of the best romantic movies I'd ever seen.

'It was more tragedy than romcom,' Katie explained as we settled around a table in the conference room of the Langham Huntington Hotel. I'd never been there before, but it was a calming, regal place with a pastel brick facade, and the room overlooked a gorgeous Japanese garden. 'I want to avoid getting typecast as the queen of the weepies, but everything I write myself is inexplicably morose. I've looked at adapting novels, but none of them get me in the gut. Nothing did, until I read your script.'

There were seven other people around the table – Frank, his assistant Sheena, two male execs from the studio and three reps from Katie's production company. They all seemed to love the screenplay, but I'd learned early on not to believe a word out of a Hollywood executive's mouth. They are the ultimate lick-arses, as my mother would say.

But Katie seemed different to any other director I'd met. She was a woman, for one thing. She had long blonde hair that looked like spun gold, big blue eyes and an energy that I just vibed with.

'Of course, I want some changes,' she said, laying her cards on the table. She had to let me know who was boss.

'I do too,' I countered. 'I know this script has the potential to be a hit, and I want the right collaborator to make that happen. I want all the magical pixie dust available to sprinkle on this movie and make it amazing.'

Katie grinned at me, and I had a good feeling. But this was Hollywood. I couldn't get too excited.

An hour after I arrived, it was all over. It all felt like a blur. Frank insisted we go to lunch, just the two of us. He wanted to know all about what had happened with my mom, so I drove us both to Chef Tony's downtown for some dim sum. Frank is a low-key guy, and over beers and steamed buns I filled him in on what had gone down. I didn't tell him everything – it was up to my mother to disclose her CML diagnosis – but chatting for a couple of hours was cathartic.

'I've always felt very protective over your mom,' Frank said as he drained his third Tsing Tao. 'She has this quality, where she's tough but you still want to take care of her. I know your old man felt that way.'

'I wish I knew more about him. As an adult, a person, you know? It's weird only having this childhood impression of my father, and then everyone else's opinion of the public figure that he was.'

'I wish he'd stuck around to see you girls grow up – he'd be blown away. Your pop was a complicated guy, but he really loved you all. When I was a movie reporter way back when, there was nobody I'd rather shadow than Roberto Rizzi. And he looked after me, you know? When I was an up-and-coming agent, he let me look after his memoir. That set me up, and it's why I'll always be there for your family.'

I saw a tear sparkle in his rheumy eye and felt a surge of affection for Frank. 'Okay, big guy. Your cardiologist will kill me if you keep drinking beer in the afternoon. I'll give you a ride back to the Langham. Book yourself into the Chinese spa for some R&R.'

As I kissed him goodbye at the hotel valet, Frank was ebullient. 'You killed it today, kid,' he said proudly. 'You had everyone in the room eating out of the palm of your hand. You're your father's daughter, no doubt.'

'I don't know if romantic comedies would have been my dad's thing.' I laughed.

'Roberto liked talent, Portia. He liked good storytelling and professionalism. He would be so proud of you right now, just like I am.'

I felt tears welling up, but I blinked them away. Nothing had happened yet, and probably wouldn't for months, if ever. If I'd learned one thing about working in show business, it was never to get your hopes up too high. It was time to wait.

I have never been a patient person. In fact, that's a massive understatement. But until I heard that the project was officially green-lit, there was no point hoping. I forced down my excitement, tamped down my dreams, and prepared to bide my time.

In the days following the meeting, I realized something. Whatever fleeting desire I'd had to go back to New York had left me. Since the news of my mother's illness, I wanted to be near her and nowhere else. I thought about my beautiful apartment sitting empty, and knew that I couldn't keep avoiding the thoughts of going back east, even just to sort stuff out. I felt too much in limbo to even begin to deconstruct my life, and not for the first time of late, thanked the heavens for the privileges my family's money afforded us.

I took to sleeping in Dessie's bed at night and spent hours researching her condition. She'd made a grand return to social media to assure her followers that she was not only fine, but fabulous, and because they trusted her, they believed her. But I wasn't so easily convinced. I learned through my reading and chats with her doctors that Chronic Myeloid Leukaemia isn't always fatal, and Dessie was right in saying that patients can live with it for decades. But the angry bruises snaking up her limbs frightened me, and she was weak and nauseous most of the time. I hated seeing my strong, resilient mother suffering.

I had been purposely avoiding thinking about Jason and Sandra because it was too difficult. But in the time passing after Dessie's collapse, whenever I wasn't worrying about her, I was thinking about him. It was like a switch had been flipped when everything slowed down and my emotions were raw and exposed. It was utterly bizarre that I hadn't seen him in months; the pain was still fresh, still hurt like a fresh scald on my heart. Whatever ability I'd had to put him out of my head when things were busy was gone, and Jason was living rent free in my mind, 24/7.

I didn't know what Jason was doing, who he was with, where in the world he was, and that bugged me. The possibility of him being with Sandra seemed less and less likely, because I was sure I'd have heard something from the network of family spies in Ireland if it was true.

At night, when Dessie was snoring away softly beside me, I lay awake and wondered if I'd been too rash in fleeing New York the way I did. Seeing my mother in this vulnerable state had rattled me on so many levels, including bringing forth an unwelcome sense of mortality I hadn't experienced before. People often asked me who'd look after me when I was older if I didn't have kids of my own, and I shrugged their comments off with a smart response. But watching how much Dessie was relying on us all for support, help, company . . . it shook me. I wasn't invincible, nor was I an island. I didn't want to be alone for ever.

I wondered if I should have given Jason more of a chance to explain himself; if what we'd needed was time together to work things out. And then I worried I'd never know.

@LifeWithLRS

5 September 2022

Today's blog post is all about my wonderful mom! We've been spending so much time together since I've been living in her gorgeous home, and we spent hours poring over old photo albums together that we'd love to share with you all. It's inspired me to print out photographs of my own little ones, and not have them all living in the cloud.

Click for some never-before-seen photos from my childhood featuring @dessiedaniels and my sisters. Remember just how important it is to cherish your memories with your loved ones. Patreon subscribers get even more unseen pics!

33

One Saturday morning in September I was making my mother a date shake, her Palm Springs favourite. It sounds gross – a whizzed-up concoction of ice cream and medjools – but it's fantastic. Absent-mindedly, I was listening to Ariel and my mother shout to one another from their rooms.

'Mooooom, where's Dad?'

'How am I supposed to know? I don't have a tracking device on the man!'

A thought occurred to me from nowhere. The previous year, when I'd got my new iPhone, Jason had been setting it up to communicate with all my other devices. We'd permanently shared our location with one another on our cells, joking that we'd always know where to find the other. 'No more wondering which dive bar I'm propping up now, babe!' he'd joked, and I'd swatted him playfully. Was the secret to where in the world he was right there on my phone?

Breathless, I grabbed it and went to the Find My app. There was no guarantee he was even using the same cell or that he hadn't blocked me, but when the app zoned in, there he was. A flashing beacon on the map in . . . I did a double take. Orange County?!

Date shake forgotten, I ran to find Dessie. '*Mom!*' I shouted.

'Jesus, what? I'm supposed to be taking it easy, Portia – don't frighten the shite out of me!' I found her in her closet wearing a pink Versace robe, eye patches, her hair in a ponytail. She was scribbling in her Filofax.

'He's in California, Mom! Jason is in Newport fucking Beach!'

'Are you sure, love? Why would he come to LA and not call you?'

'I don't know – because he doesn't give a shit about me? Because he's in a relationship with his sister-in-law?'

'Do you want me to call the network and do some digging? Sweetheart, he might not even know you're here . . .'

A voice piped up from the doorway. 'He knows.'

Our heads turned to see Ariel hopping from foot to foot. She had something in her hands, an envelope.

'Before you get mad, this only happened yesterday. I didn't tell you yet because I wanted to make sure you'd want to know . . .'

'Ariel, what?'

'Jason came by. He didn't ring the doorbell or call, but he put this in the mailbox.' She held out the envelope. 'He was being sneaky, but I saw him from the window. I went out and got it, and I thought I'd keep it safe until I was sure.'

She saw my thunderous expression.

'I knew I'd be sure really quickly! I was going to tell you like, asap. I just wanted to hear you say something, like you missed him or whatever.'

'Ariel, have you learned nothing from the past few months?' I asked, my heart thumping out of my chest. 'We don't keep secrets, and we don't interfere with other people's business.'

'But you're just starting to do better!' she groaned. 'I wanted to make sure you'd want to hear from smelly old Jason.'

'Ariel, he is neither smelly nor old,' my mother scolded. She snatched the envelope from Ariel and handed it to me.

I walked away from them, clutching the envelope in

both hands. Out by the pool, I turned it over and, when I saw his familiar handwriting, my heart lurched. This was something from Jason, my Jason, after months of nothing. Would opening it be like opening Pandora's box? Or would it answer the questions that had never stopped whirling around my head?

Letters had always been our thing. I took a deep breath and slid out the pages within.

Dear Portia

I've written and rewritten this note to you what feels like a hundred times over the past few months, but I've never known what to say until now. I haven't seen you in so long, but the feeling of missing a limb hasn't left me, like I thought it might with time. Then when I saw the news about your mam, I knew I had to reach out. But I wanted to wait until I was nearby, so we could talk properly.

I don't know where to begin, but I want you to know that you were right about Sandra – but not about me. She left Mick and told me she loved me, and I flew home to deal with the fallout. But I didn't, don't, feel the same way. I never have. I was ashamed that you were right, that I'd been so stupid and couldn't see things with her for what they were.

Everything is messed up because Sandra got the wrong idea about us, and I know now that's partially my fault. I've been in Ireland trying to sort it out and, in truth, trying to sort my own head out. I was leaning on her when I hit a rough patch, and I didn't realize it was inappropriate because I didn't know she had feelings for me. Then I was offended, because I thought you knew that. It's taken me until now to look at it from your point of view, to realize how it looked from the outside. I am so, so sorry.

Before coming back to the States, I went to Sydney to see Tiernan and Liza, and the new baby. He arrived in early August. They called him Louis, and he's perfect.

I've taken a new job, as an executive producer in charge of development, so I won't be freelancing any more. The powers-that-be have tasked me with creating and casting new reality shows. It means being based on the West Coast, a lot of travel and a lot of money, which is great. But everything feels hollow without you to come home to.

Right now, I'm working in the OC on the latest Ladies franchise and renting a place in Newport on the water. I hope you're still at your mam's – I know you're not at the place in New York (I've had Frida downstairs keeping an eye on things and haven't been back there myself). I thought with her being unwell lately, you might have stayed close to Dessie.

I'm sending a letter because you may not want to hear from me and calling and texting just doesn't feel like enough. I'm putting the ball in your court.

I still love you more than anything, and I'm here if you want to talk.

Jxxx

I must have read and reread the note fifteen times before I even looked up from the page. Jason said that he still loved me. This was my chance to find out.

He was an hour, ninety minutes at most, away by car. He wanted to see me. Without even talking to anyone, I stalked through the house, grabbed the keys to Vinnie's car and tore out of the driveway, wheels spinning.

It took two hours to get to Jason's location with traffic, and I was terrified the blue dot signalling where he was would move before I got there. I didn't allow myself to think, to hope: I was focused on breathing and driving along the I-5. But certain things were still niggling at me – why was he in touch with Frida downstairs? Why didn't he get in touch with me sooner? Was this just a pity letter because my mom was sick?

According to my phone, he was in a house on Balboa Island. As I indicated off the interstate and found myself in the swish environs of Costa Mesa, I started to get nervous. I'd never really liked Newport Beach; it always felt like a sort of fake place to me. Everyone there is white, thin, conservative and ultra-rich. But Balboa is cute, I remembered, as I crossed the little bridge on to the man-made enclave. It was like stepping back in time, with small, independent businesses lining the streets, cedar-shingled New England-style homes and lots of American flags flapping in the breeze.

When I pulled up to the address at Diamond Avenue indicated on my phone, I paused for breath outside. I looked at my reflection in the rear-view mirror, smoothed my hair and tried to gather myself before walking up the path and pressing the doorbell. I took a deep breath.

The door opened, and I steeled myself to look into those icy blue eyes. But instead of being face to face with Jason, a blonde woman with gigantic, hard-looking breasts was staring at me quizzically. 'Oh, I'm so sorry! I'm looking for Jason Dempsey?'

I realized then when she tried to smile that this woman's face wasn't puzzled, it was just her normal face. 'Oh yes, honey, he's two doors that-a-way. Lovely guy.'

I thanked her and turned to see Jason standing on a porch nearby. He was laughing, and my stomach lurched at the sight of him. 'Wrong gaff,' he called, and looking at him, it felt like no time at all had passed.

We'd always fitted together perfectly, Jason and me. My

shoulder under his arms, my head under his chin. It was something that made me feel quite certain we were meant to be. That, and the fact that I felt balanced with him, like the rest of the world was tuned out. I had always been completely and utterly myself with Jason. Hugging him in that moment, it felt both so familiar and so foreign. He smelled different, but also the same.

We pulled apart at the same time, obviously both feeling a little strange. 'You came,' he said, stroking my face with his thumb. 'How did you find me?'

'Well, you didn't put an address on your note,' I replied. 'Luckily, Mr iPhone knew where you were. Well.' I grinned. 'He was off by about twenty feet.'

He laughed. 'Oh, wow. I didn't even think of that. I've been staring at my phone, waiting for a call.'

'You know, I haven't been checking in on you,' I said, quietly. 'I've been trying to forget, it's been . . . a lot.'

Wordlessly, Jason took my hand and led me into the little blue house. He pulled two beers out of the fridge and opened them, handing one to me. He walked out back on to the deck, and I followed. We both sat down.

'Wow,' I said, taking in the sparkling sea, bobbing boats and people walking their poodle mixes on the boardwalk. 'Talk about picturesque.' I looked around again. 'Hang on, is this an old person's community?!'

'Not officially.' He grinned. 'But the average age is about sixty on this stretch. It's quiet, I like it. After dealing with the Newport Ladies all day . . .'

'How's work going?' I asked, not sure of what to say.

'It's going,' he replied. 'The new gig will have me criss-crossing the globe, but I'll be based in LA. I'm thinking of trying to get a place in that block I lived in when we first met. Remember?'

308

'How could I forget?'

Jason fixed me with a look. After so many years, I knew what the look meant, and what he was remembering from those early, halcyon days. I felt a throb between my legs, a rush of pure chemical attraction in my gut. But I wasn't going to let this get physical, no matter how much I wanted to.

'Why did you write to me?' I asked plainly.

'Because I miss you, and I love you,' he said, shrugging. 'I kept waiting to feel better, but the pain isn't going away. In fact, it's getting harder. When I heard about Dessie being in hospital, it nearly killed me not being there for you. But I didn't want to just contact you from Australia and ask how you were. I figured I'd wait until I was back here.'

I nodded, believing him.

'It all happened so fast back in New York,' he was saying. 'I told you how I'd been feeling, things got weird and then, all of a sudden, you were gone. I was so mad at you.'

'My sister needed me, and things between us . . . I couldn't stand being so at odds with you, I felt like I was crawling out of my skin. I didn't know what to do, so I bolted.'

'It's not like you, Portia. You don't run away.'

'But whose fault is it that I did?' I snapped. 'Remember how it all came out in the wash? Remember, your inappropriate pen pal?'

He looked down at his feet. 'The whole Sandra thing was a complete nightmare; you were right about that. But I never intended it to happen that way, and I was so pissed you didn't trust me enough. I have zero romantic feelings for Sandra, she was just someone to talk to . . .'

'But human beings aren't just people to talk to, Jason. Unless you're paying a professional, someone you bare your soul to will consider you to be in some sort of close relationship.' I was angry again. 'Surely you know that? Women aren't just a sounding board for angst-ridden men!'

'I thought she was safe – she's my brother's wife!'

'Yeah, well, you thought wrong!' I yelled, surprising myself. I was furious. 'And the biggest problem is that you weren't talking to me! Don't you see that? I was right there!'

'I was scared!' Jason stood up and was shouting now too. 'I was scared during the pandemic. I was freaking out about death and mortality. And then when I realized I did want to have kids, I was scared of exactly what happened, happening. I knew once I told you, you'd freak. And then you were gone and I was lonely and terrified.'

'Well, good for you, Jason, because I had no idea of how you were feeling or what was going to happen and was completely blindsided!' I roared.

I saw Hard Boobs two doors down peering across the fence; maybe nobody had screaming fights on Balboa Island.

Jason sat back down, head in his hands. He looked defeated.

'I'm sorry, Portia,' he said, and I could hear the tears in his voice. 'I'm truly sorry.'

'I am too, Jay. I'm sorry that you felt you couldn't confide in me. But I don't know what we can do about it now. It feels . . . broken between us.'

He just sat there, his handsome face contorted with misery, and my heart couldn't take seeing him so sad. I walked over and knelt in front of him, my hands on his knees. 'When you told me the truth about wanting to be a . . . father.' I gulped. 'I wanted to be able to give you what you wanted, if it meant you and me were going to be okay. Even though it wasn't what I wanted, I was thinking about going against my own instincts for you. And if the whole Sandra thing and Vinnie's drama hadn't happened, I probably would have just said *oh, fuck it*, and given it a try so I didn't lose you. But the Sandra thing did happen. And then you certainly didn't waste any time . . .'

'You're saying that I'm the one that ruined everything?'

'You didn't help. And now so much has gone on, I don't think we can ever get back to where we were.'

I was openly crying now too, and we were clinging to one another.

'I can't just have you gone from my life,' he managed. 'I need you in it, in some way.'

'What, like friends? I can't, Jason . . .'

'Not just friends, like best friends, like my soulmate, like you've always been. I don't even know what's going on with you. What are you working on? How's Vinnie? I want to catch up, hang out.'

I stared at him, and it dawned on me that he truly thought we could still be that close after everything. As if we could click back in to spending time together, as if I could fill him in on the life I was attempting to cobble together. He didn't realize that, because of him, I still wasn't sure where I was going, what I was doing. I didn't know where I was going to live, if New York was even still home for me. The last few months of my life had been on pause, while his was ongoing without me.

'Jason, I'm sorry. I still love you too much to even pretend to be able to be friends with you. I'm glad I've seen you, but I don't think we should do this again. It's too painful.'

'But what if things were different?'

'What if? Jason, we can't live our lives on what-ifs. And we can't fake it, either. Even if we forgot about everything else, all the lies of omission and the fact that I'd struggle to trust you ever again. The fact remains that we want different things.'

He leaned forward, took my face in his big hands and kissed me on the mouth, as if he could stop me speaking the truth, as if he could kiss the past few months away. I let him for a few beautiful seconds, the feeling so safe and so sweet. But I broke away, because the more I let him back in, the harder it would be to leave him again. And I had to, because nothing had changed.

I walked purposefully out of the house and got into Vinnie's car before he could come after me. But he didn't. I drove off and continued for thirty minutes before I pulled into a gas station in Santa Ana and let the tears come. I took out my phone and blocked Jason's number and location. It was the only way I'd survive.

34

Over the next days and weeks, Dessie became a lot brighter and more like her old self. It was early fall, her favourite season, and she was enjoying pruning her rosebushes and hiking with Vinnie in the hills as the summer heat abated. She certainly appeared strong and able and was back to looking ageless and spry.

I'd taken to helping her in the garden, and with the dogs. Bubbles and I had grown close, seeing as I was sharing the bed with him and Dessie, and I found myself wondering if a dog of my own was feasible, wherever I ended up. The three of us spent hours bingeing box sets and watching old *LOLA*s, howling at her mid-noughties outfits and cooing over baby Ariel on screen.

We didn't talk about anything serious, didn't mention our problems. She never asked what happened with Jason and though I worried about it, I never bothered her about her prognosis because I knew she didn't want to talk about it. We just hung out, with me keeping a watchful eye on her, and it was restorative.

In full 'get over Jason for good' mode, I had gone on a few Raya dates, but none of them interested me much. I'd come home from Newport and had a day of sobbing before deciding that while our situation was sad, it wasn't a matter of life and death. I had to try and move on, to live the only life I had. I could see how a brush with mortality could shake someone, even Jason and Sandra.

So, I gave the app another try, but wasn't vibing enough

with any of the guys to want to see them naked. Vinnie was trying to give me dating pointers, which was rich, coming from her.

'You're not exactly banging your way around town, sis,' I pointed out. 'I don't know why you're trying to give me advice.'

'That is by choice, while I figure out my own sexual quandary,' she replied smugly. 'And I am also a mother-of-two with a much bigger profile than you. It's not that easy for me to get laid, so I want to live vicariously through my single big sister.'

'Touché. But none of them are doing it for me.' I shrugged.

'Do you think seeing Jason put you back a little, in your recovery? Like, you were going cold turkey and doing so well . . .'

'No, I think it will be better in the long run. There was a bit of closure because not ever seeing him again would have been too weird. But I don't think I'll ever get over it fully. He acted like a selfish idiot, but we adore each other. We just want different things.'

'Are you going to sit and rot like Miss Havisham, pining for your great love?'

'Nice literary reference, Vinnie.'

'I watched the Ethan Hawke movie version.' She stuck her tongue out at me. 'What if he changed his mind again?'

'Not likely, Vin. And I'm not going to either. We are at what they call a stalemate. And that's why I just need to get over it. And I will. Eventually.'

To distract myself from thoughts of both Jason and Apple TV, who I was yet to hear back from after several weeks, I got into something of an LA routine. I started going to Barry's Bootcamp with Suz a couple of times a week in West Hollywood and bringing David lunch in the salon afterwards. He had officially leased a condo in WeHo, letting his apartment in New York go, and it was great to have him close by full time.

I went for walks with Vinnie and the boys, played chess with Giulia in the evenings, and even started showing an interest in Ariel's TikToks. I never thought I'd see myself lip-syncing to Miley Cyrus on a fifteen-year-old's social media, but that's where my strange new existence brought me.

Ariel was seeing an adolescent psychologist weekly and doing Zoom sessions along with her parents once a month. Nothing too stressful for Dessie, just some light work to foster a mutual understanding. My kid sister was being a lot more pleasant, which seemed to mean it was working.

I went to the movies with Chris Adams as a sort of chemistry test just to see for myself if there was anything there. While we had a nice time, it was clear to me that the moment for us had passed. I wasn't attracted to him that way; we were just friends, and that was for the best. Chris was easy company, and he had lots of intel on the inner workings of the romcom genre from his ex-wife, the consummate on-screen best friend. I started going to his house after that to watch his favourite romantic movies with him, purely for scholarly reasons. We devoured *Casablanca*, *The Philadelphia Story*, *Love Story* and *Working Girl* together, classics of the genre that we both loved.

'Why didn't you ever do a romantic comedy?' I asked him one evening after the credits rolled on Melanie Griffith's magnum opus with shoulder pads.

'Too sexy and rugged,' he quipped, his eyes crinkling. 'I would have liked to, but my agent said it would damage my action-hero status.' He shrugged.

'Bullshit,' I yelped. 'Did we not just watch Harrison Ford be completely devastatingly sexy as a romantic lead? He'd been Han Solo, Indiana Jones, by that point!'

'Unfortunately, Portia, I am not Harrison Ford,' Chris sighed. 'I'm much, much sexier.'

In Chris I was discovering perhaps the first ever straight guy who was truly just a friend, almost a father figure. I hadn't even realized how deep my own daddy issues went, and if there was one thing I needed to feel at that moment, it was faith in straight men.

Billy had returned from his Mexican exile and was lying low in an apartment in Valley Village. Vinnie had put their Hidden Hills home on the market and was proceeding with the divorce uncontested. She had relented and let Billy spend an afternoon with Si and Seb on neutral territory; he did that classic newly separated dad thing and brought them to Disneyland.

'I've encouraged him to get some intensive therapy to get over his penchant for barely legal ingénues,' she told me after one of their peace summits.

'Yeah, it would help if he wasn't pursuing high-school girls in future.' I grimaced. 'How were the boys with him?'

'They were happy to see their dad, but also perfectly happy to say goodbye and return to Mom's house. It wasn't some big, tearful reunion, you know?'

'I guess we should be grateful that the split isn't affecting them.'

'Yeah, until they're old enough to google and find out that their dad is a creep.' Vinnie shuddered. 'Anyway, I will be pre-empting all that long-term damage with a lot of counselling. I don't want them ending up like me,' she said.

'What, hyper-successful and beloved by millions?'

'No, blocking out every feeling they ever have with booze and drugs. Mom should have made us see a shrink after Dad died.'

'Things were different in the nineties, Vin,' I said. 'And I turned out pretty normal?'

'Oh, of course, besides the rampant accidental serial monogamy and distaste for procreation.' My sister smirked. It was good that we could laugh at these things, at least.

I'd been thinking about our dad a lot and talking to both Mom and Vinnie about him. I wasn't naive enough to think that his sudden death and his issues in life didn't affect my relationships, but I was only now truly realizing how deeply. Vinnie and I had both suffered because of turning a blind eye to problems with the men in our lives, while Dessie had chosen artifice over true love. They were safety measures; how we protected ourselves.

Vinnie was keeping her distance from India, as promised, but they still talked all the time. I could tell my sister missed her; she wasn't shining as brightly as she had in the weeks when India was the centre of her life.

But she seemed content enough – she'd started posting regularly again, which was a sure sign of improved mental health in an influencer. Giulia had wangled her a nostalgic cover shoot with other noughties supermodels for *New York* magazine, and she was so excited for it. 'Seeing those bitches sober will be an experience,' she'd huffed in the middle of a punishing ab workout. One thing about a group of former models – they're going to be competing to be in the best shape. I was glad Vinnie was doing it the old-fashioned way.

Ten weeks after Dessie's dramatic collapse, on a breezy October day, she summoned us all for an extended family brunch. Ostensibly we were meeting to watch a preview of the action-packed reunion during which she conked out; it was being teased on the internet to rabid response, now that everyone knew she was okay.

The extended family congregated on a warm autumn Sunday morning on the patio, where Dessie had laid out bagels, Kerrygold butter and cream cheese, crispy bacon, maple syrup, pancakes and fresh fruit. There was coffee, a variety of juices, and bottles of Bollinger on ice as well as fresh flowers. My mother never did things by halves.

'Wow, Mom. This is quite a spread,' I said, helping myself to a pancake and sitting down beside Suz. She'd brought her two girls, who were becoming women at a frightening pace.

'Well,' Dessie said dramatically, standing at the head of the table. 'While we will watch the reunion after brunch, in all its gory glory, I also have an announcement to make. Since it involves all of you, I thought I would tell all of you together.'

I was suddenly nervous – with Dessie it could be literally anything, and I was getting celebratory vibes – was she getting her own show? Going back to acting? Having a full facelift?

She waited until she had everyone's attention. There were twelve of us around the behemoth marble table – me, Dessie, Vinnie, Silas, Sebastian, Ariel, Manuel, Giulia, David, Suz, Sabrina and Willa.

'Darlings, I gathered you all here because I have decided to write my memoir,' Dessie announced grandly, pronouncing it 'memwaaas'. 'Giulia and Frank brought me a fantastic deal for an eye-wateringly large sum to chronicle my life thus far, from modelling for Andy Warhol to meeting Roberto, from near-destitution to a career in soaps and infomercials, to *LOLA* and business and everything in between.'

She paused dramatically for us to take it all in, Giulia looking pleased as punch beside her.

'I've turned down offers like this before because I always felt like my story was only beginning. But now I can see that I've come a long way, and every one of you has come along with me. I'm going to take the time to write my life story, and I'm going to be honest and unflinching. I hope that you will all support me in that.' She looked around the table, and her gaze lingered on Vinnie, who looked uneasy. Of course. Dessie was looking for permission to tell the truth about Vinnie's past life.

'Let's talk about it, Mom?' Vinnie eventually said, and my mother beamed at her. It wasn't an immediate no, anyway.

'Well, we will have plenty of time to talk because I have a proposition for my daughters,' Dessie said. My ears pricked up.

'I've decided that to write about my life, I must go back to where it all began. I have three months off from filming the show, and I want to spend them in Ireland. In Dingle, County Kerry, to be exact. And I'd like the three of you' – she pointed at me, Vinnie and Ariel – 'to come with me and help me. And my grandsons, of course.'

Ariel looked stricken. 'Go to Ireland? Do they even have Wi-Fi there? And what about school?'

'Well, that depends on Lavinia. Darling, what if Marjorie came with us to school Ariel and the boys?' Dessie announced. 'I don't mean to be rude, but the fabulous Marj has a Ph.D. and she's sort of been wasted on the little ones?'

Vinnie shrugged. 'I guess?'

'You've been saying you want to be home-schooled?' Mom nodded at Ariel. 'I'm willing to let you try it out for the remainder of tenth grade. Something tells me you'll happily go back to high school as a junior next September, though.'

'If I know you, Mom, I know you've already spoken to Marjorie.' Vinnie smirked.

Dessie grinned. 'I have, and she's up for it if you are, darling. Do you think Billy would give you any shit for taking the boys away?'

'I think Billy hasn't got a leg to stand on.'

We all digested my mother's suggestion along with our

fruit salads. Dessie was writing a tell-all, and she wanted to do it in Kerry. I'd decided the second she announced the book that I would be, if not her ghostwriter, then her professional adviser. If my mom was going to do this, she was going to do it right. But in Ireland? Where Sandra lived?

David was the first to speak. 'I think that's a fantastic idea, Des. I haven't been back home since before Covid, to my father's disgust. I'll let you all get settled and then I'll join you for an extended vaycay over Christmas. I have to make sure I come across well in the book, obviously.'

He buttered a bagel thoughtfully. 'I wonder if the gays back home have gotten any cuter in the past few years . . .'

Suz was swiping around on her phone. 'I'm off air for a month in the New Year,' she declared. 'The girls will be in school, so I was going to leave them with their fathers and hit the Bahamas for two weeks. But why not hit Ireland instead?'

'I can think of a few reasons,' I said. 'Climate being a big one. But yes, come! I'm in, Mom.'

My mother looked thrilled. 'So, that's arranged, then? We'll leave in a few weeks, after Lavinia's big shoot in New York and Thanksgiving. We'll have Christmas in Ireland! I have Natasha looking at houses we can rent for an extended period.' She looked around the table. 'Are you all with me?'

Everyone nodded their assent.

'Hey,' I said. 'What about you, Manny?'

He smiled, slowly. 'Dessie and I have already talked about it. I'm going to take some time for myself,' he drawled. 'I'll go home to Miami and spend Christmas with my mother while she's still with us. Maybe even take a trip to Palm Springs.' He looked me dead in the eye when he said that, and in that moment I knew that he was aware I knew his secret. I winked at him, wondering if he'd be checking into one of those all-male nudist hotels in the desert and living his best gay life.

Dessie popped a bottle of champagne and made Mimosas for everyone.

'To Ireland,' said Dessie, and we all clinked glasses. '*Slàinte!*'

Publishers Weekly

Penguin Random House acquires memoir from reality star and mogul Desdemona Daniels

14 November 2022

Putnam has won a five-way auction to secure Desdemona Daniels' currently untitled memoir.

Publishing director Estelle Brown struck a 'major' seven-figure deal for world rights from Frank Ryan at Ryan & Associates Agency. Daniels' memoir will be published in hardback in September 2023 and will be backed by a 'highly unique transatlantic marketing and publicity campaign'.

Daniels, the widow of notorious Sicilian filmmaker Roberto Rizzi, has become a huge star in her own right in recent years, due to the success of her role in reality show *Ladies of Los Angeles* and her multimillion-dollar fashion and beauty empire.

Brown says the memoir will be 'an intimate recounting of Dessie's life thus far, from humble beginnings in rural Ireland to a life of glitz and glamour in LA, all served up with Dessie's signature tenacity, grace and humour'.

Daniels says: 'I will be holding back nothing in my memoir, from my spirited childhood in rural Ireland to my migration to the glitz and glamour of New York and LA, and my family back me utterly on telling what is my true Hollywood story. I'm looking forward to writing it from my native county Kerry, with the help of my daughter, the screenwriter Portia Daniels.'

35

We arrived in Ireland on a cold December morning, after stopping off in New York to collect my passport and winter clothes. I'd sent Natasha into the apartment because it would have felt too weird to make a flying visit. She brought my knits, boots and goose-feather parka along with my documents. Then she bid us all farewell for the moment, as she was staying in the States to manage my mom's interests in her absence. You would have sworn she and Dessie were being parted for ever, the amount of snotty crying they did.

Thanks to a loan of Graham's jet, we were able to fly straight into the tiny Kerry airport and collect the rental cars we'd be using for the duration. Dessie had requested a fleet of Escalades, but as they don't exist in Ireland, had to make do with two green Land Rover Defenders instead.

Mom was in raptures from the second she stepped off the plane. You'd swear she hadn't been back to the old country in decades, but she was in Kerry just before the pandemic hit for her brother Orlando's sixtieth. I was expecting her to break out into a rendition of 'The Rose of Tralee' at any moment, or kiss the tarmac at the airport, but she held it together. Just.

Dessie was dressed for an Arctic expedition. She wore a leopard-print cossack, matching ski jacket and knee-high Uggs, which made her look like a stylish explorer. Even Bubbles was wearing a furry coat and sat proudly in her arms, taking in the views.

Marjorie and I were the only adults present with any experience of driving on the left-hand side of the road – she'd nannied for the Beckhams in London before coming with them to the US – thus we were in charge of transporting us to the Airbnb Natasha had found.

Marjorie took Ariel and the boys, I took Mom and Vinnie and their assortment of bags, and threatened my sister with violence if she didn't get comfortable with Irish roads pronto. Dessie had never learned to drive, which was probably for the best – she tends to get road rage from the back seat. She says her one big luxury in LA is her driver, Ronald, but I think saying she only has one big excess is pushing it.

I was delighted by what was to be our home for the next few months. Natasha had done well. It was a huge house on a bluff on the Dingle Peninsula that jutted out into the wild Atlantic Ocean. With three peaks, a flat, pebble-dashed facade and huge picture windows, it was a far cry from Dessie's Spanish-style modern farmhouse in Bel Air, but no less luxurious. The huge brick house had been fully renovated and refurbished with seven bedrooms and a purpose-built pub out the back. The owners explained it was a pandemic time addition and went down well with renters. It even had a Guinness tap.

What's more, Natasha had arranged to have the entire house decorated as a surprise, so we arrived to a gorgeously festive and warm atmosphere. Silas screamed bloody murder at the sight of a six-foot Santa in the hall, but even Ariel was enchanted by the old working fireplaces hung with red tartan stockings and the enormous, twinkling tree.

The kitchen was beautifully appointed, with copper pots hanging from the ceiling over an old-fashioned range. My mother said she was looking forward to doing lots of home cooking over the coming months, but I was glad to see that the huge American-style refrigerator had been fully stocked in advance. Grocery shopping was Dessie's least favourite household chore, and Instacart was a saving grace back home.

'Kerry has changed since my day!' she exclaimed as she perused Natasha's extensive notes on the property. 'You can have anything delivered! Shopping, ingredients, wine. Oh, girls, we're laughing, so we are!'

My room was on the first floor, next to Vinnie's. We were sharing a bathroom, which felt kind of old-fashioned and fun, and meant I'd get to use all her boujie products. We were both giddy, like kids at camp, only it was the bowels of winter in a mansion and, as grown-ups, we could drink mulled wine to our hearts' content – non-alcoholic for my sister, of course.

That first night, Dessie prepared a hearty Irish stew and we all sat around the dinner table together. Marjorie was googly-eyed at everything so far, and this picture-perfect part of Ireland lived up to all of her rugged Emerald Isle fantasies. She'd never spent Christmas away from her family, who were at least pleased she would be in a Catholic country and could attend Mass throughout the advent period. Dessie had promised to go with her, mostly so her own siblings didn't accuse her of being a heathen.

'So, Mom,' I began, my mouth full of delicious stew. 'What are your plans for getting started on the book?'

'Well, I think I'll take the weekend to get settled. I'm going to see the family tomorrow, and I'll fill them in on what's going on. I want them to hear about the CML from me, so I can reassure them.'

'Are you sure they won't accidentally let it slip, Mom?' I asked.

'No, darling. Your Aunt Rosalind may be the local busybody, but she's a mouth like a vault when it's important, or about me. And Jim, well, he'll probably forget five minutes after I tell him.'

'Who's Jim?' Marjorie was confused, and I didn't blame her.

'Jim is Orlando, Mom's brother,' Vinnie explained. 'Whatever about the glamorous girls in the family, but a name like that wouldn't fly around these parts.'

'She's right. He used to get an awful slagging when people found out. They called him Mickey Mouse in school,' Dessie laughed. 'Anyway, I'll arrange to do some interviews with them about my childhood next week. Then I'll stay on a tight schedule. Three months isn't a long time to write a book like this.'

'I agree, and I meant my offer of help. I'm still waiting to hear from Frank about the Apple deal, so I'm free as a bird,' I said.

'What's taking them so long, darling?'

'It's a process. Katie's wedding and honeymoon held things up with their queries and production meetings, but she feels like she'll know more soon. In the meantime, it might be better for me to interview the aunties – they're more likely to tell me the truth.'

'Oh, Portia, darling, that would be fabulous. What would I do without you?'

I glowed at my mother's praise. I was looking forward to working on this project with her and spending real quality time together.

Ariel piped up. 'And what do we propose I do in the middle of nowhere when it gets dark out at 4 p.m.? Should I learn to knit? Dig a tunnel to civilization?'

'We-ell,' Vinnie said, sneaking a look at Dessie, who nodded. 'You're going to have school with Marjorie during the day and Zoom classes with your math and science teachers in the evenings. But how would you feel about helping me out in between, while the boys are doing their schoolwork?'

'Helping you out how?' She was trying to keep her tone neutral, but I could tell Ariel was intrigued.

'Well, Mom and I have been talking about me showing

you the ropes, content-wise. You could be my intern – help making videos, teach me about TikTok transitions, even show me the ropes with what Gen Z is up to. I feel like we could help each other out, reach one another's audiences? And spend a bit of time together in the process.'

'Will you teach me how to model?' There was a glint in Ariel's eye. She'd had a growth spurt, and her new dream was to rule the world's runways – at five foot eight, she only had an inch to go before she was the standard height and she was canny enough to know that Vinnie was the perfect coach and mentor.

'That's a good idea,' Dessie chimed in, as if she hadn't already thought of it. 'After all, a modern star needs to know how to do it all.'

'Okay, deal,' said Vinnie, and my sisters shook hands across the table.

Finally, everyone was getting along. As I took a sip of Cab Sauv, I had a warm and fuzzy feeling in my chest that wasn't just from the alcohol.

That feeling lasted until about 2 p.m. the next day, when Ariel had a meltdown. She hadn't thought about the ramifications of an eight-hour time difference and was freaked out by the lack of contact from her so-called friends during daylight hours.

'My story views are in the toilet!' I heard her shriek at Dessie. 'Everyone is going to forget about me! I am *on the wrong continent!*'

We were all a bit ratty and frazzled from jet lag so, to placate and entertain her, I took Ariel to Dingle, thinking she might be charmed by the winding streets and coloured facades. She was not.

'Why are there, like, ten bars on this street alone? Is that all people do here? Sit in bars? Gross!' Part of me was pleased she wasn't about to get into the Irish drinking culture, but another part was worried. This girl was going to go crazy in the countryside for three months, and I knew that would be everyone's problem. I made a mental note to plan activities that would impress her – a privileged teenager from the Golden State would be difficult to please, but I was relatively confident that Co. Kerry had enough hidden gems to shock and awe anyone, even Ariel.

That night we went to one of said pubs to meet Dessie's sister Rosalind and brother Jim and his family. In fact, Uncle Jim owned the pub, having bought it in the nineties, but he was now retired and left the running of it to his twenty-two-year-old daughter, Aisling.

I was shocked when I saw her – my cousin had been a pimply teen when I was last in Dingle, but now she was a quintessential Irish beauty, all flowing red curls and freckles. Ariel was clearly impressed by her, the witty repartee she had with the regulars and her pint-pulling abilities. Maybe I could convince Aisling to help with the wayward teen as well.

My mother's Irish accent had become about ten times thicker since she entered the pub, her vocabulary peppered with 'yerra' and 'whisht'. She was drinking Guinness, which I found hilarious until she fixed with me a green-eyed glare and said, 'It's actually a tonic, Portia.'

I got the message: don't embarrass Dessie when she's in the bosom of her family.

Vinnie was, shockingly, also in her element. It was like she'd undergone a metamorphosis on the plane and was now as Irish as Dessie. She was wearing an actual Aran jumper, and making it look impossibly chic, paired with leather Spanx pants and Barbour boots. All she needed was a fiddle and a flat cap, and she could be on an ad for the tourist board. She'd always loved Kerry as a kid but hadn't been back in eons.

Auntie Rosalind was holding court, telling tales of Dessie's misspent youth. 'Arrah, this one always had stars in her eyes,' she was saying to her rapt audience of family and locals. 'Our Desdemona was always the prettiest girl in the town, and Daddy wanted to marry her off to the posh fella that owned everything. Our da had notions, as if that isn't obvious by our names. But our mother wanted more for all of us and convinced us to go to America before we landed ourselves in trouble, or our oul' da got his wish. I didn't last, it was too noisy and filthy for me in New York, but Dessie blossomed there. I knew she was a lost cause the second we walked out of Pennsylvania Station – I was horrified by the smells and sounds, but she was captivated.'

My mother was glowing at the memory of the day she fell in love with the Big Apple. We'd heard the story from her many times, but I loved getting Rosalind's take. They'd sublet a place from their big sister Celia who was living in sin with her boyfriend in the Bronx. It was a studio apartment in Hell's Kitchen, and Dessie had taken to the city like a duck to water.

In a matter of days, she'd scored a job at a run-down Irish bar near Time Square; the Cork-born owners had taken one look at her and offered her a job without even asking about her experience. She whiled away her days serving beer and chatting to the clientele, which was mostly made up of ex-pats.

One fateful cold winter's night a model agent stopped in for a hot toddy and signed her on the spot. Dessie was a smidge too short for the catwalk, but he knew the camera would love that face.

'Yerra, I didn't even know modelling was a real job,' Dessie was saying. 'I would have done it for free, I loved just having my picture taken! But luckily this guy was the real deal. Before long, I was in catalogues and on billboard ads, and I hadn't a clue how lucky I was.'

'I remember Celia seething with jealousy,' laughed Rosalind. 'She would have given her right arm to be a model, but she was stuck selling perfume in Macy's while Dessie was in the brochure! But then Cece and Lenny got hitched, God rest them both. And I wasn't going to move to the Bronx and be a third wheel with them. I came back to Ireland, much to Mammy's delight. I got in trouble for leaving Desdemona behind, though.'

'Why didn't you ever get married?' Ariel asked, baldly, and I elbowed her in the ribs. Rosalind shooed away our embarrassed scolding. 'Well, child, I never met the right man. And marriage to the wrong one can be a life sentence, and especially true back then. But I've been quite contented by myself. I never longed for a big family of my own.'

Everyone looked at me then. It took me a second to realize they were drawing comparisons between me and my spinster aunt. But there wasn't time to dwell on it, as Aisling arrived with a fresh tray of pints. I discreetly asked for a Jameson on the rocks; the black stuff didn't agree with me at all, but I feared that admission would mean I'd be ostracized.

'Jim, I want to hear from you,' said Vinnie. 'What was Dessie like as a little girl?'

Our uncle cleared his throat, ready to deliver a sermon. 'She was a little Jaysusin' divil, so she was,' he announced, causing peals of laughter. 'Arrah no, she was always trouble, but in a funny way. We're closest in age, and her boldness was always blamed on me because she was the apple of our father's eye.' All three siblings got misty-eyed then, only it was hard to say if it was the Guinness or the memories – probably both.

'I always knew she'd be a star,' he said. 'Kerry never would have been enough for her – Ireland, even! But I never dreamt she'd be what she is today.' He raised his glass. 'I'm proud of you, sister. Look at the wonderful life you've built, the beautiful daughters you've raised. You're a credit to us all.'

It was my turn to get misty-eyed then. Something about being here with this extended family, who loved one another despite thousands of miles and decades living apart, was touching me deeply. I hoped that Vinnie and I would always be close, that Ariel would grow up into a woman I could relate to, that Silas and Sebastian would turn to me in tough times in their lives.

Right then, there was nowhere in the world I'd have rather been than this shabby pub in Co. Kerry. Everything that had happened had delivered us here, and I was surprised to realize that I was immensely grateful.

36

The days fell into a routine, as my mother had promised. Ariel did her assigned reading first thing, and then it was Spanish lessons with Marjorie. It was the boys' turn for learning after lunch, while Vinnie was on Zooms and email with her team back home. Sales had recovered in the weeks since her Instagram Live, but I could tell her heart wasn't in selling nipple pads and crystals any more.

'I have to keep food on the table,' was the response when I asked her why she was still bothering.

'Vinnie! You're hardly hard up for cash!'

'No, Portia, I'm not, but I've spent a lot of years building this business. I'm not going to let it completely go to shit. And who knows, I might even have to pay Billy alimony, or a settlement, if he's not working. I'm just biding my time, figuring stuff out. All will become clear, I know it.'

Her *New York* magazine cover shoot had gone well and was due out in January. She'd faced her old cronies and come out of it feeling stronger.

'I'd love it if all would become clear for me too,' I moaned. 'Do you think Katie Carlton has forgotten about me?'

'No way, José. All in good time, my sweet.'

'Yeah, yeah. Print that on a manifestation card.'

'Portia, as *if* I haven't already.'

Whenever she got a chance, Vinnie was teaching Ariel the ropes – how to walk, improve her posture and smile with her eyes. In return, Ariel was editing Vinnie's videos so they'd suit the TikTok algorithm, and giving her stuff a contemporary edge.

Vinnie's Irish content was going down well with her global audience. Maybe it was because she looked so truly happy hiking the Dingle Way or tucking into a chicken fillet roll, or maybe it was just the change of scenery, but her following was creeping back up. What was refreshing, though, was that Vinnie didn't really care.

'Maybe I should have been born here instead,' Vinnie confided to me one night after the boys had Zoomed with their dad and we'd tucked them into bed. They were both sleeping like the dead in Ireland, probably from all the fresh air. 'I just feel like I fit in so much better here. Maybe I wouldn't have been looking for approval all the time from everyone like I was back home.'

'Unfortunately, Vin, you would have been a natural supermodel wherever you'd been born. And people who look like you just aren't set for a normal life.'

'Jeez,' she replied, seeming shocked. 'I'd literally never thought about that before. I always thought I was only famous because of our parents.'

'You're famous because you're over six foot and drop-dead gorgeous, I'm afraid.' I laughed. 'I think it's like that old saying – a change is as good as a rest. And Vin, you've had a lot of changes recently.'

I knew she was still in contact with India; I heard them FaceTiming at night. But whatever was responsible for this profoundly positive effect on my sister, be it her new, undefined relationship or her proximity to the wild Atlantic, I was all for it.

I had a pen pal of my own. Noah Frost had been liking and commenting on my Instagram Stories of Ireland. 'Man, I've always wanted to go there,' he DMed me one night. 'Although if all the women are like your mom, I don't think I could handle it!'

'She's one of a kind,' I typed back. 'But there are lots and lots of sheep and cows here for you to photograph. You'd be in your element!'

He replied with a single laughing emoji. Noah was a man of few words, but I liked that about him. It meant that when he messaged, he really meant it.

Ariel was behaving too. Once she settled into the time zone, she seemed to chill out a bit. She was hanging around with Aisling a lot, and her own Irish content was doing well. Vinnie's help and attention was like a tonic for her and being around all of us in close quarters just seemed to suit her.

'Yerra, *anáil na beatha an t-athrú*,' my mother mused when I expressed all of this to her. 'Change breathes new life.' While I appreciated the sentiment, if she kept this up, I'd soon need a Dessie Duolingo.

Aisling had promised to introduce Ariel to some young people during the Christmas holidays, which could only be a good thing. She was already too precocious from being with adults all the time – as long as she didn't smoke crack with the local youth, I was happy. But then I ate my words when she came home drunk and freezing one night after partaking of a 'bag of cans' in the local field. 'It's a local speciality,' she hiccupped. Her hangover the next day was punishment enough, but our mom read her the riot act anyway.

Dessie and I locked ourselves away every day from ten to six and worked on the book. She was scribbling things down as they came to her, and it was my job to sort through her haphazard notes and anecdotes and shape them into a narrative. Rosalind came by most days to reminisce on tape, and by Christmas week, the project outline was taking some shape.

Three days before the big day, everyone was excited because David and Giulia were coming to stay. We had done 'the big shop' in preparation, an Irish festive tradition, according to

Rosalind. The house was full to the brim with potato chips, huge boxes of cookies and chocolate, and every kind of meat and fish you could imagine – spreadable, smoked, boiled, brined and to-be-baked.

David was bunking in with me, because our beloved Giulia wouldn't dream of sharing a room with anyone. She would take the guest suite, and Dessie had decked it out to her liking, with extra pillows and a heated blanket. 'The woman doesn't cope well in the cold,' Dessie explained. 'I can't have the hole freezing off her entirely.'

Even though it had only been a matter of weeks since I'd seen them, I was thrilled when David and Giulia arrived at the house and delighted that they thought it was fabulous. I'd become attached to this big mansion on the shore and had hoped it wasn't beneath their LA standards.

David was full of gossip from the States, filling me in on the fact that Frida the Vegan from downstairs was being lined up to appear on a new V Network show, *Downtown Moms*. 'Apparently that's why she was always all over Jason,' he told me excitedly. 'She was trying to get on TV, not in his pants!'

I realized then that must be why Jason was in touch with Frida. Oh well, I thought. It doesn't matter any more.

'The show is like *LONY*, but about young, alternative moms instead of older, drunk ones,' David was saying. 'The network is excited about it, but I smell a flop. The girls they've cast are so boring. Jason has his work cut out.'

I flinched every time he said Jason's name, and if David noticed, he didn't say anything. He knew all about our rendezvous, and also knew I didn't want to talk about it. Changing the subject, he said, 'I helped Manny find a good hotel in Palm Springs for New Year's.'

This piqued my interest, and I raised an eyebrow at him. 'Oh, you did, did you?'

His expression told me everything.

'*David!* How long have you known?' I asked, amazed.

'Oh, for ever. Your gaydar is terrible, Portia. He's definitely on the DL, but come on! The man is still camp as Christmas!'

'I just thought he was, you know, international,' I groaned, weakly. 'Suave, stylish, Latin.'

'Gay, gay and gay,' David laughed. 'Hand in your ally card, please.' He eyed me slyly. 'You're lucky I never went there myself, you know. He's such a Daddy.'

'*Gross*, David!'

'Speaking of Daddies, any more from Chris Adams? He could crush my windpipe with his quads and I'd say thank you.'

'We talk all the time, but we're just friends, I'm afraid. He's dating some girl that was on *The Bachelor* now; she's perfectly blonde and vacant.'

'Miaow! Jealous?'

'Not even slightly. We were not meant to be.'

'I always say it – heterosexuals are wasted on one another.'

37

The following night, Vinnie, David, Marjorie and I geared up for an Irish festive challenge known as the Twelve Pubs of Christmas. There were exactly a dozen drinking establishments in the town, so it felt right. The rules were simple – an alcoholic beverage must be consumed in every pub, and you must wear something ridiculous and festive.

Vinnie was allowed to skip the alcohol part, obviously. I noticed she'd cut back on smoking since she'd been in Ireland, probably because her favourite brand of menthols was outlawed. Either that, or the clean country living was having an impact.

Marjorie was excited to have a night off. Dessie and Giulia were minding the kids, much to my aunt's chagrin, and Dessie had told Marjorie to go and 'get locked', that she could have the next day off as well. Marjorie had allowed Vinnie to give her a makeover and looked like a complete and utter bombshell with her hair wavy and cheekbones accentuated. The men of Dingle weren't going to know what hit them.

Vinnie had driven an hour to Penneys in Tralee, having finally conquered her fear of driving on the wrong side of the road. She'd bought festive accessories for everyone: reindeer ears for David, a cute miniature Santa hat for me and Christmas-tree earrings for Marjorie. Vinnie herself was wearing a Mrs Claus sweater dress, but of course she made it look impossibly chic.

David was excited because his father and brother were meeting us for a drink in pub number ten. They had a farm closer to Killarney but were making the trip to see us and staying in a B&B in Dingle. 'Why didn't you invite them to the house?' I asked, but he batted my offer away, claiming a lack of space and not wanting to impose.

As predicted, we made waves in the first pub we stepped into. I don't think the men at the bar were expecting to see an overexcited Venezuelan, a vaguely recognizable six-foot bottle blonde and a pale, flamboyant man clad in Gucci show up that night. As the least stand-out member of the gang, I elected to get the round in.

As luck would have it, the bartender was more than a bit cute. He was young, probably mid-twenties, and giving Paul Mescal vibes with his messy brown mullet and strong arms visible underneath a crisp white shirt. 'What can I get ya?' he asked in an adorable accent.

'Two pints of Guinness, a red wine and a diet Coke, please,' I replied, and he nodded.

'Nice hat,' he said as he was pouring the pints.

' 'Tis the season,' I flirted back.

'Are you part of the gang that's been causing a ruckus round here?'

'I don't know what you could possibly mean!' I faux-gasped. Dessie's presence had resulted in a bit of a stir with the locals, which was understandable. The local gal done good and home for the holidays was a rite of passage in Irish celebrity culture, and she'd already turned down an 'at home with' shoot for *VIP* magazine.

The cute Paul lookalike handed over a heavy pour of Chilean Malbec. 'Let me know if you need me to show you guys the sights?' He grinned cheekily. 'The name's Sean, and you'll find me right here.'

I paid him and scurried back to the gang, who had noticed the interaction and were teasing me. Vinnie took out her phone and pointed it towards us. 'Okay, guys, time to capture the "before" shot from pub number one.'

We all beamed for the camera, and I felt happier than I had in ages. 'Send me that,' I said to Vinnie, and it became my first Instagram grid post since the spring.

By pub six, we were merry. We made an impression in every establishment, and Marjorie was being drooled on by men on each stop. She'd already got two numbers in her phone and was thrilled. 'In LA, I am a five out of ten!' she kept saying. 'In Ireland, a nine and a half!'

David was enjoying himself more than he expected. I knew he felt vaguely uncomfortable being his fabulous self in Ireland, but people were far more taken aback by Vinnie's height, startling beauty and the fact that they knew her from somewhere than they were by David's loud shirt and directional haircut.

Ireland had come a long way, it seemed, from the days of his youth. When he was fifteen, he'd worn a striped Broton top to the local disco and endured weeks of being called Marcel Marceau, his mates only communicating with him in mime.

An elderly man in pub eight produced some mistletoe and secured kisses from each one of us, most keenly from David, and the barman gave us a free round of sambuca shots, which were a very bad idea. We were full of the fizz of the festive season, and we were all singing Christmas songs enthusiastically between each pub.

I noticed my phone blowing up with notifications, and saw they were all from Instagram. My first proper post in months had surprised and delighted my friends and family, but it was one Like that stopped me in my tracks. It was from Jason. My heart dropped when I saw it, but there wasn't time to freak out because I was being dragged to the next bar. I hadn't blocked him on Instagram because he barely used the app.

There was a 'Fairytale of New York' sing-song in pub nine, which, combined with Jason's interaction, made me feel vaguely weepy. I ordered a sparkling water with my wine, but it was too late. By the time we entered pub ten, David, Marjorie and I were all rat-arsed, and Vinnie was delightedly documenting everything.

But that was where we met the Family O'Shea. David screamed when he saw them and launched himself into his father's arms. I knew they'd spent a lot of time chatting on Zoom during the pandemic, and David felt more connected to his dad now than he had growing up. While he'd been the consummate provider, Mr O'Shea worked too much to ever be truly present in David's life. We all shook hands with him, and he insisted we call him Fionn.

Vinnie and I expressed amazement that this was the first time we were meeting him. He was a handsome man, tall and sturdy with dark eyes and features – the polar opposite of David.

'Ahh, I never had time to head down to Ballybunion when ye were all nippers,' he said wistfully. 'A farmer's life is a regimented one. Didn't allow for many frolics, sadly.'

'We need to get you out to Los Angeles,' said Vinnie. 'You need to see for yourself the empire your son has built.'

Just then, a tall man strode out of the gents and joined the group. I did a double take. '*Luke?*' I exclaimed.

'In the flesh! Come here to me, you big ride!' I was scooped up and spun around, and couldn't believe the gorgeous specimen in front of me was David's baby brother.

'What has it been, twenty years?!' I asked in amazement.

'Easily,' he replied. 'I'm thirty-two now, big and bold.'

The last summer we'd all spent in Ballybunion had been when I was eighteen, before I was too grown up and busy to head home with the family every year. I'd been back to

Dingle over the years, but the last time I'd seen Luke, he'd just hit puberty and was spotty, horny and incredibly annoying. Now he was a man, a huge man with a bushy beard and twinkling eyes. And he was staring at my sister like she was an apparition.

'Lavinia, I can't quite put you and this pub together in my head,' he laughed, hugging her. 'You're much too glamorous.'

'And I can't believe you're not a little twig any more!' she gasped. 'David, why didn't you tell us your brother had become a lumberjack dream guy?!'

'Because: *ew*, that's why. He might be burly and bearded now, but he's still a massive pain in the arse.' Luke got David in a headlock, spilling his Prosecco and ruining his artful hair.

'I see we've got some catching up to do, anyway,' said Fionn.

'Now Dad is semi-retired and not up with the larks, he's able to relax and enjoy himself,' said Luke, getting the barmaid's attention. 'Two double Jameson, neat, and whatever this crowd is having,' he said. 'And then we're going for a boogie.'

Technically, we only did ten pubs, because the last one was a hilarious nightclub on the road out of town. It had a couple of stripper poles and a nineties playlist, and because it wasn't even 11 p.m., it was empty. After securing videos of each of us swinging on the pole, we decided to head back to the house and forgo the final pub, which Luke said was 'a bleedin' shithole'.

Fionn was reluctant, but Luke and David cajoled him. 'Come on, Dad! Everyone else will be in bed, we can sit out in the shed bar and catch up. It has heaters!'

But when we arrived home, there were lights on in the kitchen. We found Dessie and Giulia with an open bottle of bubbles on the table, and Christmas carols playing low. The blessed women had prepared sandwiches for us, knowing we'd be ravenous after a rake of drinks.

We all piled into the kitchen hugging and kissing, but David's dad hung back. My mother was trying to disentangle herself from Luke's embrace when she turned at the sound of my voice and set eyes on Fionn. She paled dramatically, all the colour draining from her face. It was as if she'd seen a ghost.

Fionn stepped forward and took both her hands in his. 'Hello, Dessie,' he said, staring into her big green eyes and smiling. 'It's been a long time.'

38

I panicked that Dessie was going to keel over again, she looked so spooked. Yet despite the drinks, it dawned on me that she was having a visceral reaction to Fionn O'Shea's presence rather than a medical issue. Giulia was sitting at the island with her mouth hanging open, while Vinnie and I were like nodding dogs, looking between our mother and David's dad.

Dessie eventually recovered with aplomb. 'Well, this is a big surprise!' she managed. 'Come in, come in and make yourselves comfortable, please. Will you have a sambo? A cup of tea?'

Suddenly, she was the hostess with the mostest, heating a heavy-bottomed pan to cook the cheese-and-ham toasties and plying everyone with more alcohol. I noticed her hand trembling, though, as she filled the kettle.

There was something going on, but I was half-cut (a new term I'd learned) and also distracted by a buzzing on my hip. My phone! But who would be calling me at this hour? Frank, that's who.

'Portia, hon, I know it's late in Ireland, but I've just got the call from LA.'

'What call?' I hiccupped.

'Oh good, you're already drunk. Well, keep drinking, baby. Apple TV+ is buying your screenplay, and Katie Carlton has officially signed on to direct. You did it!'

I sat right down on the floor in the kitchen, which caused the merriment around me to stop as everyone gawked. 'I did it?'

'You did it, sweetheart. I'm so proud. Merry Christmas!

I'll call you next week with details and send over contracts. Congratulations.'

I don't remember much else about that evening, other than it being one of the happiest of my entire life. Bottles were popped, there was dancing and a sing-song, and I felt a deep contentment that only comes from a sense of true pride in oneself. Ariel woke up thanks to the noise, but instead of throwing a fit she joined in with the fun and frolics.

I must have drifted off on the sofa because when I woke up at 6 a.m., the house was silent, it was Christmas Eve and the tree was twinkling.

It took me until much later that morning to corner Dessie about the awkwardness with Fionn, because she was suffering from a filthy hangover. We were instructed by Giulia not to bother our mom if and when she rose from the bed, at least not until we were spoken to.

When she did appear, Dessie was mooning about the kitchen assembling different drinks and icing her face while moaning softly. I was itching to find out what the hell was going on, but I knew I'd get nothing out of my mother until she was good and ready.

Vinnie was fresh as a daisy; when she joined us in the kitchen she had already been for a brisk walk with Bubbles and the boys and was rosy-cheeked and invigorated. Sometimes, being a recovering drug addict had unforeseen perks.

Giulia was fine; she has a high tolerance for – well, everything. Marjorie, on the other hand, was yet to surface.

Once Dessie had consumed two shots of espresso, a pint of sparkling water and two effervescent Solpadeine, she joined us at the table. 'I think I need some hair of the dog,' she said weakly. Giulia looked at her watch. 'I will make the *vin brûlé* in one hour, you must last until then.'

December 24th was Giulia's annual day in the kitchen. Christmas Eve is a big deal in Sicily, perhaps even more important than the big day itself. There, they celebrate the Feast of the Seven Fishes, so Giulia spends the entire afternoon making a seafood feast, as well as antipasti, mulled wine and desserts. It's one of my favourite days of the year.

'So, Mom, why were you so weird with Fionn last night?' Vinnie asked, beating me to the punch.

Dessie sagged and put her head on the table. 'Giulia, I'm not able. Can you tell them?'

Our aunt looked thrilled with her task. 'It was long, long ago in the Bally of Bunions . . .'

'It's Ballybunion, you thick!' Dessie cried. 'And it wasn't there, it was in Killarney. Oh, I'll tell them myself.'

Giulia huffed off, not thrilled at being called a thick, I imagined.

'Do you remember when we were in Palm Springs?' our mother asked.

'Vaguely,' I replied, and I wasn't being facetious – that trip felt like it had been years earlier, not months.

'Oh my god!' Vinnie squealed. 'He's not . . . Oh, wow!'

My mother nodded sagely, but I hadn't a notion what the two of them were talking about. Vinnie saw my clueless face. 'Portia, don't you remember? The sheep farmer?'

Then it all clicked. My mother had told us of her longlost love, the one that had chosen her best friend, broken her heart and been the catalyst for her leaving Ireland.

'*No!*' I gasped. 'It was Fionn? David's *father*!'

'Stop shouting, Portia. Poor Marjorie is in bits and trying to sleep it off.'

Dessie dramatically swept over to the sofa, where she lay prone, and we followed her like two fools. 'Yes, it was Fionn O'Shea. He was the man I loved back in 1979, and seeing him

345

last night brought me right back to the second he smashed my heart into smithereens.'

I flopped down on the easy chair. 'I don't believe this. Does David know?' Then another thought occurred to me. 'Did you know he was David's father?!'

She sighed, with the air of somebody settling in to tell a long tale.

'When I was a teenager, my best friend was a girl called Maeve O'Malley. She had long strawberry hair and porcelain skin, and the divil in her. I loved her madly, but so did all the boys. She was much more fun than I was, and far less serious.

'When I wanted to get married and settle down to be a farmer's wife, she told me I was mad. I guess that's what attracted Fionn to her, that fiery, wild side. When he dumped me and fell for her, I was horrified. I tried not to hold it against her, but I was devastated. So, I ran away towards the bright lights of New York City, not knowing whatever became of them and, quite frankly, not wanting to.'

Vinnie and I were rapt. 'And?' I encouraged.

'When you both were young, your father and I decided we wanted our girls to know where we came from, and to be familiar with our homelands. Every summer, we said we'd bring you back to see where we grew up and spend time with our families. Roberto's commitment to these trips didn't last long; he always had something else going on. But I was thrilled bringing you little girls back to Kerry.

'The third or fourth summer, I was here with you all by myself and we'd rented a cottage by the sea in Ballybunion. And who was in the cottage next door, only Maeve O'Malley and her little boys? When I saw her, the past fell away. After all, I was madly in love with your father by then. But I was still shocked to hear that she was now Maeve O'Shea and married

346

to Fionn. His father had died and he'd inherited the family farm. He was too busy to come with her.'

'But why did he marry her if he was such a free spirit?'

'She'd gotten pregnant, you see, and that had clipped her wings and seen them running up the aisle. But the poor thing had had a miscarriage quite late in the pregnancy, and she was never right after it. They went on to have David, but she suffered dreadful with her nerves.'

I knew this was Irish code for depression, and it tracked – any memories of David's mother I had were wispy, not fully formed, because that's always how she seemed. Sombre, maudlin, barely there. The antithesis to her outgoing, flamboyant son.

'I tried to be a good friend to her. Fionn sent her off to the beach to recuperate in the summers. He thought the fresh air and sunshine would be good for her. He never came, and I have to say, I was grateful for that. But he knew I was there, minding her.'

'Are you saying that you haven't seen Fionn since you left for New York in 1979?' I was incredulous.

'Never, in the flesh. I saw pictures of him, we talked about him. But last night was the first time I've looked into those black eyes in decades, and it knocked me for six.'

'Woah.' I exhaled. We were all silent for a minute, until Vinnie piped up.

'Sorry, you never mentioned if David knows or not?'

'That's because I don't know myself. I've certainly never told him that I loved his father, and that he broke my heart by going off with Maeve.'

'I wish you had.' We all turned at the sound of David's voice. He had tears in his eyes. 'Thank you for being kind to my mother,' he said, and knelt before Dessie for a hug.

'Arrah, pet, I adored her. It was so sad to see her so broken.

347

She had her good days; she always said having you was her saving grace. And she rallied a bit when Luke was born; she was proud as punch of both of you. But she never got over losing a daughter like she did.'

We all knew the rest of the story. Maeve had died of breast cancer when David was in his early twenties, and Dessie had summoned him to the States to work for her.

'I can't believe you never told me about you and my dad,' he said sadly. 'He and I were never that close when I was younger, he was always so busy and I was so . . . different, I think, to what he expected his son to be like. It was only during the pandemic, when I was talking to him on Zoom, that we actually, you know, talked. But neither of you ever let on that you had a past together.'

'We were kids, David. I didn't even know if the man would remember much. I thought I might have even imagined the intensity of it all. But when I saw him last night, Jesus, it all came flooding back. For me, anyway.'

'For him too,' Vinnie said. 'Remember, I was sober. He kept gazing at you, Mom.'

'Yerra, whisht!' said Dessie, but I could tell she was thrilled. 'I am far too old for that nonsense.'

Any further discussion was null and void, because my mother had miraculously sprung back to life. 'Giulia!' she called. 'Do you need help, love?'

David, Vinnie and I looked at one another, unconvinced by her sudden recovery.

'Are you guys thinking what I'm thinking?' Vinnie said.

'Oh yes,' I grinned. 'Mission *Parent Trap* is a go!'

'Ohmigod!' David squealed. 'We're really going to be sisters!'

In the end, we didn't have to do anything to get our parents together. Luke and Fionn came that night for the feast, invited the previous evening by our aunt, and it felt completely natural to have two new additions at the celebration.

Marjorie was still hungover, the poor thing, so she wasn't up to much. But everyone else was in flying form, including Ariel. She'd been helping Aisling in the bar that afternoon, which surprised everybody. Our cousin had gifted her a book of Irish sayings, and she'd found solace in the words of George Bernard Shaw explicitly. She said he spoke a lot about 'the haters' and was designing a post for Instagram with her favourite quote of his – 'Hatred is the coward's revenge for being intimidated.'

'That, like, totally speaks to me,' she enthused.

'So, how was the manual labour today?' I asked her. 'Did you break any pint glasses, chat to any locals?'

Her eyes shone. 'OMG, it was so fun? Once you get over the smell of everything in a pub, it's pretty cool. Everyone was, like, so happy to meet me? And not because I'm Mom's daughter or Vinnie's sister but just cos I'm me!'

It was nice to see Ariel happy, because what's rare is wonderful. She'd met everyone in the village aged five to ninety-five that day, all of them calling into the pub for the traditional Christmas Eve pint. All and sundry had been charmed by her overt LA lustre, enchanted by her teenage otherness and spunky attitude, and unimpressed when she showed them her TikTok.

'They didn't care about my millions of followers, which I thought was so weird. But, like, so much less pressure?'

She'd also made seventy-five euro in tips – 'It's like Monopoly money!' – and she kept mentioning one boy's name over and over. I texted Aisling, who assured me that this Niall Flynn was in fact a sixteen-year-old lounge boy, and not a predatory man. We'd had quite enough of those.

I grinned at Vinnie as Ariel chattered about her day without

Wi-Fi and how she didn't even care. Maybe that's what Ariel had been in need of – her own real-life identity, to be made to feel special outside of our family's fame and her own online notoriety. I'd always said she needed to get off her phone and into the real world, but perhaps it took getting out of LA for her to truly get away from it all.

'I'd like to propose a toast,' said Fionn, raising his glass of white wine. He seemed a bit pissed, but also a bit nervous. 'To our hostess, Desdemona. It's been eons since I've had the pleasure of her company. To Dessie!'

We all raised our glasses, and I felt myself getting misty-eyed. It seemed like everything was getting better – Mom was reconnecting with her past, feeling stronger, and I was getting my movie made, Vinnie was thriving, and even Ariel was happy. For the first time in ages, I dared to feel a little bit hopeful.

39

Over the holidays, Dessie and Fionn became inseparable, and made no secret of their mutual affection. I wasn't sure if she'd told him about the CML, but the day after Christmas I'd caught them slow-dancing in the kitchen while everyone else was playing Monopoly. Vinnie had also spied them smooching in the garden under a blanket. I had never seen Dessie happier. She had planned to work through the holidays, but the book-writing had stalled as she went on adventures with Fionn, seeing all the places they remembered from their youth and catching up with old friends.

I was also enjoying watching a lovestruck Luke hitting on Vinnie every chance he got. He was waiting on her hand and foot, accompanying her on hikes and even bonding with the children in order to impress her.

'Vinnie, you should totally go for it,' I told her one night, in that strange space between Christmas and New Year. 'I know it's Luke, but we're not kids any more. He's turned into the most amazing guy, and you deserve it!'

'I can vouch for the fact that he's not a fuckboi, otherwise I wouldn't have let him near you,' David piped up. 'Luke is a good guy, much as it pains me to say that about my idiot little brother.'

Vinnie smiled magnanimously every time we brought it up but said nothing. I didn't know if she felt like it was too soon, too complicated with the distance, or even too close to home in terms of our families. But no matter how hard Luke was trying to hook her, she wasn't yet biting.

I was glad of the break from working with Dessie, because I had work to do on my screenplay tweaks. While everyone else was lying around eating Quality Street and watching movies, I was beavering away on my laptop and making progress.

Frank had sent me over the contracts, and it had finally hit me – this was happening. The pre-production wheels would be set in motion and casting would be underway imminently, with principal photography expected to start in New York City in the summer for a Valentine's Day 2024 release. I'd even wrangled a co-executive producer credit thanks to Frank's great negotiating skills and Katie's collaborative nature.

Suz arrived on 31 December and looked like a fish out of water as her Uber dropped her on the gravel driveway. It was dark at 5 p.m., the wind was biting cold, and she couldn't have looked more like a famous Los Angeles celebrity if she tried, with her Louis Vuitton trunk, travelling cape and bemused expression.

I showed her around the house while Luke hefted her trunk upstairs. Marjorie had gone home to Venezuela for a visit, on Vinnie's insistence. 'I've come to realize that I can in fact look after my own children,' she'd laughed when Marjorie opened the plane tickets on Christmas morning and dissolved into grateful tears. 'I'll see you back in LA in a few weeks.'

Suz was impressed with the house, particularly the kitchen. As she shrugged off her Max Mara cape, I noticed she was holding herself differently, clutching at her tummy, and she looked a little peaky. But it was only when she refused a glass of champagne that I guessed – my friend would *never* turn down a chilled glass of Dom Pérignon unless she was . . .

'Pregnant! I'm pregnant,' she beamed. 'Fourteen weeks already. I didn't want to tell you until I knew it was real, with everything you've all had going on. I thought babies might be a tricky subject for you.'

'Suz, as long as there's no baby inside me, I'm so thrilled for you,' I cried, tears spilling down my face. 'But how? Who?'

'I'm going it alone,' she smiled. 'A sperm donor, a great doctor and my own fabulous eggs, and hey presto! I thought I'd have to do *in vitro*, but it worked liked a charm.'

'And the girls?'

'Are ecstatic. Sabrina was worried about me being an empty nester in a few years, and Willa will love having a baby brother.'

I burst into tears again. 'It's a boy?' I managed.

'I found out yesterday, I had some early blood tests done. It's a beautiful baby boy,' she said, taking the scan photos out to show me. I couldn't think of a better way to start the new year, and I told her so.

'I have a favour to ask,' she said.

'Anything.'

'Will you be my person, when the time comes? Hold my hand, tell me to breathe and all that? I can raise a baby by myself, we all know that, but I don't want to give birth alone.'

'Suz, I would be honoured.' I pulled her into a bear hug. 'Come on, let's tell everyone else!'

The evening passed like they all had in Kerry, comfortably and happily. Dessie and Fionn were curled up together on the couch, Ariel was watching Jools Holland's annual *Hootenanny* with a surprising degree of interest, and Luke and Giulia were playing cards as David and I kept everyone's glass filled. Suz had fallen asleep on the couch, exhausted from the travelling and hormones.

It was getting close to midnight, and everyone was relaxed – Vinnie so much so that she kept dozing herself.

'Come on, it's nearly time. I know Luke is just dying to lay a big fat kiss on you when the bell tolls,' I laughed.

Just then, there was a knock. 'I guess the neighbours are jumping the gun,' I said, running to answer the door.

I swung it open, and standing on the front step was Jason.

I didn't believe it at first; couldn't believe my eyes. But it was him, in his old Patagonia fleece, taking up all the space in the doorway with his bulk. The corners of my vision felt blurry, and my equilibrium was off. I stared at him, unable to speak.

'Can I come in?' he asked politely, and I stood aside. Jason looked as gorgeous as ever; his sandy hair was a little longer, and he was deeply tanned.

He saw me noticing. 'I've been casting in South Africa,' he explained. 'Yet another new Ladies franchise. I wanted to come for Christmas, but I couldn't get away.'

I was so confused. Come for Christmas? But all I managed to say was 'Oh.'

Unable to speak, I walked into the kitchen, and he followed. I automatically put the kettle on, confirming my metamorphosis into an Irish person.

'I saw your Instagram post, and Portia, it was like a sign from above. I decided to come and surprise you for New Year's Eve. Once I made up my mind, I couldn't wait to get here.'

'What do you mean, you've made up your mind?'

'Come here and I'll tell you,' he said, his arms open. When I demurred, his face dropped. 'Come on, P, I've had quite a trek to get here.'

I went to him because I'd never stopped wanting to go to him. I was still bemused by both his sudden appearance and the fact that he obviously had something to get off his chest, but he drew me in like a magnet, as always, and I folded myself into his arms.

'Portia,' Jason said into my hair. 'Forget everything I said

354

before this moment. I have been the biggest fool on planet earth, and the last nine months have proved that. I'm sorry I made you feel like you can't trust me. I've realized that I just want you, for ever. I want to end this awful year on a positive note.' He moved backwards, and as if in slow motion, I saw him getting down on one knee. 'Will you do me the honour of marrying me and being my wife?'

For the first time in my thirty-nine years, I was genuinely lost for words. I could hear my family cheering and clinking glasses in the other room as the clock struck midnight, but I may as well have been on another planet.

Jason was still kneeling before me, looking a bit freaked out. I realized I hadn't answered him. This was all I had wanted, right? For him to come back to me and say he was wrong, that he regretted blowing up our lives, that he couldn't live without me. That he'd made a mistake and I was enough, we were enough. Was this to be my happy ending?

I looked at him again, kneeling and proffering a diamond ring, hope and love in his gorgeous blue eyes.

'Yes,' I said.

40

There was communal ecstasy at the news of my engagement. Nobody seemed to notice that I was pretty shaken; they'd all been on the fizz, and who doesn't love a grand romantic gesture at New Year's? Except this wasn't quite *When Harry Met Sally* – more When Jason Shocked Portia.

Within minutes, Jason had been warmly welcomed back into the bosom of the family, the fact that he'd shattered my heart months before seemingly forgotten. Suz kept weeping at the sight of my ring, at the big romcom moment. I knew it was the hormones, but I was tempted to give it to her, just to shut her up.

Dessie introduced Jason to the O'Shea men, who clapped him on the back and shook his hand.

To be fair, David and Giulia didn't seem quite as thrilled as everyone else. They'd gone through the motions of admiring my ring as I sat on the sofa in a daze, but I saw them muttering to one another when they thought I wasn't looking.

Suddenly, I was exhausted. It was all too much – the shock, the celebration, even just being physically close to Jason again. I wanted to sleep for a thousand years. I told him as much, and he made a big show of picking me up in his arms and carrying me off to bed. Over his shoulder, I saw David watching us with an unreadable expression.

Waking up the next morning, it all felt like a dream. But when I rolled over in the bed, there was Jason, softly snoring, and yep, there was a rock on my finger. After all those months of turmoil and heartache, I couldn't quite believe he was there, that this was real. I reached out and touched his face to make sure he wasn't a mirage, that I hadn't imagined it all, and he stirred.

'Good morning, fiancée,' he said, and smiled sleepily.

I truly didn't know how to feel; my mind was abuzz with unanswered questions and an awful, niggling feeling that I was making a mistake. Did he mean what he'd said? Was I enough? Was I denying him his heart's true desire? Could I trust him? Did I even want any of this?

My soul was conflicted, but my body responded to Jason in the way it always did, and my hips rose to meet him as he rolled on top of me. As we made love, I clung to him like a limpet to a rock.

When we finally went downstairs everyone was hungover yet again and swearing off booze for the foreseeable future. 'New Year, new me,' croaked David as he lay on the cool kitchen floor in the foetal position. Vinnie made a big show of throwing away her last four cigarettes, and Dessie whizzed up green juices for everyone.

I noticed Luke had slept on the sofa; that meant Vinnie had once again spurned his advances.

The dreamlike feeling hadn't left me. I sat at the kitchen table clutching my juice and felt like I was wrapped up in cotton wool. I was aware of everyone around me but felt insulated somehow from the activity and conversation.

I looked down at the two-carat cushion-cut diamond twinkling on my finger, set beautifully in a yellow gold band. But my hand looked utterly foreign to me, like it belonged to somebody else.

I remained in that dreamlike state, cocooned in the bosom of the clan. I suspected that my family were slowly noticing that I wasn't as thrilled as a newly engaged woman ought to be, especially in the cold light of day without a load of booze inside them. Or maybe we just all had The Fear.

On 2 January Jason wanted me to come with him to Limerick to break the news to his parents and celebrate with them. I said it was too soon; I didn't want to face them yet after the Sandra debacle. I knew he was irked, but also terrified to rock the boat.

So, off he went on his own, albeit reluctantly, to tell the extended Dempsey clan and fetch his things, promising them that there would be a big engagement party once everything had settled.

I didn't want to admit it, even to myself, but I felt relieved when he drove off after dramatically kissing me goodbye. As I waved him away, it was like a weight lifted from my chest but almost instantly that was replaced by a shiver of worry. What was I doing?

I threw myself into my work with Dessie, who kept giving me funny looks, but said nothing.

When he returned the next day, Jason bore flowers from his mother and the news that everyone was thrilled for us. Well, except Mick, who knew that his brother had not intended to emotionally seduce his wife but was still too raw about the whole thing to be able to be happy for Jason. 'He's stopped wanting to smack me, though!' Jason proclaimed, delighted.

I learned that even though Jason had rebuffed her romantic declaration, Sandra hadn't returned to the family home and still intended to divorce poor Mick, who was probably better off in the long run.

'The whole town is amazed at her causing so much trouble,' Jason declared. I wondered if he felt at all complicit in said trouble, or if he'd talked himself out of any guilt by association. But while I wasn't ready to talk about any of it yet, or ask leading questions, everyone else in my family was devouring the gossip. Even David was interested, thrilled at his sober distant cousin's about-turn to dramatic homewrecker.

Of course, we hadn't spoken about Jason's own about-turn on the baby situation – we simply hadn't had the time, or the inclination, to bring up such a messy subject when things felt so strange. The mood was celebratory, but also tenuous, and I soon learned that Jason wasn't finished dropping bombs. The next day, he told me that he still had obligations in Cape Town and had to get back as soon as possible.

I was aghast. 'Sorry, you've come here, changed everything, and now you're fecking back off to South Africa?'

'Excellent use of the word "fecking"!' he beamed. 'We'll make an Irishwoman of you yet, Portia Daniels. Will you be Portia Dempsey when we get married, do you think?'

'*Stop* changing the subject, Jason,' I snapped, rattled. 'You can't just walk in and discombobulate everything and then leave!' I screeched.

'You're misunderstanding me, babe. I want you to come with me. You can work from anywhere.'

'Who says? I'm working with my mother –' I attempted to interrupt, but he was in his flow.

'. . . and you'll love it there! The food is amazing, the wine, the weather. And the Ladies are hilarious – you'll love them.'

I couldn't believe him. Once again, the man had absolutely no concern for my life, my feelings, my own responsibilities. He still wanted his way, after everything that had happened.

At the mention of the Ladies, my mind snapped back to a question that had been niggling for months. 'Jason, did anything happen between you and Sybil Simpson?'

He went bright red, which told me everything I needed to know.

'It was a one-time thing, I swear,' he babbled. 'It was after you left and I thought I'd lost you for ever. I was in bits,

Portia. I wasn't thinking straight, and she threw herself at me. But she knows nothing is ever going to happen again – and, in fairness, I think it's all in the thrill of the chase for Sybil. She got what she wanted.'

'I bet she did,' I muttered.

I couldn't say much: I hadn't been a born-again virgin myself and didn't want to get into the details. But I felt a glimmer of vindication, a tiny shift in the power balance.

His admission closed the door on any further South Africa talk. We spent the next couple of days with everyone else, as their time in Ireland was coming to a close. That was my excuse for rarely being alone with Jason – that Giulia and Suz were soon heading home and back to reality.

I didn't know what was wrong with me. Surely if I'd just been blindsided by his proposal, the shock would have worn off by now? Surely I should be happy if this was my happy ending? But that thought just chilled me, and I clung on to Jason for dear life.

Before they left, we obligingly took Suz on a whistle-stop tour of Kerry. We went to a sheepdog demonstration, to see the Gap of Dunloe and Ladies' View, and experienced a jaunting cart in Killarney. The latter proved too much for her, with shrieks of 'Oooh, Lord help my pregnant ass!' ringing out around the national park.

But those tourist activities couldn't satisfy her. Suz wanted more diddly-aye, more paddy-whackery and more *craic agus ceoil*. So we pointed her in the right direction and watched her Instagram stories as she pranced in fields wearing a flat cap, discovered fairy forts, marvelled at ruins and talked the ears off every Irish person she met.

She and David even took a bus tour to the capital and danced into the wee hours at the gay hotspot, the George; of course, the drag queens of Dublin adored her, and Suz blew their minds by FaceTiming Dessie in their company. One of them was a Dessie tribute act called Messie Daniels, and my mother was utterly thrilled at the sight of her enormous, leopard-skin-clad bosom and huge brunette wig.

Suz toured Trinity College, posed for selfies at the Guinness Storehouse and fed the deer in the Phoenix Park. 'This country is restorative,' she told her Instagram followers, and it did indeed seem to have done her a world of good. Everyone seemed better off after a stay in Ireland. Everyone except me.

I could still sort of appreciate the magic, even in my suspended state. But I wasn't having the same holistic experience as the rest of the family, not since Jason had arrived. I didn't know what to do about it all, but one thing was for certain – I wasn't going to Cape Town, and I told him so.

'Babe! After months away from you, I don't want us to be apart any more.' He gave me the big blue-eyed gaze. 'Do you?'

'Jason, I didn't know you were going to show up and propose. I have obligations, and besides, I don't want to go to South Africa and sit around while you work.'

He huffed around for a few hours, but I was unmoveable. Eventually, he conceded that I was right, that he'd be back in a few weeks, and he'd miss me every second. I said I would too, because it was easier to do that than to try and unpack my own feelings, let alone explain them to anyone else.

As I waved him off once again, that instant feeling of relief returned. I had a couple of weeks' grace with the baby conversation, and a couple of weeks to work out why I was feeling so strange having got everything I'd wanted for months – Jason back, a commitment, and no ultimatum.

Over the previous few days, though, something had been niggling. I was noticing a trope in mine and Jason's relationship, something that, as a screenwriter, I would have picked up on right away at work. Over the years, Jason had always been the one to move things forward in our storyline, while I followed. His job brought us to New York, but that was okay because I wanted it to. But it was undeniable that his work dictated our lifestyle, and the baby bombshell had been a step too far.

I'd realized that he was always the one in control, while I bobbed along, fearful of rocking the boat and disrupting our nice, unproblematic even keel. Until I couldn't get on board with having a child, which made us flounder. And then Sandra sunk the ship.

I turned back into the house and saw my mother standing in the hallway, watching me.

'Oh, Portia. You don't love him any more, do you?'

'What?' I snapped. 'Don't be ridiculous.'

'I've been keeping an eye on you. A mother knows. You're not in love with Jason. You don't want to marry him.'

I scoffed. 'Are you an expert on love now, Mother? Now that you've been having a holiday romance with your first boyfriend, you're an authority on all things relationship?'

'I don't like that snarky tone.'

'And I don't like you assuming things about me! I mean, you're hardly a pro at marriage, are you?'

She recoiled as if she'd been slapped. 'No. No, I guess I'm not. Just don't do anything you're going to regret, darling. Learn from my mistakes. And speaking of my mistakes, come on. We've got book work to do.'

reddit.com/LifeWithLRS

10 January 2023

pollywoo77: guys, I live in Dingle, Co Kerry, and I've met Lavinia about ten times since she's been here. She is the sweetest! And omg she is so gorge IRL

gracefromwithin2008: She seems happy in Ireland. Maybe she should stay there? Not being bitchy fyi

lifethrualens98: nah, she'll be back in LA selling her shit soon. That's what they all do, take a break from their reality cos they're so rich.

rumourhasit: I hear there's a rebrand coming . . . she's dropping the S, to begin with.

pollywoo77: I think she has a boyfriend here, some gorgeous beardy guy is always with her and the kids. He's Irish!

theillest_LA: Nah, I get gay vibes from her.

rumourhasit: Maybe we'll get a big Irish wedding!

41

A week after Jason returned to South Africa, Vinnie came storming into the office as Mom and I worked.

'I'm about to do something, and I want you both to be prepared for it,' she said, wheezing with what seemed like nerves, and flapping her arms. 'I've been in denial about something, but not any more. It's time to come clean. I'm in love with India Ames, and I'm going to tell the world!'

Neither Dessie nor I had time to even digest this information, let alone respond, before Vinnie was shouting again.

'I've been too afraid of what people think of me, but I don't care any more! If I was straight, I would be taking Luke O'Shea up on his offer to make beautiful green-eyed babies together. I would have at least slept with him. But no! Despite a gorgeous, kind man who is not a sexual predator declaring his love for me, my heart belongs to someone else. A woman. Can you believe it?' She paused and looked at both of us, and then we all burst into hysterical laughter.

'Lavinia, darling, are you saying that you're . . . coming out?' Dessie asked. 'Publicly?'

'I am, Mom. I'm making a grand romantic gesture, and then I'm flying back to Los Angeles to get my girl!' I had never seen my sister so animated.

'She's been holding back because she thinks I'm ashamed of her, but I'm not. I just didn't know myself well enough to commit to her until right now. But I'm in love! Woohoo!'

Vinnie exited the room as quickly as she'd entered it, and Dessie and I just stared at one another. 'Well,' she said. 'There must be something in the water around here.'

Vinnie's subsequent Instagram post became her most liked of all time. In it, she declared that she had fallen in love with a person who just happened to be female. She hoped her followers could accept her relationship but said it didn't matter if people didn't – that she had finally accepted herself.

She also alluded to her past issues, telling her fans that she'd never fully believed in who she was until that very moment. 'This is me, laid bare. If you want to continue to follow my life, you are more than welcome to, because I love sharing it. I won't be hiding anything from here on out. I'm not perfect, but I am myself.'

Of course, there were detractors. Vinnie lost another million followers but gained over a million new ones. Before she even landed back in LA, there were think pieces and talk-show segments devoted to her news, as well as salacious stories about her past hijinks during her wild days. The conservatives who'd held her up as their ideal mother figure were losing their minds, while the gay community was overwhelmingly welcoming.

But Vinnie didn't care about any of it – nothing but India, who had been at LAX's private terminal to meet my sister and the boys when they landed. There had been an emotional reunion, and then a more intimate one, after which Vinnie had texted me: 'I'll never look at another dick again.'

And then there were four in the house, which was starting to feel rather big and empty. Ariel had opted to stick around after the others left, because, surprise, surprise, she was loving Ireland. She'd made friends with a gaggle of local girls, she had her cousins, and of course she had her new love interest,

Niall. She was on her best behaviour with her schoolwork and around the house, for fear of being grounded and not allowed out to see her mates. It turned out that all it took for Ariel to be a normal teenager was to be around other normal teenagers.

I had never enjoyed my little sister so much before, and it was truly heartening to see her happy. She hadn't given up on the Irish wisdom either – her social media was littered with quotes from the greatest thinkers of the Emerald Isle, from Wilde to Swift to Stoker. My personal favourites were the girly-pink font she chose to illustrate Beckett's infamous 'Fail again. Fail better' line on Instagram, and the interpretative dance she made up to go with Shaw's greatest soundbites.

Her new motto was 'Happy is the man who can make a living by his hobby', although she changed 'man' to 'person' and 'his' to 'their', because Shaw's own words were 'like, totally reductive'.

David had decided to stay in Ireland with us and spend more time with his family. The salons in the US ran themselves, and off the back of his association with our notorious family and their generally fabulous hair, David had found himself quite in demand on Irish morning television and in the newspapers. The four of us were all busy and distracted for the most part.

That left Dessie and me trucking away on the book, which was close to a finished draft and far better than I'd ever thought it would be. If her publishers were expecting fluff and frivolity, they'd be in for a surprise – nestled among the glamour and gossip were heartbreaking stories of loss, struggle and love. I was proud of Dessie, and what's more, she was proud of herself.

It would soon be time to leave. Jason was coming to get

me, and we were all going back to the States just in time for spring. So, why was I dreading his return?

'Are you excited about Jason coming back?'

'Huh?' I glanced up from my laptop to see David looking at me inquisitively. 'Yeah, of course.'

'Yeah, you seem thrilled,' he snorted, half to himself.

'I heard that! I'm just busy, David. I've to get these script amendments over to Katie's team.'

'Mm-hmm. And it's providing a great distraction from the fact that your fiancé is returning today.'

I turned to look at him. 'Okay, David, spit it out. What is it you want to say to me?'

He paused for a moment, considering whether to speak his mind. Then he sat next to me, and his expression changed from catty to kind. 'I'm just a bit worried about you, P. I have been ever since Jason put that ring on your finger.'

'And you haven't found any time to talk to me about it until now?'

'Have you found time to talk to *him* about any of it? Wedding plans, engagement party – oh, I dunno, the fact that he demanded a baby from you and has suddenly done a complete one-eighty on the subject?'

He had me there. I knew it was bizarre that we hadn't discussed the kid thing in detail, but how can you have that conversation over FaceTime? Or in the wake of a joyous reunion when your extended family are staying in the same house? I said as much to David, who at least didn't scoff.

'I'm not one to talk, because my longest relationship was about eighteen days,' he said, swallowing hard. 'But I know you. And I think you're avoiding the issue because you know it's going to disrupt everything again.'

I sighed and slammed the laptop closed.

'Fine, you're right, David! Does that make you feel better? I don't want to bring up his sudden change of heart because it's weird, and it doesn't make any sense. I had just come to terms with getting over him when he told me that actually, no, he just wants me again with no contingencies. So, I'm not excited to have any sort of deep and meaningful conversation with him because it scares me. I don't really believe him. Happy?'

David shrugged. 'Kind of, to be honest. Portia, I just want you to be true to yourself. You'd made some real progress over the months you guys were apart, and I was seeing a new and even more brilliant side to you. I don't want you being snowballed by Jason Dempsey and his flights of fancy any more.'

'What do you mean?'

'Well, I've never exactly taken the whole baby thing superseriously,' David shrugged. 'Jason enjoys an uncomplicated life, he's very independent. I think being a father is a fantasy of his, and the reality would be very different. That's why I was so glad you didn't just capitulate and get knocked up.'

This was news to me. David noticed my galled expression. 'I'm not saying he'd be a bad father,' he protested. 'Just that I think he has, like, an idea of what it would be like. Bringing them to the playground on Bleecker, carrying them on his shoulders to a baseball game. I don't think he's exactly romanticizing changing nappies and night feeds, you know?'

David was saying out loud everything I'd secretly thought. For the first time, I felt like I had a true ally, someone who really understood that Jason wanted a Kodak moment more than he did an actual, real-life family situation. But I'd been afraid to admit that to anyone, for fear of being dismissive or unkind. After all, there are people for whom parenthood *is* a sudden epiphany and vocation.

'Of course,' said David when I vocalized this. 'But that's not the case with Jason. He's a big kid himself; he wants a plaything. And I'm sure the whole bloodline, family name thing comes into it too, if you're having some sort of mid-life crisis.'

I was amazed by his sudden candour. I'd been too close to the whole thing, too shocked by Jason's about-turn to see things as clearly as David did. But he was right. Even if Jason did truly want to be a parent for all the right reasons, I knew he wasn't thinking about it in the same way I was. For him, it would be an addition to his life, an enrichment. For me, it would be entirely life-altering. I'd be the one doing the rearing, while he carried on with his career and his life. There was never any indication he was willing to give any of that up to fulfil his dream – the expectation was on me to bend to his will, as usual.

I'd been distant in the weeks Jason had been in South Africa, and glad everyone was too busy to drill me on it. I'd been throwing myself into work, both the book and the screenplay, and putting in crazy hours to talk to the publishers in New York and filmmakers in LA.

Conversations with Jason had been snatched moments, as his own schedule was punishing. It suited me not to go deep, but that excuse would no longer fly because Jason was en route from Shannon airport as we spoke.

'Hey. I love you, David,' I said, tears springing to my eyes. 'I don't think I tell you that enough.'

Uncomfortable with overt displays of emotion, he squirmed. But he dropped a quick kiss on my head and squeezed my shoulder. 'Me too.'

He gathered himself, preening in the mirror. He was trialling some new products an Irish distributor wanted to put out with his name on them, and I had to admit, he was looking amazing.

'Right,' he said, puffing out his chest. 'I'm going to meet someone for one last Irish hurrah. But ring me if you need anything, okay? I am never too busy to pick up the phone – I'd even stop mid-ride, for you.'

And in a cloud of Tom Ford's Fucking Fabulous, he was gone.

42

Three hours later, Jason and I were lying on my bed in our own post-coital haze. Thankfully, Dessie and Ariel had both been out when he'd pulled into the driveway – 'Free gaff,' Dessie had winked at me as she left for her lunch date with Fionn – so we hadn't even made it to the bedroom at first. In a sure sign of getting old, though, sex on the stairs had done something bad to my hip.

'Ouch,' I grunted, reaching for my cigarettes.

Jason raised an eyebrow at the sight of me lighting up. 'I thought you quit?'

'What made you think that? I don't smoke often, just when I feel like it.'

'I don't know. I just thought you'd stopped is all. I thought a lot of things had changed while we were apart.'

I scowled. 'Like what?'

'I dunno.' He shrugged. 'Your sudden love of Los Angeles, for one. Not being on social media. You haven't even been as much of a workaholic.'

'Jason, if I were you, I wouldn't use such a holier than thou tone when talking about people changing. Because, to use a Dessie-ism, you change like the weather.'

'What's that supposed to mean?'

I blew a stream of smoke out the window, stubbed out my cigarette and pulled on my dressing gown. I sat on the bed and looked him square in the eye.

'You are the one who changed everything,' I said calmly. 'You came to me and told me that you wanted to have children,

371

and that was the end of us because you know that I categorically do not. But then you came here and told me that you were wrong. You don't want kids, you were just having some sort of crisis. Correct?'

Jason was looking at me as if I had ten heads. Sitting up in bed, he pulled the duvet up around his chest. Perhaps this wasn't a nipples-out conversation.

Slowly, he spoke. 'I didn't say that, exactly.'

It was my turn to look baffled.

'Portia, I said that given the choice between being with the love of my life, or having kids, I'd choose you.'

'Woah, woah. Hang on. Are you saying that you still want a baby?'

'Are you listening to me? I said I want you!'

'Yes, but you also haven't answered me!' I cried. 'To me, you and I were already a family, so forget that word play. Answer me straight. Do you still want to be a father? Does any part of you still hope to have a child?'

He held my gaze for a moment, before looking away. 'I don't know how to answer it.'

My stomach dropped and my instincts were confirmed in that moment. I stood up and started to get dressed.

'Okay, fine!' he shouted. 'Imagine you came to me tomorrow, or next year, or in five years and said, "Do you know what, Jason? I would like to raise a kid." Would I be on board with it? Yes, I would. Even if it was adopted, or via surrogate, I'd be happy. I think we could have a beautiful family together. I'd like to experience being a dad. But is the random thought of potential future children enough to not have you in my life any more? No, it's not.'

I stood there half dressed, shaking.

'I've done nothing but think of you for the last few

months, Portia. What we have is special, and I don't want to give that up for a what-if.'

I don't know if it was the repeated use of the word 'I' in his monologue or the fact that we clearly still were not on the same page, but in that moment, everything became clear to me. I realized that whatever we'd had that was special, it was gone. I had loved Jason more than I thought possible, but I'd also idolized him. But he wasn't perfect, he was far from it. And this dramatic about-turn and grand gesture was just proof of that; it was all about what *he* wanted and had very little to do with me.

'Jason, you're right. I've changed. Everything has changed. And I'm so sorry, but I can't do this any more.'

'What do you mean?' His face had taken on a nasty quality, his features contorted.

'I'm not the woman for you. Or perhaps it's more accurate that you're not the man for me. I can't marry you. I think that we need to draw a line under us, for good. Whatever we had together, it's gone now.'

He just couldn't take in what I was saying. Here was a man who wasn't used to being told no, who always got what he wanted, when he wanted. He'd been willing to compromise on the kid thing for me, and I still wasn't content. I could see the machinations on his gorgeous face. 'Jesus, Portia! You're never happy.'

Jason stomped off into the bathroom, and when he came back, his eyes were red. He looked resigned.

'I'm sorry, P,' he sighed. 'I thought I was doing the right thing, coming back to you. But if I'm honest with myself, it hasn't been the same.'

I nodded, sadly. 'No, it hasn't. I don't want to deny you anything in this world, Jason. You should have it all. I think

I'd feel guilty for the rest of my life if you gave up being a dad for me. But thank you for trying. If that was our only problem, well, it'd still be a huge one.'

I slid the ring off my finger and held it out to him. Jason accepted it and sat down heavily.

'Thanks for giving it back. That'll buy me a new place to live,' he smirked, through his tears.

We were quiet for a while, both lost in thought.

'I've been thinking about leaving New York,' I said. 'You're right, LA has grown on me. And living in the city wouldn't be the same without you.'

'Okay.' He scrubbed at his nose. 'Can you handle the sale? Because I think it would send me round the bend, getting rid of it.'

'Of course. I'll look after it.'

We lay there for what felt like hours. I watched the late-afternoon winter sun stream through the skylight and move around the room before the sun set and the room was bathed in darkness. Eventually, without a word, Jason switched his bedside light on, got up and started packing.

He left an hour later, heading back to his mother's place in Limerick while he sorted things out. I think the others could sense that something had happened, because nobody came near the room after Jason was gone. And I was glad, because it gave me time to lie there and think, to shed a few tears. Even if calling off the engagement was the right thing to do, it was still so very sad.

Eventually, there was a soft knock at the door and Dessie stuck her head around it. She didn't say anything, but the tears came again at the sight of her. I was now officially the biggest cry-baby in the family, after years of arid ducts. Dessie sat on the bed with my head in her lap and I bawled like a baby.

'Hush, love. Let it all out. My poor, poor Portia.'

'You were right, Mom,' I managed between sobs. 'It's over, for good this time.'

'Arrah, I thought as much. But isn't it good that you tried?'

As usual after a crying binge, I must have fallen asleep. When I woke up it was still dark out, Dessie was curled up beside me, snoring softly, and David was lying across the foot of the bed, fast asleep. I looked around and saw Ariel in the foetal position on the futon across the room.

And in that moment, I knew I'd be okay. I may not have Jason any more; that chapter of my life was firmly closed with no wondering left to do. I had my family, I had prospects, and I had been true to myself. Despite the sadness, there was still hope.

A few weeks later we were halfway through March and all packed up and ready to get back to LA. Ariel was moping, upset at leaving her new friends. 'You have friends in LA, honey,' I told her.

'Yeah, shit ones,' she bit back. I had to laugh.

It was bittersweet, leaving the house. So much had happened within its walls – Vinnie's revelation, Dessie and Fionn's love story, my final goodbye with Jason. David had even seduced the Paul Mescal lookalike barman, Sean, who had in fact not been flirting with me during the Twelve Pubs and firmly played for the other team. 'He just thought your hair was cool,' David informed me gleefully. 'Which I, of course, took credit for.'

Even if we'd wanted to stay on, we couldn't. The house was booked from St Patrick's Day right through the summer months, and would host countless hen parties, girlie weekends and couples holidays all season long. As we packed up the remaining Land Rover, we all paused to take pictures of the rainbow arching above the roof of our safe haven.

Only Dessie seemed chill about leaving, which made me think she had something up her sleeve. She and Fionn reconnecting had seemed like much more than a holiday romance and her leaving him behind happily would have been surprising.

It took until we were sitting in Aer Lingus business class about to depart Shannon airport that she took off the dramatic elbow-length gloves she'd been wearing and I caught her smiling at her left hand.

'Is that what I think it is?' I asked, incredulous.

'It is, love,' she beamed, showing me a glistening diamond Claddagh ring. 'I told Fionn about the CML back in January. Arrah, I'd been dancing around it before then, but I came out and told him everything. I made him think about it, really think about what it would be like, planning any sort of life with someone who has a cancerous disease. So he did, and . . . well, Fionn asked me to marry him on Valentine's Day. Yesterday, I accepted his proposal.'

'Mom, I'm so happy for you!' I squealed.

'Sssh, you're the only person that knows. I was going to wait and tell everyone together when I got back, but I've said yes. What is it they say, the fourth time is the charm?'

Her eyes were twinkling, and she couldn't wipe the grin off her face. I examined the ring, which was simple and beautiful – completely unlike her past sparklers – but it was perfect. It was very Dessie and Fionn, whose love story after all this time was simple and beautiful too.

'Wait, where will you live?'

Dessie looked around to make sure nobody was listening. 'I'm quitting the show,' she whispered. 'I've been talking to Manny every night, and he's agreed it's the right thing to do for everyone involved. I want to move back home to Kerry for a simpler life, and I'm hoping Ariel will agree to come with me.'

376

'Are you kidding?' A squawk from the row behind us. 'Of course I'll come with you! Oh, Mommy, I'm so happy!' Ariel tried to get out of her seat to hug my mother, but she was out of luck – we were taxiing down the small runway, about to take off. So, she made do with putting her arm through the gap between the seat backs and holding Dessie's hand until the captain switched off the fasten seat-belt sign.

SimonSays.com
Leaving Los Angeles!

17 March 2023

It's a St Patrick's Day miracle! Irish star of *Ladies of Los Angeles* Desdemona 'Dessie' Daniels has revealed she is sensationally QUITTING the hit reality show and moving back to the motherland to marry her childhood sweetheart.

In a statement released today on her Instagram, Daniels explained that she's been living with a chronic illness, and her recent visit to her native Co. Kerry to write her memoirs opened her eyes to the fact that she missed home. 'My soul was telling me to write the book in Dingle, but little did I know that it was leading me back to my soulmate,' she wrote. 'As such, I have decided that fifteen years on a reality show is more than enough for any woman, and my youngest daughter, Ariel, and I will be relocating to the south of Ireland at the end of the summer.'

Fans are speculating about the nature of her illness, but Dessie promises that her book will be a true 'tell all', not hiding any details. Not one to ever leave her fans high and dry, though, Ms Daniels will also record her own special miniseries called *Dessie's Fourth Time Lucky*.

The show will follow her as a sexy sexagenarian gearing up for her fourth and final big day, before she heads off into the sunset with her betrothed, Mr Fionn O'Shea.

Who will replace the OG of LOLA? Fans are betting that her daughter Lavinia Rizzi is in with a shout . . .

43

Dessie and Fionn had decided to get married in Kerry. That didn't exactly thrill the V Network, which was filming the entire preparation for the wedding and the big day itself. Dessie wanted to exit the reality-TV world on a high. Filming in Ireland made things far more complicated. But Dessie wasn't backing down – Killarney was where she and Fionn had met, and in Kerry they would wed. V would just have to deal with the logistics.

Dessie was working with wedding planners, commissioning lighting installations and instructing builders on her dream location. Producers, stylists, caterers and florists were all coming and going from the Bel Air house as soon as we got back there. And despite taking care of all the finer details, I don't think I'd ever seen her as relaxed about a project.

'That's because it's not a project,' she said, when I mentioned as much. 'It is my happy ending, Portia. Cameras don't bother me; hard work doesn't bother me. It is a last hurrah, the pot of gold at the end of the proverbial rainbow. Then I'll take it easy, darling, I promise.'

I was happy to be back in California and throwing myself into pre-production on the movie. The plan was to spend the summer in New York while the film was shooting and tie up all my affairs while I was there. I had decided to permanently relocate back to the West Coast, and Vinnie and India were helping me look for a suitable place. It made sense; they were looking for a home of their own, and they knew the current state of LA and its property market better than I did.

I was surrounded by little love bubbles. Not only were Vinnie and India (LavIndia, as the tabloids had named them) joined at the hip, but Fionn had come out to LA to be with my mom for a few months before she made the big move to Ireland. He was spending his days bonding with Ariel, seeing the sights with David or filming with Dessie. Luke had officially taken over the farms, meaning Fionn was free to play the straight-man sidekick to Dessie's ebullient bride on the wedding spin-off show.

'Jesus, Portia, I can't even go for a piss in peace,' he sighed one afternoon. 'They keep asking me how I'm feeling about things and putting make-up on me.'

I gave him a reassuring pat on the back. 'I don't envy you, but it's only short term. And look how happy it's making her,' I said, indicating Dessie with a nod.

She was being filmed looking at her old wedding dresses and photo albums in her gargantuan closet. 'If it ain't broke, don't fix it!' my mother was saying to the stylist who had been hired to nod along on camera. 'Sustainability is important these days, so my youngest daughter, Ariel, is helping me adapt an old Oscars dress from the seventies along with bits from my own mother's wedding dress into a new gown. But the silhouette will be a Dessie classic, I think. Snatched to the heavens, boobs to the sky!'

Fionn laughed and turned back to me. 'The things we do for love, eh?'

They say good things often happen in threes, and when it came to property and the Daniels women, they did. Dessie was thrilled because she'd made an offer on the house in Dingle in which we'd all stayed, and the owners had accepted. They'd had no plans to sell until Dessie Daniels charmed the knickers off them and, come September, it would be all hers and Fionn's.

The plan was that Dessie, Fionn and Ariel would be fully moved in before the year was out, and they were calling it Teach Tuar Ceatha, which translated to 'The Rainbow House'.

'Of course, they're co-opting our symbol,' David had stage-whispered to Vinnie when this particular gem was revealed, only half joking. 'Dessie can't let the gays have anything to themselves!'

Vinnie and India had bought a place in Oak Knoll, Pasadena, a gorgeous, tree-lined enclave in a great school district with the perfect yummy-mummy clientele for another Pilates outpost. My sister had also declared a plan to go back to education and finally get her degree from CalTech. 'I'm going to put my business brain to good use,' she told me. 'India and I are going to pool our skills and resources and focus on actual wellness, not hawking crap.'

I feigned horror. 'Does that mean no more vagina crystals?'

'Don't worry.' She grinned mischievously. 'I'll make sure you have a lifetime supply.'

But the best news of all came when the offer I'd made on a house by the Venice Canals was accepted. I was with Manny when I got the news.

'I can't believe it!' I cried. 'I bought my own house, with my own money, all by myself!' I threw my arms around my stepfather. 'God bless Katie Carlton!'

'God bless you, Portia. Katie Carlton wouldn't have a movie without your story, don't forget that. We're all so proud of you. When can you move in?'

'Oh, it's a total fixer-upper. Mom is going to renovate – her big conclusion of *Dessie Decorates*.'

'Wow. That's a lot, even for her.'

'I keep worrying that she's taking on too much, but she says she's fine, and so do her doctors. We'll all just have to keep an eye, make sure she's not overdoing it.'

I appraised Manny thoughtfully. 'You know, I'm not sure I ever really apologized to you for how I acted when I found out Mom was sick.'

He shrugged. 'You didn't need to. You were going through a lot, and it was a crazy thing to take in. I was distraught when she was first diagnosed with CML, and Ariel is just so young to have to deal with this. But things are going okay. Life happens, and then it's what you make of it. Whatever will be, will be. We're a family, and we'll cope.'

'Manny, we've all been so caught up in ourselves. I haven't even thought about what you're going to do next.'

'Don't worry about me, sweetheart.' He grinned. 'I always have something up my sleeve.'

Three days after my fortieth birthday, I was in the final throes of pre-production when the call came about Suz. Not just a call, but *the* call. She was in labour, earlier than expected, and she needed me immediately.

Suz had taken early maternity leave from the show when she puffed up like a balloon in her thirty-second week. Doctors feared pre-eclampsia because of her age, but it turned out she had just been overdoing it.

More modern birthing techniques weren't flying with Suz, though. 'These Lamaze class people keep asking me if I have a doula, and if I've considered pain medication,' she'd scoffed to me. 'As if it's even a consideration? Child, I have squeezed two children out of this body, and I was in my twenties then. Give my forty-year-old ass all the drugs!'

Suz was enjoying being off work for perhaps the first time ever. Her life was all pregnancy yoga, V Network reruns of *LONY* and spending time with her daughters. Sabrina was thinking about what colleges she'd like to attend the following year, and I went with her to visit Stanford and the University of Washington while her mom was laid up.

It was Willa who called me, frantic, when her mother's waters broke. 'It's too soon, Portia! She's only thirty-six weeks!'

'She's also over forty, baby,' I cooed. 'Try not to freak out, your little brother is thoroughly cooked by now, and we knew this might happen. Call Dr Knowles and find out what you need to do. I'll be there right away.'

I quickly called Katie to cancel the production Zoom we had planned for that afternoon. She was in the office in New York, and I was scheduled to join her later that week.

When I got to Suz's modern gated estate in leafy Sherman Oaks, things were a lot calmer than Willa's call had led me to believe. Suz was bouncing on an inflatable ball and sipping a green juice, while Sabrina was rubbing her lower back. Only poor Willa seemed frantic, pacing the floor and reading something on her phone.

'Okay, Mom. Contractions are now eight minutes apart. I think we should get to the hospital.'

I, too, had called Dr Knowles on the way over, who told me to bring Suz in whenever she felt ready, but that if things continued progressing as they were, she was better off in a warm bath for an hour or two. I ran the water while attempting to soothe Willa's jangled nerves, and when it was ready, I helped my friend into it. She was swollen and sore all over, but Suz exuded an air of calm.

'I didn't think I could do this again at my age,' she huffed as she eased into the water. 'But it turns out, the more people you have around that care about you, the better – especially your own near-grown kids!'

I sat on the floor next to the tub and read aloud as Suz soaked. She had tried hypno-birthing on Willa, and it had triggered more anxiety because she's so Type A. Dr Knowles had told Suz a hyper-focused birthing plan was perhaps not for her, so this time all she wanted to hear were the wise words of Jackie Collins.

'Read me the sex scene in *Hollywood Wives*,' she instructed. 'The one where the guy has a heart attack and dies from getting his dick stuck in his mistress.'

I did as I was told. It was certainly a unique method, but I was down for whatever relaxed my friend.

Three hours later, things hadn't progressed much on the contractions front, but we were in situ in a private suite in Cedars-Sinai's maternity unit. By then, Suz was in pain but not dilated enough for an epidural. Her face was stoic, but I could tell she was suffering by her clenched fists and whispered requests.

I felt totally helpless, but all I could do was rub wherever she asked me to and keep her stocked up in ice chips. I was also good at distracting her with tales from *Us Weekly* and *DeuxMoi*. Her favourite activity was guessing the blind items, and it usually turned out that she was right.

The girls were in the waiting room with David, who had brought them per Suz's request. 'This is not a free-for-all,' she'd wheezed. 'I am not going to pull the baby out with my bare hands like Kourtney Kardashian. Tell them to stay outside.'

David was thrilled; he didn't want to see a woman's nether regions at the best of times, and besides, he's too much of an empath. He'd be having contractions with her.

This was all well and good for the mother-to-be, but I was feeling out of my depth. I'd never been present at a labour before. I would do anything for Suz, but the smells, sights and sounds were utterly disconcerting. Between her little yelps of pain and the bleeping of monitors, I was totally on edge.

'Aren't . . . you glad . . . you never did this?' Suz huffed at one point. The contractions were coming faster, and she was nine centimetres dilated.

'Uh, I can't say I'm not pleased,' I grimaced, as another wave took hold of my friend. She squeezed my hand so hard I thought for sure she'd broken it.

'It's not pretty,' she panted as the contraction abated. 'And right now, I'm asking myself some questions. But it will be worth it.' She smiled, weakly. 'This little baby is going to make my life even better than it already is. I chose some primo sperm.'

I smiled at her with tears in my eyes, perhaps partly from the pain of my throbbing hand. I was sure that she was correct, that for Suz, this baby was a blessing and a gift. But if I'd had any sliver of a doubt before this experience, any iota of hesitance, it was gone.

Forget labour, forget childbirth – which is apparently what women have to do so they can go through it again – it wasn't just the harrowing stuff I was uninterested in, but the whole shebang. I realized that I'd been carrying a sort of guilt about that, deep down. I'd been harbouring subconscious thoughts my whole life that I was strange, selfish and even unnatural to not want children of my own.

It was as if Suz read my mind, or perhaps I was just wearing my emotions on my face. 'You're not wrong,' she panted. 'This isn't for everybody, P. And you're not a bad person for not wanting it. I promise.'

Then she let out an almighty roar that brought the medical team running into the room. I was swept aside so they could help Suz, and just like that, I was out of my own head and present in the moment. I stood by her side and let her squeeze my poor hand as hard as she could as she sweated, pushed, screamed.

I spoke to her coolly and calmly as she cried that she couldn't go on. I literally mopped her brow and told her she could do it, just like they do in the movies. And when finally, at 3.03 a.m., Jethro Adonis Peterson made his entrance in the world, I broke down and wept.

When he was all cleaned up and swaddled like a tiny burrito, I stood over Suz's shoulder as she gazed upon her son. 'A boy,' she marvelled. 'I never thought I'd have a boy. I hope he doesn't mind not having a daddy,' she whispered, a tear rolling from her eye.

'Hey, now. You told me before – you're a rich man, remember? And he may not have a dad in the truest sense of the word, but he has all of us. This little guy will never want for anything.'

Suz beamed up at me. 'I knew you were the right person to be here with me,' she grinned. 'David owes me a hundred dollars; he said you'd pass out.'

I laughed. I'd had my own doubts about my suitability as a birthing partner, but David was one to talk. 'Don't worry,' Suz said. 'I told him he was thinking of himself, not you. Portia . . .' She tore her eyes away from Jethro and looked at me again. 'Feel free to say no, because I know you're not religious or spiritual, and kids aren't your thing. But will you be his godmother?'

'Are you kidding me?' I replied, tears coming down my face now in earnest. 'I'd be honoured.'

The door swung open, and David and the girls appeared, as well as Suz's dad, Kyle. They were all laden with gifts, blue balloons and teddy bears and even a cake. Everyone crowded around the bed to coo at the new arrival.

'I told them they were projecting gender norms on to a newborn,' David whispered to me. 'But even I couldn't resist the little blue teddy.'

Sabrina was holding up her phone, and on a split screen I saw my mother and Fionn, Vinnie and India, Ariel, Giulia and Manny. 'Say hi, everyone! Guys, meet Jethro. Or Baby J., as the girls have been calling him.'

'Ew, Suz!' Ariel exclaimed. 'You grew a tiny penis inside of you!'

I realized right at that moment that I hadn't just been placating Suz minutes before; this child really did have a whole big, strange, loving modern family looking out for him. As I waved to the screen and gently stroked the baby's cheek, I felt happier than I can ever remember feeling before.

44

Being back in New York confirmed that buying a house in Los Angeles was the right move. My mother had thrown herself into the renovation of my new home, and the four-bed, two-bath on the quietest stretch of water behind Venice Beach was in the process of becoming a two-bed, one gigantic office, two-and-a-half-bath under her guidance. I'd left a list of non-negotiables – I wanted a soaking tub and an outdoor space – but I trusted Dessie. She knew my taste, this was her wheelhouse, and if there was one thing she excelled at, it was bossing people around.

Not only did the apartment Jason and I had shared feel as strange as I predicted, New York itself also felt stifling. Normally, I loved how close everything was on the island of Manhattan, but after a year of wide-open California living I was feeling suffocated in the city and in the building itself. I wasn't adapting well to the changeable high-summer weather, everything was too loud and when I watched a guy take a dump on the street at 11 a.m., I realized it wasn't our place that had shrunk, but me that had grown.

Plus, I couldn't move in the apartment without being reminded of our relationship. It hurt at first, coming across a photo of Jason and me when we'd been so happy, or a stray sock of his. But as the weeks of filming went on, the hurt turned to a sting, which turned to a sort of dull pinch.

Jason had been in and cleared out his stuff while I was in LA, so at least I didn't have to deal with his personal belongings.

But having the place half empty was also jarring, as was deciding what to bring with me to the West Coast.

On Vinnie's advice, I hired a crack team of organizers and gave them instructions to pack, sort, toss and donate my belongings before putting the apartment on the market. I'd come home at night after a long day on set to piles of my things with little notes and question marks. I had no idea how I'd managed to accumulate so much useless stuff and was profoundly grateful that I didn't have to go through it all myself. My mother always taught us that having money wasn't the be all and end all, but these were the times I was grateful to be comfortable – when it meant that I got to delegate the logistics of my long-term-relationship break-up to somebody else.

Work was going well. Writers are never really much of a presence on set unless they're a star, so I'd never experienced the thrill of watching my material come to life before. But Katie was every bit the workhorse I'd taken her for, and a close new friend. Even though it was hot as Hades every damn day on location, the material coming back every evening was showing real promise. We were shooting interiors on a soundstage in Brooklyn, so each day was different.

I also wasn't chained to the set like Katie was. I could break for lunch with Amy – I'd eaten with her and her bouncing baby girl, Gina, a handful of times since I'd been back – and found time to meet Dessie's book editors at Putnam whenever I could.

Still, the days were long and intense. But I never felt exhausted or burnt out. I felt as if I'd been waiting my entire life to do this, and full of excited energy.

One way of working that energy out was the dalliance I'd been enjoying with the stunt coordinator. Yes, even romantic comedies need one – anything physical, from driving a car to a staged fall, requires expert personnel to oversee it. Theo

Andre was enormous, like a human climbing wall, but when he confided that his mom calls him Teddy, I totally believed it, because he's as squishy as a stuffed bear on the inside.

It was very much a situationship, the on-set version of a holiday fling, but I was enjoying myself. The sex was good, uncomplicated and satisfying, and nobody was at risk of catching feelings. Teddy was into Crypto and Crossfit, all things that would give me the ick if I thought about them in any real way, so we kept it strictly sexual. He liked a light cuddle afterwards, which was fine by me, but then it was clothes on and out the door.

Raya was also interesting in the city. I hadn't deleted the app for fear of having to go to the back of the queue if I ever wanted to use it seriously, and from time to time I browsed what was on offer in New York. I got a fright one day when Andy the pool cleaner slash bodyguard from Dessie's house popped up – turns out, he *was* Jason Momoa's body double, and they were in town shooting the latest *Aquaman* instalment. My mother found it hilarious when I told her over the phone. 'Oh, I miss that big ride every day,' she purred. 'I may have finally found true love, but the sight of Andy cleaning the pool in his micro shorts really had a way of soothing me to sleep at night.'

He invited me over to his hotel room after a bit of chat, but I demurred – I was still embarrassed about what had gone down in LA, and he reminded me of a time when I was not myself. Visions of those rock-hard pecs and bulging arms had me think about it for a long second, though.

One morning, I was leaving the apartment to head for the West Village production office, my AirPods in, arms full of scripts and a KeepCup full of coffee in hand, when I literally collided with someone on the stairs. It took me a second to realize that it was Frida, my earth-mother neighbour who was soon to be a burgeoning V Network star.

'Portia!' she exclaimed. 'Sorry, I was just coming upstairs to see if you had any spare coffee. I have a house guest this morning who needs it to function, but I don't pollute my body with caffeine.' She shrugged and grinned in that holier than thou way of hers, as if abstaining from coffee somehow made her the most special woman on planet earth.

'Sorry, Frida. I always have a supply of delicious, habit-forming coffee beans, but I'm late for work.' I indicated the scripts in my arms.

'Oh, I heard! Jason told me you're shooting a movie. That's amazing!' She beamed.

'Ahh, yes, I heard you were working with him.'

'He's one of the executive producers on our new show. Ohmigod he is *so* great. I was sorry to hear you guys split.'

'Yeah.' I grimaced. 'Me too. But it's all for the best.'

We were standing awkwardly on the landing outside her door, so I moved to make my exit. 'There's a Starbucks on the next block. Call over later on and I'll give you some legal stimulants.'

She looked blank.

'Coffee?' I laughed.

'Oh, yes!' She tittered. 'You are so funny, Portia.'

She swung the door to her apartment open, and I saw a guy standing in the hall. I did a double take, just as the door shut in my face. Either I was having a stroke, or the guy was Noah Frost.

By the time I got home that evening, I was out of sorts. It had been a tough day getting a tricky scene laid down, mostly because one of the supporting actors was fond of ad-libbing his lines. But in all honesty, I'd been irked since that morning.

Why on earth was Noah Frost in Frida's apartment? Was he one of her many conquests? Why was he even in New

York, and why hadn't he texted me? We were Instagram friends; he'd have known I was in the city.

But then, why would he text me? It's not like we were very close, more like vague acquaintances. Yet there was something about Noah. He had truly been there for me, for all of us. I'd spent my lunch break trawling his profile on Insta, but it gave little away. There was one story that day, a shot of the bodega on the corner around 11 a.m. It *was* him!

I hurried up the stairs and past Frida's door quickly, for fear of running into either of them. But I did as promised and made up a little bag of ground arabica beans. As I hung them on her door handle, I debated leaving a note but thought the better of it. Frida might be a bit dim, but she'd surely know they were from me.

As I turned to walk away, the door opened, and there was Noah in all his louche, sexy glory, scruffy-haired as ever.

'I thought there was a little rat scratching at the door,' he grinned. 'But turns out, it was you.'

I couldn't help but smile. 'Well, well. What are the chances of running into you here? Are you stalking me, by any chance?'

'No,' he said bluntly, and I gulped. I'd forgotten how forthright he was. 'I've been back east visiting my mom and doing some work in New York for a bit. But this is a nice coincidence! It's good to see you.'

'Yeah, same!' I said, shrilly. 'Are you out here for long?'

'No, I'm just on a job for this week. It's so hot, I don't know how you do it.'

'You'd miss the wide-open plains of the Serengeti and Sunset Boulevard,' I joked, and he smiled.

'I hear you got engaged. Congratulations.'

'Huh?' I was taken aback. 'No, no. Well, I did, briefly. My ex came back and . . . yeah. But no, it wasn't . . . it wasn't going to work, it's over. It's just me now.'

He looked thrown. 'Oh, wow. I'm sorry, I'd heard that you . . . Bad information, I guess.'

'Yes, well. I hope you figure out what you're doing here!' I blustered, suddenly mortified. 'And Frida is a lovely girl! Well! Good luck!'

I practically ran up the stairs, and stood with my back to the door, panting. Of all the apartment blocks in all of New York, Noah Frost had to walk into mine and hook up with my irritating, health-crazed, sexually liberated (to put it politely) downstairs neighbour. Thank god I was moving. Getting off that island was definitely for the best.

45

If I thought my life would calm down a little after a summer of shooting on the movie wrapped, I was mistaken. As an exec producer on the project, I was due to spend the fall and winter in the LA office on post-production. Along with Katie and the production team, I'd have a say on everything, from score to trailer. Then we'd be preparing for the publicity trail that would lead us to Valentine's Day.

The wrap party was a lot of fun, considering I was sleep-deprived after the final intense days of early-September shooting – some epic set pieces at iconic New York landmarks like the Freedom Tower and Central Park meant pulling all-nighters to avoid the tourists. But I couldn't – wouldn't – miss the party, so I rallied. I drank three venti iced lattes, put on my shortest, tightest, littlest black dress and highest boots, and joined the rest of the crew at the Bowery Ballroom to celebrate the end of principal photography. Reshoots were unlikely unless the edit bombed with test audiences, so everyone was jubilant and letting their hair down.

I also knew it would likely be my last hurrah with Theo, which was bittersweet. It had been nice having a warm body to turn to, and it would be a pain to find another one with such a good mutual understanding. But he was moving on to his next production, and I was heading back west.

I was also aware that if we spent any longer fucking one another's brains out, there was a slight chance it would move from casual hook-up to relationship of convenience. The habits of a long-term serial monogamist die hard. But Theo was not the one for me, and I was becoming a little sceptical that such a thing even existed. This from a woman who had just written a romantic comedy – the irony wasn't lost on me.

Still, I was down for a swan song. So, when Theo gave me the look across the room – a raised eyebrow, a tilt of the head – I downed the last of my Martini and followed him out of the party. He pulled me into a dimly lit supply closet down the hall, and in seconds had my panties off and on the floor somewhere, my back against the cinderblock wall, legs around his waist and his thumb on my clitoris. What can I say, the man was an expert stunt coordinator.

'It's been nice knowing you, Portia,' he wheezed when we'd finished, as I looked around for my knickers. 'You're one hell of a woman. If you're ever in town . . .'

'Stop.' I whirled around, thong in hand. 'Don't say it.' I walked over to him and planted a big kiss on his lips. 'It's been amazing, Teddy. Thank you for the orgasms, and for the expert cuddles. You're a great guy. I'll see you around.'

I knew that walking out of the supply closet with my panties in my bag, and not even allowing him to politely allude to future hook-ups, was exactly the kind of cool-girl behaviour that could have hooked him. But I truly wasn't trying to. If the past year and a half had taught me anything, it was that I had to live my life on my own terms, and nobody else's.

Shrugging off any residual societal shame I may have almost felt about shagging my conquest in the cupboard and not feeling anything, I returned to the party and allowed myself to have an absolute ball. I deserved it.

When I made it back to Los Angeles, there was the small matter of my mother's book launch in late September. It was being released before the holidays and marketed as the perfect gift for the reality-show fan in your life, so that meant squeezing in a lot of promo before the wedding at the end of October. The press was clamouring to speak to my mother, and Giulia had a list of interview requests a mile long. But what I hadn't expected was any attention on me as her co-writer.

'Don't ghostwriters stay firmly in the background?' I'd beseeched my aunt. 'Aren't they called that because, in the world of the book, they don't exist?'

'Ah, but you do exist in the book, *bella*,' Giulia soothed. 'You not only made this book the masterpiece that it is, you're also her wonderful *bambina*!'

I expressed doubts about my interview abilities. 'Hey, you are going to have to get used to this life, Portia. I'm lining up movie press with the studio now as well. You're about to become a big deal in your own right. This is only the beginning.'

That was a sentence that both thrilled and frightened me, but I had to remember that any notoriety coming my way had to do only with my own work. This wasn't about being adjacent to my family's fame, this was the big time off my own steam.

Thankfully, my aunt was willing to give me some media training and, between that and a session with Dessie's stylist, by the time the first interviews rolled around, I felt somewhat prepared.

Our first joint chat was with an old friend of Dessie's, Emily Rutherford of *People* magazine. As such, we met her for a faux-casual drink at Chateau Marmont. A haven for the rich and famous in West Hollywood, it's known for being anti-tourists, and you'd be as likely to find yourself sitting next to Ozzy Osbourne as Meghan Markle.

We exchanged some pleasantries, and she and my mom caught up before Emily turned to me. 'Well, Portia. You've avoided the spotlight for a long time, but now you've got this book and a movie coming out early next year. What does it feel like, at forty years old, to be really coming into your own as a writer of both books and movies? Do you feel like you're following in your late father's footsteps?'

I took a deep breath. I was prepared for this. 'Considering my dad didn't live past his own forties, it's an honour I don't take lightly,' I replied. 'I'd never really seen the parallels in our careers until recently. If I inherited even a shred of his talent, I'll be doing very well indeed. I'm so proud to be his daughter, and I hope that, wherever he is, he's not embarrassed by me writing a memoir and a romantic comedy!' I laughed, remembering to be self-deprecating and warm. This was so much harder than my mother made it look.

Emily was shrewd, though. 'Speaking of romance, I believe you had your own unhappy ending not so long ago.'

I wasn't shocked, exactly. Good journalists have a way of finding out everything they need to know about their subject. But I was surprised. There was no way I was using what happened with Jason to sell anything.

Luckily, my mother interrupted. 'Emily, you wagon! I may be willing to whore myself out to the press every now and then, but Portia's love life isn't the story here.'

'Oh, Dessie, I didn't mean to cause offence. It's just I thought any personal heartbreak might be relevant to her writing.'

'It's okay, Mom,' I interjected. 'Yes, I'm single since spring and I've just moved back to California, where I've bought a place by myself –'

'Which you can see me decorate on the forthcoming finale special of *Dessie Decorates* on HGTV!' my mother butted in, always on brand.

'Uh, yes, that's right. But I'm not on any sort of schedule, imposed by myself or by society. And I don't think you have to be in a long-term relationship to be able to write about true love. As long as you've experienced it, that's enough.' Dessie visibly relaxed, happy I could hold my own. 'My adventures in dating are fodder for my projects – let's call it real-life research. And I still believe in love. I'm a true romantic. I just know that life isn't only about romantic love.' I realized as I said it that that was the truth. I was a believer, but I was also just fine by myself because I had my family and my friends.

'Amen, sister,' my mother said, and the three of us clinked glasses. It was only then that I noticed Emily's own bare ring finger and realized that I was preaching to the choir.

People's exclusive was a hit, and some of my comments went viral. It seemed the public couldn't get enough of our family, and the fact that I'd never courted the limelight before made them want to know more. Suddenly, I was something of a feminist icon and getting requests to write think pieces for *Vogue* and appear on high-profile podcasts and morning shows.

As a result of the coverage and my mother's international fan base, the book was a smash. Before we even attended the official launch party in LA, we knew that it was going to be a *New York Times* number-one non-fiction bestseller.

The night of the event, Mom had called in all her glam-squad reinforcements. David had a team of hairstylists in one cottage at the Beverly Hills Hotel, while Axel and his gang had commandeered another. Three different stylists had been employed to make me, Dessie, Vinnie and Ariel look like our absolute best selves, and Giulia was running around making sure everything was on schedule.

When I asked her if she was getting glam herself, she rolled her eyes. '*Bella*, this doesn't need glam.' She said the last word as if it was the most ridiculous thing she'd ever heard. 'I am already fabulous, and this party is my crowning glory as a publicist! I'm back, baby!'

Vinnie was nervous because it would be her first official red-carpet outing with India on her arm, but her partner's calmness soothed her ruffled feathers.

'I told her, what's the worst that could happen?' India intoned in that zen way of hers. 'Even if she fell on her face, I would still love her. We all would. So, screw it.'

It was amazing, like Vinnie had uncovered her own private tool for coping with her anxieties – one who also happened to give her the best orgasms of her life. When she started trying to teach me about lesbian sex techniques, though, I was out. There are some things that are just too much information where your sister is concerned.

I was dressed in a slimline skirt suit, something I'd never have looked twice at on the hanger but that suited me down to a tee. It was a deep ruby colour which accentuated my lingering tan from days shooting outdoors and it was cut dangerously low. 'Now, if I wore that, I'd be arrested,' Dessie had exclaimed when she saw me in it. 'I'm telling you, Portia. Small breasts are decidedly chic.' I'd laughed because I had to agree.

I was feeling like myself, proud as punch of our mutual achievement, and loving the results of the afternoon of pampering. Axel had given me glistening cat eyes and deceptively large lips, and as I posed for pictures I surprised myself by feeling comfortable in the spotlight.

Before we left for the party, my mother clinked a dessert fork on her champagne glass in the cottage we had all convened in. 'Darlings, Manny has an announcement to make!'

My stepfather was propelled forward by Giulia, and he cleared his throat. 'You all know I love the spotlight,' he said drily. 'But I wanted to tell everyone that I'm moving to Palm Springs after the holidays. An old contact of mine from the music business has invested in a hotel, and he wants me to be his guy on the ground, schmooze the VIPs and generally make the place the best it can be. After nearly two decades living with Dessie, I guess I've learned a thing or two.'

'And I'll take all the credit for teaching you!' My mother winked. 'Now, cheers, everyone. Let's get this show on the road!'

Dessie had invited a heap of her V Network colleagues to the launch party, both to promote the book and in the spirit of collaboration. I saw Natasha being chatted up at the bar by a very married cast member of one show, and Manuel deep in conversation with the supposedly straight ex-husband of one of the New York Ladies. Ah, Hollywood, I thought.

Then I felt a hand on my arm, and it was Frida, formerly of downstairs. Of course, her new show was premiering that week on V, so she was in LA doing press. 'You look gorgeous, Portia! You're so cool!' she squealed.

I had to admit, she scrubbed up well too. I was tempted to ask her if her false eyelashes were ethically made, but I decided against cattiness. This was the new me.

'You too, Frida. How's everything going? Where are the kids?'

'Oh, they're back in New York with their dad. This is Mamma's week to let her hair down!'

'Their dad?' I was confused. 'But I read on your blog that you –'

'Oh, the turkey baster? No, I made that up. You need a hook these days online, you know? Their dad is my ex. He didn't want to be involved with them at first, but he is now.'

'I see . . .'

'And doing the show has, like, totally opened up new ways to meet men. I have my eye on that journalist over there,' she twinkled, casting a glance to a tall, dark and hipster man at the bar. 'A little LA fling!'

I tried to appear nonchalant. 'You're not seeing Noah Frost any more, then?'

She wrinkled her little nose. 'Who?'

'Noah, the photographer? I saw him at your apartment that time in New York. You were looking for coffee for a house guest. Sorry, I presumed you guys were dating.'

She threw her head back and laughed. 'The guy who the network sent to take photos? Ohmigod, no! Totally not my type.'

I froze.

'He was just shooting pictures for the show's promo in my place and around the city. They like his "urban style" of shooting, or something like that. He did a day or two with each of us. I liked him – he made me look good! But I'm not into that rumpled look.' She screwed up her nose again. 'I have a thing for really slick guys – you know the type? Work in finance, wear expensive suits. But I've actually been practising conscious celibacy for the past eighteen months. I wanted to, like, get myself into the most, like, zen space where I didn't need men to, like, validate me? I have a high libido, and I didn't want to embarrass my mom on TV, so I, like, went to this sex therapist . . .'

She kept talking, but I wasn't listening. I was tempted to pull out my phone and text Noah then and there to explain my mix-up, but I stopped myself. He probably hadn't even noticed or cared. Dammit, why was I so awkward?

I felt a slight twinge of regret. I would always think kindly of Noah Frost. He'd been the man to resuscitate me when I was barely alive, the one who'd helped me to feel something when I was numb. And he'd been incredibly kind to my family, and to me. Far more than was necessary, in truth.

I shook myself off. I was sure he knew that I was grateful to him. And at the end of the day, he was just a guy. I didn't know why I had such visceral reactions to him; it was all probably tied into the fact that it had been such a strange time in my life. And he was my first, after Jason.

I saw my mother beckoning to me across the room and excused myself from Frida, who, I had to admit, wasn't too bad. I hoped the journalist she was eyeing up was worth breaking her self-imposed sex ban for.

'I want a big family photo,' Dessie declared. Everyone was there; Suz and her kids, with Jethro in a leopard-print baby carrier strapped to her front; India, Silas, Seb and Vinnie; David, Fionn, and even Luke, who'd flown in for the festivities; Giulia, Manuel, Ariel and her Irish beau, Niall, who had special permission from his parents to be by her side. I thought it was all a bit much, but Ariel was beaming and well behaved. Who was I to argue?

'Now, darlings,' my mother cooed as the photographer set up the shot. 'Stick out your chest and say "Boobies!"'

46

When Graham's jet landed in the tiny Kerry airport – as a wedding present, my mother's colleague was allowing Dessie to use her plane as a shuttle bus for the family – I was greeted by the most beautiful autumnal vista. There were still leaves on the trees, but they were turning amber. The air was crisp and mild and the sun shining. I breathed it all in, relishing the moment and truly happy to be back in Ireland.

I'd travelled over with Ariel, Manuel and Giulia, as well as Axel and Fiona, Dessie's wedding stylist. When we arrived at Teach Tuar Ceatha, there was frenzied activity. Two massive, elegant marquees had been erected in the garden, and there were people everywhere. It was all so *Father of the Bride* I expected Franck to pop out at any moment – I laughed out loud when I saw peacocks roaming the grounds, and a newly installed pumpkin patch on the lawn.

'Darlings!' my mother shrieked when she saw us. 'I'm so glad you're all here.'

Dessie had been in Ireland for the past two weeks, making sure the house was going to be ready in time and fine-tuning all the logistics involved in a transatlantic wedding. Mom had rented every property in a three-mile radius for the wedding, so it was like a movie set, complete with TV cameras and half of Hollywood rolling into town. She'd thrown money at every obstacle, including relocating the families meant to be occupying said houses to the Parknasilla resort in Sneem. If she hadn't been such a national treasure, I'm sure she'd have had a lot more difficulty.

403

'Bono offered the house in Dalkey, but I told him it had to be Kerry,' she'd told me one night on the phone. 'I don't know why he has a reputation for being a pox – the man is a pet!'

The cameras were rolling, and I instinctively ducked when I saw them over my mother's shoulder. But then I remembered – this was her last hurrah, and we were all going to play ball.

'Hi, Mom.' I kissed her on the cheek and gave her a squeeze. I'd missed her. 'How are you doing? Are you minding yourself?'

'I'm grand, I promise. Portia, love, did you remember everything on your list from New York? The bridesmaids' dresses from Vera, the rings from Harry Winston?'

'Of course.' I swatted away her worries. 'Everything is under control, I promise.'

Her shoulders sagged with relief. 'Oh, fabulous. Would you believe it, I'm getting nervous.'

'If you weren't, it would be weird,' I soothed. 'This might be your fourth wedding, but it's your first in Ireland and the first to be broadcast internationally on TV. And it's the one that's going to last for ever.'

'Oh, Portia. I needed to hear that. You're the best, sweetheart.'

I was staying in the house next door for a week, bunking with Vinnie, India and the boys. Suz and her kids were also staying with us, and David too. But he was highly in demand, falling into bed exhausted at night after cutting, colouring and styling every strand of hair even remotely involved with the big event.

Dessie and Fionn had eschewed the traditional American rehearsal dinner, with my mother wanting to save her energies for the day itself. 'This will be a proper Irish wedding,' she had told me. 'Those LA bitches won't know what hit them when they're doing "Rock the Boat" on the floor at four in the morning.'

I had to agree and was glad when the night before the ceremony was just us gals, and David of course.

Dessie was sharing my super-king bed for the night, and she had bought us all matching pyjamas for the occasion. She and David had been spray-tanned early in the evening, and there was a distinct scent of digestive biscuits in the air.

'Are you still nervous, Mom?' I asked, as we settled down for a big bowl of pasta and some red wine.

'Not really,' she answered, digging into her dinner. 'If I was nervous, I wouldn't be mainlining carbs. I'm excited, but I want it all to go well, you know?'

'It will. You've planned it perfectly,' said Vinnie, adding a salad bowl and some crusty bread to the table. 'Now you just have to enjoy it.'

'I'm bloody nervous!' David exclaimed. He looked bizarre, the spray tan congealing around his freshly dyed eyebrows. 'I have to give her away, in front of everyone.'

'Oh, love. Don't be silly. Literally nobody will be looking at you.' Dessie grinned.

Only Giulia seemed quiet. When I asked her why later, she laughed ruefully. 'It's *stupido, bella*. But this is your mamma's fourth wedding, and I have never even had one.'

I was surprised. 'Did you want one?'

She shrugged. 'I would have liked a choice in the matter, you know?'

I nodded, because I did know. I had never felt much like a spinster myself, having been in relationships my entire adult life. But with a roundy birthday came a lot of feelings, which I knew since I'd turned forty. Giulia was now sixty, and I'd never known her to be in love.

'Have you ever come close?' I enquired gently.

She sighed. 'Twice. The first was when I was at college in New York. The *bastardo* cheated on me and broke my heart. The second, well . . . it was more complicated. He wasn't a good guy.'

'Why not?'

'He was one of your father's colleagues. But not in the movies, if you know what I mean.'

I was confused for a second, until it dawned on me. 'Oh, Giulia. He was . . . connected?'

'To put it politely, yes. He was a made guy, originally from Sicily as well.' She rolled her eyes. 'What can I say, the heart wants what it wants.'

'What happened to him?'

'I don't know,' she said, resigned. 'I like to think witness protection. I think that is perhaps naive, though. All I know is that he went out one night, and never came back.'

'Oh, Giulia. I'm so sorry. No wonder you and Mom were always so worried about Roberto.'

'*Sì*, what do they call it? PTSD? I think we both have it. But this was 1986. Since then, there has been nobody that interests me much.' A slow smile spread across her face. 'Well . . . not until recently.'

'Giulia, you sly dog! Is there a guy?'

'There could be. If he shows up tomorrow, then I would say yes. But it's not about me. In the morning, we get to watch our beloved Desdemona marry the love of her life and get her happily ever after. You and me, *carina* – we'll be okay, no matter what.'

'You're some woman for one woman, Giulia.'

'Ah, sure I'm grand,' she replied, a glint in her eye. 'Now, let's get ossified.'

But, as Dessie had planned, it was a tame night, which we

were all glad of the next morning when David started his military shtick. We were called to hair and make-up according to a roster he'd drawn up, and nobody was allowed a second more than the time they were allotted – even if they had an eyelash hanging off their face.

His strict schedule worked, though, and when I saw my mother for the first time all done up, I nearly cried my make-up off. We'd jokingly been referring to her dress as Frankenstein's Monster, made up as it was from bits and pieces of other gowns. But the result was spectacular. It had long lace sleeves, a modest V-neck, a cinched waist, and a silk fishtail silhouette with a flowing train. Dessie was wearing a cathedral-length veil, an emerald pendant on a delicate gold chain, and her bouquet was a stunning mix of fiery orange, deep purple and greenery. She looked ethereal, like an autumnal fairy queen from another dimension.

The rest of us were in forest-green silk; Dessie had allowed us to choose any cut we liked so we felt our best. I was in a one-shouldered number, while Vinnie's was strapless. Ariel's was a Bardot-style prom dress, and David was wearing a three-piece dark green suit with a silk waistcoat.

Only Giulia was different, in her signature Dolce florals. But she'd bowed to her beloved Dessie and was sporting an autumnal colour palette alongside her signature lip. She'd even let Axel do some contouring. Giulia was performing the ceremony, having taken a celebrant course at Dessie's behest. To quote my mother, we were all 'feckin' gorgeous'.

The wedding itself was beautiful, and as intimate as an event with three hundred people and multiple cameras can be. Once Dessie and Fionn had said their vows, exchanged rings and shared a kiss, the festive atmosphere kicked in instantly. Waiters roamed the tents with champagne and canapés, the music was turned up, and it was party time.

I knew Jason would be there because my mother had asked my permission to invite him. I wasn't surprised when I saw him across the room at the reception, nor was I surprised that he had brought a date. I made my way over to him, and my heart only constricted slightly at the sight of those eyes up close.

'Portia,' he said, as he leaned in for a kiss on the cheek. He had a new hairstyle, and I was momentarily thrown but I recovered well. 'You look gorgeous.'

'You scrub up well yourself.' My eyes fell on the woman behind him, who was both stunning and obviously in her twenties.

'Let me introduce you to Abigail,' Jason said, propelling his date forward. 'Abigail, this is Portia Daniels.'

I took her hand; she had a firm grip. 'Really pleased to meet you,' I said, marvelling at my own maturity. When I looked in her eyes, though, I saw how nervous she was, and I relaxed. This was a lot for any new relationship, meeting the ex at her famous mother's wedding.

'I've heard so much about you, Portia,' she said, and I detected a California accent. We made polite chit-chat for a few minutes, until Abigail excused herself. 'I'm sure you guys have some catching up to do.'

'Wow, Jason,' I said as I watched her tiny bottom walk away. 'Beautiful and smart. Where did you find her?'

'Abigail is the daughter of one of our new Newport Beach Ladies,' Jason said, raising his eyebrows. 'Before you ask, she's twenty-seven, and yes, I am a cliché.'

'Oh, god,' I laughed. 'You truly are. She seems lovely, though.'

'She is. I was reluctant to get involved, but behind the obvious wealth and beauty, she's quite normal. She reminded me of someone,' he said, bumping gently off my shoulder.

'I'm happy for you, Jason,' I said, and I realized I meant it. 'You'll have her knocked up in no time.'

He threw his head back and laughed, and that set me off. We were standing there in our finery, in absolute stitches. I'd never been a big believer in fate, but at that moment it felt like that's exactly where we were meant to be.

The biggest surprise of the night was that Giulia's fella showed up, and it was none other than Chris Adams. I gawped when I saw him arrive.

'Don't worry, Portia. I'm not here for you.'

'I was just going to say, it would be a bit much to show up at my mother's wedding,' I laughed, kissing him on the cheek. 'Not to be rude, but why are you here?'

'He's with me,' said a voice behind me, and his eyes lit up at the sight of Giulia.

'My god, you're gorgeous!' Chris twirled my aunt around, and she simpered, something I would have thought her incapable of.

'You've kept this quiet!' I demanded of her as he made the rounds saying hello, and Giulia laughed.

'I bumped into Chris over the summer and he eventually convinced me to go on a date. I said I didn't want your sloppy seconds, *si*? But I knew nothing ever happened with you two, and Chris says he's enchanted with me. I wasn't sure if he'd show up to something as public as this, but here he is.' She gestured grandly. '*Bella*, I have taken a toy-boy. Thirteen months my junior. Aren't you glad you never slept with him now?'

'You won't believe how glad.' I beamed, delighted for both of them.

The rest of the evening was uneventful in terms of scandal, but one of the greatest nights of my life. I gave a toast, and Luke made a hilarious best man's speech. There were tears and laughter, and everybody loved the photo booth with specialist TV lighting.

It was unquestionably bizarre to see the Dingle cousins mingling with scions of Beverly Hills, and to see Giulia dancing with Chris. But it was beautiful, a merging of my mother's two realities, and wonderful in its strangeness.

When the cameras packed up around midnight, the party really got started. Trays of shots did the rounds, Riverdance was played, and the Americans were giving as good as they got.

I was lingering outside the tent sneaking a cigarette when Vinnie ran up.

'Give me a drag, quick, before India sees.' My sister's girlfriend had managed to almost cure her of her most dangerous habit, but I was pleased to see that Vinnie wasn't entirely changed.

'Clean living is great, but a drag of a menthol is one of life's greatest pleasures,' Vinnie said, sighing with pleasure as she blew out a stream of smoke. 'How are you holding up?' she said, sneaking another puff.

'I'm great. You know me, Vin. I can hold my own with the Irish.'

'I don't mean the drinking.' She laughed, and nodded towards Jason, who was holding Abigail tight. 'I meant with being here alone.'

I looked at her, puzzled. 'I'm not alone, though. In fact, I've never felt less alone in my life.'

'God, you are so well adjusted.' She sighed. 'Why didn't I get even a bit of your chill? Why did I have to get the addict genes, the anxiety genes?'

'Because you also got the supermodel genes, and you can't have it all.' I poked her in the ribs.

We stood together, watching everyone sway in time to the

music. Michael Bublé had just started his set, and everyone was twirling around the dancefloor.

'Now, this may not be a romantic comedy, and my Prince Charming isn't going to materialize and ask me to dance,' I said. 'However, it can be just like the end of *My Best Friend's Wedding* if I can prise my gay husband away from sexy Sean the bartender. Care to join me?' I said, offering my sister my hand.

'Hell yeah,' she said. 'Although now David is our step-brother, it's kinda weird to be calling him your gay husband.'

I did manage to separate David and Sean, but not without a lot of pouting.

'If he runs off now with Andy Cohen, you're dead to me,' David said, taking both of our hands and twirling Vinnie and me around the floor.

'Andy did mention how Sean looks just like Paul Mescal . . . I'm joking, I'm joking!' I laughed. 'You can relax. Axel has Andy backed into a corner. Besides, you owe me a spin.'

The song changed, and India sidled up to us. 'Vinnie, may I have this dance?'

David held me close as we watched them waltz off, looking like an Amazonian power couple. Michael started singing his version of the ballad 'Home'.

'Can you believe it, Portia? Our parents are *married*!'

'I can, and it's the best. My mom is radiant.' I smiled, dreamily.

'As are you.' He gave me a squeeze. 'Portia, I'm rarely a serious person, but I want you to know how proud I am of you.'

I went to reply, but he shushed me. 'Let me get it out. I've always known you were strong and smart and independent, but you've shown me over the past eighteen months that we should never accept anything less than exactly what we want. You're an inspiration, okay? Never forget it.'

411

My eyes were wet. 'It's funny. In the past, if I thought of myself being single at forty, I'd have considered myself a failure. But I've truly never been happier. Who needs a man?'

'Oh, I do,' he snorted. 'Make no mistake of it. And I suspect you'll have a romcom ending too. But the beauty is, you never know when it's going to be – just look at your mother. And you're not going to sit around waiting in the meantime.'

Over his shoulder, I saw waiters distributing breakfast rolls. 'Oh, goodie,' I said. 'They're bringing out the soakage.'

David took my hand and led me off the dancefloor. 'Come on, gorgeous. We could both do with a good sausage to end the night.'

Epilogue

I was nervous. Actually, screw nervous. I was petrified. It was early February, and the movie was being screened that night before its theatrical release the next morning. On Valentine's Day it would also land on Apple TV+, streaming to every corner of the globe – well, everywhere with good Wi-Fi. Even though I'd spent every waking moment of the last few weeks preparing for this night, the reality of it was seriously different.

Vinnie and I were in the Venice house, getting ready. It had been finished just two weeks prior and was everything I'd hoped it would be and more. Dessie's team had done the most incredible job – my bedroom was an oasis of calm, with an emperor-size bed, white walls and lots of green plants. I had my own terrace to grill on, and a Juliet balcony off the main suite. But the best part was my enormous en suite office, complete with a squishy leopard-print couch, my old white oak desk, and a gallery wall of photo stills from my parents' careers. I'd originally wanted my dad's old movie posters, but seeing those on the walls reminded me of creepy Brandon Leary. My favourite photo was the one on my desk from Mom's wedding, though. My whole extended modern family, mugging for the camera.

Vinnie, David and I were all in the office space with Axel, getting glam. David was trying to calm me down and doing a bad job of it.

'You've been to dozens of premieres before, Portia. It's no big deal.'

'Oh, feck off, David. This is *my* premiere! It's a huge deal!'

'Yeah, shut up, David,' Vinnie interjected from the next chair. 'You're making things worse. Portia,' she said, above the noise of the hairdryer, 'you have every right to be nervous, but let's turn that energy into excitement. That's not nausea, it's butterflies in your stomach.'

'Oh, you can go and shite as well,' I yelped. 'Next you'll be teaching me breathing techniques.'

After that, everyone wisely remained quiet and left me alone with my thoughts. I was chewing my newly extended fingernails, jigging my right leg and downing glasses of sparkling water. I'd chosen a bad month to finally give up cigarettes entirely. What can I say, a combination of LA living and new-year-new-you dogma had finally got me.

'I'm sorry, guys. I'm just really scared.'

'Well, don't be,' said Vinnie. 'We will all be right there with you. This is your moment, sis. Revel in it.'

An hour later, I was in the back of a limo on the way to the red carpet. I'd chosen to go alone, thinking I needed to conserve my social energy for the press line and the after-party. But I felt lonely. I pulled out my phone and FaceTimed Dessie, who was in the car behind me.

'Darling, are you all right?' she answered, looking concerned.

'I'm great, Mom,' I replied. 'Would you just sit on the phone with me until we get there? You don't need to say anything, I just like knowing you're on the other end of the line.'

'Oh, I'm here, sweetheart. And so are Fionn, David and Luke. And Vinnie, Suzanna, Ariel and India are in the other car. Giulia will meet you there; just do as she says. Honey, we are all so bloody proud of you. This is your night. Enjoy every second.'

I felt better, just knowing they were all rooting for me.

By the time the car pulled up at the theatre, I felt ready. I checked my make-up in my light-up compact one last time and smoothed down my magenta Bardot-style dress by Self-Portrait. My hair had grown a little, and David had swept it up in a chic bouffant; the whole look showed off my shoulders and my skin, and I felt truly sexy.

I took a deep breath and opened the car door. The noise hit me like a ton of bricks, as did the flash of light bulbs on the red carpet. I had to keep reminding myself that it wasn't for me. Chris had been slated to arrive just before I did, so I knew the applause and shrieks were for our very own superhero. It was good of him to show up and support, but then, he'd do anything for his beloved Giulia. If I had my way, Chris would be making his own romcom debut sooner rather than later.

I stepped on to the carpet and went on autopilot for the photographers. The plan was to do my stroll alone, and then chat to reporters while I waited for my family to catch up. Katie wanted to walk the red carpet with her husband, which I totally understood.

You can do this, I told myself. You can handle it all.

After the snappers were done with me, I felt a strong hand grasp mine. Giulia, in full PR mode, gave me a reassuring squeeze and then propelled me towards the velvet rope which kept the showbiz journalists off the carpet. Once I got talking, I felt a sense of zen wash over me. I could do this. I could wax lyrical about this film in my sleep.

'Portia, I'm Laura Lynn Richards from *The New York Times*. Is it true that Apple TV+ has tapped you for another three projects?'

'It is.' I beamed at the reporter. 'I've just signed a contract to write and develop original material with the studio, and I couldn't be happier,' I said, allowing Giulia to move me down the line. But then I noticed my aunt moving away from

415

me, and I presumed that meant that the rest of my family had arrived. I looked down the press line, waiting to see who would accost me next.

The guy that appeared before me had messy hair and a louche expression and was pretty casually dressed, which was unusual – the people that work red carpets are normally almost feral in their enthusiasm and rigorous in their grooming. That's probably why it took me a minute to realize that this guy was no reporter.

'Hey, Portia,' he said, in that easy way of his. 'Noah Frost, proud interloper. Let me ask you, do you have a date to tonight's premiere?'

My breath caught at the sight of him, and a warmth spread through me. I cleared my throat.

'Um, no, actually. I'm much too busy and important for a date tonight. A guy would only hold me back.'

His face fell a little, which was so cute I almost reached out and touched it.

'I'm kidding!' I cried. 'I'll meet you inside once I'm finished here. Would you get the popcorn?'

He laughed, and when his eyes met mine, I felt something I hadn't felt in a long time. Turns out, the thunderbolt can strike twice.

Variety

The Romcom is Back! Carlton and Daniels prove a dream team

6 February 2024

Apple Studios has a massive hit on its hands, as the weekend box office numbers and rave reviews signal a roaring comeback for the romantic comedy genre. Newly minted superstar director Katie Carlton and writer Portia Daniels have thrilled audiences and critics alike with *Starting Over* and brought in a $50 million domestic take on opening weekend. The movie is perfectly positioned as a Valentine's Day treat for couples or gaggles of girlfriends, and cinema-goers are making an effort to see the flick in theaters even though it will premiere on Apple TV+ this week.

With a five-star review from this publication and talks of another collaboration for Carlton and Daniels in development, it seems the future is bright for these rising stars.

Acknowledgements

First and foremost, I'd like to thank Patricia Deevy for taking a chance on me and making a lifelong dream come true. She is the most remarkable editor with such a kind, keen eye and sensibility. Thank you for pointing out how fond I am of certain words and idioms – they are now stricken from my vocabulary. Thank you also to Sarah Day and Claire Pelly, whose careful work has made this novel far more engaging and endearing than my initial draft – and also, legible!

I'd also like to extend my warmest thanks to the wider Penguin Sandycove team – Cliona Lewis, Sorcha Judge, Louise Farrell, Carrie Anderson, Joyce Dignam and Leonor Pestana Araújo. Having been on the receiving end of promotional pitches during my years as a magazine editor, I know just how much work goes in to spreading the word about a debut and I appreciate you all so much. Also at Penguin in London, thanks to Ellie Smith and Annie Underwood behind the scenes, making sure the book gets into production smoothly and on time. And an especially big shout-out to the art team for the gorgeous cover – to designer, Charlotte Daniels, art director, Richard Bravery, and studio manager, Rosie Hellier.

Huge thanks to my agent, Faith O'Grady at Lisa Richards, for being so supportive and acting so quickly when approached about representing me. I love a decisive woman! She's the cool head I've always needed.

None of this would have happened if I hadn't tipsily confessed my desire to write fiction to Aimée Johnston at the VIP Style Awards in 2022, or if she hadn't told her former colleagues what I'd said. For that, I thank her from the bottom of my heart, and take it as proof that you should always run your mouth at awards ceremonies.

To my friend Sarah Breen, thank you for always being my mentor and allowing me to copy your professional movements so graciously. Having you in my corner has always gone well for me!

Thank you to my mother, Denise Notaro, for being my very first reader and being so wholly enthusiastic and lovely about the book. She didn't think it needed any editing, and that's the kind of confidence only a mammy can have in you.

Thank you also to my friends who read drafts early on and gave me hope, praise and support – Marian Keyes (who is living proof you should always meet your heroes), Caitlin McBride, Lucy Redshaw and Conor Behan.

Thank you to Patrick Kavanagh for coming up with the title, and to Rebecca Brady, Aidan Corcoran, Katie Gilligan, Trevor Carroll and Laura McAllister for all the encouragement along the way.

Thank you to Ilona Duffy and Rachel Purcell for medical advice about Dessie's condition, and to Glenn Jennings for helping me get to a place where writing this book was possible. To my walking buddies Laura Fox and Thor, you helped air out my brain when it was most needed.

Thank you to Visit California for all the help with the itinerary for my research trip to Los Angeles and its environs.

I wouldn't have conceived of this novel if I hadn't spent hundreds of hours watching reality television during and after the pandemic. Going to BravoCon on a press trip in 2022 allowed me to write an event like V-Palooza convincingly, and was one of the most exciting weekends of this nerd's life.

Thank you to the women (and, indeed, men) who share their lives with us all through reality TV and social media.

Every Real Housewife, momager, influencer and Instagram star I've ever observed has informed this novel and its inhabitants.

Thank you to my secondary-school English teacher, Ro Aitken. Every novelist just wants to impress the person who nurtured their love of writing, and Ro did that through making literature accessible and psychology interesting.

The biggest thanks go to my incredible family. To my dad, Eugene, for teaching me to read before I started Junior Infants, and my Mam Denise and Nanna Phyllis for encouraging my love of books throughout my childhood. Those trips to Tallaght Library and Eason on O'Connell Street were the foundations of my career as a writer.

Thank you to my amazing in-laws, Rita, Shelley and Jack, for being as excited about all of this as I am.

My dog, Jacko, is my constant companion as I write, snoring away in his little teepee beside me. Bubbles is based on him, with unending love.

Last, but certainly not least, thank you to my husband, Joe, to whom this book is dedicated. People talk about love and support, but you show me both every single day. None of this would have been possible without you, and thank you for making it so easy for me to follow my heart since the day I met you.